Also by Marlene Morgan

Revenge I Will Have

SLEEPING
WITH A WALL STREET
BANKER

JAKE LOGAN #1

MARLENE MORGAN

ARCHWAY
PUBLISHING

Archway Publishing books may be ordered through booksellers or by contacting:

Archway Publishing
1663 Liberty Drive
Bloomington, IN 47403
www.archwaypublishing.com
844-669-3957

ISBN: 978-1-6657-4137-8 (sc)
ISBN: 978-1-6657-4136-1 (hc)
ISBN: 978-1-6657-4138-5 (e)

Library of Congress Control Number: 2023905558

Print information available on the last page.

Archway Publishing rev. date: 6/2/2023

To Daniel, who has been a rock of stability in my life.
To Mom: Everything you did made me stronger.
You made me the person I am today.
And to my father, whose loving spirit sustains me still.

You can spend minutes, hours, days, weeks, or even months overanalyzing a situation; trying to put the pieces together, justifying what could've, would've happened … or you can just leave the pieces on the floor and move the fuck on.

—Tupac Shakur

CONTENTS

1

Greenwich, Connecticut

The ambulance raced through Greenwich. Its sirens, which could be heard for miles, fell silent as it turned into Greenwich Hospital.

A police show of force awaited the ambulance outriders, adding to their numbers. Hospital security tightened as the media circus gathered outside. The ambulance's lights extinguished seconds after it stopped outside the emergency entrance.

Jake Logan had arrived at the hospital two minutes before the ambulance pulled up to the entrance. He stood inside the entrance and watched as the paramedics, Pete and Liz, whisked the stretcher into the emergency department's operating theater.

"The patient is a female in her early thirties," Pete told the gathering emergency team. "Assistance, please!"

Liz and two members of the emergency department helped Pete roll a scoop stretcher under the patient and lift her onto the hospital gurney. Pete continued to brief the team while they removed the scoop. As he spoke, he turned his head toward Dr. Milner, who was checking her vital signs.

"The patient was confused at the scene," Pete said. "We were unable to verify many of the details relating to the incident."

"She's unresponsive!" Dr. Milner said. "Her breathing is abnormal. Crash team!"

In an instant, roles changed. The crash team commenced CPR. Seconds passed.

"She's defibrillating!" the monitoring emergency medic said. "Clear!"

The nurse giving CPR ceased chest compressions. Another team member moved in with a defibrillator. Once the electric shock was delivered to the patient, all eyes turned to the monitor, searching for a heartbeat.

In the visitors' waiting room, Jake paced back and forth. *She was so still—not moving. Not breathing. Stop! You don't know that. What the hell happened at the house?*

Douglas, his limousine driver, had called and said Miss Alice had been stabbed and was on her way to Greenwich Hospital. He had given only a few other details: he had seen a woman go into the house, and when Miss Alice, who was always punctual, had not come out to the car at her appointed time, he had gone into the house and found her in a pool of blood. Jake could not help thinking that Jessica had something to do with this disaster.

Annabel! I did not call Alice's sister. He pulled his cell phone out, but there was no cellular reception in the waiting room. Continuing to thumb through his phone contacts, he walked out of the waiting room and toward the hospital's front entrance.

Outside, Jake entered 44, the international dialing code for England, in front of Annabel's cell number. She answered on the fifth ring. She sounded drowsy, but that did not surprise him; it was after midnight in England.

"I'm sorry to call you so late, but—"

Annabel stumbled to her feet as Marcus turned on a light. "Jake, what's wrong? Alice—where is Alice? Is she OK?"

"There's been an incident, a bad incident, and Alice is in the hospital."

"What? Are you serious? No, you can't be serious. What incident?"

I think my ex-girlfriend gutted her. Jake composed himself. "I don't know who did it or why, but she's been stabbed and is in the OR as we speak."

"OR!"

"Sorry. Operating theater," he said, remembering English terminology.

"Can you tell her mother?"

"Me? Why me? This can't be happening."

Jake looked up and saw the reporters in front of the hospital. "Listen to me, Annabel. I promise you this terrible news is real; it won't be long before some news reporter calls your mother."

"OK, OK."

He could hear Marcus in the background, asking her what had happened. "I know this can't be easy." He did not say more.

"I will call you back." Annabel ended the call.

Jake's gaze went back to the reporters. He recognized Edward Bernstein of the *Wall Street Journal*, a close friend of Alice's. He was embracing someone—a fellow colleague, Jake assumed. Bernstein was staring over the colleague's shoulder directly at Jake. *He knows. Fuck, he knows.*

Jake turned to go back into the hospital but stopped when Bernstein called to him. The sound of his voice came closer. Jake felt his hand gently touch his arm. He turned to face him. The woman was at his side.

"Hey, I thought it was you. Alice has told me so much about you."

And you think she did not talk to me about you? Jake did not want to sound defensive and, hoping he could quickly get rid of him, said, "All good, I hope."

Bernstein just smirked. He turned to face the woman. "This is

Zara, a colleague and friend. We worked together at the *New York Times*. Zara, this is Jake Logan, a friend of a friend."

"There's a lot of excitement around here. Are you visiting somebody in the hospital?" said Zara.

Bernstein did not wait for Jake to reply and said to Zara, with his stare fixed on Jake, "What's the latest on the hospital victim? Do we have a name?"

Zara shook her head. "No. A spokesperson for the police just announced they'll hold a press conference once the next of kin has been contacted." She grinned and could not contain her excitement.

"In the last update I received, the police were not ruling out a connection between this incident and this morning's discovery of a man's body in an apartment in New York," Edward said. His eyes pierced Jake.

Jake fought to hide the shock on his face. He was desperate to take his leave of them.

"Have the police identified the owner of the apartment?" Zara asked.

"Yes. Jessica Brooks."

"Who's Jessica Brooks?"

"An aspiring art dealer." Bernstein did not add where he had heard the name or that he had heard it before that day. He continued his eye contact with Jake.

Why do these people enjoy train wrecks? "I thought you were with the *Wall Street Journal*. Isn't a dead body outside your job spec?" Jake asked.

"Still with the *Wall Street Journal*," Edward replied. "My sources inform me there's a connection with Wall Street."

Jake struggled to contain his anger. *You smug jerk. It's clear to me now why Alice and you never got to first base.* "Sorry, guys, but I don't want to miss visiting time. Nice meeting you, Edward." His shoulder turned gently to the right. "You too, Zara." He walked away and back into the hospital.

2

London, three years and nine months earlier

When Jake walked into the main room at Tate Modern, his attention was drawn to the woman at the other end. She was animatedly talking with a host from the KBW accountancy firm. He observed not only how she talked but also how she listened attentively. She was dressed in a charcoal-gray suit with a silk scarf draped on her arm. When she laughed, her smile radiated throughout the room.

As the woman meandered through the collection of modern and contemporary art, Jake followed at a distance. He noted the graceful way she moved and how elegant she looked as she went from room to room.

Several rooms had been cordoned off for the KBW event. The firm had invited clients from a variety of business sectors. Jake didn't take his eyes off her as she walked over to the buffet table. She stopped close to him, placing her glass on the table. Her pose was attractive, and the sweet aroma of her perfume stirred his senses. As she leaned forward, the silk scarf on her arm slipped off and fell to the floor.

"Alice, your scarf." Jake bent, reached for the scarf, and handed it to her.

He thought she faltered when he called her by name. He watched her gaze as it moved down to her identity badge, which read, "Alice Francis, legal counsel, International Gaming Limited (IG)." Then he engaged her with his eyes.

"Thank you," she said, composed once again.

He held out a hand to greet her. "Jake Logan."

"I detect an American accent." She shook his hand.

"Yes. I lived in New York and worked on Wall Street until three years ago, when HK Bank temporarily transferred me to London."

Jake was disappointed when their host intervened, turning the conversation back to business and ushering them into the adjoining room for the presentation.

"Fuck!" he said under his breath. He had missed his opportunity to ask her to join him for a drink later.

Several attendees entered the room at the same time, forcing Jake and Alice in opposite directions. He saw her to his left. When his eyes met hers, she blushed and looked away. He tried to focus on the fifteen-minute presentation, but thoughts of her kept distracting him. He stole another glance at her.

When the last speaker wished the audience a good evening, the people to his left stood up to leave. Jake turned, hoping to catch Alice's attention, but the seat she'd occupied was empty. When he spotted her in the crowd, she was making her way out of the room.

He looked on, but he could not get around the people on either side to stop her from leaving. Just then, he looked down at the program in his hand. "Alice," he whispered.

Within seconds of the presentation closing, Alice rushed out of the building and into a taxi. Jake arrived outside the entrance of the Tate as Alice settled into the backseat. Initially, he could not see her face, but when she raised her head, she had her phone in her hand. As the car pulled away, Jake fumbled with the program in his hand and retrieved his phone from his pocket. He sent Alice a text: "Hey,

Alice. I was pleased to meet you and would like to continue our conversation."

Jake raised a hand to flag a taxi, and at the same time, he checked his phone. As the taxi he'd entered drove away from the Tate, his phone beeped.

Alice replied, "Ditto," with a smiley emoji. "How did you get my number?" There was another smiley emoji.

Jake chuckled to himself. On the back of the event program, KBW had provided a list of all attendees and their business contact details. He sent another text to Alice.

"That's for me to know and for you to find out. Dinner?" He smiled.

Alice and Jake's first romantic meeting was on a cold evening in late March. It had snowed earlier in the week, but most of the snow had cleared. It was one of those rare days in London when the gray sky gave way to a clear bright blue. A few buds had started to appear on the bare trees. Spring was creeping in, and the days were getting longer. But winter had not let go at its appointed time.

Although it had been a mild day, the evening was cold. This presented a problem as Alice contemplated what to wear. How could she dress in a manner that would appeal to a man but allow her to stay warm? She carefully eyed the array of clothes in her wardrobe. *It's too late to hit the shops.* She sat down on her bed in despair. Then she spotted it—the perfect dress.

She slipped on the sleeveless black Armani dress and turned to face the mirror. The dress had a bubble hem that softly fell just above her knees. The top of the dress was cut in a slight racerback style, which revealed her slender, toned shoulders. The lace brocade fit snugly on her shoulders and finished just above her breasts. She could not wear a bra with the dress. While it didn't show bare cleavage, it left an admirer with no doubt that the wearer had full, voluptuous breasts. Alice also wore a pair of black lace boy-cut panties and lace-topped stockings. She completed her look with a pair of four-inch

Prada pumps. For this occasion, less was more. She looked elegant but felt sexy.

She smiled when her thoughts went back to the day they had met at Tate Modern. Initially, she had been astonished that Jake had gotten her telephone number and email address. That he had contacted her excited Alice. Leaning back in her seat and closing her eyes, she was curious whether a friendship might develop between Jake and herself. To the outside world, Alice appeared to have followed her career at the expense of relationships. Internally, she was soul-searching and opening her mind to her true feelings. She yearned to find a loving relationship.

Earlier that day, Alice had sent Jake a text message, asking if he had seen the movie *There's Something about Mary*. She had laughed to herself when he said he had. She'd teased him with a second text suggesting he masturbate before their date, so he could get sex off his mind and get to know her better.

Wearing two more layers of clothing to keep the chill out, Alice arrived at Claridge's Hotel. Claridge's was in the heart of Mayfair, placed perfectly for the city, shopping districts, and Hyde Park. It dated back to the first half of the nineteenth century. Alice had an interest in architecture and interior design, so she knew that the de-signer of Harrods had rebuilt Claridge's from the ground up. In the latter part of the twentieth century, Claridge's had updated its heritage with a modern twist. The foyer had been revitalized with a modern art deco feel and a stunning Dale Chihuly chandelier.

Alice entered the foyer, where stars, socialites, and the crowned heads of Europe had been kibitzing for more than a hundred years. She was fifteen minutes early for her date with Jake. She made her way to the bar.

The bar's original art deco features were complemented beauti-fully by a silver-leafed ceiling, a green glass chandelier, and red leather banquettes. Each round, shiny table was decorated with a dark red rose. The bar played host to Mayfair's socialites. Champagne and cocktails lined the tables. It was not that Alice did not know that world, but she had never been comfortable sitting at a bar alone. Instead, she searched for a place to leave her coat.

After checking her coat, she went to the ladies' room and inspected her attire. She was wearing an off-white peplum jacket over the dress, and her long dark brown hair fell neatly over her shoulders. She picked up her clutch bag and the small blue gift bag she had been carrying and headed back to the foyer.

Though usually bustling with live music, the foyer—a popular place to take afternoon tea or sip evening cocktails—was quiet. She seated herself on a sofa and waited.

Sometime later, Alice looked at her watch. It was ten minutes after seven. Where was he? She disliked tardiness. Twenty-five minutes had passed since she had arrived. It did not matter that she had arrived fifteen minutes early; she was not pleased and did not discount the first fifteen minutes. She felt self-conscious that she had been sitting alone for twenty-five minutes. She surveyed the foyer discreetly to see if anyone had noticed. The bellboy was standing by, opening and closing the door as people entered the hotel. The man at reception seemed engrossed in paperwork. A few other people were also passing time in the foyer, but most of the noise emanated from the restaurant.

Alice stared at her watch; it was seven fifteen. She concluded Jake was a no-show. She retrieved her mobile phone from her clutch bag to see if he had called. She stared at the phone, wondering whether to call him or to call it a night and go home. Her disappointment showed on her face. She fumbled to find his number as she stood up to leave. Holding her clutch in one hand and the small blue gift bag and mobile phone in the other, Alice looked ahead. Staring directly at her was a tall, dark, and handsome man. He smiled at her.

This was not their first meeting. Still, she was stunned by his facial features. Jake was proud of his Irish heritage; he had boasted about it in their text message exchanges. He had inherited his ancestors' black Irish genes: wavy dark hair, blue eyes, and a dark complexion. Standing six feet, two inches tall, he was wearing a dark navy pin-striped suit and a smile that lit up the room. Alice's annoyance dissipated into nervousness. Butterflies hit her tummy, and she struggled not to drop her clutch.

Jake had just finished the eighteenth hole on the recently modernized Wentworth Club West Course. He smiled. He had played well. It was his first time on the West Course since the renovation had been completed. He had birdied the challenging par-five eighteenth hole.

As he and the business associates with whom he had played that afternoon headed to the bar, he found himself thinking about his date with Alice. He was looking forward to spending time with her. The day was perfect—an afternoon of playing golf, followed by a date with a beautiful woman.

By the time Jake had drinks with his business associates, he was running late. The car he had booked was waiting outside. Wentworth Club was in Virginia Water, Surrey, on the southwestern fringes of London, not far from Windsor Castle. He had a distance to go, and he hoped traffic would not be too congested.

Jake thought Wentworth Club was special. Leaving aside the privilege of treading in the footsteps of the game's great players from the last eighty-five years, the world offered few more glorious natural settings for golf than that stretch of heathland surrounded by woodlands of pine, oak, birch, and vibrant rhododendrons, which added color. Outside of work, golf was Jake's life.

The car stopped outside Jake's Kensington apartment. He asked the driver to wait as he ran inside to shower and change. Ten minutes later, he was back in the car.

En route to Mayfair, his thoughts turned to Alice. He was intrigued. She was intelligent and had a sense of humor. They had been emailing each other for several weeks, and each evening, he went home excited to read her emails. They had engaged in many light debates. It did not matter which side he chose; Alice would argue the opposing side eloquently. Jake's father and brother, like Alice, were lawyers, and he had grown up with plenty of debates around the breakfast and dining table.

Early in their email exchange, Jake had asked Alice if she had lived or would ever consider living in another country. He'd discovered that she had traveled extensively, both for pleasure and for business. She had lived in the United States for several months at a time. While it had been lonely at times, she said the foreign travel and time spent in the United States had been good life experiences. Her summation struck a chord with Jake. He had been working in London for the last three years, and while it had been a good experience, he had been lonely. As Jake had read that email, he'd sensed Alice had given thought to his question before replying. She had concluded the email by saying she would not want to live in certain countries unless it was essential but that she had not ruled out the possibility of living in another country. Yes! Jake had his answer. He smiled. Although he would have been a little off balance if his best friend had said, "You're falling for Alice," he certainly thought she was special, and he found himself drawn to her more and more.

The car pulled up in front of Claridge's.

Even at a distance, Jake detected sadness in her hesitant smile. *Fuck!* He had not sent a text to let her know he would be late. He walked over to where she was standing.

"Sorry I'm late." His eyes engaged with hers and then glanced at the mobile phone in her hand. "Sorry I didn't call or text." His eyes did not move from her. *She's still upset.*

Alice smiled. "Apology accepted." She regained control of her composure, jammed her mobile phone into her clutch, and looked at Jake to see who would make the next move.

"Would you like to go to the bar for a drink before dinner?" He looked at his watch. "I've made a dinner reservation at C London for eight thirty. We still have time."

Alice glanced at the gold Rolex on his wrist. It complemented his tanned arms. "Yes," she replied.

Jake took a step back so she could pass in front of him. Walking closely but slightly behind, he followed her into Claridge's bar.

Once inside, they realized no tables were available.

She leaned toward his ear. "I'm comfortable standing. We're not staying long."

Jake bought a glass of champagne for Alice and a gin and tonic for himself. His gaze darted around the room, looking for somewhere to sit.

Alice tugged his sleeve gently. "We can stand over there."

Jake paid her no mind; he pulled ten crisp fifty-pound notes from his wallet and slipped them to the waiter. Her eyes opened wide. Minutes later, they were seated.

Jake sat looking intently at Alice. His warm facial features reached out to her, pulling her gently toward him. She studied Jake while trying to hide her surprise at what had just transpired. She did not know why she was surprised, given the reputation bankers had for extravagant spending. A silence fell between them, but she did not feel uncomfortable, and from her detailed study of Jake's demeanor, he appeared relaxed. She stared into his blue eyes. Seated across from her was a man who appeared to believe money was power and that if you had it, you could buy anything you wanted. Although Alice had thought she would see a person without a soul, she did not. All that radiated back to her was angelic warmth. She came back to reality and realized they had been silent for a while. She reached down, picked up the gift bag, and handed it to Jake.

A surprised look registered on his face. "What's this?"

She smiled. "It's my way of saying thank you for the lovely date I'm anticipating."

How did she know it was going to be a nice date? She looked at Jake, and she had her answer. Alice was an independent woman and was looking for a partner, not a meal ticket. She did not want to run the risk of appearing dependent by not offering to split the bill or causing offense by not allowing him to pay. The rule in relation to who should pay on a first romantic date had become confusing. Alice had decided not to offer to split the bill. Instead, she had bought a small present to express her thankfulness.

"I decided to give it to you now because it would be silly to carry it around and run the risk of leaving it on a chair or table. We can leave it at the cloakroom and retrieve it later."

Jake peeled off the blue plaid wrapping paper, which complemented the bag. Inside was a copy of *Blink*. The book had been on the *New York Times* best-seller list, and from the knowledge she had gained from their email communications, she guessed he would enjoy it. *Score!* He appeared genuinely pleased.

"*Blink*. Interesting." He looked up and smiled. "Thank you. This is one of the titles on my reading list. The book is about the kind of thinking that happens in the blink of an eye—the first two seconds of meeting a person or encountering a situation. Gladwell believes those instant conclusions are powerful, important, and generally reliable. Is this your way to ask about my blink moment when we first met?"

She laughed. "Are you confessing to having a blink moment? Tell me about your thoughts in those first two seconds of our meeting."

He smiled. "They were all good."

Alice detected a rush of emotion in Jake.

He stared at the book. "I can't recall any of the women I've dated buying me a present. Thank you."

Alice listened not only to what he was saying but also to his soft American accent, which Jake had told her originated in the Midwest.

"The women you've dated didn't give you gifts?" Her tone was jovial when she touched his arm. "I don't believe you."

She pondered his statement. If true, she wondered what kind of women he had been dating. She did not think she had done anything special. The gift had been her answer to the bill dilemma.

Jake raised his glass, finished his drink, and placed two fifty-pound notes on the table. "We should make our way to the restaurant."

Alice tore her eyes away from the two fifty-pound notes on the table, tucked her clutch under her arm, and walked with Jake toward the cloakroom.

3

When the Claridge's bellboy opened the door, cold air smacked Alice and Jake in the face. Without fail, the remnants of winter were encroaching in places they were not welcome. Alice pulled up her coat collar to prevent the cold from wrapping itself around her and seeping inward. Earlier in the evening, when Alice had arrived at Claridge's, office workers had been spilling out of the pubs. Gone now were the men with their ties pulled loose, laughing and joking with their female coworkers or friends they had arranged to meet for an after-work drink. The hard-core partygoers had taken over.

"The night is cold for walking, but there's nothing to be gained in taking a cab," Jake said. "It's a short walk to C London from here. The damage the cold would do in the time it would take to flag a cab outweighs the short walk."

They walked briskly down the street. Alice, a mere five feet, four inches, took two steps for every one of Jake's. She looked up at him. The rate at which he was moving suggested he might be regretting not wearing an overcoat. He was not the only one who was cold. If she stayed outside too long, the biting wind would permeate her legs and numb her toes. The night called for, at minimum, forty-denier tights, not nine-denier stockings.

Alice's thoughts went back to the way Jake handed out fifty-pound notes as if they were five-pound notes. She could not cry outrage; that would have been melodramatic. She contemplated if the tips were Jake being overly generous or if there was a deeper meaning to his behavior. She was cognizant of the general complaint that investment bankers awarded themselves fortunes while the public denounced their selfishness. She was not sure whether his excessive spending indicated a lack of moral probity or uprightness of character. Judging him because the reputation of bankers had hit an all-time low was not fair.

Jake's voice broke into her thoughts. "I hope you like this restaurant. I have my reservations about C London's new name, but it's one of my favorite restaurants in London."

"The restaurant owners didn't have a choice," Alice replied. "C London was forced to change its name after its owners lost a High Court battle with the Hotel Cipriani in Venice."

They turned the corner onto Davies Street. The pavement outside the entrance to C London was crowded. As they approached, the assemblage were recognizable as paparazzi. Jake stopped to talk to a man holding a zoom-lens camera and then turned to Alice.

"There's a rumor Sir Elton John is dining within."

In the foyer, they received a warm welcome from the restaurant manager.

"We have a reservation for two under the name Logan," Jake said.

"Yes, Mr. Logan," the restaurant manager replied. While assisting Alice with her coat and jacket, he asked if they would like a drink at the bar before dinner.

"No, thanks," Jake replied.

Alice could have been fooled into thinking the manager had been waiting for Jake and his guest to arrive. Her gaze wandered around the room. C London was an iconic restaurant. Modeled on the famous Harry's Bar in Venice, it formed part of the Cipriani worldwide brand, with other venues located in New York, Hong Kong, and Los Angeles. It oozed old-school glamour and elegance, boasting a stunning wood-paneled dining room with immaculately dressed tables topped with the crispest white linens.

Jake stared at Alice. She looked stunning. She had long, toned, slender arms. He could see her bare shoulders through the fitted lace brocade top. Her shoulders looked like those of an Olympic swimmer. Jake observed that Alice was not wearing a bra, and judging by the way the soft, seductive silk fabric cradled and fell over her breasts, he guessed she was at least a D cup. The dress revealed little else. Jake's curiosity was driving him crazy. He could barely contain his sexual desire. It was unlike him to lack confidence, but in that moment, he wondered whether she liked him. Walking behind but not too close, he watched her every elegant and graceful move as she followed the restaurant manager to their table.

The manager stopped at a corner table in a discreet part of the restaurant. The two chairs were adjacent but at a right angle to each other. The manager pulled the table out so that Alice could slide across the first chair to the second chair. Jake sat on the second chair. They both looked up and thanked the manager. Before they could utter another word, he disappeared, replaced by a waiter, who introduced himself and handed them menus. A second waiter appeared and asked if they preferred still or sparkling water. Jake motioned to Alice with his head.

"Sparkling, please," she said.

Jake studied the wine menu and then turned to Alice. "Do you prefer white or red?"

Alice glanced at the wine menu. The list was dreamy, but she was at C London, and the signature drink had to be the Bellini. "I would like a cocktail, please. A peach Bellini would be nice. And my preference is white wine with dinner."

When Alice spoke, Jake heard her singing quietly and softly to him. He was in a trance for a few seconds after she had finished her last word. The waiter waited patiently

"Jake?" Alice said.

He snapped out of his hypnotic state and ordered a gin and tonic. He asked the waiter to give him a few more minutes with the wine menu. When the waiter returned with their cocktails, Jake ordered a bottle of Monfortino Riserva Barolo, 2000 vintage.

When a second waiter arrived with bread and olive oil, Alice ordered marinated salmon and asparagus, and Jake ordered a veal chop and salad. Alice waited until Jake had finished ordering and then said, "Your wine choice is interesting. Did cost play a part—expensive means quality wine—or do you have an interest in wines?"

After the first waiter returned with the wine, offered Jake a taste, and filled their glasses three-quarters full, the conversation resumed. "I'm interested in wines," Jake said. "My knowledge has increased in the last three years that I've been in London. I attended a few wine tastings and have read many publications about wines." He added to the exposition she had received from her mother, saying that Barolo, a dry Italian wine, was considered one of the finest and longest-lived wines, often referred to as the king of wines and the wine of kings.

Alice excused herself. Jake stood; pulled the table out; and, upon allowing her exit to go to the ladies' room, absorbed the beauty of Alice and the dress she was wearing. His fixation on the dress troubled him. He lapsed into his past and Jessica, his cost center, the name he used to refer to his ex-girlfriend when he was in friendly company. Jessica had known two addresses: Fifth Avenue, New York, and her apartment address, which was within walking distance of Fifth Avenue and an array of designer shops.

Like most men, generally speaking, Jake hated shopping. He had spent his time sitting on sofas and perusing sports on his iPhone while Jessica shopped, looking up only to hand his credit card to the sales assistant. He had no desire to date another woman who viewed extravagant shopping sprees as a recreational pursuit. Then he forced himself to stop. He could not allow Jessica to spoil this special evening.

"Jake?" Alice called.

"Sorry. I was miles away." Jake stood so Alice could sit down.

The food arrived. The drink he had consumed had enhanced his appetite. After he ate a few mouthfuls of his veal chop, his thoughts turned back to Jessica's addiction to shopping.

"The dress you're wearing is beautiful. Is it a designer dress?"

Alice smiled. "Why? Do you have an interest in fashion design too?"

Jake smiled. "I asked first. You answered a question with a question. Not fair."

Alice smiled and lifted her fork to her mouth to avoid answering the question. From the many weddings, dinner parties, and other events Alice's mother had catered for public and family gatherings, she had some knowledge about wines. Her memory trailed back to a family dinner party following a vacation to Italy, where she had traveled through Alba, a town and commune of Piedmont, Italy, in the province of Cuneo. Alice's mother had told her that the experts had recently named Francia in Serralunga d'Alba—where the Barolo Monfortino Riserva grapes were grown—Italy's top vineyard. She was aware that a bottle of Monfortino Riserva Barolo, 2000 vintage, could cost in the region of £280, not including the restaurant's markup. She was not going to discuss the label on her dress or its price tag. Her defenses crept up, but her reaction also made her feel like a hypocrite. Throughout the evening, she had been the one watching how much Jake spent. The flow of conversation stalled. Alice focused on her salmon.

"Alice," he said, "your dress is as beautiful as it is unique. That's why I asked if it was a designer dress."

Why couldn't he let it go? Her annoyance was building; she did not have to justify herself to this man. Alice, who was used to cross-examining the witness, was in the witness box. She chewed the food she had just put in her mouth. *Is he worried I might be high maintenance? I'm an independent woman—I pay my own way. Didn't he read that in me? Is he even worth a second date?* She longed for the loving

relationships her sisters and friends had and decided to give this connection a chance. Alice was cognizant of what she had to gain if she let
his persistent questioning fly over—she faced loneliness if she allowed
sensitivity to consume her.

"Yes," she said, "it is a designer dress, but shopping and labels are
not who I am."

She did not feel pleased with herself at that noticeable, even if
minor, outburst. She had to make amends. She put down her knife
and fork, took a sip of wine, and explained to Jake that when she was
growing up, her mother had made pretty and unique clothes for Alice
and her sisters. By the age of eleven, taught by her mother, Alice had
been able to make her own clothes. She had developed a keen eye for
fashion trends, quality fabrics, and the cut of a garment. Virtually all
the clothes she had worn then were made by her own hands.

Continuing her narrative, she told Jake that she had polished her
skills when she worked for a renowned designer and attended the
London School of Fashion. But a time had come when, because of her
busy career, she no longer had the time to design and make clothes.
By then, Alice had become used to wearing quality clothing—the
extra fabric in a skirt or dress and the haute couture finish.

"I struggled to find clothes that met my standards on the high
street," she said in a calm voice. "You might be surprised to learn
that by careful shopping, a person can buy reasonably priced classical
designer clothing."

"That's an amazing story. Why law and not fashion designing?"

She explained that fashion was not a secure industry. "Hoping to
make a living in the world of fashion is not so different from seeking
a career as a singer or an athlete," she said. "Few aspiring designers
achieve their big break."

Jake felt guilty. He was aware that he had offended her. Why had
he brought Jessica to this date? He felt like an idiot. He should have
allowed Alice's character time to unfold and not tarred her unjustly

with the same brush as Jessica. He should not have let Jessica control his thoughts. He had ended his relationship with her—well, strictly speaking, she had ended the relationship. Closure was for the best, so why was he still letting her haunt him? Jessica's email the previous night had said she had been wrong to walk away and that she was convinced he still loved her. Jake still had feelings for her, but he knew he would be crazy to ruin what he might have with Alice before they even got to first base. Not wanting to put her on the spot again, he excused himself to go to the men's room. *I'll change the subject when I return to the table.*

While Jake was away, the waiter brought dessert menus. Alice perused the list of delicacies. When he returned, she gave him the menu and pointed to her favorites.

Jake did not know for sure if his knee touched hers or if Alice's knee touched his. Either way, she did not pull away. The warmth and sensation she radiated excited him. His eyes were engaged with hers. He broke his gaze when she blushed but not before he followed her eyes down and noticed her erect nipples.

Jake was not a dessert person. An appetizer and main course sufficed. Alice expressed that her appetite was satisfied as well, but Jake was determined not to break the knee contact. He encouraged her to have dessert, drawing her attention to the dessert trolley and agreeing to share her choice.

Dessert's cameo did not disappoint. Every time their knees separated, they engaged again, sending sensations to Jake's core, teasing until he was hard. With every mouthful of lemon tart Alice leaned forward to take, her aroma increased his desire to love and please her. Dessert—memorable but short—played its role.

Soon the plate was empty. Alice did not want coffee, but Jake was in no position to stand. He placed his black American Express card on the waiter's tray and scrutinized the bill to turn off what she had turned on.

Outside the entrance to C London, Jake observed Alice, wishing he could wrap his arms around her to keep her warm. He had to go back to Claridge's to collect his book. He suggested Alice accompany him. She could wait inside in the warmth while the doorman flagged a taxi. He was contemplating how he could spend more time with her. He could not—would not—let her go. He stared into her eyes and tried to woo her with his thoughts.

Please spend the night with me.

The cool air silenced them as they headed back to Claridge's. It was nearly eleven. The streets were quiet. The homebound partygoers were not due for at least three hours.

When they reached Claridge's, Alice approached the bellboy to ask him to flag a taxi to Langley Park.

"Alice," Jake called, "please stay and have a nightcap with me."

Jake did not have to wait long for a reply. She smiled at him and followed him into the deserted foyer.

This time, Alice either did not notice or did not care when Jake greased a pocket or two. She sat on a sofa, her feet thawing with every sip of the tea Jake had ordered. Jake was drinking a bottle of Budweiser. He felt her eyes on him, observing with an unspoken but knowing tenderness.

Every drink had a lifespan. Jake watched as Alice drank nearly three cups of Earl Grey tea before she relaxed and released her hands from the cup she was cradling. Warmth had returned to her body, he guessed. She was finally satisfied, and Jake could not persuade her to drink any more tea.

In the light of the foyer, Jake could see that she had a natural beauty. She wore minimal makeup, and her lip gloss accentuated her full lips.

He leaned forward to place his empty bottle on the table. He did not return to his original position. Turning slightly toward Alice, he aligned his lips with hers. When she did not pull away, he kissed her gently. When she did not resist, he kissed her again, holding the kiss longer.

The kiss was patient. Jake experienced the allure of Alice's tender, sensual lips and her heart beating heavily but rhythmically against her chest. The odor of her warm breath was fragrant with a hint of cherry that flavored her full, soft lips. Alice was silent, as was Jake.

Alice could have waited inside the entrance to C London. It would not have taken long to get a cab. But her intrigue and her warmth for Jake were escalating, and as she thought, a little more time with him was nice.

For all the alcohol she had consumed that night, Alice was fully aware of what was happening, but she felt powerless to resist, nor did she want to. She had a strong attraction to Jake, yet she had been drinking, and she did not want to wake up the following morning knowing she had had an amazing night but not remembering much of it. She preferred to experience and remember every kiss, caress, and thrust.

Knowing it had to stop and feeling tired, she put a hand on Jake's arm. "I've had a great evening with you, but I'm sleepy and should be leaving. I have an early start tomorrow."

Alice was a little taken aback by his demeanor. He looked confused and seemed to be asking her if he had done anything wrong. Yet the confidence he exuded was still there, silently telling her he had mistaken her feelings for him.

"I can get a room at Claridge's."

"No, thank you," she said. Alice did not hide that she was annoyed.

"Alice, I'm sorry. You said you were tired, and I know you have a fifty-five-minute journey to get home. I would invite you to my apartment, but I thought a hotel would be more neutral and comfortable. I honestly did not mean to offend you."

How naive does he think I am? He's treating me like a high-class call girl.

She stopped her train of thought. She was being defensive.

"Jake, I am tired, but no way am I spending the night in a hotel with you. I enjoyed spending time with you," she added, lightening her tone a little. "But sex tonight? No." Calmer now, Alice admitted to herself that she did not want the night to end at Claridge's. "I will accept the sofa in your apartment. No sex, though. Understand? I was not making excuses. Set the alarm. I have an early start tomorrow."

"You have my word, Alice. I understand. No means no."

He collected his book and Alice's coat from the cloakroom, and minutes later, they were in a black cab on their way to Jake's apartment.

4

The cab passed Royal Park and then went by Green Park, a refuge for people living in, working in, or visiting central London. By day, it was filled with sunbathers and people having picnics. On that night, it was sleeping.

The taxi passed Hyde Park on the right and slowed as it reached a fork in the road. To the left were Brompton Road and the bright lights of the iconic Harrods department store. The taxi bore to the right, continuing past the 180-foot Victorian bronze gilt statue anchored in Kensington Gardens. The statute had been Queen Victoria's tribute to her husband, Prince Albert. Even in the dark, it was easy to see, a symbol of a royal love story that, like the statue, had stood the test of time.

The conversation in the cab was scant. Jake was comfortable with moments of silence, feeling no need to force anything. He could see that Alice was struggling to keep her eyes open and was exhausted. Alice had told him that she woke every morning at 5:30 a.m. and left the house at six fifteen to journey to work. Her day ended anywhere between six thirty and seven thirty. Often, she did not reach home until eight thirty.

Fifteen minutes later, the taxi pulled into the grounds of Jake's apartment in Kensington. Jake held Alice's hand as she emerged from the cab. He did not let go as they walked into the concierge building and out the door on the other side. Jake stopped for a couple of seconds to nod at the security guard on duty.

"Good night, Mr. Logan," the security guard said.

Jake would have told Alice about the history of the building, but a combination of the dark sky and fatigue encumbered Alice's ability to observe her surroundings.

Inside the apartment, he watched her as she stepped out of her shoes, leaving them to the right side of the door. The lighting in the apartment was on a dimmer mechanism. It was set to a nighttime setting, low enough so that she would not trip and fall but bright enough to allow her to take in the interior design. *Hm, she didn't wait for me.* In a world of her own, she wandered down the apartment hallway, passed the living room and the kitchen, and failed to see the left turn that led to the bathroom and the guest bedroom.

Jake watched, slightly amused. He thought Alice was endearing. She turned right into his bedroom and sat on the left side of the bed at the head, resting her head against the leather headboard. Jake wondered if that would be Alice's sleeping position for the night.

"Alice?" he said.

Alice opened her eyes. "Yes. Can I please have a shirt to sleep in?"

Jake opened his closet, thumbed through his T-shirts, and selected a gray sweatshirt with *Nantucket* printed across the front. He turned back to face Alice and paused as he watched her remove her stockings. Her legs were as toned as her arms, and though she was not tall, her legs were long and in proportion to the rest of her body. He wanted her. He wanted to hold and kiss her. He took a step forward and then remembered his promise.

"Here," he said. "You can sleep in this sweatshirt."

Alice took the sweatshirt and thanked him. She held it for a moment, looking at him. "Please, can you turn around so I can put it on?"

Jake had thought that in her fatigued state, Alice might forget he was in the room. He turned and waited until Alice indicated it was OK to turn back.

Initially, Jake had sat at the bottom of the bed. Now he sat on the top half, waiting for Alice's next move. She did not move. Her eyelids closed. Jake held Alice's hand and moved closer to her. She opened her eyes.

"Jake, no sex. You promised." Alice leaned forward. "I need to sleep." She kissed him on the lips before lying down and passing out.

Jake, also tired, removed his suit and stripped down to his boxer shorts. He thought about Alice. She had made him promise not to force himself on her. He thought about her words. He tried to reason with himself but found that he kept coming back to the fact that Alice was in his bed. She was supposed to be sleeping on the sofa, and he had planned to offer her the guest room. How had she ended up in his bed?

He turned to go to the guest room but stopped. He had tried to sleep in that room before, and he had had a restless night. Jake was a creature of habit in his personal life and did not adjust well to change. He looked at the king-sized bed. Feeling sleepy, he told himself she had not said he could not sleep in the same bed. There was plenty of room, and he would stay on his side. Tired, he lay down.

It was late, after three in the morning, but Jake could not settle into sleep. It had nothing to do with Alice being in his bed. That was where he wanted her to be—next to him, for now and maybe forever. No, it was not Alice. Then it struck him. He sat up.

Alice was on his side of the bed!

He contemplated how he could move her to the other side of the bed without waking her. She stirred and turned to face him. She was breathing lightly, and her aroma enchanted him. All thoughts of disturbing her dissipated. Jake lay back down and, eventually, was overcome by fatigue.

It was just after six in the morning when he opened his eyes. The morning light was dawning. Emerging slowly to consciousness, he wrapped a hand around his erection and massaged it back and forth. He paused. It wasn't working. He needed to go for a jimmy. He rolled out of bed and went into the en suite bathroom.

He looked around. Something seemed strange. He washed his hands and splashed cold water onto his face. Then he realized he had approached the bathroom from the left side of the bed.

Alice! Fuck! She's in my bed!

He looked down and realized he was completely naked.

Fuck! Where did I put my T-shirt and boxer shorts?

He knew she would not believe him if he said he had removed them in a sleeping state, and his cheeks burned red. The more he thought about Alice and the previous night's events, the harder it became to relax and ease his erection.

Jake wandered out of the bathroom and knelt on the bed. He watched Alice sleep. Her long dark brown hair fell softly on her shoulders. He thought about the dimples in her cheeks when she smiled. He was lost in another world, obsessed with this woman, not only her beauty but also her intelligence.

Wrapped up in his fantasy, Jake closed his eyes and did not notice Alice turn so that they were face-to-face.

"Good morning, Jake," she said softly, not wishing to startle him.

The softness of her voice did not achieve the desired result. Shocked, Jake snapped back to reality and opened his eyes. Alice's eyes were closed. Hoping she had not seen him, he lay down on the bed with his face to hers. Alice opened her eyes, reached out to him, and kissed the corner of his mouth. Jake moved his mouth a fraction of an inch so that it locked with Alice's lips. They kissed slowly and tenderly. He reached down and lifted the sweatshirt over her head. Jake kissed and caressed every part of Alice's body. He kissed her passionately and teased with his tongue until their bodies intertwined and became one. Jake did not need to ask. There was no confusion. He felt the lower part of Alice's body throb. When her moment of ecstasy came, her muscles tightened around his cock, teasing and triggering his explosion.

Afterward, Jake lay motionless, overcome with emotion and a heightened sensitivity to Alice's feelings. He was sure she had orgasmed, but he still wondered if she had enjoyed their intimacy. He had a desire to continue exploring the strong attraction he was experiencing for her. He decided to make the next move, determined not to let her leave.

"Would you like a glass of orange juice?" he asked. "Let me make you breakfast. I can cancel golf with my friends. Spend the day with me."

When Alice first opened her eyes, she rubbed them, not sure if she was dreaming. Either it was a dream, or she was watching a private screening of a girl's soft porn movie. Then the previous night flooded back. She was aware now that she was not in her own bed and that Jake's hand, wrapped around his cock, was moving back and forth. He was oblivious, ignorant that Alice had opened her eyes. Alice was stone-cold sober, but her sexual desire for Jake was as strong as it had been hours earlier. Maybe she should have been shocked and displayed her outrage, but that was not how she felt. She was aroused. Alice closed her eyes and allowed her lower body to ache for Jake.

Their intimacy intensified Alice's affection for Jake, yet she feared that giving in to her feelings so soon was counterproductive for a long-term relationship. She contemplated whether there had been sufficient courtship between their meeting and their having sex. She had broken the dating rule of no intimacy on a first date. Alice smiled. It was not the first date if the email exchanges counted. And if the emails did not count, Friday night counted as the first date and Saturday morning the second.

Screw the rules.

She could not see the point in denying sexual intimacy on date after date, only to discover she had connected with a man mentally but not physically. Both elements, in her opinion, were essential to an enduring relationship. She was not in her late teens or early twenties. She was approaching thirty and knew what she wanted. Any man who would judge her in that way without getting to know her was not the type of man she wanted to date.

Jake's offer to make breakfast brought Alice back to reality. Her hand fell to the side of the bed. She lifted her watch and looked at the time. It was 7:45. She was meeting her younger sister, Annabel, at nine.

"Jake, I must go. Annabel and I have an appointment at the bridal shop. I mentioned she's getting married the last week of August, and I'm her maid of honor."

"Can we have dinner later?"

At first, she did not answer. Then she became conscious that her delayed response made it appear as if she did not want to see him again, which was not true.

"I can't have dinner, because I've accepted an invitation to my cousin's thirtieth birthday party."

She could see his disappointment, realizing he was not sure if she was telling him the truth. She smiled inwardly. *You've no idea how elated I am about the previous evening and this morning.*

Alice was conflicted. Her cousin had thrown several previous dinner parties, and on each occasion, Alice had given a genuine excuse for being unable to attend. She felt guilty at the prospect of sending yet another apology. She wished she could spend more time and another night with Jake, but time was running out. She had to leave. Her mind raced as she tried to decide how she could convey that she was not brushing him off. Then she suggested she would show her face at the party and then leave. They could have a late supper.

Jake's facial features relaxed. "Perfect!" He walked over to his desk and picked up the phone to arrange a car for her. "Are you going to your house in Langley Park?"

"Yes." She was sitting on the edge of the bed, stuffing her stockings into her clutch bag. "Thank you. Now I don't have to go searching for a cab while looking like I spent the night on the street." She picked up her dress and slipped it on.

He handed her a notepad. "Please, can you write the zip code for Langley Park?"

Soon the car was arranged. Jake was nothing if not efficient. He showered quickly, shaved, and dressed in his golf attire. A few minutes before eight o'clock, he closed and locked his apartment door. He and Alice walked across the courtyard and through the reception area, where the concierge office was located, to their waiting cars.

While walking from Jake's apartment to the car, Alice kept her head down. She was conscious that she had not showered or changed her clothes from the night before. Behind the car in which Jake's friend Ben was waiting for him was a black limousine.

Alice tugged Jake's sleeve. "Will I appear ill-mannered if I don't say hello? I would prefer to meet Ben another time when I don't look like I've just emerged from a nightclub."

"No problem." He kissed her. "I'll see you tonight."

Once Alice was inside the limousine, the driver confirmed her destination as Langley Park. Alice checked her watch. It was two minutes after eight. Provided traffic remained light, she would be home in time to shower and meet Annabel.

Minutes after Annabel's wedding had been announced, planning for the wedding had commenced. Annabel was no different from any other bride. The wedding consumed her every waking moment. This was the fifth bridal shop she planned to visit to find bridesmaid dresses. The internet did not help the situation; it churned out more bridal shops. Alice did not think it was her imagination that the shops were getting farther afield. The only saving grace was that Annabel's taste was discerning. Two of Alice's friends had married recently. Both brides had looked beautiful, but the bridesmaids had looked hideous. Brides often feared the bridesmaids would outshine them, so they dressed them down, but Annabel believed bridesmaids should complement the bride and add to the beauty of the day. Alice was looking forward to the wedding, though she wished Annabel would lighten up a little. It would have been nice to go home, drink coffee, and tell Annabel about Jake, but that would have been considered a lack of focus on what was important: the forthcoming wedding.

Alice looked at her watch. She was making good time. The car had passed through Victoria. A few people were entering the tube and mainline station, but it was early Saturday morning, and Victoria was still waking up. The car crossed Vauxhall Bridge, a Grade II–listed bridge in central London. It crossed the Thames in a southeast–northwest direction between Vauxhall on the south bank and Pimlico on the north. It did not matter how many times Alice crossed that bridge; as she neared the south-bank side, she always looked up at the MI6 secret intelligence service's building, the SIS. The SIS, located at Vauxhall Cross, had, in the past, focused its activities on the Russian threat, but that mandate had been cut back to focus on the prevention or detection of serious crime.

The opposite side of the MI6 building was Saint George Wharf Tower, also known as the Tower, a residential skyscraper that was still under construction. Alice had watched the building's construction from its inception. When built, it would be the tallest residential building in the United Kingdom. She gazed at the apartments before looking away and back toward the river. She closed her eyes and imagined sharing a river-view apartment with Jake. She rubbed her eyelids and tried to replay the moments of their lovemaking that morning. Her flushed cheeks burned.

Jake would have preferred to have dinner with Alice, but he was prepared to make any compromise, provided it would result in Alice agreeing to spend time with him. As he came closer to the car, he noticed that Ben had a mischievous grin on his face. Jake wondered how long it had taken him to put two and two together when he saw Alice coming from his apartment in evening wear. They had been close friends for three years. Ben should have known that where intimacy was concerned, it was out of character for Jake to engage in one-night stands. But this was Ben. What he had learned about Jake would make no difference. He had a one-track mind and would be waiting to hear a rampant sex story.

"How much longer are you planning to keep me guessing?" Ben asked. "I want to know everything that happened last night—and spare no details."

Jake laughed. "Do you think about anything other than sex?" He laughed again and then provided Ben with the details of his date, leaving out the intimacy earlier that morning.

Ben was astonished. "You agreed to have a beautiful woman in your apartment and not make a play for her? I can't believe you. If I were in your shoes, the rules would be simple: no nooky, no bed."

Jake liked Ben but had long ago given up on him where women were concerned. Ben was married to a beautiful Russian woman. He controlled her because he controlled the money and the key to her green card.

Jake did not want the conversation to go any further, so he sought to end it. "I respected her wishes and, thereby, earned her respect."

"Are you planning to see her again?"

Jake did not hesitate in his reply. "Yes. I don't think you appreciate how difficult it is to find a beautiful woman you can connect with both mentally and physically."

He fiddled with his phone and sent a text to Alice to help break the conversation: "Send me a photo that shows a side of you I don't know."

He was pleased when the buzz of his phone indicated that Alice's response had arrived. He opened the message to find a photo of her modeling swimwear. *Wow!* Jake could not believe what he was seeing. The photo depicted Alice wearing a scant two-piece bathing suit on a catwalk at a fashion show.

"Planning to share?" Ben asked.

Jake smiled. "I'm looking at a picture of Alice in swimwear, but it's for my eyes only."

They both laughed.

"Are you free this evening to have dinner? Helena will want to learn more about Alice."

Jake accepted the invitation gladly.

5

Alice fumbled in her clutch bag for her wallet as the limousine pulled to a stop in front of her house. The driver exited the car and held the door open for her. With purse in hand, she stepped out.

"How much do I owe?" she asked. She would have preferred to settle the bill before getting out of the car.

"The gentleman has taken care of the bill, madam," the driver replied politely.

Alice thanked him and walked to her front door while searching for her house keys.

Five minutes later, Alice stepped out of the shower and put on her bathrobe. She jumped when a sharp knock on the door hit her ears. *Annabel!*

Seven minutes early, Annabel was standing on the doorstep, expecting Alice to open the door fully dressed.

"It'll only take me two minutes to get dressed," Alice blurted out before Annabel could say anything.

Annabel's annoyance registered on her face. "Alice, you had plenty of notice. Why can't you take my wedding seriously?"

Alice thought Annabel was being unreasonable. They had agreed to meet at 9:00, and it was 8:53. She was not late. Alice did not answer the question. Looking past Annabel, she saw their mother sitting in the car. It would not be an easy day.

Alice said, "I haven't had breakfast. Please, can you buy me a cappuccino and a Danish pastry from Caffè Nero? Feel free to grab something for yourself and Mother." She handed Annabel her wallet. "I'll be dressed and ready to go by the time you get back."

Alice opened the door just as Annabel was about to take her anger out on the door knocker. Alice touched her mother's shoulder as she sat down in the backseat of the car. Annabel was in rally mode as she put the car in gear and headed for Kingston upon Thames. Alice savored every bite of her naughty-but-nice Danish pastry. Mother and Annabel were neither eating nor drinking. They had probably been awake since five that morning to discuss the wedding and had long since had breakfast.

"Alice, did you forget to set your alarm clock?" her mother asked.

Alice let the comment fly and continued to indulge in her pastry. She blocked out her mother and Annabel's heated debate about the menu for the wedding breakfast. They had no idea of the brain damage they were causing each other and those around them.

Alice was startled when Annabel, having lost the latest round with her mother, asked her what she was smiling at. She knew Annabel thought she was amused by their discussion of the menu, but she had been lost in her thoughts about how much she had enjoyed the previous evening and morning with Jake.

She was saved from explaining herself when her phone vibrated with a text alert. She stopped the name Jake from falling from her lips. Instead, she said, "The office." Jake would be her little secret for the moment. She was not concerned that she was encouraging the belief that her career was more important to her than marriage and starting a family. The text message was from Jake.

"Wow! When do I get to see you in that swimsuit?"

Alice's reply was nebulous: a smiley emoji.

Jake's was right on point: "Can I see you in the swimsuit if I take you on a vacation to Hawaii?"

He had asked about her favorite holiday destination during one of their email exchanges. Alice had replied that it was the Caribbean but that she dreamed of going to Hawaii, which was probably what had prompted his text.

Tempted to say yes, Alice resisted and texted another smiley face in reply.

Jake's reply was quick: "You're a tease."

"Tease?" She inserted an emoji of a pink bikini.

To Alice's amazement, later that morning, Annabel found her dream bridesmaids' dresses. They made an appointment for the bridesmaids' dress fitting, at which time Annabel, or their mother, would settle the final color.

The drive back home was jovial, until Annabel gave one more display of the power she was wielding. Alice, who was eager to get home to finalize a legal document for her Monday morning meeting, noticed her sister had taken the turn for London. Believing it was a mistake on Annabel's part, Alice drew it to her attention. Annabel fired back sharply that she had an appointment at the Pronovias bridal shop in Harrods to view the tiaras she had selected. She wanted Alice's opinion.

"It would have been polite if you had forewarned me," Alice said, not wanting to provoke an argument.

"I am planning a wedding," Annabel replied. "Do you know how difficult it is? Forgive me if I forget to notify you about one appointment."

Alice thought Annabel was missing the point, but she did not reply. Alice's text alert on her phone sounded. She looked down. It was another message from Jake: "Do you have any food preferences or dislikes for supper?"

"No, a light snack will suffice. My mother is the caterer for to-night's party, and I will be expected to partake in the buffet."

"OK."

The three women stopped for lunch in a café on Brompton Road before going into Harrods. It was four in the afternoon before they were back in the car and headed to Langley Park. Alice, because of her late Friday night, fell asleep during the journey.

When the car pulled into Alice's driveway, Annabel looked back over the driver's seat and told Alice she would pick her up at six forty-five that evening for their cousin's birthday party.

Alice opened the car door and stepped out. She stopped and con-sidered saying something about taking her car that night, but she was aware that her mother anticipated she would have a glass or two at the party and that Annabel would take her car. Annabel would not be drinking, because she was working the following day. An inquiry would follow on why they were taking two cars. When her mother discovered Alice planned to leave the party early, her lecture on the importance of family would surely follow. Alice decided to keep her mouth shut.

"Six forty-five," she said. "Bye."

She hurried up the drive before she changed her mind and said something.

Alice's autopilot sent her straight to the bathroom, where she ran a bath, pouring in bath oil and adding an extra measure of bubble bath. She needed it and deserved it after a full day with her mother and Annabel.

She was packing an overnight bag, when her phone pinged. Her body stiffened. Men had, in the past, notwithstanding a connection and weeks of dating, canceled on her without any explanation. Her heart sank. *Jake. He's canceling. Please, God, don't let him cancel—not now. He's special. I like him.* She picked up the phone, expecting the worst.

"Honey, park your car in front of the reception area, and hand your keys in at the concierge desk; a valet will park the car. I'm hav-ing dinner with Ben and Helena and expect to be home early, but if you arrive before me, the concierge will give you the key to my apartment. Make yourself comfortable. XX."

Alice stepped into the steamy bubble bath, inhaling the bath oil's scent. She lay back and stretched her aching body. She relaxed, calm and soothed, as she lost herself in her sanctuary.

The house was silent. The fading light in the bathroom and the approaching dusk outside alerted her that it was early evening.

She was not sure how long she had been in the bath, but the cooling water signaled it was time to get out. She reached for her terry cloth robe.

Back in the bedroom, she selected a dress. After one final look at herself in the full-length mirror, she put the gift vouchers she had bought for her cousin into her clutch bag and went downstairs to wait for Annabel.

She stared at the document in hand, trying to remember why she had thought law was her calling. *Practicing law is something I just happen to be good at, a profession that's respectable and that guarantees me a nice income. Now, in my thirties, I'm bored with my career path and life, but the thought of trying to change it scares the hell out of me—it feels like it's irreversible.* She closed her eyes and thought about Jake. *It's not too late for love.* She turned back to reviewing the document.

Alice had almost finished reviewing the document for her Monday morning meeting regarding IG's sponsorship agreement of the Valencia Football Club, when Annabel's car pulled into the driveway; the headlights illuminated the living room. Alice put the document in her briefcase laptop bag and went outside.

As Alice approached the car, Annabel lowered the window to greet her. On reprieve from the wedding, Annabel smiled at Alice warmly. This was the Annabel Alice loved. Leaning into the car window, Alice explained that she had a date later that night and would be taking her car.

Annabel smiled cheekily. "Mummy won't be pleased that you're leaving the birthday celebration early."

Alice returned her smile. Had she not passed her eighteenth

birthday a decade ago? "Mother forgets sometimes that we're adults. I'll follow you."

They arrived at the party fifteen minutes later. Alice wasted no time. Her plan was to make sure the birthday girl and a few carefully selected guests saw her face and then leave.

Alice had just finished a conversation with her cousin, when she noticed her mother over by the buffet table. A twinge of sadness hit her heart. She had been close to her mother once, but their relationship had started to change as she approached age thirteen. It had not been adolescence that caused the distance between them; it had been her mother's divorce from Alice's father.

Her mother had dated other men after the divorce, but she had not found happiness, and over time, her daughters had become a substitute for a husband. In the early years following the divorce, she had depended emotionally on Alice. Things had come to a head in the years that followed Alice's move to London to pursue her dreams. Breaking their loving bond had been painful. It should have been simple, a child leaving the nest, but it hadn't been. Alice had taken away the crutch she had volunteered to her mother. She was not present emotionally to the extent she had been previously. She could not speak for her mother's feelings, and now was not the time to explore any guilt she should or should not have been carrying. The issue was that she had allowed her mother to become dependent on her and then pulled away that support. As a result, Alice's mother had painted her as the disloyal daughter. Her bitterness had prevented her from forgiving Alice for the perceived wrong.

Looking at her watch, Alice saw that it was five minutes to eight. She had been at the party for almost an hour. She had to leave. She could not delay the lecture any longer. She approached her mother with trepidation. Her only saving grace was that they were in a public place. Her mother was unlikely to make a scene.

Alice approached her mother, who was standing with Annabel, and praised her for the buffet. Alice's mother, in Alice's and others' opinions, had first-class skills in that field. After a forced conversation between mother and two daughters, Alice informed them she had to leave for a prior engagement.

"Prior engagement?" her mother replied. "Alice, you've known about this party for months."

Before her mother could say another word, Alice turned and walked away, raising a hand to wave goodbye.

Inside her car, she checked her mobile phone for messages, punched Jake's address into the GPS, and set off for central London.

6

lice pulled up in front of the iron gates of the gated development where Jake lived. The security guard emerged from the guardhouse and approached her car window. Alice lowered it and explained that she was visiting Jake Logan. It was apparent that the guard knew Jake was not home but was expecting her, because he did not call through to Jake's apartment. Having passed through the first round of vetting, she steered her car up the drive and parked in front of the reception building, as Jake had instructed.

Inside, a uniformed concierge greeted her. Behind the desk were two more security guards. The reception area, a majestic communal hallway, had plush purple and beige sofas. The aroma from the floral display, which featured orchids in vases, wafted through the room.

"Mr. Logan is not home yet," the concierge said. "These are the keys to his apartment. Do you need a porter to walk you there?"

"No, thank you," Alice replied.

Alice thanked the concierge, handed him her car keys, and headed to the door on the other side of the reception, which opened out into the courtyard, gardens, and apartments.

As Alice let herself into Jake's apartment, she was greeted with the same dim lighting from the previous night. She noticed the reception room to the right and the hallway desk to the left. As she passed the desk, she saw it held an iPhone, scattered coins, and a Bridgestone B330 golf ball. The remote control for the lights sat millimeters away from the golf ball. Although Jake probably had not planned it, the remote control was acting as a fail-safe that secured the golf ball and prevented something from disturbing its balance and causing it to roll off the table into the reception room and under the sofa, where it would have been lost to Jake's world of golf.

Alice headed for Jake's bedroom. She set down her night bag and returned to the hall desk. She picked up the remote control without disturbing the golf ball, but as a precaution, she moved a pile of coins in front of the ball to stop it from rolling off the desk. She studied the remote for a while before she figured out how to brighten the lighting in the hallway.

The nighttime lighting changed to normal lighting, and she noticed that on the center of the desk was a golf figurine. Alice guessed by the weight and feel of it that it was polyresin. It stood about seventeen inches high and depicted a man driving a golf ball.

Setting down the figurine, she noted that hanging above the desk and on the adjacent wall were tastefully chosen pieces of modern art.

She put the remote back on the desk and went into the reception room, where she found two sumptuous beige sofas. On the sofa to the left sat a Callaway RAZR X Black driver, not that the label meant anything to Alice. But she was quickly learning that designer golf equipment was, to Jake, what fashion designer labels were to women. Alice made herself comfortable on the sofa facing the frosted French doors through which she had passed to enter the reception room. She picked up the television remote from the marble-topped coffee table and selected Sky News. She had not listened to the news or read a newspaper that day. The headlines were mainly about the US president's forthcoming visit to London.

Minutes later, she heard a key in the door.

"Alice?" Jake called.

She turned off the TV and walked into the hallway to greet him. Jake put his keys down on the table next to the set of keys Alice had used to enter the apartment and then turned and wrapped his arms around her, kissing her on the lips.

"Did you pour yourself a glass of wine? Are you hungry?"

"I arrived five minutes before you. I haven't discovered the kitchen or the wine."

Jake took Alice's hand and led her into the kitchen. It was in keeping with the rest of the apartment. A massive stainless-steel Sub-Zero fridge complemented the other stainless-steel appliances. A normal round glass table offered a place to relax and eat dinner. For breakfast, there was a granite bar with stools. Alice sat at the bar as Jake poured wine and laid out nibbles—chicken, cheese, fruit, shrimp, olives, and whole-wheat crackers. He nibbled at the cheese and relayed how Helena and Ben had grilled him for information about her.

Alice excused herself and went to the bedroom to find her clutch bag and check her messages. When she turned to leave the bedroom, Jake was standing behind her. He put his hands on her shoulders and moved her dress's sash shoulder straps to the side. The dress fell to her ankles. She stood naked down to her panties. He lifted her onto the bed and kissed and caressed her, venturing to tease where he had not dared to go the previous night. When Alice could not contain her excitement any longer, her back arched at the height of her orgasm. Jake's body interlocked with Alice's, allowing them to move together in ecstasy. Jake thrust until he achieved his climax. Alice lay in Jake's arms and fell asleep.

She woke up around three o'clock in the morning. Low but audible music emanated from the living room. Jake was sound asleep. She watched him; he was at peace. His chest rose and fell gently with every breath. Alice heard Sade's "The Sweetest Gift" playing in the background. She directed her attention to the sleeping man she had met by chance and the joy he was bringing into her life. Alice was an optimist, not naive. She was still getting to know him, but in her heart, she knew this was the kind of happiness that might happen once in a lifetime. Relaxed and at peace, she drifted back to sleep, thinking that for as long as she lived, she would always remember that moment.

Jake was still sleeping soundly when she opened her eyes at eight o'clock. His head was tucked under the pillow and pinned down with his arms. She peeped under the pillow. He opened his eyes.

"It's the birds," he said.

Alice was puzzled until he emerged from under the pillow and explained.

"The birds' chirping disturbs me early in the morning. It doesn't sound like singing. It drives me crazy, and if I can't block them out, if I can't silence the birds, I'll get my BB gun and shoot them until they chirp no more."

"They're just little birdies tweeting," she teased.

"I can't believe you hear sweet singing."

She smiled. "Point me in the right direction. I'll brew coffee."

She put on the sweatshirt she had worn the previous night and went into the guest bathroom. When she walked into the kitchen several minutes later, she saw that Jake had started to brew coffee. Two glasses of fresh orange juice sat on the granite bar with the morning paper. The mixed aromas of the brewing coffee and bagels toasting floated through the air. Jake was barefoot and dressed in knee-length white shorts and a white T-shirt with *Florida* printed across the front. Alice climbed onto a barstool and picked up a glass of orange juice.

They read the papers, sipped fresh black coffee, and ate bagels.

"One of the things I miss about New York is having freshly baked bagels and coffee in the morning," Jake said. "I can't get fresh coffee and bagels before my run in the morning, because the Starbucks in London doesn't open at six."

Alice returned to the bedroom, made the bed, and went into the en suite bathroom to run a bath. The phone rang and then stopped at the same time Jake's mobile began to ring, and then it too stopped. Alice guessed he had switched it to silent.

The bathroom smacked of decadence. On one side was a luxury bath for two. The other side featured a double shower with power showerheads placed strategically to hit every angle of the body. In the center was a double vanity with separate his-and-hers basin cabinets.

The bathroom floor was heated, and towel warmers completed the setup.

Alice was not planning her usual soak; she had forgotten her shower cap and did not want to get her hair wet by taking a shower. She ran a bath with the bath wash from her overnight bag, but her curiosity got the better of her, and she could not stop herself from peeping into the bathroom cabinets. The left, Jake's side, was minimalistic. It contained shower wash, shaving foam, razors, a toothbrush, toothpaste, and deodorant. On the right side, women's toiletries fell out of the cabinet. The only thing missing was her choice of perfume. Alice's heart sank.

Jake walked into the bathroom right as she closed the cabinet, leaving no doubt to an observer that she had seen its contents.

Regardless of whether she stayed or picked up her things and walked out the door, she needed to get cleaned up and dressed. She stepped into the bathtub, refusing to acknowledge Jake until her nakedness was covered. Jake watched her beautiful, if not perfect, body slip under the bubbles. He knelt at the edge of the tub and put a hand in the water.

"Can I wash your back?"

"Shouldn't you be washing the back of the woman whose things currently occupy your love nest?"

He sighed. "Please let me explain." He ran through the bare facts. "Jessica, my ex-girlfriend, lived in London for a few weeks, but it didn't work out, so she moved back to New York. The items in the bathroom cabinet belonged to her. I should have thrown them out, but they're in the cabinet I don't use, and getting rid of them slipped my mind."

Why should I believe you?

He appeared to be studying her face while waiting for her to respond. She remained silent.

"It's the truth! Please don't spoil this day."

Alice maintained her poker face, giving no indication of whether she believed him.

Alice had listened intently as if she were in a courtroom, observing Jake to see if his body language confirmed his words or raised suspicion. She had not had much sleep in the last forty-eight hours. Her head swam with questions. She had seen no other signs of another woman in the apartment. She was not certain she should, but she decided to give Jake the benefit of the doubt. She eased her body into a standing position. Jake reached for a towel and wrapped it around her.

Alice surveyed the bathroom. The contents of the cabinet still bothered her. She needed to protect her heart from Jake and put up a barrier—a brick wall he could not penetrate. Her mind dug the foundations, knowing that once the first brick was laid, in no time at all, the wall would be complete.

Back in the bedroom, she peeped into the closet for signs that she had made the wrong decision. Jake was in the kitchen, cleaning up after their breakfast. She found nothing out of place. His story seemed genuine. Alice relaxed. Erecting the wall was put on hold. She still had the towel wrapped around her when Jake put his head around the door.

"Did you bring any clothing other than cocktail dresses?"

"Yes, I have a casual outfit," she said, a little surprised at the question.

Jake smiled at the shocked expression on her face. "Some women have only one look: high-end designer from head to toe. If you have casual clothes, it would be nice to walk in Kensington Gardens."

When Jake reentered the bedroom five minutes later, Alice was sitting on the bed, brushing her hair. She wore black leggings and a white georgette shirt. He walked over to her. The outer sides of his calves and knees touched the insides of her thighs. Jake moved his hands from her shoulders to the second button on her shirt.

"Take your clothes off?" he asked.

A little puzzled after their conversation about casual clothing, Alice did not reply. *Does he not like what I'm wearing?* She lifted her head to look at him, and her eyes traveled up his tall, toned body. Her eyes did not reach far enough to engage with Jake's. She stopped when she saw his erection, which Jake's loose-fitting pants could not hide.

He finished unbuttoning her shirt and then kissed and caressed her body as he slipped off the rest of her clothing.

Jake, with Alice beside him, lay on the bed in a state between wakefulness and sleep, when the apartment's landline rang for the third time. He jumped up. Only one person knew his landline number. She wasn't likely to go away. She didn't take kindly to being ignored either. *Not today*, he thought. He reached for the phone and pulled out the cord. He'd deal with it later—there was no way he could risk Alice hearing the stream of profanity Jessica would unleash if she did not get her way. His ex had no filter when it came to her anger. The phone continued to ring in the reception room.

"Why are you ignoring the phone?" Alice asked after several rings.

He hesitated before explaining that it was an unsolicited call. "Probably somebody trying to sell something I don't want to buy."

The phone stopped and then, minutes later, rang again.

"Have you considered answering the phone and threatening the caller with the privacy laws?" Alice asked.

London differed from New York in that respect. If a number was not listed in the public directory and permission had not been given regarding using personal details from the voters' roll for marketing, residents rarely received unsolicited calls.

"I'm not very familiar with British privacy laws," he lied.

He owed her an explanation, but he struggled to come up with one due to the enormity of the emotions rushing through his head. Jessica had ended their relationship, but he still had strong, if not screwed-up, feelings for her. Alice was special, rare, and his feelings for her were growing in ways he was powerless to control. She deserved the truth, but he could not work out which version to give her.

In his head, he corrected himself. No sane person could explain Jessica. The thought caused him to question his own sanity. While Jessica lived, he wondered if he could ever have a life apart from her.

He thought about the easy option: no explanation. He could let Alice go to find happiness elsewhere. *I can't and will not let her go—I want her.*

Jake revisited how he had been unable to do simple things with Jessica, because she was always dressed in expensive designer clothes whose only function was to be admired.

Alice isn't Jessica, and I will not let my experience with Jessica control this relationship. I need to move forward, not back. It was the start of day three of his weekend with Alice. She was intelligent, patient, and kind. *Still, I know the difference between Nike and Armani leggings—designer clothes. Eventually, she'll become another Jessica.* He feared falling in love again only to discover he and that person were not compatible. He would risk all in business, but his heart—he fought to keep that off-limits. He wanted to believe that Jessica was outside the norms of any relationship and that he should let things with Alice play out. In that case, he had to contain Jessica before Alice's alarm bells turned on. He also had to deal with another romantic encounter that had wounded him so deeply emotionally that he had not healed. Until now, he had buried that relationship. The closer he drew to Alice, the more his history caught up, and the excuses to run niggled at him.

He turned to Alice and kissed her. "Let's go for that walk in Kensington Gardens."

7

By the time Alice and Jake stepped out of the apartment and walked across the courtyard, it was almost noon. Alice had not appreciated the architecture of the building on her previous visit. The original house, now apartments, had been built in Jacobean style. Jake told her that toward the end of the eighteenth century, it had been converted into a girls' boarding school, but it had been destroyed in a fire in 1870, and a replica had been built. Eventually, the replica had been converted into luxury apartments, an exclusive gated development with concierge service and underground parking.

"How much would a buyer pay for a two-bedroom apartment in this development?" Alice asked.

"Apartment fifty-four, it's rumored, sold for sixty million pounds. That apartment had five bedrooms. I believe two-bedroom apartments sell from five to seven million pounds."

"Where's the car park?" Alice asked.

He reassured her that her car was parked safely underground.

"Show me," she said. "And here's your challenge: guess the model and make of my car."

Jake turned and opened a door that led back inside the building. Heading toward the underground car park, they passed the communal pool and gym. Along the way, he guessed BMW, Mercedes, and Audi, but none were correct. Alice looked around the car park but could not see her car. He teased her, saying the concierge had probably taken it on a joyride.

She smiled. "My Porsche can't go anywhere without me."

"Wow! What model?"

"Cayman S," Alice replied.

"Nice! Cars are fun, but I'm not obsessed with them. I'm blown away to hear that you drive a Porsche; it's not generally perceived as a girl's car." In the office, talk of Porsches fueled the boys' testosterone.

Jake surveyed the car park. "Alice, you might not be worried, but I feel responsible. I was the one who said the concierge would take care of your car."

"Trust me, Jake, the car can't go anywhere without me. An alert is sounded when it moves outside a set range from my security fob. The security fob is in my purse. If the Porsche had moved outside the per-mitted range, the monitoring company would have received an alert."

After leaving the car park, Alice and Jake crossed over Kensington High Street and headed toward Kensington Gardens. She had lived in Britain all her life, but she took many things for granted. As they entered the gardens, Alice thought about their history. Kensington Gardens covered approximately 250 acres and originally had been part of Hyde Park. The gardens, with their magnificent trees, were the setting for Kensington Palace, the birthplace of Queen Victoria, who had lived there until she became queen. Like Green Park, the gardens were particularly popular for sunbathing and picnics in fine weather. They were also popular as a healthy walking route for commuters. Joggers and cyclists also used the paths extensively. The place was a refuge for people living in, working in, or visiting central London.

They held hands as they walked through the gardens, but Alice realized she had not let go of the bathroom cabinet incident entirely. *He doesn't want to be reminded of his ex-girlfriend, but he must know the questions are coming. If we've any chance of going forward, he can't be evasive with me.*

"Jake," she said slowly, "tell me about Jessica." They were headed toward the Diana, Princess of Wales, Memorial Playground—a fantastic adventure for kids. The memorial was also a reminder of how a third party, Camilla, had encroached upon Prince Charles and Princess Diana's relationship.

He took a deep breath before telling Alice that he had dated Jessica for the past five years on and off. Jessica was friends with a colleague's wife, which was how they had been introduced. "I had been single for just under a year and was looking for companionship. In the beginning, Jessica was fun, and I closed my eyes to the obvious. Right from the start, though, I realized she was not interested in me; she was dating a bank balance." Jake paused for thought. "Jessica was not so different from other women I dated in New York."

"What happened?" Alice asked.

"Opposites attract," Jake replied. "But they also repel. Conflict ensued. Jessica shopped, spending anything from hundreds of dollars to several thousand dollars on each occasion. During the work week, she expected me to hang out with her and her socialite friends from the art world in bars or clubs until early hours of the morning. I didn't mind sharing her recreational pursuits some of the time, but Jessica didn't share any of my interests. A suggestion that we go cycling, go hiking, or stay home and watch television would result in an argument."

"What did Jessica do for a living?"

Jake winced. "Can we change the subject?"

Alice sensed he was still hurting from the failure of his relationship with Jessica, so she did not push for an answer. They passed the Broad Walk Café located next to the Diana Memorial Playground. Until that moment, Alice had not appreciated how much Kensington Gardens was steeped in romance. She thought about the Italian Gardens, the 150-year-old ornamental water garden located on the north side, near Lancaster Gate. It was believed to have been created as a gift from Prince Albert to his beloved Queen Victoria.

It had been some time since breakfast, so Jake suggested they stop for refreshments at the café in the Italian Gardens. Alice had tea, Jake had a Diet Coke, and they shared a large slice of cheesecake. After Jake put the last piece of cheesecake in his mouth, Alice leaned forward, and her lips brushed against his ear.

"Take me home, Jake Logan," she whispered, "and make love to me."

Back in the apartment, Jake put the groceries in the kitchen, and Alice went into the bedroom to take off her cardigan. She opened the closet, placed the sweater on a clothes hanger, and then stepped back to close the closet doors.

Jake came up from behind and pressed his erection against her. "Your desires are mine to grant," he whispered as he wrapped his arms around her waist. He kissed her neck gently, turned her around, and lifted her onto the bed.

Once they exhausted their desires, Jake bent over and kissed Alice and then slipped out of bed, put on a pair of jogging pants and a shirt, and headed to the kitchen.

Jake had revealed in their discussions that he enjoyed cooking in his spare time, and it was more fun when he had someone for whom to cook. She hesitated for a few seconds before she said, "You've not asked about my past relationships." She paused and watched him as he prepared the chicken, stuffing it with onions and squeezing lemon juice onto the outside. She knew she had to choose her words carefully. *There are no good words to use here.* "Why is it so difficult for you to discuss your ex or her occupation if you've both moved on?" Before he could reply, she said, "Are you ashamed of what she did for a living?"

"Please don't spoil this beautiful evening."

She detected an urgency in his tone.

"I didn't say I wouldn't talk about Jessica—but not now."

You did, and it's never a good time.

Before she could speak, he walked out of the kitchen and said, "The movie is about to start. We can talk relationships another time."

The aroma of the chicken roasting filled the kitchen and hallway. At intervals throughout the movie, Jake paused to baste the chicken. After the movie finished, Jake and Alice returned to the kitchen to finish cooking and set the table.

It was approaching nine o'clock when Alice cleared the table and settled back into the living room to watch the late news with Jake.

The landline rang. He did not answer it. It rang a second time. Alice had the urge to pick it up, but it was neither her apartment nor her landline. Jake unplugged the phone. Almost immediately, his mobile phone started to ring. He did not answer it. Alice looked at him. He was visibly disturbed. He grabbed his left arm and pressed it against his chest to ease what appeared to be discomfort in his chest. Visible beads of sweat appeared on his forehead as his breathing shortened. His mobile stopped ringing. Within seconds, it started again.

Alice looked on. *He's having a heart attack!* "Are you OK?"

"Stop! Jessica, stop!"

The words were barely audible, but it was clear to Alice what he had said. He switched his mobile phone to silent and stared at it as if willing it to stop ringing.

"Jake," Alice said, "is there a reason you can't answer the phones?"

"The calls are from Jessica," he said. "She won't stop calling. She won't leave me alone." He sounded and looked exasperated, lacking the will or the energy to lie.

"Is the relationship finished?" Alice asked. "You said it was over. Is it really?"

"Yes."

For the second time that day, Alice felt his anguish. Something was not right. She was cognizant that she did not have the full picture, but she felt that unless Jake was hiding something, Jessica's behavior bordered on stalking.

"What is it that you're not telling me? Why does she keep calling?"

"She would still like us to reconcile."

Alice touched his shoulder. "If you can't be open and honest, I don't see where we go from here." *This, whatever it is, is not for me.* Feeling choked up, she went into the bedroom to prepare for work the following day.

✦ ✦ ✦

Later that evening, Jake had made the arrangement for his car for the following morning. Earlier in the day, Jake had given Alice the heads-up about his Monday morning routine. On Mondays, he woke at 5:55 a.m. and walked out of the apartment at 5:58 a.m., dressed in his gym gear, having brushed his teeth and picked up his suit carrier. He achieved a three-minute turnaround. He had a car collect him at 6:00 a.m. to take him to the gym located near his office in the city. After a vigorous workout, he showered, dressed, and went to the office for a breakfast meeting at 8:00 a.m. with the team he managed.

After he finished, Jake called the concierge desk and requested that Alice's car be made available at reception at 6:00 a.m. He was still talking to the concierge when he walked into the bedroom to pack his personal items and put his suit in the suit carrier. Alice sat on the bed. When he finished his call, he kissed her on the forehead.

"Honey, I've arranged for your car to be brought to reception at six. Is that time OK for you?"

"Perfect," Alice said.

Jake lay down next to her. Their shoulders touched gently. He then rolled onto his side to show her the iPod touch he had purchased recently. Alice, who, through her own choice, had never even owned a Walkman, was impressed.

Jake played Pete Yorn's "Just Another," as he did often when he thought about Jessica. His thoughts about Jessica mixed with the lyrics: "Our worlds were so different. I know there were doubts about the future, but you shouldn't have behaved the way you did."

His mind jumped back and forth as he tried to convince himself that he had made the right decision to end his relationship with Jessica.

"Jake, this is an emotional yet beautiful song. Who's the artist?"

"It's Pete Yorn's 'Just Another.'" Jake enjoyed spending time with Alice. When he looked into her eyes, he saw her intensity and intellect matched with innocence and a kindness he had never experienced. He could not fool her, and he sensed a cross-examination was coming. It was better adjourned for another day. To head it off, he kissed her and said, "It's late, and we have an early start." He pulled the duvet around her shoulders and fell asleep.

8

New York, Sunday

It was six o'clock in the evening in New York, and Jessica was alone in her apartment. She had not been outside all day. She thought about taking a shower and ordering takeout. She stared at the almost-empty container of antidepressant medication on the table and the half-empty bottle of red wine. If she ordered takeout, she would have to face the delivery man, and she could not do that in her present state. She had been playing Buckshot LeFonque's "Another Day" repeatedly for the last thirty minutes. She made a mental note to text her new favorite song to Jake: "Another day staring out of my window, thinkin' 'bout tomorrow, wishing things would clear."

She was not sleepy, just tired of the way she lived. "No, the way I'm not living," she said. She picked up the bottle of wine, went into her bedroom, and used it to wash down a couple of sleeping pills. She fell across the bed.

Why does he constantly ignore me, run away from me, hang up on me, keep me hanging on plans, stand me up on actual plans, and ignore my phone calls? He doesn't take my calls when I call him at work. He unplugs his land-line. He doesn't return texts ever. Why does he constantly shut off his phone when I call?

She was crying uncontrollably. The voice in her head would not go away.

He has taken you to the brink of hell and back a thousand times.

She thought it was an exaggeration, but the voice in her head disagreed.

No, it's not an exaggeration. It's probably more like one hundred thousand. Why? Have you asked yourself that?

"My love for Jake runs deep. God only knows why," Jessica whispered.

No! Wrong. Jake is your best option—your only option, the voice said.

Jessica hit the redial button three more times. The calls went straight to Jake's voice mail.

"Fuck you!" she shouted into the phone. The message recorded, and she threw the phone across the room.

London, Monday

Alice turned and put her arm around Jake's. She was half asleep, so her aim was a little off, and she touched the tip of his erection. *Oh!* She yanked her hand away.

"Not so quick," Jake said. "If you touch, you have to play." He rolled over and kissed her. He moved his hand down her back and lifted her silk nightdress.

Jake did not stop her when she slipped out of bed shortly after their early morning play. She could not dress as quickly as he could, so she needed a head start. He was already drifting back to sleep.

Alice took a long and refreshing shower. Out of the shower and three-quarters dressed, Alice went to the kitchen and poured two glasses of orange juice—one full and the other only half full. Based on Jake's schedule, they would not have time for breakfast. Coffee would have to wait until she was in her office.

Back in the bedroom, she handed Jake the half-empty glass. Over the weekend, Alice had watched Jake as he poured a full glass of orange juice but only drank half.

"This is all you can have, because you've been wasting your orange juice," she said with a cheeky smile.

He smiled back as he accepted the glass. "Are you spanking me?"

Alice giggled. She had put aside her doubts of the past night, convinced that he was falling for her, and his past was just that.

At reception, the concierge handed Alice her car keys and informed her that her car was parked in front of the reception building. Alice thanked the concierge and caught up with Jake, who had already collected the morning paper and was heading out the front reception door.

Jake recognized Alice's Porsche as the Cayman S. A colleague at work had recently become the proud owner of a Cayman S and had treated the office to photographs. Jake's colleague had boasted that the car reached sixty-two miles per hour in just 5.2 seconds and topped out at 172 miles per hour. The photographs had not exaggerated the interaction of convex and concave curves and the nineteen-inch Porsche Turbo wheels.

"Nice car," he said as he kissed Alice goodbye.

When she hit the accelerator, he did not miss the audible hallmark of the characteristic Porsche sound coming from the stainless-steel twin tailpipe integrated into the car's rear end.

Jake settled himself into the limousine. The journey to his office was approximately fifteen minutes. He opened the morning paper. The president's forthcoming visit to London was still dominating the news, but Jake was too distracted to care. He could not stop thinking about Alice. Leaving out the Jessica incidents, they had had a perfect weekend. Desperate to hear her voice, he reached into his pocket for his phone. On the screen was a text from Jessica: "Good morning, big babe. Did you play golf this weekend? I called. Call."

He deleted the text and forced himself to focus on his work.

Jake often felt like a run-of-the-mill agent for his investment bank. HK was organized into four business groups: commercial banking, retail banking and wealth management, global private banking, and global banking and markets, or investment banking. Jake worked within the last group. He did not create anything, and he did not buy anything. He merely punched the numbers on company mergers, stocks, and shares the bank sold, and he made a lot of money doing it.

He planned to spend a large part of the upcoming week making introductions to sell companies. Jake was considering the best way to distribute risk to maintain the bank's liquidity. In the current climate, one bad judgment call could throw the balance sheet out, leaving the bank at the mercy of the taxpayers. Most of the financial institutions were walking a tightrope. Like many Wall Street bankers, Jake was aware that he was only as good as his last deal. The party had come to an end. The market had a limited scope to diversify. The previous week, Jake had introduced buyers and sellers of two large corporations. He needed the guys on his team to make a deal happen. The bank did not have anything invested; the only things at stake were his time and the bank's share of the market.

Jake reviewed his emails. It was ten minutes after six. There was a one-line email from Jessica: "Babe, did you lose your phone again? Call when you get to the office. I miss you."

He inhaled a deep breath and moved to the next email. A colleague was asking where he was. He informed Jake that he should come into the office as soon as possible to send out a status report. The US office had sent information to which Jake had not yet responded, so a cloud of panic had descended. At the very least, he had to take a shower and dress in office attire before the onslaught.

Minutes later, Jake crossed the trading floor en route to his office. With 700 seats, 1,000 computers, and 2,500 monitors, the bank's trading floor was average, if not small by some standards. The floor was home to traders, technology support, and executives. The bank had around six thousand offices in eighty countries and territories across the world. HK had assets of $2.1 trillion. It was the world's third-largest bank in terms of assets under management and the ninth-largest public company. HK had an initial listing on the London Stock Exchange and was a constituent of the FTSE 100 Index. It had secondary listings on the New York Stock Exchange and the Hong Kong Stock Exchange. The bank dealt in almost every type of asset class and traded across almost every region.

Jake barely had time to greet friends and colleagues as he hurried toward the elevator. The elevator door opened on the fifth floor. Jake had just reached his office, when a colleague's PA handed him a hard copy of the marked-up version of the status report in question. Most of the changes consisted of adding or deleting commas and changing font sizes. His PA met him at the door to his office and said, "Jessica called—she said it was urgent that she speak to you."

"Thank you." He entered his office and closed the door.

At his desk, Jake reviewed, accepted, and made additional revisions before arranging for the final version to be sent to the team in advance of their 8:00 meeting.

At the meeting, the investment banking team told the group about the buyers interested in the introductions the bank could arrange and the meetings that had already been set up. Jake, listening vaguely, worked on a pitch document for an initial public offering, or IPO, in the background. He hit Send, and the draft IPO pitch was sent to the directors, who would be at the meeting that afternoon.

As lunchtime approached, Jake allowed his thoughts to return to Alice. He had to call to let her know he was thinking about her. *To be fair, I should have been up front and told you that my move back to New York is imminent.* He pondered whether their relationship could withstand long-distance dating. He would be back in London on a regular basis, and she could visit him in New York.

Back in his office, Jake thought about his time in London. He stared out the window. He had been valedictorian at Princeton. He was acutely aware that his educational background and time in the Special Forces had paved the way to his working in the corporate offices of this old investment bank located in a historic seventeenth-century building in London. The experience had been an opportunity of a lifetime. Over the years, with a thorough understanding of the business needs of its management and how its employees interacted with clients, the bank had gone through architectural and interior design changes to bring it up to date with modern requirements. State-of-the-art technology systems had been installed and coordinated into the design, but in most areas, the bank's interior design retained the building's great historical bones and matched customized adornments to them.

Every morning when Jake entered the bank, he admired its key feature: the reception area, with its large, hexagonal central hall and grand open area that housed the client services functions. It evoked and retained the elegant feel of the entire building, which always impressed clients. The stained-glass ceiling echoed the building's style and form. Everything in the client zone was custom, including the tall wooden doors with stained-glass windows, the chandeliers, the oak-paneled walls, and the marble floors. Casual everyday dress code might have become the desired and appropriate work environment for many companies, but for HK Bank, a gentlemen's club atmosphere worked better.

The employees' offices were located on floors one to five. The directors' offices, including Jake's office, featured marble-inlaid fireplaces, marble mosaic floor tiles, and beautiful ceiling cornices that had been retained from the original construction.

Jake was staring into his office's fireplace, thinking about how strong his feelings for Alice were, when his PA announced that Jessica was on line one. He instructed his PA to inform her that he was in a meeting. Seconds later, his mobile vibrated. It was Jessica. Jake ignored the call.

A text message popped up: "Fuck you! What is wrong with you? I'm calling your office in New York. You will not have a job when I am finished."

Jake's heart sank.

9

London, two weeks later

Alice's day started at 5:45 a.m. She was slow to wake up and switched her body to autopilot. Her first task was to make a cappuccino and take it back to her bedroom, where she would take in the unfolding events on Sky News. Back in her bedroom, she put the coffee mug to her mouth to take a sip. The aroma rushed up her nostrils.

Alice put the cup down and barely made it to the bathroom in time. When she went back to the bedroom, the aroma of the cappuccino filled the air and sent her straight back to the bathroom to vomit. She thought about what she had eaten in the last twenty-four hours. For lunch, she had taken a small portion of quiche to work, which had been freshly prepared by her meticulous mother. In the evening, Jake had cooked dinner. The fish, albeit overcooked, had been fresh. She could not compare notes with him, because he did not like fish and had prepared chicken for himself.

Alice put a tissue over her nose, went back into the bedroom, opened the window, and then took the coffee down to the kitchen to dump it out. She did not feel great, but she decided to go to work anyway. If her condition worsened, she could return with the files she needed and work on them between spilling her guts.

Alice hit the road ten minutes later than her normal time. She turned on her iPod touch. Jake had bought it the previous Thursday as a gift and surprised her with it during dinner that evening. He had put John Legend's "Once Again" on it to get her started. Every day for the last two weeks, he had called to let her know she was in his thoughts. She had no disagreement. The last few weeks with Jake had been fun. They were still in the honeymoon phase, but Alice had good feelings about him and their relationship.

Feeling better now that her stomach had settled, Alice hoped it would hold and that she would get through the day and to her dinner with Jake at Scott's that evening. In an email exchange with Jake, she had told him that Scott's of Mayfair was her favorite seafood restaurant. He always remembered the small details.

Alice's thoughts turned to work. Over the last three years, she had advised International Gaming on legal matters relating to e-commerce. The latest issue related to a sponsorship contact. The company had agreed to pay £15 million to Valencia Football Club in return for access to the exploitable commercial potential associated with the club. The company had agreed to the sponsorship with the expectation of commercial gain, even though, on Alice's advice and that of the chief financial officer, Bob, the numbers did not tally. Her part in the negotiations had become a butt-covering exercise, and she had tuned out. She thought, *Success and a good credit score can't love me or give me an orgasm. Is this how it's going to be forever? Is this all there is? God, I hope not.*

Alice gave up her lunch to fit in a workout session at the gym. For the remainder of the afternoon, she put nonurgent calls on hold and finalized the mortgage documents. The transfer of funds was the only detail preventing the majority shareholder and the director, Richard, from signing what Alice called "the suicide deal."

It was a relief when Alice finally picked up her bag and headed to Jake's apartment. She had spoken to him briefly earlier in the day.

He'd said he missed her and was looking forward to dinner that evening. The day had passed without any more trips to the bathroom to empty the contents of her stomach. Just the same, Alice decided to stay away from coffee after dinner.

Jake was getting dressed when Alice arrived at the apartment. No longer wearing his work attire, his dress style was distinctively American. He wore a polo shirt and khaki pants. She followed him through to the bedroom and placed her overnight bag in the closet.

"Help me choose which sport coat to wear," he said.

"This one." She pointed to a tweed coat that picked up the beige from his khaki pants.

They engaged in a conversation about women trying to change his appearance, which continued in the taxi on their way to Scott's.

"Jessica bullied me to wear the latest designer clothes and insisted I dye the two strands of graying hair she discovered and wax my body. At first, I gave in, but the clothes made me feel uncomfortable. Now I vehemently resent being told how to dress."

Alice smiled. "The hair is still there—all of it! What happened to the wax?"

Jake laughed. "Ouch!"

She vowed to be cautious and considerate when making comments on his style of dress.

She touched his hand. "I'm interested in the man, not his wardrobe. I can't comprehend meeting a man with whom I connect on many levels and then setting about changing or rejecting him because he isn't fashion-conscious. Can I be honest with you?"

"Of course."

"On the odd occasion, you have dressed beyond your years, but I would describe your dress code as classic, in no way offensive, and certainly not an issue to be made a bone of contention."

At the restaurant, Alice and Jake sat at a right angle, adjacent to each other. They preferred it to sitting opposite. Their table looked onto Scott's elegant oyster and champagne bar.

Jake looked up from the menu. "My father is unwell and will be having surgery as soon as next week. It will mean a trip to Florida."

"I'm sorry to hear that," Alice said. She conveyed her wishes that all would go well. "I lost my father when he was sixty-two. It was painful. I recall how I expected life to stop the day he died. For years afterward, I could not think of July Fourth as a happy day. No matter how I felt, I realized that life went on.

"At the hospital the day he died, my family passed the maternity ward, and though I did not appreciate it at the time, we passed through a replica of nature's laws in miniature—birth and death combined. For all the lessons they pass on, good or bad, parents do not teach children how to cope with death. Life goes on; that much I learned. Jake, your dad will be OK. He's in his seventies and still kicking."

They both realized the sadness of the moment. Jake changed the subject to his arrangements to play golf the following day. Meanwhile, Alice was overcome by emotion. She did not know why. Her dad had died eleven years earlier. She had long passed emotional breakdowns when she spoke about him.

After dinner, Alice was tired and asked Jake if he would mind if they skipped drinks at a bar and went home. Alice was quiet during the taxi ride. She was conscious that Jake discreetly looked over at her. She sensed he was learning how to read her and how to allow her moments of silence but to be there for her.

That night, he held her close and made tender love to her.

"I'm falling in love with you," he whispered, and then he turned over and fell asleep.

The next morning, Jake was set to tee off at 8:30. He was up and out of the apartment by seven. Alice was tired and did not leave the apartment until eight. All memories of the previous day's stomach upset had faded.

Before heading home, she stopped at Caffè Nero. On her way out, she raised her coffee cup to her mouth. It did not even touch her lips before she felt nauseated. She dropped the coffee into the trash and ran into the bathroom.

Before she settled back into her car, she searched for a plastic bag in the event that her stomach had not settled and she needed to vomit while driving home. As Alice searched through her handbag, she saw the tampons she had put in the bag two days earlier and realized her period was two days late.

10

"**N**o!" Alice shouted. She threw her handbag into the backseat, started the engine, and hit the accelerator as if on the starting line of a Formula One race. A traffic jam ahead saved her from getting a speeding ticket or, worse, causing an accident. Alice calmed down, but her heart was still pounding as she thought about the enormity of the situation. She took deep breaths and tried to focus so she could locate the nearest Boots pharmacy.

Ten minutes later, she walked out of Boots with a Clearblue two-in-one digital pregnancy testing kit.

"How could we be so careless?" she cried when she was back in the car. She headed for home with tears rolling down her cheeks.

When Alice pulled into her drive, she had convinced herself that it was nothing more than a late period. Any other symptoms she had experienced, including the fact that her breasts were swollen and aching, were mere phantoms.

Leaving her handbag on the car seat and the car unlocked, she picked up the Clearblue kit, unlocked the door to her house, and ran upstairs to the bathroom.

She opened the kit and read the instructions three times before she was satisfied that she did not have to test with the first urine sample of the day. After she had taken the test, she went into her bedroom to wait for the result. The two minutes seemed like an eternity. The downstairs door slammed shut in the wind, and she remembered her handbag. She ran downstairs to her car, collected her things, and locked the car door.

"No! No!" she screamed when she picked up the test monitor moments later.

She was pregnant.

11

lice's thoughts raced back to the first time Jake had made love to her. He had not pulled out! *Why did he do that?* She had not told him it was OK to come inside her. Alice was not ready to accept that she should not have let him enter her without a condom and should not have dismissed his coming inside her simply because she did not think she was ovulating at the time.

Why didn't he pull out? she asked herself again. *We were careless on one occasion! The test is wrong. I'll do it again.*

She ignored the fact that she had read three times that it was 99 percent accurate if taken after the day her period was due.

The second test was also positive. Alice sat staring at the two monitors in her hand, which read, "You are pregnant, and you conceived one to two weeks ago." Lost to the world, she was brought back to reality when she received a text message from Jake confirming that evening's dinner reservation.

She replied and then lay on her bed, wondering how she could fix the problem. She could not. Her mother had brainwashed her on that score. Her mother's first career had been as a nurse. She had told Alice and her sisters horrific stories about abortions. She had talked of women who had abortions and could no longer have children and of babies' body parts left in dumpsters in the hospital sluice room after late-term abortions. Maybe her mother's depictions of the horrors of abortion were exaggerated, but if a child grew up hearing that kind of indoctrination, it penetrated eventually. No, this could not be fixed; she was not having an abortion.

Alice forced herself to go running to clear her head. She ran five miles in forty minutes and then lay on her bedroom floor and stretched. That was when the reality of what she had just discovered came back into sharp focus. *What will I tell Jake?*

She showered and went to the grocery store. Wine was off her shopping list. What did pregnant women eat? She went back home, confused, having bought no groceries other than a pint of milk, water, and fresh orange juice.

This situation would cause a major adjustment in her life. She could call Charlotte. She was a mother and would know what to do. *Maybe not.* Alice typed *pregnancy* into Google and started reading. She knew she would have to have a conversation with Jake, and a feeling of foreboding overtook her.

12

The journey to Jake's apartment was consumed with thoughts of how to tell him that she was pregnant and what his likely response would be. Alice did not expect Jake to marry her; they barely knew each other. Maybe he would offer financial support. If he did not, she could support the baby and herself if she went back to work. What if he suggested an abortion? That was the scenario Alice dreaded.

Jake was waiting in front of the complex's reception area when she arrived. He opened the car door, and Alice rotated her legs around and raised herself to a standing position. Jake kissed her on the cheek and held out a hand to take her car keys. The concierge took them from Jake, and then Alice and Jake walked hand in hand down the path to flag a taxicab.

It was a short drive to the restaurant. Alice was too distracted with her own issue to notice Jake was preoccupied. The cab stopped in front of Electric Brasserie in Notting Hill. Jake opted for a table at the back. Alice was relieved. She could not have the necessary conversation with him while seated at the high-decibel bar. Discreet conversation was on the agenda. It was a celeb-spotting restaurant with a distinctly French feel to both the food and the service.

As a result of her stressful day, Alice had not eaten adequately.

What was it people said? Mothers-to-be were eating for two. From her extensive research earlier that day, she realized that was not true and that she needed to eat a balanced diet and increase her calorie intake but not excessively. Alice ordered steak frites and a green salad. She declined a cocktail and had a glass of freshly squeezed orange juice instead. Jake ordered a bottle of wine. When the waiter poured Alice's glass, she lost the nerve to decline, knowing Jake would notice and that she would be forced to explain, but she pushed the glass away.

"Have you had any news on when your dad will be admitted to the hospital?" she asked.

"It could be as soon as next week."

"That's good news. Your dad didn't have to deal with a long waiting list. I'll be in Spain on business the following week but contactable."

Jake asked for the bill after Alice had eaten a quarter of her main course and put her fork down, indicating that she had finished. They had eaten a meal together—or, rather, Jake had eaten his meal—and Alice had not found the courage to raise the fact that she was pregnant. Part of her felt Jake had a right to know, but another part of her wanted to run. She did not need his support. Alice put her napkin on the table and picked up her handbag. She was barely able to stand. She felt dizzy.

"Jake!" Alice put a hand on the table to support herself. It was too late. Her limp body fell to the floor—her head missed the table by centimeters.

"Alice!" Jake cried. He bent down to see if she was OK. He looked up at the waiter. "Call 999!"

When Alice regained consciousness, she was in an ambulance, and Jake was holding her hand. She squeezed his hand but did not speak.

Upon arrival at the Chelsea and Westminster Hospital, Jake arranged for Alice to be taken to a private room. Alice heard him giving the contact details for billing purposes.

"Alice, we will be carrying out a few tests to discover what caused you to faint," the doctor said.

Alice looked at Jake and then turned her head back to face the doctor. She opened her mouth, but the words would not come out. Tears filled her eyes. She took a deep breath.

"I'm pregnant."

"That would probably explain why you fainted," the doctor said. "Do you know the first day of your last menstrual period? I would like to take a blood sample."

Alice turned her head away and closed her eyes while the doctor took a blood sample. Jake walked over to her and held her hand but remained speechless.

The doctor sent the sample down to the lab. "If the blood tests indicate that all is well, there is no reason you can't go home tonight."

Meanwhile, he took her blood pressure and examined her pelvic area externally before he rushed to his next patient.

Forty minutes later, the door to Alice's room opened, and the doctor entered. "Congratulations," he said, confirming the test result she had received earlier. "I advise that you see your GP as soon as possible. You have low blood pressure, and to combat fainting, you should not stand up suddenly." He congratulated Alice and Jake once again and then left.

It was just after ten o'clock that night when they stepped into Jake's apartment. Alice was exhausted. The pregnancy explained why she had felt so tired lately and why she had become so emotional the other night when she told Jake about her father. For the foreseeable future, raging hormones would control her emotions. She showered, brushed her teeth, and lay on the bed.

After Jake had checked his landline for missed calls, he lay down next to Alice.

She turned to him. "Please, can we talk?"

"Honey, not tonight. I'm tired."

She had watched his loss of coordination; he had swayed as he lowered himself onto the bed. She raised her head to talk to him directly, but he was already asleep.

"Jake! How can you sleep at a time like this?" She shook his shoulder gently; his response was slurred. "Jake." Alice shook him again. "What's wrong, Jake?"

She was not sure what was happening. Jake had had a couple of glasses of wine, but his demeanor was that of a drunken person. She was concerned. She shook him and called his name, but he had lost consciousness. His breathing was regular, so Alice decided not to call an ambulance, but she did not sleep well that night, out of concern for him.

On the way to the waiting cab, Jake remained silent. During the cab ride, he did not volunteer any conversation. He pushed himself back in the seat and stared into space. Jake's mind exploded. *She was so quiet at the restaurant—and in the ambulance. I thought she was onto me. In the hospital, that was on another level. Did I hear right? Alice is pregnant? Jessica will lose her mind. I don't understand. I was careful. How can Alice be pregnant?* Then it all came rushing back: their first romantic meeting, their dinner at C London, and the next morning—the first time they had made love. *Fuck! I didn't pull out. Fuck! I fired come into Alice.* He glanced at Alice; he did not know what he should say and could not find the words. *Sorry! Sorry I was so careless. I don't think that will cut it.* Regret turned to panic and a feeling of being overwhelmed.

Jessica. Fuck! What can I tell Jessica? This is a fucking nightmare! What have I done? Jessica will lose her mind when she finds out. Fuck!

He opened the door, and he and Alice entered the apartment. He threw his coat onto the sofa and headed for the bathroom. After he closed the bathroom cabinet, he sat on the edge of the bathtub and put his head in his hands.

Minutes later, he walked back into the bedroom. He climbed into bed, closed his eyes, and blacked out.

13

When Alice woke in the morning, she smelled the aroma of omelets. Jake walked into the bedroom with breakfast on a tray and the morning paper. Alice sat up as he set down the tray.

"Jake, I was worried about you last night. You were in a very deep sleep."

"Sorry, honey. I took zolpidem to help me sleep."

Alice asked him to take the coffee away because it made her feel nauseated. When Jake walked back into the bedroom, Alice was enjoying the omelet he had made for her. He sat on the end of the bed and picked up the *Times*.

"Why did you need something to help you sleep?" Alice asked.

He apologized and said that work was stressful and that Jessica had been stalking him. "Please believe me. I've tried several times to make Jessica understand that she's no longer a part of my life. Jessica calls me two or three times a day at work and at least four or five times during the evenings. You've witnessed the calls. And ..." He fell silent.

"What?" Alice asked.

"Then I found out you're pregnant."

"Yes, I'm pregnant." She waited for his reply.

"Can we talk about it after breakfast?"

Alice did not reply. She pushed aside her omelet. They spent the next hour reading the Sunday papers, speaking only when they wanted to share something they had read. Eventually, Jake put down the paper and asked Alice if she would like to go jogging.

They jogged along a road stretching between Notting Hill Gate and Kensington High Street and adjacent to Kensington Gardens. The road contained some amazingly expensive houses that were home to some very wealthy residents. The road was nicknamed Billionaires' Row. Many of the houses were former embassies, and some were still used as embassies or ambassadors' residences. Jake said he ran the route often because, like Alice, he was interested in architecture.

They turned into Kensington Gardens and ran through to Hyde Park and up to Hyde Park Corner. Their path took them around and back to the entrance to Kensington Gardens. From there, they walked along Kensington High Street and back to Jake's apartment. Once in the apartment, Alice headed into the bedroom to take a shower.

She turned on the shower, removed her running gear, and stepped under the stream of water. Her mind was preoccupied with Jake's total silence about the pregnancy. She did not know what his thoughts were on the matter, and he appeared to have no intention of discussing them.

Alice noticed Jake in the doorway, observing her. Obviously aroused, he opened the door and stepped into the shower. He kissed and caressed the back of her neck. The water hit their bodies and bounced off. She turned, and their bodies locked together to make passionate love.

When they were finished, Jake wrapped a towel around her and looked into her eyes. "Alice, you have no idea how strong my feelings are for you."

Alice smiled, unsure. The message Jake was conveying to her did not tally with his previous refusal to talk about the pregnancy. "Jake, we need to talk about the baby I'm carrying."

"We can talk over lunch. I suggest we have a pub lunch. Is that OK with you?"

Jake did not wait for a reply. He made a quick exit from the bedroom and made a reservation at the Punchbowl in Mayfair.

✦   ✦   ✦

The taxi pulled up in front of the Punchbowl, an old Georgian London public house that dated from circa 1750. Although it had been altered over the years, it retained many period features. Jake asked Alice if she was aware that the pub had been featured in the documentary *I'm Going to Tell You a Secret*, which followed Madonna and her ex-husband Guy Ritchie on a night out at their local pub. The information was news to Alice, but she did know that Ritchie and Madonna had bought the pub.

Alice and Jake ordered the fish and chips. Alice put a hand out and touched Jake's hand. Her intention was to raise the subject of her pregnancy, but she did not. If Jake did not want to talk about it, she was not sure what there was to discuss. Instead, she asked about Jessica.

"Do you have a photograph of her?"

Jake searched through his iPhone and handed it to her.

Jessica was not what Alice expected. A peroxide blonde with visible signs of aging, she had been a pretty woman once. Her attempt to mask her age with makeup had done nothing for the wrinkles at the corners of her eyes when she smiled. Alice handed the phone back to Jake.

"I'm curious as to why Jessica and you didn't take the relationship to the next level, given that you were together for a long time."

Waiting for their fish and chips to arrive, Alice guessed, gave Jake time to reflect on his answer. He placed his hand on top of Alice's, indicating he did not need to think long. His gaze into her eyes was reassuring to her that he cared for her. She smiled, hoping, knowing the relationship could only survive if he opened to her, and that meant the truth.

Alice's changing body dictated a quick bathroom break. He raised his hand as she stood and walked in the direction of the bathroom.

As she entered the bathroom, she looked back. He was studying her, seemingly in deep thought.

Alice walked back to the table just as their food arrived. Not long after she put her first bite of fish in her mouth, Jake said, "After I dated Jessica for a year, I proposed to her. We found a nice house to buy, and the wedding plans were in full swing. It was set to take place in New York."

"What happened?" Alice's curiosity was bursting. She had to know what had happened.

Jake paused. "I could not go through with it." He whispered, "Poor Jessica—I jilted her. I didn't show up for the wedding. She never completely recovered or forgave me."

Alice's eyes widened, and she looked directly at him. "You jilted her at the altar, and she still wants to be in a relationship with you?" When she spoke, her voice trailed slowly, as if her words were unwilling to take flight. "Unbelievable." *Who are you?*

"Jessica and I split for a while but picked up the relationship later. I'm not proud that I didn't go through with the wedding, but at the time, I wasn't sure if Jessica and I were right for each other. If I'd married her, I would have been forced to divorce my entire family and all my friends, who Jessica hated passionately."

"And you couldn't let her down before you arrived at the altar? I don't understand the on-and-off dating for five years—you knew Jessica was not right for you the first time you split. What changed when you picked up the relationship the second, third, and fourth times?"

Jake let out a deep sigh. "Please try to understand that I'm not proud of my behavior. I didn't do the right thing and stay away when we split. I didn't make the right decisions, and as a result, both Jessica and I paid—and are still paying—the price."

Alice felt numb. All thought of discussing the pregnancy flew out the window. She contemplated whether she had any kind of future with Jake. It was one thing to have jilted the woman at the altar. She supposed it was better than entering the marriage while knowing it was not right and then divorcing her later. But the on-and-off rela-tionship in his thirties did not seem normal. Alice had a lot to digest. She considered the subject closed for the moment.

In the taxi back home, Jake broke the silence. "Are you free to have dinner at my apartment Wednesday evening? I'd like to make baked ziti for you." He described it as a classic Italian American com-fort food of pasta baked with sausage, tomato sauce, and all kinds of gooey, yummy cheeses.

Alice's mouth watered. *Sounds delicious, but I can't say the same about you, not now and maybe not ever. This issue with your ex is fucked up.* "Wednesday?" She was uncertain whether she wanted to see him again. Alice lied when she said, "An old friend is in town, and I agreed to meet up—I'll try to rearrange."

Alice's morning routine had changed. A cappuccino was out. Before leaving the house on Wednesday, she nibbled a whole-wheat cracker to combat her morning sickness. By the time she arrived at work, she was able to digest breakfast. On Thursday, she had a doctor's ap-pointment scheduled. She packed an overnight bag. That evening, she would talk to Jake for the sake of the child she was carrying. Evading the issue was no longer an option.

Alice received Jake's text message at ten in the morning. She had seen the message at nine thirty but had been unable to read it, because she had been in a meeting: "I'm flying to Florida at noon today. I mentioned to you that my dad is having an operation. I'll be in touch."

Alice checked to see if Jake had called. No. Her eyes watered. She wiped her eyes and blinked furiously. Alice looked over her shoulder, fearing somebody had witnessed her distraught state but praying no one had. She hurried to her office, closed the door, and cried uncontrollably.

Midmorning on Monday, Jake relented and took one of Jessica's calls. She seemed to believe that if he loved her, as he had told her often when they were dating, and she loved him, they should be together. In Jake's mind, *love* was the operative word. He still cared about her well-being, but he no longer loved her. Jessica disregarded the fact that on their last vacation together, she had thrown a bag of rocks at his head. The bag had narrowly missed. *She came close to killing me.*

Upon reflection, he realized he had not allowed sufficient time between his breakup with Jessica and the start of his relationship with Alice. He could not deny that he had lingering feelings for Jessica that conflicted with his strong feelings for Alice. He had no desire to turn back the clock, yet he could not discard his concern for how Jessica would cope going forward. Her behavior had become increasingly erratic. She was desperate to marry and have children. *News of Alice's pregnancy will push her over the edge.* He muttered, "Jessica, eventually, I'll have to tell you about the baby and that I intend to marry Alice."

On Monday night, Jake left his office to attend his leaving party. It was not the best day of the week to be partying, but he had opted for the correct day. Thursday or Friday would have clashed with his father's operation. The guests were city boys. He did not think the fact that it was Monday would concern them. They had been his work colleagues, and some of them had been close friends for more than three years. It was a good way to get them all together to say goodbye.

The party was at the McQueen bar and restaurant in Shoreditch. Jake had heard about such parties, which could go on until six in the morning. He thought about all the work-related issues building in his email inbox. He wished he could party into the early hours, but he did not have the time. He would stay for a couple of hours and then slip away.

Jake arrived at McQueen at eight o'clock. The party organizer did not disappoint. Guests were treated to lashings of Louis Roederer champagne, Iceberg vodka, and strippers. Jake felt uneasy that he had not mentioned the party to Alice. The strippers were a good reason not to tell some women about the party, but the strippers were not the reason Jake had avoided disclosing it. They would have laughed and joked about them. He had not mentioned the party because she would not laugh about the fact that he was moving back to New York, especially now that she was pregnant.

Unnoticed, Jake managed to leave just after ten o'clock. In the taxi back to his apartment, he checked his missed calls. Jessica had been calling all evening. He turned the phone off. Wall Street would be closing soon. He had to check his phone one more time. He scrolled to his emails. Jessica's email hit him in the face:

> When you were next in the US, I just wanted to have fucking dinner. And you are such a weak pussy and spineless coward that you can't even be a fucking man and fucking call even! Who the fuck acts like that? You are a fucking douchebag, loser, idiot, asshole, and piece of trash! You are a complete piece of garbage to treat me to more of your sick manipulation, lies, and bullshit head games.

Jake's head hurt. With the stress at work, Jessica, Alice's pregnancy, and his father's forthcoming operation, his heart was overworked. He felt as if it were about to explode.

14

Alice had no idea how long she had been crying, when she heard a knock on her office door. She pulled three tissues from the box on her desk and dried her eyes. Nicola opened the door. She noticed Alice's red eyes right away and asked if she was OK. Alice replied that she was feeling unwell. Nicola suggested she go home. Alice agreed. She asked Nicola to collect the Valencia file from Bob. Whether her health was good or bad, a mountain of work still had to be done on the deal.

When Nicola closed the door, Alice's eyes watered again as her thoughts returned to Jake. He had called every day for the last three and a half weeks. She could not understand why he had not picked up the phone the previous night or earlier that day to give her a heads-up on his flight to Florida. She put her things in her bag and waited for Nicola to return with the file.

In her car en route to Langley Park, the floodgates opened again. Alice was not sure why she was so upset. It was her decision to keep the baby, and it was not as if she had known Jake long enough to expect him to be a full-time father to her child. Her emotions were out of control. She had to pull herself together. She had received a few text messages from Annabel inviting her to spend Easter weekend with her and Marcus, and she could not spend the weekend crying.

Jake did not contact Alice on Wednesday. By lunchtime, she had surrendered all hope of a telephone call. He was in flight and would be out of contact for the rest of the day.

Alice's mother was waiting at Alice's house when she arrived. She had baked lasagna. Her mother sat at the kitchen table and talked about Annabel's wedding plans and Easter. Alice was prepared to take her mother's love in whatever form it was available. For a couple of hours, she did not even think about the baby or Jake.

Alice was on leave—if it could be called that, given the fact that she was on call 24-7 because of the Valencia agreement—from Thursday through Monday. She agreed to drive her mother to Annabel's house after her appointment the following day.

Easter weekend arrived, and Alice still had not heard from Jake. She convinced herself that his father was seriously ill, and that was why he had not touched base with her. On Thursday afternoon, she had sent two text messages inquiring about his father's health. Alice had expressed that she feared something bad had happened, but Jake had not replied. She genuinely feared the worst and was desperate to reach out to him.

She began to lose patience. Surely if what she feared had happened—his dad had passed—he could at least have let her know. Or if the problem was that he did not want to have any further contact, good manners dictated that he at least advise her of that.

On Friday, when she still had not heard from Jake, she sent a text inquiring whether she could collect her running shoes from his apartment. No reply.

Alice had come to expect disappointment from relationships, but this one was different. She had paid a price—the child she was carrying. *I wanted a family but not like this. My career—I can't contemplate changing it now. I must support my baby, and the father is a Pandora's box.* Alice tried to put Jake and her pregnancy aside and enjoy the Easter break and discuss plans for Annabel's forthcoming wedding.

On Saturday, Annabel and her mother went shopping. Alice's

excuse for not joining them was the need to attend to pressing matters at work. She stayed at Annabel's house and worked on the Valencia file. She managed to shut Jake out for the better part of the morning—until she received a text message alert. She picked up the phone, expecting it to be Annabel. It was Jake.

"Hi, honey. Dad's operation was successful. I sent you an email. Did you receive it?"

Alice was not sure whether she should text the f-word back to Jake or be relieved. It had been three days since he had contacted her in the form of a text message, and he was acting as if he had called daily. Alice stared at the message. Ten minutes passed before she read his email. Realizing she had to download pictures, she turned on her computer.

A sane person would have deleted the text and email. Alice's finger moved to the Delete button. She hovered over it for the next minute, thinking that it would be good if the baby knew his or her father. She was overcome by emotion. Mother Nature was working her magic. That was good, but she needed to make a rational decision.

Alice delayed for another minute and then hit the download button. Photographs appeared of an apartment Alice believed to be Jake's Sanibel Island condominium. The dining room featured basket-woven chairs that no one would have sat in for long. In the reception area, an off-white sofa was paired with hard basket-woven armchairs. The walls had generic art like what one would find in a hotel. There was nothing personal. Nothing. *Does he even live here? This looks like a magazine photo. What is his point?*

She scrolled down the page. Finally, she reached the text: "This will all be yours after we're married."

Alice's relief that Jake was writing about their future together, which included marriage, dissolved quickly into anger. "He didn't contact me for over three days." She paused to contemplate. "Why would he think I would be excited at the prospect of owning an apartment that, at best, could be described as an acquired taste? With its cold and uninviting decor, it's only value is as a critique." She needed to talk about the baby, not material possessions.

Alice shut down her computer and resumed her work on the Valencia file. Raging hormones or not, she had satisfied her curiosity by opening the email, but she had no intention of replying.

It was late afternoon when Jake's second text message arrived: "Alice, I sent you another email."

What did he want? More photographs of the cold life she could live with him? Jake's Sanibel Island condominium was nothing like his London apartment. But he was renting his London apartment, so the interior design could not be credited to Jake. Alice opened his second email. She stared at a photo of Jake holding a diamond ring with the price tag dangling. She reached the close of the email and thought about how surreal it all was.

He finds out I'm pregnant, takes zolpidem, refuses to discuss the matter, and ignores me for three days. Then, on the fourth day, he proposes marriage and selects a seventy-thousand-dollar round, six-pronged, classic two-carat Tiffany engagement ring. "Kumbaya! I don't think so."

He suggested in the email that she could have a Cartier ring if she did not like the Tiffany ring. He said maybe he should make an appointment at Cartier to view their rings. "That will give me something to do," he wrote.

Is he for real? This must be a joke.

Alice did not reply to his second email either. She was tired, so she put her head down on Annabel's sofa. Although her mind was filled with Jake's strange behavior, the baby had a stronger claim. She drifted into sleep.

Alice jumped when Annabel put the key in the door, waking her. She had slept for almost two hours. Her sister and mother had shopped all day. Seeing the bags falling out of their hands, Alice rushed to the door to help them. How could one wedding be so time-consuming? Would they ever run out of things to buy? They were both quick to blame the hours spent on shopping on the Easter shoppers, only to report ten minutes later that they had expected more people to be out shopping, given it was a holiday weekend.

Annabel fussed about dinner. She preferred to have Marcus come home to dinner, not shopping bags. That would not be a problem. Having two chefs in the family was an advantage. Good meals could be served in a relatively short period of time. With the shopping bags stuffed behind the sofa, Annabel and their mother set about cooking shepherd's pie.

Marcus's timing was perfect. He walked through the door just as dinner was laid on the table. The three women and Marcus sat down at the table, talked, laughed, and enjoyed the shepherd's pie. Alice had not shared news of her pregnancy or Jake's strange behavior with her family. Still, she felt comfort in being with people who cared for her.

Alice was relieved when she finally put her head down to sleep. The day had passed without any emotional outbursts on her part.

✦ ✦ ✦

The next afternoon, Annabel was preparing the table for Easter dinner, when Alice received a text from Jake: "Honey, how are you?"

Alice ignored the text and asked Annabel if she needed any help. Her phone rang. It was Jake. She excused herself and went upstairs to the bedroom. She answered as if she did not know it was him.

"Hey, honey," he said.

"Jake," Alice replied.

"Did you receive my texts and emails? Are you OK?"

"Yes." She paused and held back from letting him know how annoyed she was with him. "Jake, you flew to Florida last Wednesday, and you haven't called since. Your dad is unwell. Did it not occur to you that I would fear the worst?"

"Sorry, honey. I sent a text."

"Three days later, Jake."

"Sorry, honey."

Honey, she thought. *One more* honey *from him, and this conversation is over.*

Seemingly oblivious to her annoyance, Jake inquired as to whether she had read his email about the engagement ring.

"Yes, I read your email." She pulled her mouth away from the phone. "Are you for real? You're not playing with me?" She could not warm to Jake, but she did not want to be rude. She put the phone back to her mouth. "Are you referring to the Tiffany—"

Jake cut her off and volunteered that he had given a one-and-a-half-carat Tiffany ring to Jessica, and he could not buy anything less for his honey. He went on to say they could look at Cartier if that was her preference.

If Jake had been standing in front of her, Alice, though not a violent person, would have punched his lights out. Jake continued, oblivious to how what he had just said had affected her. He suggested she start making wedding plans, because it took time to plan a wedding.

To whom did he think he was preaching? Between Charlotte's and Annabel's weddings, she had learned enough to become a professional wedding planner. He volunteered that he was not an expert on wedding dresses but that New York girls opted for Vera Wang.

"Jake, you're planning a wedding without even asking the key participant if she will marry you."

Jake shot back quickly that he had asked her. He had sent his honey an email. Alice replied that she had only received two emails from him: the one about the Tiffany engagement ring and the one with photographs of his Sanibel Island condominium.

"That's the email," Jake said. He added that he wanted Alice to know what would be hers when they were married. "I'll send you my guest list. We can touch base tomorrow. Love you."

That was it. That was his proposal of marriage. He had asked Alice to marry him, and now he expected her to start planning a wedding.

Alice finished her call just in time to join the rest of the family at the dinner table and say grace. Annabel's wedding dominated the conversation. The debate was whether Annabel should stay at Coombe Abbey on the eve of the wedding. Her mother insisted she stay at another hotel, because the bride and bridesmaids had to *arrive*. By that, she had in mind the wedding car driving down the tree-lined Coombe Abbey driveway. Annabel did not want to entertain the idea of booking in and out of hotels on the most critical day of her life.

"Jake asked me to marry him," Alice blurted out.

Her pronouncement did not register for the next thirty seconds.

"Alice, I'm so happy for you," her mother said finally. "Have you set a date?"

Annabel appeared concerned. Alice realized she was worried about Alice upstaging her wedding. She was cognizant that there was a window in any year to have a wedding, and time would be needed to plan Alice's wedding as well.

"Alice, have you set a date?" Annabel asked. "Finding a nice venue in August and September will be difficult. I'm sure you're not planning your wedding before next year. I'm not ordering your special day, but if you're working on getting married in the most reliable months for good weather, this year is out."

Alice could not believe what was happening. The pressure had started already. She should not have opened her mouth. She refused to answer their questions beyond saying, "I haven't made any plans with Jake yet."

Her mother could not keep from making an announcement. "Jake's role is limited to attending the wedding."

Alice thought about Jessica. That could be a problem in itself. Would Jake ditch Alice at the altar too?

It could have been guilt on Annabel's part—Alice had no way of knowing—but she backed off and told Alice that she could borrow her bridal gown catalogs.

"Thank you," Alice said, getting up. "I'd like to stay longer, but I agreed to drinks with Charlotte later."

The drive back to Langley Park was tranquil. It was a fifty-minute drive, and ten minutes into it, Alice started to unwind.

Her phone rang. She thought it was Annabel, but when she looked at the screen, it was a US number she did not recognize. She answered the call.

"Hey, Alice. I'm Patrick, Jake's brother."

Alice was stunned. Jake had not given her a heads-up that his brother would be calling.

"Congratulations on your engagement and forthcoming wedding to my brother," he said. He added that he had heard many good things about her from Jake.

"Thank you," Alice replied. "Jake said your dad's operation was a success. How is he? Is he home from the hospital?"

"Dad is home, and we are pleased with his progress."

They talked about the differences between the US and the English legal systems. Then Alice plucked up the courage to ask something more personal.

"Patrick, tell me about Jake. Will he be a good life partner?" She laughed. "You don't have to answer that if you don't want to."

Patrick laughed. "I'll try to be objective. He's a good person and successful in his chosen career."

Would he rat on his brother? No, she doubted it. Alice felt her relationship with Jake was moving at a fast pace. He had surprised her with his marriage proposal. Although Patrick's call had come out of the blue, she derived comfort from speaking to him. She hoped that meeting Jake's family would help her get to know him on a deeper level.

The next day, Alice was surprised when her mother knocked at her door. She had keys and did not need to wait for Alice to answer. Her mother had barely entered the kitchen, when she began to speak.

"There's no time to delay. This year or next, we need to get started on your wedding."

Her mother did not take a breath before questioning Alice's decision to postpone the wedding until the following year. Alice explained that Annabel was the one who thought it best to postpone.

"Alice, if you're planning to move to America, you and Jake should get married. The wedding can take place either the week before Annabel's wedding or the week after, depending on the availability of reception rooms for the wedding breakfast."

Alice's mother had the brochures for all the places Annabel

had rejected and pointed out that many of the hotels still had dates available.

"What about a wedding dress and cake?" Alice asked.

"You won't find one if you sit there all day. I've made you an appointment at Harrods this afternoon."

Between the fatigue of carrying the baby and the stress of the Valencia issues at work, Alice did not have the energy to argue. Ten minutes later, she was in the car with her mother, driving to Harrods.

Alice tried several dresses before her mother found the perfect one. Alice did not dispute that the dress was beautiful. It was silk and finished with handmade lace and a train befitting a royal wedding at Westminster Abbey. But she had a few issues. First, her mother was not listening to her wishes. Second, by the time the wedding came around, the dress would have to fit two. Most importantly, the dress, although beautiful, was heavy. On her wedding day, they would need to hire a crane to move her from one location to the next.

The shop assistant was not listening either. She demonstrated for Alice's mother how the train could be buttoned up after the service. She rushed away to find a veil. Alice stopped protesting and placed the order for the dress—anything to go home and rest.

Twenty-four hours after Alice had announced her wedding, her stress level had spiraled. Although Annabel was helpful by sharing wedding information, places to buy invitations, and the latest bridal magazines, her concern that Alice's wedding would upstage her own was written all over her face. She did not like the fact that she was no longer the center of attention—even though Alice had explained that marrying Jake would mean she could work in the United States.

During a discussion on the practicalities of two weddings so close together, Charlotte let it be known that she thought Alice was plain selfish and could not understand the rush to marry Jake.

Alice could not understand why her sisters were not pleased for her. She thought she was being overly emotional and blamed her mood on her hormones. Upon reflection, she realized there was no way she would walk down the aisle while six months pregnant. A registry office ceremony with a church blessing and a celebration after the baby was born was Alice's preferred option, but her sisters were being too mean to allow her to arrive at that decision. Alice's wedding was turning into the event from hell, and she no longer wanted to talk about it or plan it.

Then there was Jake. Tears filled Alice's eyes. She would have liked to believe her hormones were out of control and preventing her from acknowledging that something did not add up. The call from Patrick had been followed by a call from Jake's niece, Victoria, who also had welcomed her to the family. Jake's brother was divorced, and his niece had lived close to Jake when he was in the United States.

Alice had bonded instantly with Victoria. During their conversation, Victoria had opened up to Alice and said she loved Uncle Jake but had been estranged from him for the year toward the end of his relationship with Jessica. In her words, Jessica was not a nice person.

Alice did not know what to think. The only thing she was sure of was that she was carrying Jake's baby and would like the baby to know his or her father. She had strong feelings for Jake, but his behavior seemed odd at times.

Later that evening, with the excitement of the day over, Alice decided to go to bed early. She was setting the alarm, when the phone rang.

"Honey, it's Jake."

Alice asked him if all was well. She had expected him to be on a flight back to London.

"I'm at the house in Greenwich, Connecticut," he said. It was one bombshell after the other. He launched into how much Patrick and Victoria had enjoyed their conversations with her.

"When are you coming back to England?"

"I'm not," he replied. "I'll be working out of Wall Street for the foreseeable future. I'll call you tomorrow, honey. Love you."

With that, the phone went dead.

15

Greenwich, Connecticut

J ake ended his conversation with Alice and then sent a text to Jessica: "Our conversation tonight will be brief. My friend's wife died."

Then he turned on the sports channel, put his feet on the coffee table, and settled down with a bottle of Sierra Nevada to watch golf.

His phone flashed a text from Jessica: "I sent you a text."

Jake scrolled through his texts: "Fuck you, Jake. Your excuses reach a new low every time you open your sad, alcoholic, lying mouth. You're such a waste of time it's ridiculous. I hope your friend finds out what an asshole you are for using his poor dead wife as an excuse for not doing the right thing. You truly are the lowest of the low. Go fuck yourself, Jake. You truly are trash."

"And you're unhinged. Fuck you," he said aloud. He put his iPhone down. Tiger Woods was about to hit his shot. Jake thought about pausing the television but changed his mind. When Tiger finished, he picked up his iPhone to reply to Jessica.

"I'm not trying to avoid you. I've got my hands full," he wrote.

Then he switched off the phone and returned to watching golf.

London

Alice lay in her bed, too numb to cry. She resolved to call Jake the next day and set him straight. It did not matter how she felt. The only reason to continue seeing him was the baby, and that was not good enough. He could be part of the baby's life if he chose that path but not part of hers.

Tears filled her eyes. *God, please don't let this happen to me—I love him.* It was like tripping over what she felt was beyond her control. "I know he's far from perfect, but don't I deserve some happiness? And the baby—he or she needs a father." A tear rolled down her cheek. She thought about how she had come to this moment in her life. *He isn't threatened by my independence, and our shared views on politics, religion, and work put me at ease in his company.* Those were the objective reasons she had connected with him, but she realized there had to be more. *In my heart, it is his presence—his smile, his eyes, the feeling of togetherness we share whenever we meet or talk. I love him, and I loved him long before the hormones started raging.* She sobbed. "I'm hurting, and love can't cure that. Was it just lust?" she whispered. "The baby is my priority." She cried herself to sleep.

When she awoke the next morning, she searched for a reason other than work to get out of bed. Jake's blasé attitude about his relocation to Wall Street and his refusal to talk about the pregnancy still cut deep. She did not want to interact with people, but where work was concerned, she had no choice. She had a morning meeting, a lunch appointment at the bridal shop in Harrods, and an early evening flight to Spain.

She sat up in bed, put her feet on the floor, and allowed herself to adjust before standing. She planned to cancel the appointment at the bridal shop, use the time to pack, and leave early for Madrid.

The meeting at work lasted just more than an hour and covered the scope of her authority regarding the discussions with Valencia's lawyers the following morning. IG had arranged for a Spanish inter-preter to assist Alice at the meeting—the only sensible action they had taken so far. For the convenience of both parties, the meeting was taking place in Madrid. IG's director, Richard, hoped to attend, but if he could not, Alice had her instructions.

As soon as the meeting was over, she rushed back to her desk to call Harrods. She told her appointed sales assistant, Maria, that some-thing had come up at work, and she would not be able to make it. She would call back to arrange another appointment. Then she punched Nicola's extension and told her that she was leaving the office but would be working from home until she left for the airport.

As Alice drove home, her thoughts turned to Jake. She could not put off calling him any longer. His phone rang and then went to voice mail. Alice did not leave a message. She was still trying to make sense of the events since the previous Wednesday. Maybe the turning point had been when she told Jake about the baby.

Alice was distracted momentarily when a policeman stopped her car to inform her that she could not cross Vauxhall Bridge. He di-rected her toward Westminster Bridge instead. He did not offer any explanation for the diversion even when asked.

Alice did as she was told and made a note to call Nicola to pay the congestion charge. As far as Alice was concerned, the ticket was a work-related expense.

After crossing Westminster Bridge, turning right on the round-about, and driving toward Langley Park, she tried to call Jake a second time while sitting in traffic. Then she sent him a text: "I tried to call a couple of times today. I'm leaving for Madrid later today. Call, please."

No call came from Jake during the drive home. Alice did not want to end the relationship by text or email, but he was forcing her into a corner.

Once home, she sat in the dining room, in front of her computer, and sent him another text, asking if he was sure about his marriage proposal.

Alice did not like to rush, so she decided to pack her overnight bag for Madrid. If she did not hear from Jake by the time she finished, she would send him an email ending their relationship—if she could even call it a relationship.

Nicola had brought Alice's flight forward to 4:00 p.m. The car to Gatwick Airport was collecting her at 1:40. Alice checked her watch. It was noon. She was not herself, because until then, it had not occurred to her that New York was behind by five hours. That would explain why Jake had not returned her calls. She decided it was not appropriate to email him yet. She settled her mind on the Valencia papers while she waited for her car.

When Alice boarded her flight at 3:30 p.m., Jake had not called. He had not even sent a text to say he had received her missed calls and text message and would call later. She had a bad feeling. She had to deal with this situation. Stress was not good for the baby.

Exhausted, she started to drift into sleep before the airplane left the runway. For the first time, she contemplated how she would work for the next seven months.

Alice slept for the entire two-hour-and-ten-minute flight. While the airplane taxied down the runway, she checked her phone for messages. Jake had not called. It was seven o'clock in Madrid; there could be no mistake over time zones. She resolved to email him and end the farce as soon as possible.

Alice disliked Madrid's major airport, Barajas, but it was the major gateway to the city. The international airport was the busiest and largest in the country and had been ranked the eleventh busiest globally and the fourth busiest in Europe. Although the airport was paved with restaurants and shops to make life easier, getting from one gate to another was a pain, taking up to forty minutes after clearing security.

Alice observed Madrid on the drive to the InterContinental hotel in the city center. Madrid was the capital and largest city in Spain. The city's modern infrastructure preserved the look and feel of many of its historic buildings and streets. She passed landmarks, such as the Royal Palace of Madrid and the Teatro Real.

The cab stopped outside an impressive landmark on Paseo de la Castellana, an eighteenth-century palace and the inspiration for the InterContinental Madrid. Alice had opted for the hotel because of its location in the cultural and business district, where Santiago Bernabéu Stadium and the Real Madrid Museum, the elegant Serrano shopping street, and Madrid's historical center were located.

Shortly after Alice checked in, she pulled out her computer and sat down to write an email to Jake.

Hi, Jake,

I hope you're well and have settled back in the United States.

She paused, struggling to find the words. Tears filled her eyes. She could not end the relationship. She did not want to let Jake go. She continued her email.

Is it possible for me to collect my running shoes from your Kensington apartment? I'm back in England Wednesday night. I can collect them on Thursday or Friday and would be grateful if you could inform the concierge in advance. Thank you.

Best wishes,
Alice

Coward, Alice told herself after she sent it. She did not owe Jake anything, and his behavior was odd by any standard. She reached for her jacket. She was suffocating and needed fresh air.

She walked out of the hotel toward Bernabéu Stadium and the Real Madrid Museum. As she strolled alongside the stadium, life-sized photographs of David Beckham jumped out at her. Beckham could have been a catwalk model if he had not been such a talented footballer.

Having heard Bernabéu Stadium was a must-see venue for tourists visiting Madrid, Alice had arranged a private tour. Her tour guide escorted her to one of the stadium's eight panoramic elevators. From there, she followed him into the trophy room, which featured so many trophies that Alice could not take them all in at once. According to the museum, they made up "the most impressive track record any football club has ever had." In the trophy room, Alice also viewed historical kits, pictures of players from the first team, boots, and equipment.

From the trophy exhibition, she walked around the pitch, which gave her a view of how spectacular the stadium was from the ground. Next, she toured the presidential balcony, reserved for Real Madrid board members, those from visiting clubs, important personalities, and special guests. It was also the place where numerous Real Madrid captains had received many of the titles the team had won. She finished with the players' tunnel, the access point to the benches, and the coaching area. Feeling tired, Alice skipped the dressing rooms.

After the tour, she took a cab to Botín, a traditional restaurant that offered Mediterranean cuisine. According to *The Guinness Book of World Records*, it was the oldest restaurant in the world. She knew the restaurant was a tourist spot, but Spaniards still went there to sample the excellent food. She was also interested in its architecture. The restaurant was housed in a sixteenth-century building in the old part of Madrid, and friends had advised her that it was a must when visiting Spain's capital.

Back in her room, Alice checked her iPhone for missed calls and emails. Jake had not responded. Her frustration reached a peak. She settled down in her bed and hoped against all odds that he had a good reason for his insane behavior.

The early Wednesday morning meeting with Valencia was a waste of time, just as Alice expected. Valencia insisted on execution of its promised on-demand financial installment, and IG was beginning to realize that it had agreed to pay millions without something up front and that it had to pay despite the fact nothing had been delivered. Alice gave 100 percent in the meeting, but the signed contract did not support her contentions. The meeting started at 9:00 a.m. Ninety minutes later, she was heading back to the airport.

Alice arrived in Langley Park late that afternoon. She had checked her phone in the cab, and Jake had not called. She wondered whether she would ever hear from him. She resolved never to email, text, or call him again. The only message she had received was from her mother, asking if she had decided on a veil and stating that she would like to see it before Alice made her final decision.

"Fuck you, Jake!" She had accidentally hit the Backspace key and deleted the report she was writing. It was hard to concentrate. She checked her phone again. Nothing.

She stared at the blank screen. The company needed a plan, and Jake needed to call. She checked the clock: three hours to go before she could shut down her computer and call it a day.

Although Alice tried, she could not stop thinking about Jake. It was Thursday night, and he still had not called. She lay in bed and thought about whether he had given any thought to the fact that he had fathered a child. Logic dictated that he would disown the baby, deny paternity, or suggest an abortion. Jake had cut all ties. She was in her sixth week of pregnancy and alone. Alice did not want her baby to be stressed and suffer from anxiety in life. Scientific research said that stressed mothers produced stressed children. Feeling guilty about her selfishness, she flicked through her iTunes library to find a song that would help her relax.

Alice placed her iPhone on loudspeaker, but before it could start playing, it rang. It was Jake. She did not take the call, and it went to voice mail. She dialed in and listened to the message.

"Hey, honey. It's Jake. Just checking to see how you are. I'll call you later."

Alice's stress level hit an all-time high. *Is this man normal?* she asked herself repeatedly.

Twenty minutes later, her phone rang again.

I should put an end to this madness, answer the phone, and tell him not to call again.

"Hi, honey. How have you been?" Jake said when she answered. "I've missed you. How are the wedding plans?"

Alice could not believe what she was hearing. "Jake, you haven't called since Sunday. You never talk about our baby. It's difficult for me to believe you want to be in the baby's and my life."

Jake was silent. Alice was tempted to hang up.

"Honey, I was scared."

The excuse sounded pathetic. Did he think she had been celebrating since she found out she was pregnant?

Jake went on to explain that he wanted to be with her and that he had been busy at work. But the bottom line was, he had fears about fatherhood. He told her he would be in England on Saturday and would like to meet her mother. Alice responded that she would like that, but she could not face the further embarrassment of arranging for him to meet her mother and having him not show.

"Jake, I'm pregnant. I can't cope with the stress."

"Honey, I promise I'll be there," he told her. His tone was soft but sincere. "I was scared, but I'm sure now. I want you. I love you. I give you my word. I'll call tomorrow to finalize the details."

Alice wanted to believe Jake but had doubts. She was struck by anxiety as she processed what Jake had said. *Surely it would be a problem if I wasn't anxious, because there's a difference in life between being brave and being foolhardy. Am I brave because I want to trust him? Is that why I have these feelings?* Her thoughts lingered. She whispered, "For my unborn child, I must take a chance and do a reset with Jake."

16

The previous night's conversation with Jake was the first thing on Alice's mind when she opened her eyes the following morning. She did not know whether to trust that he would get on a flight to London later that day. She debated whether to put her mother on notice or say nothing. By the time Jake boarded his flight, it would be eleven o'clock at night in London, too late to be calling Mother. If she waited until Saturday morning, her mother might have other plans, not to mention the lecture Alice would receive about the short notice.

Alice nibbled at a whole-wheat cracker while pulling on her running pants and a long-sleeved T-shirt. She looked at her running shoes and thought, *I ought to replace them.* Then she remembered that she had bought a new pair, the pair at Jake's apartment.

She put on her old shoes and jogged toward the park. As she picked up speed and obtained a natural breathing rhythm, she thought about Jake. She was cautiously excited about seeing him the following day.

Forty minutes later, Alice's run brought her back to the house. She checked Runkeeper. She had run five miles. She stretched in the bedroom before taking a shower.

Feeling exhilarated by the run and the hot water, she thought about the day ahead. She had to follow up on the report she had sent to the company following the Valencia meeting and draft a letter before action to Valencia. It troubled Alice, because she struggled with the grounds on which her company could maintain an action against Valencia. IG was about to part with its first £5 million, and it had not received anything in return. The company was in denial and refused to accept that it had not legally bound Valencia to provide anything under the contract. IG expected that Valencia would push visitors from its website to the IG website to place bets on soccer games and use the other gaming services IG provided.

Alice also had a late-morning doctor's appointment. She had been experiencing light cramps in her pelvis, and she needed reassurance that it was nothing to worry about. At her first visit following her positive pregnancy test, the doctor had offered screening tests that could detect structural abnormalities, such as spina bifida, a defect in the development of the spine, or chromosomal disorders, such as Down syndrome. She had planned to discuss the tests with Jake but did not want to delay making an informed decision on whether to have them.

After breakfast, she sat down to draft the letter before action to Valencia. She identified several key steps IG had completed. Additionally, she identified steps Valencia had not completed. She concluded the letter by asserting that Valencia was not entitled to exercise the on-demand finance agreement IG had signed entitling Valencia to the first installment of £5 million from IG's bank.

Task accomplished. She addressed the letter to IG's directors, chief operating officer, and chief financial officer for approval and then hit Send. Then she picked up her car keys and set off to the doctor.

Alice was relieved after the doctor examined her. The doctor confirmed that it was not unusual to have cramps in the early weeks of pregnancy during the implantation stage as the embryo embedded into the uterus, and she told Alice that everything appeared normal. Alice's first scan was scheduled for twelve weeks. After the scan, with sonograms of the baby in hand, she planned to tell family and friends that she was pregnant. She had contemplated waiting until sixteen weeks. *Scheduling—I should talk to Jake about this.* At the thought of him, her doubts that he would show the following day crept back.

No test could guarantee her baby would be born without an abnormality, but Alice was trying to decide whether to have the tests anyway. She had thought about what she might do if the tests suggested her baby did have an abnormality. The doctor had informed her that if a test suggested a higher chance of a chromosomal abnormality, she would be offered further tests, which would give a more definite diagnosis. Her concern was that the tests carried a small risk of miscarriage at twelve weeks, the earliest point at which the tests could be undertaken. Alice was not sure she should have them. *This is something I should discuss with Jake.* She tensed at the thought. *What if he doesn't show? I'm building the baby's and my life around uncertainty.*

Driving home, Alice whispered, "For the sake of my unborn child, I must put aside my doubts and give Jake one more chance." She would make plans for him to have dinner with her mother and trust that he would get on the flight to London.

After arriving home, she cut the call twice before allowing it to connect with her mother's mobile. Mother was her usual self. She did not inquire after Alice's health or give Alice time to inquire after her health. She sought immediate confirmation that Alice had not made her final choice on a veil and asked whether she had contacted the church to find out its availability.

"Mother!"

Her mother paused. Alice had a window to talk, and she did not waste it. She explained that Jake would be in London the following day and would like to meet with her.

Her mother could not contain her excitement. "Alice, I hope you're planning to give more than a cup of tea."

It was no time to argue. Alice said she was hoping her mother would cook Sunday lunch.

"Alice, there's hope for you yet. I knew there had to be more to you than those books you've spent your life reading."

The comment hurt Alice, since both her father and her mother had encouraged her to read as a child, and her love of books had resulted in a successful career as a lawyer. She remembered the words of the therapist she had seen briefly after her father died, and she let her mother's comment slide. She told her mother that she had to work on urgent office matters but suggested she stop by the house later in the afternoon so they could discuss the menu. Alice would also give her some money for grocery shopping.

As Alice hung up her landline, her mobile rang. It was Jake.

"How's my li'l' honey?"

Alice tried to hide her shock that he had called. He said he was in Grand Central Station, on his way to the office. He told her he planned to leave the office at 3:00 p.m. His flight to London was at 6:00 p.m.

"Honey?" Jake said, questioning her silence.

Alice was still trying to accept that Jake might show. "Jake, you're coming to London." She realized how simple she sounded.

"Yes. I told you last night when we spoke."

Alice relaxed. She told him she had arranged for them to have Sunday lunch with her mother. Jake asked if she wanted him to bring anything. Alice could not help but let Jake know that she would be happy if the only thing he did was show up.

"I'll ask my PA to email you my itinerary. I think she's booked me into the Berkley Hotel in Knightsbridge. Honey, I'm going into the subway. I'll call you later."

✦ ✦ ✦

Wall Street, New York

Jake's limousine driver opened the door, and Jake got in and settled into the backseat. Throughout the past week, he had thought about Alice and Jessica. He had not been fair to Alice, and he intended to make that right. On Thursday night, he had called Jessica. She had asked repeatedly why they could not let bygones be bygones and give their relationship another chance. He had explained that he was nothing more than a backup plan for her, and that did not feel good to him. She had argued otherwise, but he was skeptical. She had asked if he was seeing anyone. He had lied to her and sought to comfort her by saying he still cared for her. But upon reflection, he realized that things had changed for him. He thought, *During that time, you were seeing other people, which I do not and did not begrudge you.* "At the same time, you can't have expected my life would stand still. A year ago, you were the center of my life. Over the past year, that has not been the case," he muttered. He had not heard from Jessica since then.

He was excited about seeing Alice again. He checked his phone and replied to a work-related email. Then his finger moved to press the off button. He did not get that far. Jessica's text stared him in the face. He did not know why, but he had a sense of fear as he opened it.

> You deeply and permanently hurt me. Do you get that, you stupid asshole? Do you think I should be skipping down the street all day long? I'm struggling hard to get through the abuse you inflicted on me! Sorry, but it's normal to have a hard time because of the trauma you put me through! I have fucking post-traumatic stress disorder (PTSD) because of what you put me through! I am in serious therapy.

Jake's happy spirit dissipated. *PTSD? Fuck.* Was she mentally ill?

The limo stopped in front of the airport terminal, bringing him back to the present.

Inside, security was the usual murder scene. He removed his belt, put his hand luggage through the x-ray scanner, and passed through metal detector.

Jessica has PTSD. I'm not perfect, but how is that my fault?

As Jake walked around JFK Airport, his mind went back and forth between his past relationship with Jessica and his growing love for Alice. He went into one of the outlets and bought Alice a pair of earphones for her iPod touch. The earphones supplied with the iPod he had bought her tended to fall out of her cute little ears.

He could not understand his feelings for Jessica. It was a relationship that could not be. Trying to avoid thinking about her, he went into Crabtree & Evelyn to buy a bag of goodies for Alice, but his resolve to move on with his life and focus on Alice continued to fail him. He could not rid his head of Jessica's texts, emails, and calls. Hoping to drown her out of his thoughts, he entered a music outlet and listened to a couple of tracks before he bought Kelly Clarkson's *All I Ever Wanted* album. He planned to play a certain track for Alice.

Jake settled in at the airport lounge bar to wait for the call to his gate. His thoughts wandered back to Jessica. He cared about her, but it was over. Too much broken glass lay shattered on the path between them. Jessica's words played in his head: *Sorry, but it's normal to have a hard time because of the trauma you put me through.* How could he get on a plane and leave unfinished business?

Jessica was not in a good place. He had failed her. She was the weaker party in the relationship. Why had he allowed his emotions to cloud his better judgment? He should not have rekindled a hopeless relationship repeatedly. He had to make sure she was OK.

Jake ignored the calls for his gate, the calls for him personally, and the announcement that the flight was leaving. He was deep in thought, weighing the guilt he carried in relation to Jessica against the responsibility he owed to Alice, the woman he loved, and their baby, when the receptionist from the lounge reception desk tapped his shoulder.

"Mr. Logan, your gate is closing. I'll call ahead to let the flight attendants know you're on your way."

Startled, Jake thanked the receptionist and then rushed out of the lounge, not knowing whether he would turn left and head to his gate or continue straight ahead and exit the airport.

17

When Alice went to bed Friday night, her cautious optimism was at level nine. Jake's PA had emailed his itinerary. It was a trip he was making to meet her mother and spend time with Alice. No business was involved.

Jake had called her en route to the airport. He'd called again while he was in the bar, waiting for his gate. He had also emailed the concierge at the Berkley to expect his "wife" in the morning and give her full access to their room. The concierge had also been given full instruction to take care of the Porsche. Jake had sent Alice a text that said he had something to take care of but would be at the hotel no later than 11:00 a.m.

Alice thought about his apartment. Had he given it up? He was staying in a hotel. If he had given up the apartment, when had he given notice? Her brain was working overtime. She did not want to spoil the moment. She could ask Jake about the apartment later that day. For the moment, she felt she had reason to smile.

She stretched a hand to the bedside table and picked up her phone. It was 5:30 a.m., still too early to expect a call from Jake. His flight, if on time, would land in thirty minutes. She could not sleep and would not relax until she had confirmation that he was on the runway at Heathrow. Jake had promised to call as soon as he landed.

Alice got up. She needed to do something to help pass the next thirty minutes. She thought about what to wear. The baby was not showing, though she was entering her seventh week. However, her stomach felt bloated, and some of her jeans and skirts felt tight around the waist. She had bought maternity bras but did not want to buy or start wearing maternity clothing before her twelfth to sixteenth week.

Jake's first text message came at 5:55 a.m.: "The bird has landed."

The second text arrived at 6:10: "Will call you when I get through immigration and am in the car."

Alice could not contain her excitement. She slowly clapped her hands and twirled around.

Knightsbridge was just waking up when Alice arrived later that morning. She handed her car keys to the doorman at the Berkeley Hotel and walked to Harrods, where she planned to buy Jake a gift.

Alice always entered and exited Harrods by the same entrance. It made navigating the huge department store much easier. She stepped onto the escalator and traveled up to the sports department to find the golf shop. The shop assistant helped her select a golf range finder, a Callaway rain hood towel, and a Titleist divot tool and then gift wrapped them for her.

Afterward, Alice walked back to the Berkeley to meet Jake. She was excited about seeing him again but curious as to whether she would still have the same feelings for him, given the events of the previous two weeks.

The Berkeley was a luxurious and iconic London hotel at the heart of the Knightsbridge scene and was known for the Blue Bar, a popular and exclusive London celebrity hangout. She approached the reception desk and asked for the key to Jake's room.

The receptionist handed her the key card and smiled. "Mrs. Logan, Mr. Logan is waiting for you in room three fifty-four."

Alice took the elevator to the third floor. Rather than using the key card to open the door, she knocked. When the door opened, standing in front of her was the tall, dark, handsome man she loved. Jake smiled at her. Any concerns she had about her feelings for him disappeared. Jake embraced and kissed her. Then he took her hand and guided her into the room.

Once inside, Jake did not delay. Alice's clothes needed to come off. Although she wanted to comply, Jake's behavior made it feel like a first date. She needed to slow the situation down.

To calm Jake, Alice handed him the presents she had bought. Jake, the eternal little boy, smiled in excitement. He loved surprises. As he opened his gift, his eyes sparkled, which made her feel good and carefree. This was the Jake she loved. It was as if Christmas and his birthday had come at once. He was particularly excited by the golf range finder. He had been thinking about buying one for a while.

Jake had not arrived empty-handed. He gave her the Crabtree & Evelyn bag, which contained bodywash, body lotion, a bottle of perfume, and hand lotion. In another bag were the earphones for her iPod touch and the Kelly Clarkson CD.

"Let's listen to track one, 'My Life Would Suck without You,'" Jake said.

Alice did not warm to the song. The songwriter presented a woman's relationship with her boyfriend as fluctuating and tumultuous; the two were depicted arguing and throwing each other's belongings, mirroring the sentiments of the song. *My life would suck without you. I didn't tell Jake that I want anyone but him. Maybe he is trying to relay to me that his life would suck without me—a strange choice of lyrics.* Alice could not help thinking that Jake had had Jessica in mind when he bought the CD. Jessica was the one who regretted telling him goodbye. However, Alice allowed the headlong pleasurable feeling she had for Jake to color her judgment and did not open her eyes to the fact that neither Jake nor Jessica appeared to have completed the healing process of their broken relationship. Alice told herself naively that it was the thought that counted. Even if she could not relate to that track, she liked other tracks on the CD.

Jake moved closer to her. He took the CD case from her hands and kissed her. There were no more excuses, and Alice did not want to make any. She had missed him. Jake caressed her arm and pulled her gently toward him. He kissed her soft, full lips as he slipped her clothes off. Jake teased her body with his mouth, and then their bodies locked together.

A little while later, Jake pulled the sheet around Alice and held her in his arms. Alice wanted to talk. She had many questions, but she did not want to spoil the moment. Jake broke the silence, suggesting they order room service. After he placed the order, he told Alice he had stopped by his Kensington apartment to say goodbye to the guys at the concierge desk. Alice asked what had happened to her running shoes and his personal belongings.

"I shipped everything to Greenwich, Connecticut."

Alice looked at him in surprise. "I thought you were relocated to Wall Street on short notice."

"It was short notice, but my relocation has been in the cards for a while."

"Is that why, when we exchanged emails initially, you asked if I would be prepared to live in another country?"

"Yes."

After they ate, Jake told Alice he had an appointment at Tiffany in Harrods. She was not entirely satisfied with Jake's answer in relation to his relocation, but for the first time in a while, she felt optimistic about their relationship going forward.

The Tiffany sales associates were expecting Jake and had a round, six-pronged, classic two-carat engagement ring in a size six for him to view. The sales assistant handed the solitaire to Alice, inviting her to try it on for size.

The Tiffany legend had not been exaggerated. The quality of the diamond was evident even to the naked eye. Alice knew a diamond's brilliance was determined by the amount of white light it returned to the eye. This diamond maximized that effect.

"Do you like the ring?" Jake asked.

Alice could feel the excitement, joy, and anticipation beaming from her face. "Yes!"

"Mr. Logan, would you like to take the ring now, or would you like me to put it on hold?"

"No, thank you. I don't plan to purchase the ring today."

His words registered slowly in Alice's mind. *What did he say? I thought the plan was to purchase the ring. He could at least indicate that he intends to purchase it at some point. After all, it's not the first time we've discussed the ring.*

She pulled the ring off her finger and watched as the sales assistant took it away. She could tell Jake sensed he had let her down, but he did not offer an explanation as he led her away and attempted to put Alice through a similar exercise at Cartier. It was becoming increasingly apparent that he was merely window-shopping. Alice's demeanor changed—the smile was gone, and her disappointment was visual when she realized that trying the ring on for size was as close as she would come to owning it. She refused to play what appeared to be a sick game on his part.

At De Beers, she viewed but declined to try on the ring. She turned to Jake and said, "It's beautiful. Can we go now?" She smiled at the shop assistant said, "Thank you." She turned and walked out of the shop, leaving Jake to choose whether he followed her. "Jackass," she muttered. "He seems to derive a perverse pleasure from building my hopes only to dash them." She took a deep breath. *I'm not canceling lunch with Mother—I can't deal with the drama.* She took another deep breath. *And I'll not spoil the weekend by behaving badly, but he's not getting away with the bizarre show he put on today.*

As they walked out of Harrods and toward the Wilton Arms, Alice turned on him. "Why the exhibition? Did you really think it was necessary to put me through that charade if you had no intention of purchasing a ring?" She thought she saw his face register guilt but not for long.

"It's important for me to know that you like the ring."

"That question was asked and answered over the weekend you were on Sanibel Island."

Jake was silent, and Alice did not push the issue any further. She could not cope with explaining a no-show to Mother. He was not off the hook yet.

They spent the rest of the afternoon in the Wilton Arms, Knightsbridge, known locally as the village pub. The Wilton was bustling with people, but Jake spotted a couple of comfortable high settees. He made getting to the settees his mission before anyone else noticed the seats were vacant. That afternoon, Chelsea was playing Manchester City. Chelsea won two to nil. All the big names recently added to Manchester City still needed to put aside their egos and learn to play together. Later in the afternoon, Alice and Jake walked back to the Berkeley.

Because of her pregnancy fatigue, Alice liked to nap whenever the opportunity presented itself. Back in their hotel room, Jake lay on the bed and held her close. She absorbed his affection for her and fell asleep in his arms.

He was still out when she slipped out of the bed. She sat on the bed and observed him. He woke suddenly from what she assumed was a nightmare. When he said he was OK, she headed into the bathroom.

She soaked in the room's Jacuzzi tub before showering and dressing for dinner. Jake had booked a table at the Wolseley. Sometimes the strangest things brought back an early childhood memory. For Alice, the combination of being in a bathroom and that night's dinner reservation at the Wolseley made her think about her father and their family home. In the bathroom in the house in which she had grown up, her father had created a border of pictorial ceramic tiles. The Wolseley 1903 was one of the cars displayed on the tiles. Historically, Wolseley Motors Limited had commissioned a prestigious showroom in Saint James, Piccadilly. The Wolseley restaurant and café had opened in the former showroom in November 2003.

Alice missed her father, both as a loving parent and as a friend. She wished he was meeting Jake the following day. Her father's love had not and could not have compensated for the love found in an intimate relationship, but after he'd died, she had felt alone, and her need to be loved had intensified. She paused and reflected that she had enjoyed a strong, loving bond with her dad. He would have supported her but been disappointed with her for becoming pregnant outside of marriage. She did not doubt Jake's feelings for her; his strange behavior at times was the issue. Their visit to Harrods to view engagement rings—what had that been about? In that moment, Alice was not sure she would have introduced him to her dad.

Jake was tired from his flight to London and did not object to a moment of rest. He lay on the bed and snuggled up to Alice. Although he had not mentioned the baby, he put a hand on her tummy and massaged it gently. He was overcome first by emotion and then by the feel of her soft skin and her sensual body aroma. Intimacy ensued, and then he cradled Alice as she fell asleep in his arms.

Jake's thoughts went back to the baby she was carrying. He rubbed his sweating forehead in the sheets as he felt the increased pace of his heart beating. "Becoming a father is a life-changing event," he whispered. *Jessica begged me to be the father to her babies, and I refused. I'm thirty-three, so why do I feel so unprepared mentally for the reality of fatherhood?* He had not had enough of the good life to let it go. He had spent the last few weeks stressed and gloomy when he contemplated how everything he loved about his life would have to be sacrificed. Tired, he finally fell asleep.

It was seven o'clock in the evening when Jake woke up. He had been dreaming. In his dream, Jessica had found out about the birth of Alice's baby. There had been a police alert. Jessica had been missing from the mental institution, and the baby had been missing from the hospital. Sweat dripped down his forehead.

"Jake, are you OK?" Alice asked. She sat on the bed, intently observing him.

"Yes, I had a nightmare. I'm OK. I can barely remember the details."

He could, though, and the dream sent shivers down his spine.

I must resolve the Jessica issue. I honestly don't know what that involves, but I know it will kill her if she finds out about Alice and the baby.

Jake stepped into the bathroom and observed Alice. For him, one of the hardest things would be watching her sexy body change during the pregnancy. He did not believe he would find her attractive as her bump became pronounced. He did not want to contemplate childbirth either. She would expect him to share the moment, but he did not want to see her endure pain no man could comprehend. Jake was aware he was being selfish. He could never share such thoughts with Alice.

On Sunday morning, Jake ordered, and stirred Alice from sleep with, fresh orange juice and whole-wheat toast. Jake did not talk about the baby, but he remembered her current aversion to the aroma of coffee. They planned to run in Kensington before a full breakfast.

Alice and Jake entered Kensington Gardens just below the Princess Diana memorial. Their run took them up to Hyde Park and then down into Green Park. The Runkeeper registered seven miles when they were finished. Then they headed to the gym in the Berkeley, where Jake lifted weights and Alice stretched.

In the elevator on the way back to the room, Jake suggested they buy wine and flowers for her mother. If Jake was nervous about meeting her, he did not let it show.

At noon, they walked to Harrods, where Jake bought wine and flowers. Alice's Porsche was waiting outside the Berkeley when they approached. Jake had arranged for the concierge to park it in front of the hotel at 12:30. He placed the flowers in the space behind the passenger's seat and settled into the seat, and then they set off to Langley Park.

As they drove, Jake contemplated meeting Alice's mother. Such a first meeting was often tricky, and Alice had not talked much about her. Jake had the three Cs in mind: compliment her outfit, compliment her cooking, and compliment her daughter.

Forget your interests, he reminded himself. *This conversation is not about golf.*

He could talk about cooking and how he wanted to learn to cook more complicated dishes. That would be easy because he really was interested in cooking. It would be OK. Jake smiled to himself. At his recent drinks with the boys, he had told them he was taking a trip to London to meet his future mother-in-law. His friends had attempted to scare him with tales of their first meetings with their mothers-in-law. He reminded himself that Alice and her mother's relationship was not that unusual. As far as he was concerned, the relationship between this mother and daughter had been long discussed and troubled over. If Alice's mother did not warm to him immediately, he should not take it personally.

Alice's mother was waiting outside the door when they arrived. She was warm and welcoming. She offered tea but let Jake know she had beer or something stronger if he preferred. Alice's glance told him it was OK to accept a beer.

The conversation at lunch was easy. Alice's mother had made chicken chasseur, a French recipe that combined chicken, red wine, shallots, lardons, and other ingredients into a tasty casserole. She had placed the chicken on a bed of saffron rice and complemented it with asparagus. Jake enjoyed lunch and had several questions about cooking.

Jake discreetly observed Alice and her mother throughout lunch. He was curious on two levels. First, he wondered whether he had met her mother's approval. Second, he looked for signals from Alice that she had no complaints. Midway through lunch, he discerned that Alice had exhaled. He was at ease with her mother, and she was genuinely warm to him. However, there was a moment toward the end of the visit when Alice became tense once again. Her mother leaned close to her in the doorway as they prepared to leave, and although her voice was low, he heard her say, "I thought you would be wearing an engagement ring." Jake lingered to hear her, but Alice did not reply. She kissed her mother and hastened her approach to the car.

Although lunch had been a success, he was relieved when they said their goodbyes and headed back to the Berkeley.

Shortly into their journey, Alice turned to Jake. "When are you planning to introduce me to the people you love and care about?"

"Sooner than you think."

"Oh yeah? When?" She told him she had not used up her annual leave from the previous year, and now, as May approached, she had not taken any leave. "When do I get to meet your mom and dad?"

Jake paused before answering. The more time he spent with Alice, the more he was convinced that she was the One. He drifted back to the Tate Modern event. When he had plucked up the courage to approach her, he had spoken to her briefly. Thereafter, he had emailed Alice every day for almost three months. He had to know every detail about her. That night in March, they had talked until the early hours of the morning. He found Alice interesting and exciting. Over time, he had also found her to be loving, thoughtful, and considerate not only of his well-being but also of other people around her. Jake loved Alice, though he could not find any enthusiasm for the baby she was carrying. Who wanted to go to the same park in the freezing cold for the seventh day in a row to push a fucking swing? Who really wanted to watch *Sesame Street*? And who really wanted to read the same book night after night? *Certainly not me.*

His thoughts returned to Jessica. His lips moved, but no sound emerged. *I don't want to do this to her, but she's no longer pivotal; Alice is, and I can't let Jessica control my life. That relationship is over. I must move on, and so must she.*

"I can arrange for you to come to New York next weekend," he said finally.

"Perfect," Alice replied.

What have you done, Jake? You must undo this mess. You can't do this to Jessica.

Jake's love for Alice silenced his mind. "I'll make the arrangements, honey."

He was not sure what he would do. He would be safe from both Alice and Jessica once he was back in the United States. He struggled to neutralize his feelings for Jessica, but his mind was drowned with her pleas and Pink's "Please Don't Leave Me." He was not sure where to hide, but hide he would.

18

lice could not help analyzing Jake's lack of focus in the car the previous day. For a minute, he had disappeared to a different place, as if he had suffered a blackout, and he seemed totally unaware that he had lost a minute. She considered whether she should suggest he see a doctor but thought that might be overstepping the mark. The rest of the day had been uneventful. They had discussed her travel dates for the forthcoming trip to New York. She would leave Friday, stay for a week, and return the following Monday.

Alice did not have any problems arranging her annual leave for the trip to New York. She would be traveling with her phone, a personal computer, and the knowledge that the company owned her 24-7.

Later that morning, when she checked her personal email, she found an e-ticket to New York from Jake signed, "Love you, honey." Alice replied, thanking him for making her flight arrangements and reminding him to text or call when the bird landed.

Alice did not leave the office until seven thirty that evening. Jake had called just after five to let her know he had landed and was en route to his office. Her plan was to attend meetings through the early part of the week and revise documents toward the end of the week during her time in New York. She was forced out of the office because she had arranged to meet her friend Jonathan for dinner.

Jonathan was one of her oldest and dearest friends. They had known each other since the start of their legal careers and had traveled a path together that had almost resulted in intimacy. However, because they worked in the same office, Alice had insisted they remain merely friends.

When she arrived at the restaurant, Jonathan was waiting in the bar area.

"Alice!" He stood and greeted her with a kiss on the cheek. "I ordered you a gin and tonic."

Alice embraced him. As she released their embrace, she asked, "Is our table ready?"

"Yes."

Uneasy about sitting at the bar, she turned to see if a waiter was available to take them to their table.

"Alice, your drink," Jonathan said, holding it up for her.

"Thanks, but I'm not drinking tonight. My workload is too heavy."

After Jonathan and Alice were seated at their table and placed their orders, she told Jonathan about Jake and their plan to get married.

"Wow! I'm—" Jonathan hesitated before he said, "Are you sure?"

Alice cut him off before he could say more. "I know. I'm just as surprised at how quickly our relationship has advanced."

"Lightning speed," he muttered under his breath.

"I've a good career and would be lying if I denied being scared about starting a new life in a new country." Alice neglected to tell Jonathan about the baby. She did not deliberately intend to mislead him by withholding essential information, but it seemed sensible not to make any announcements about the baby until she was at least three months along.

"Hm, you've known him how long?" Jonathan paused when he registered the serene look on Alice's face, and having recently married, he added, "I only wish for you to find the happiness I've experienced since finding the right person to love."

"Seriously?" Alice smiled. "You're in favor of me giving up my career to be with Jake?"

"I don't know Jake, but if you're serious about him and he's serious about you, emigrating might be the only way to move forward with the relationship." With a cheeky grin, he said, "You might have to let the pink in you emerge to secure this love."

"Are you suggesting that independent women aren't girlies?" she asked, smiling slyly.

Jonathan's wife had given up work after they were married. He was quick to explain that he was merely implying that there was nothing wrong with allowing another person to take care of her until she found her feet.

Friday morning finally arrived. Alice had butterflies in her stomach on her way to the airport. She traveled frequently on business and had spent many hours in airport lounges, but this was her first time in the Virgin Atlantic lounge. On Virgin's website, the description of the lounge read, "There is nowhere else like it." The claim was not an exaggeration. If Virgin Atlantic had announced Alice's flight to New York had been delayed until 9:00 p.m., Alice would have gladly stayed in the lounge and treated herself to a massage, a shower, and a wash and blow dry. It was hard to distinguish between the bar in the Virgin lounge and most of London's top bars and restaurants. It was an experience Alice would have highly recommended to anyone.

She ordered salmon and scrambled eggs for breakfast. If not for the baby, she would have ordered champagne. She had delayed calling Harrods, Pronovias. It was a call she had to make, preferably before she boarded the flight to New York. Over time, Alice had thought about the wedding and what she wanted. She did not want to up-stage Annabel's wedding; that had not been her intention when she announced the engagement. Nor did she want to endure Charlotte's wrath, and she feared disappointing her mother, but she did not want to wear the royal wedding gown.

She called Harrods, Pronovias. When the call was transferred to Maria, she explained that her wedding plans had changed and that she and her fiancé were considering having their wedding in New York. If the plans were confirmed, she would require a simple dress. Maria agreed to put the present order on hold until after the weekend, when Jake and Alice would confirm their plans.

The trip would not be Alice's first time in New York. Alice's father had lived in New York City, and her first time there had been to visit him. Subsequent visits had been for both pleasure and business. Alice, like many others, thought of it as the cultural capital of the world. As a European, Alice could not fail to notice how densely populated New York was. As many as eight hundred languages were spoken by its ten million residents, making it the most linguistically diverse city in the world.

Jake had arranged for a car to meet Alice at JFK. The driver had been instructed to take her to Wall Street in Lower Manhattan, which functioned as the financial capital of the world and was home to the New York Stock Exchange, the world's largest stock exchange by total market capitalization of listed companies. Security measures were in place that prevented the car from accessing Wall Street itself, so the driver parked at an entrance. Alice called Jake, and two minutes later, he was in the car, lighting up her world in a way only he could.

19

Jessica stood across the street from the bank. Jake was in such a hurry that he had not seen her. She followed him as he walked down Wall Street, picking up pace when he did. She saw him get into a black limousine. She thought she saw a woman in the car, but she could not be sure.

"Fuck! The antidepressants!" she shouted as she tripped over the elevation between the street and the sidewalk. She brought he leg forward fast enough to prevent the fall. She could not think or see straight. She tried to flag a cab, but as far as she was concerned, the drivers were in fucking cahoots with Jake and ignored her. Jessica ran down the street that joined Wall Street, shouting, "Stop that fucking car!"

When a policeman stopped her to ask if she was OK, she took a deep breath before telling him she needed a taxi to get home. The policeman suggested that if she walked a little farther up the street, she would be more successful.

By the time she hailed a cab, it was too late to follow Jake. Jessica gave the driver directions to her apartment. Her mind worked overtime on whether she had seen a woman in the car. Jake could move on with his life but not before he had paid his dues to her.

I have no man who loves me besides Jake. Jake owes me, and he's not

*going to walk away. He owes me. This can be easy or as fucking hard as he
wants it to be.*

She sent him a text: "Call, you fucking asshole. I want to know
about that fucking bitch in the car with you today."

Jessica was relieved when her therapist agreed to see her on short
notice. She walked into the waiting room of Bethany A. Jones, MD;
bypassed reception; and headed straight into Beth's office without
knocking.

"Jake's fucking behavior is unacceptable!" she wailed.

"Your lack of etiquette is unacceptable. There is ten minutes until
your appointment. Please leave my office and check in at reception.
Otherwise, I can't take the session."

Jessica did as Beth instructed. Seven minutes later, the receptionist
knocked on Beth's office and showed Jessica into the room.

Jessica did not waste any time in telling Beth about the events on
Wall Street.

"What were you doing at Wall Street in the first place?" Beth
asked when Jessica finished her tirade.

"Please don't waste my time. Why the fuck do you need to know
why I was at Wall Street?"

Jessica told Beth that Jake's abusiveness, whether the result of
intoxication or not, would result in his pleading his love for her one
day and then, the next day, acting as if he hated her.

"He's damaging me mentally and physically." She said that two
weekends earlier, he'd been probably the meanest he had ever been,
outside of the horrible behavior he had inflicted on her by leaving
her at the altar. "How could he move on with his life and forget our
relationship?"

"Please correct me if I'm wrong, but Jake abandoned you at the
altar three years ago, right?"

"That's right. He turned his back and walked away, leaving me
alone at the fucking altar."

"At the time, you were an attractive woman with a promising career, and even now you can turn your life around. Why have you allowed Jake's leaving you at the altar to consume your every waking thought?"

Jessica paused before answering. "I can't forget him leaving me at the altar until he makes it right. That's what I believe. Jake making up for what he's done is the only way I can ever be whole again."

"That's not the only way; you can choose to be free of Jake or let him destroy your life."

Jessica! It's the only way! Jake must make good. He destroyed your life. Tell her about the cruel text. The voice belonged to Jess, a loud, demanding voice in Jessica's head.

"It was a living nightmare all over again, reading his texts!"

"Are you referring to the texts suggesting the need for you both to move on with your lives?"

"Yes. I didn't deserve to be treated so coldly, and Jake had no idea how painful it was to read the things he wrote. His words were unnecessarily acrimonious and just awful. They sounded like acid in my ears. Words hurt, and he has never been crueler and more heartless. Jake's lack of emotional maturity was on full display in those strange and cruel words."

"I read the texts. Jake said he could not be reconciled with you and that you should move forward with your life."

"What the fuck are you talking about? It was shocking and below the belt, even for him. I didn't deserve it. His texts were just wrong! He doesn't answer my calls, and he doesn't speak to me in person ever. How could he let somebody call him over and over without answering?"

"Why do you believe you have a future with such a person?"

"Jake's behavior is fucked up. It's abuse."

"I can understand that Jake's behavior upsets you at times. Can we explore why you feel he's abusing you?"

Jessica sat there in silence with her arms folded, refusing to answer Beth's question.

"Do you still love Jake? Why did you let him back into your life after he didn't go through with the wedding?"

"I'll never forget that he left me at the altar until he makes it right," Jessica replied quietly. "I know that's the only way I'll ever be whole again."

"What if he doesn't make it right? How can he make it right?"

The session ended with Jessica's refusal to answer.

20

L ife had been quiet. Jessica had not sent any emails or texts, and she had not called in the past few days. Even though Jake hoped it stayed that way, he acknowledged that for a while, Jessica's pleas for him to take her back had been a distraction, something to take his focus off his fears about becoming a father. He wondered if Jessica's silence was the first sign that she was letting go and moving forward. Yes, Jessica would be upset about Alice, but she could not expect his life to stand still. It had been Jessica's call to end the relationship, to date another man. Eventually, he had supported her decision, but he'd told her that if it did not work out, he would not take her back. He had not wished for a bad outcome between Jessica and her new boyfriend, but it had played out the way he'd thought it would. Jessica's relationship with the other man had not worked out, and now she wanted Jake back—until the next time.

But Jake vowed there would be no next time. Jessica had hurt him when she ended the relationship. Jake had cared for her and struggled to shut off those feelings. He would be there for Jessica as a friend only. She needed to be more independent, and to that end, he would support her when necessary. But now Alice was his priority. Jake was determined to get his act together and focus on Alice 100 percent. She was a good person and deserved better from him.

Jake directed the driver toward the World Trade Center site in Lower Manhattan, previously known as Ground Zero after the 9/11 attacks. He checked his phone for emails and messages. He started to read a text from Jessica but deleted it before he got to the end. This was Alice's time.

Jake explained to Alice that while the Port Authority of New York and New Jersey often was identified as the owner of the World Trade Center site, the Port Authority had acknowledged ambiguities over the ownership of the land where streets had been before the World Trade Center was built, a dispute that went back to the 1960s.

Jake had lost friends and colleagues on 9/11. He still carried the pain.

When the car pulled in front of the Hotel Gansevoort, Jake changed the subject to the hotel. He told Alice that it was credited with revitalizing the Meatpacking District, transforming it from an area of slaughterhouses and packing plants into one of New York's most fashionable neighborhoods, catering to young professionals. He believed the Gansevoort was one of Manhattan's hottest hotels.

He checked in, and they went straight up to his room. He did not waste any time in letting her know how much he desired her.

Jake did not want to leave Alice. If he'd had a choice, he would have stayed and made love to her all afternoon, but he had a meeting he could not avoid. He kissed her and explained that he had to go back to work for a couple of hours. He suggested she walk him to the subway and then explore the Meatpacking District on her own.

Down in the subway, he boarded the express 2 train to Wall Street. Seated, Jake checked his messages. He had the usual onslaught of messages. The text from Jessica jumped out: "Call, you fucking asshole. I want to know about that fucking bitch in the car with you today."

After Alice parted with Jake at the subway, she walked back through an area previously known for its slaughterhouses. Part of the Meatpacking District's transformation had been the opening of high-end boutiques. The streets were lined with cute shops, including Alexander McQueen, Theory, Puma, Moschino, and the Apple Store, as well as cafés, such as Pastis, and nightclubs, such as Tenjune. The developments had turned the Meatpacking District into Lower Manhattan's adult playground.

When Alice passed Stella McCartney's shop, she could not resist peeking inside, but for the moment, she was exhausted. She promised herself she would return the following week and then walked back to the hotel and slept until Jake called later in the afternoon. She arranged to meet him downstairs at 6:00 p.m.

Alice walked around her room. The decor was contemporary. Hints of the Meatpacking District's former industrial nature were evident in the stainless-steel sinks and leather-wrapped headboards. Luxury prevailed, including Carrara marble in the bathroom and Cutler bath amenities. Alice ran a bath and selected from the CD player, spinning Gansevoort New York's latest musical compilation, Beyoncé's "Once in a Lifetime."

Alice stayed in the bath longer than planned. She dressed quickly. A few minutes late, she rushed out of the room to meet Jake in the lobby. When the elevator opened, Jake was waiting for her. He stepped inside and kissed her. They took the elevator to the rooftop to have a cocktail while enjoying stunning views from the Plunge Bar and roof-top garden. Then they walked around the heated, glass-surrounded outdoor rooftop pool with underwater music.

They opted not to dine at the hotel, which offered modern Chinese cuisine, including shellfish and sushi. Jake preferred not to be in the same room as sushi. Alice agreed with his choice, Tavern on Jane in Greenwich Village.

21

lice's body was on Greenwich mean time. She woke every hour on the hour from midnight onward. If she had been by herself, she would not have lain in bed and forced herself back to sleep. Finally, she gave in at five o'clock. She craved a cup of hot coffee, but that was something she had learned little baby Logan would not tolerate. Instead, she sat quietly in the room's reception area and perused dresses on Pronovias's website.

Alice lost count of how many dresses she had viewed before she found the perfect one. It was suitable for a wedding ceremony, whether it took place in New York or in Florida. She checked the time. She had not realized how long she had been viewing Pronovias's new collection, which had just been released.

It was seven thirty when she made the call to London. Her excitement spilled out when she spoke to Maria and told her that on her return to London, she would call to be fitted for the dress. Alice was pleased when Maria said she had sufficient measurements to place the order and that the final details could be confirmed later. Both parties checked their calendars and then penciled in an appointment for a week from Friday.

Planning to sneak back into bed, Alice went to the bedroom. As she entered, Jake stirred.

He said, "It's early. Were you talking to your office?"

Alice sat on Jake's side of the bed, facing him, and for the first time in a while, they talked. Long-distance dating made meaningful conversation difficult. "I canceled the wedding dress I initially chose and placed another order for the dress of my choice." She explained that she had not known him long when he had proposed. "Everything happened quickly, and at the time, I felt I'd not been allowed to come to a decision regarding the marriage or its timing."

He sat up in bed, waiting to hear what she would say.

"My mother was bullying me into wearing a wedding dress I felt was too much dress, and where the reception was concerned, she found fault with every suggestion I brought to the table."

"I had no idea you felt that way. Can I suggest three options? One, we can continue long-distance dating. Two, you could move to the United States and marry me. And three, I could move back to the United Kingdom and marry you." He could not help using the moment as an opportunity to brag that he had sufficient means to live without working. "Whatever your decision is, I hope you will still accept an engagement ring. I'm planning a special dinner next week."

Alice let Jake know that two of his options were unfeasible. She had known him long enough to know that he would not survive mentally without a career. Long-distance dating would take a toll over the long term. Marriage was the only realistic option. Alice loved Jake. Marrying him did not scare her, but she wanted to be involved in the process. If he did not object, she preferred a small wedding in New York with their immediate families.

Jake was visibly relieved. He said he did not want a big wedding, and he suggested marrying on Sanibel Island. She smiled and said, "Maybe."

Jake suggested a trip to Sanibel Island before she made her decision. He bent forward, kissed her, and then pulled her into bed.

✦   ✦   ✦

Alice and Jake's morning jog followed a path through the Meatpacking District and along the Hudson River. They passed Pastis on their way back. Jake suggested they have breakfast there when they checked out of the Gansevoort.

"What?" She had not seen this announcement coming.

"I thought you would like to see my house in Greenwich."

His house in Greenwich? Why can't he be up front and share day-to-day plans with me? There was a cost factor to living in a hotel, even for Jake. She did not believe he had been living in the Gansevoort since his move back to the United States. Why were his daily plans shrouded in secrecy?

Not long after they were seated at Pastis, the waitress poured hot coffee into Jake's cup.

"No, thank you," Alice said when the waitress stepped toward her to fill her cup.

After the waitress left, Alice watched Jake stir sugar into his coffee. "Can we have a grown-up conversation about the baby?" she asked. "You behave as if you don't mind having me in your life, but I'm not so sure about the baby I'm carrying."

He looked up at her. "Alice, I love you. Please don't read my reluctance to talk about the baby as suggesting you should have an abortion. I'm just apprehensive about the unknown. We'll talk about the baby later."

"We'll talk later—your stock-in-trade answer."

"Honey, you're worrying unnecessarily—it's not good for the baby. We'll talk later."

"Don't patronize me," she snapped.

"I'm not. I promise we'll talk later."

Alice and Jake took a cab to Grand Central Station and then took a mainline train to Greenwich, Connecticut. Jake had purchased the Saturday morning newspaper, the *Economist*, and a golf magazine. He settled into his seat and inserted earphones into his ears to signal "Do not disturb." The journey to Greenwich was approximately one hour. Alice used the time to read work-related emails.

When they arrived in Greenwich, Jake's niece, Victoria, was waiting to meet them—another small matter he had neglected to mention. Victoria often used Jake's Jeep while he was in London and during the week when he was working in New York. It made sense for her to meet them. Jake would give her a ride back home or to wherever she wanted to go. After the initial introductions, Victoria agreed to join them for lunch.

Victoria, a first-year university student, seemed mature for her years, a nice but serious girl. The family resemblance was unmistakable. Victoria was tall and had long, wavy dark hair and the same strikingly blue eyes as her uncle. Her high cheekbones complemented her porcelain complexion.

Lunch passed quickly. Both Alice and Victoria agreed they should carve out some quality time together.

"Let's meet for lunch the next time I'm in Greenwich," Alice said.

22

New York

66 **I**'ve wasted four months in therapy sessions," said Jessica. *Four months, and Beth still does not understand why I cannot let go of Jake.* She did a Google search for a new therapist. She had spent the previous afternoon and that morning considering Beth's questions. What if Jake did not marry her? What if she did not get her house and the babies? *Beth doesn't live in the real world.* Jessica was running out of time. Beth had not heard the biological clock going 24-7 in Jessica's head.

Jessica had dated other men. That was never a problem with her good looks and blonde hair. But to her dismay, the relationships never lasted longer than a few months. She felt used by men. The other men had money—more than Jake could dream about—but he was the only one she could get to spend beyond the initial sweeteners. She thought about her arguments with Jake about money. *He bought me designer dresses, and even if he was not there in mind and body, I carried the credit card.* She had two obstacles left to jump. She had to get him to buy the house and father the babies. Then he could fuck off. *If he loves me, I can't see where there's an issue.*

Jessica needed to see Jake. She called Amanda, her friend in

Connecticut, and arranged to visit her later that day. Jake spent his weekends at his house in Greenwich. There was a strong possibility she could meet him there. She felt hopeful that he would feel differently if they could meet, as opposed to emailing and texting.

Ten minutes before Jake and Alice turned onto Old Post Road on Saturday evening, Jessica—accompanied by Amanda—pulled up in front of Jake's house. Jessica's disappointment registered on her face, and her stress level increased when she saw the house was dark. She rang the doorbell several times before going back to the car and complaining to Amanda. She had been able to establish that Jake was in Greenwich, because she had peered through the window and seen that he had gone out without turning the television off.

Amanda spent several minutes trying to calm Jessica, who was shouting every expletive in her vocabulary. After a while, Amanda was able to convince her that Jake's not being home did not imply anything sinister.

"On Saturday nights, people go out," she said. She said she would have suggested they return later, but she had the children for the night, and the babysitter would charge double if she stayed out after midnight. She suggested they should not waste the evening. They could have drinks at the Gray Goose and plan their next move to make Jake Logan pay.

Jessica liked Amanda's strategy. She agreed to leave and return to fight another day.

I might return sooner than she anticipates.

23

Alice guessed the style to be neocolonial, probably built in the last half of the twentieth century. It appeared structurally sound, but it was crying out for a coat of paint and the usual maintenance that should have been carried out annually.

The shrubs and trees were overgrown and in desperate need of attention. Some were even dead. A swimming pool dominated the backyard. Like the lawn, it had not been maintained regularly.

"I've been in London so much there wasn't much time for maintenance. This way," Jake said, pulling her gently by the arm.

To the side of the property was an integrated double garage. They entered the garage through a side door. Inside was a door to the house.

Immediately inside the house, to the left, was a room Alice believed Americans described as a den. A welcoming room painted ivory was complemented by a plush beige velvet sofa with purple-and-beige velvet cushions. As was usual in neotraditional houses, the flooring was wood, and it was covered with a beige velvet rug. A flat-screen television dominated the wall opposite the sofa. Two golf bags filled with an array of clubs occupied the corner to the right of the television, and to the left of the television, a putter and driver rested against the wall. On the wall behind the sofa hung two plaques that celebrated the two occasions on which Jake had hit a hole in one.

Alice followed Jake up a half staircase that led into the kitchen. Jake lived in the kitchen. It exuded minimalism and durability and was aesthetically pleasing. It featured modern light oak, with stainless-steel appliances and a range cooker. Alice could see that Jake had not lied about his interest in wine. He had a separate fridge with a glass door that housed his red and white wines in separate halves to accommodate their need to be kept at different temperatures. The rectangular work surface in the center of the kitchen doubled as a table, with barstools that faced a discreetly placed flat-screen television. Directly in front of Alice, an entrance led to the dining room. To her right, an entrance led to a small hallway.

Dashes of green enlivened the dining room. The center of the room housed a dark oak antique dining table. The piece that stunned Alice in the dining room was the dark oak grandfather clock. In response to Alice's intrigue, Jake confirmed that the pieces of dining room furniture were not reproductions. To the right of the dining room, an entrance opened into the front reception room. It could also be entered from the dining room or through the kitchen via the small hallway Alice had noticed.

Alice surveyed the room. She did not think her thought—that the reception room was a shrine to Jake Logan—was unkind. On the bookshelves were numerous books about golf and the Special Forces, as well as trophies from the many golf tournaments in which he had played and won. Alice looked at all the photographs of Jake taken with famous golfers and those of him with his family through the years. It was notable that no recent photographs were present, and some frames were empty. Alice walked out of the room, holding the thought that time had stood still there.

From the kitchen, a right turn led to the hallway and to a southeast-facing front door. The left turn into the hall led into the front reception room. Turning to the right also led to a half staircase heading to the second floor and bedrooms.

As Alice explored the remainder of the house, Jake informed her that he had worked with a couple of interior designers to achieve a look that worked with the antique pieces he had collected over the years. One of the four bedrooms on the second floor had been converted into an office. An Apple desktop computer adorned the desk. A second bedroom had been converted into a gym with a full range of exercise machines and weights. Alice took her time and walked around the room, looking at photographs on the wall taken during the period when Jake had been a member of the Navy SEALs. His time as a member of the SEALs was something Jake rarely discussed.

Alice had not doubted Jake's word, but the photographs confirmed that Jake was an ex–Navy SEAL, and they also brought home the reality of war. Memories of the first morning they'd made love came back. Alice had noticed a small keloid scar on his left shoulder and had asked him about it. Jake had revealed that he had joined the Navy SEALs straight out of college and had taken time out in his fourth year to heal, not physically but physiologically, from a bullet that should have taken his life.

"These are my friends, the good guys. We lost one member of the SEAL team and two marines that day in Afghanistan when I was injured," Jake said as he pointed out the men in the photograph.

"What happened?"

"I'm sure you understand that I can't give you the specific details."

She nodded. "Yes, just a brief outline."

"The op should have been straightforward, relatively speaking. When the target exited the building, we were to pursue and take him alive." Jake smiled. "Mac—I have good memories of him—said, 'Let's catch and cage the Bat.'"

He paused and stood silently staring at the photographs on the wall. "On the day of the op, we had coffee with Grace, an operative from the CIA. She had been assigned to the team for that op. Usually a focused person on the day, she seemed distracted and talked about how her eighteen-month career with the CIA had stagnated. Mac asked her to concentrate on the task at hand. He promised to discuss her participating in fieldwork later. Grace often complained that equality did not apply to roles for women in combat positions.

"The team believed she understood her role in the op. Grace was tasked with identifying the target, whom we called the Bat. She was also our lookout for the enemy, who could get in the way. She had seen the Bat's face in person. He had undergone surgery that rendered the photographs in the CIA database unreliable." The tone in Jake's voice changed. "Maybe she didn't appreciate that her role was vital, but during the early stages of the op, we heard her mumble that she was finished with acting as the team's personal assistant.

"When the target emerged, Grace told us the Bat was on the move. At that point, we went to radio silence. Grace had been instructed to hold her location until we made contact. Her part in the op ended when she identified the Bat. In fairness to Grace, she had no means by which to contact us, so when she realized that she had, in fact, identified a decoy, she could not let us know that the Bat was headed in the opposite direction. Every second that passed put the Bat out of reach. Grace did not wait; she pursued him. I couldn't help but wonder what she was thinking.

"During the investigation held later, Grace conceded that had she been focused on the task at hand instead of her stalled career, she would not have mistaken the decoy for the Bat. She could not defend herself, because her capabilities, training, and firm instructions were against her following the Bat.

"When we caught and neutralized the decoy but could not contact Grace, alarm bells sounded. Grace's response eventually came through our earpieces in the form of screams of torture. Using a tracking device attached to her person, we located and, ultimately, paid a high price to rescue Grace from her captors."

Jake paused and turned his face away from Alice, but she had already spotted the tears in his eyes. She knew Navy SEALs were heroes, and heroes were tough, but it was clear that his lingering memories and his personal conflict tormented him. Finally, he turned back to Alice.

"Can I finish this story another day?"

Alice would have liked to hear more, but she nodded.

In silence, they finished the tour of the house, which ended in the master bedroom.

Later that night, Jake introduced Alice to *Smallville*, an American television series based on the DC Comics character Superman. Relaxing by watching action movies was one of their shared interests, and Alice had never seen *Smallville* before. They watched three episodes before she fell asleep in Jake's lap. That was Jake's cue to go to bed, as he had a 7:00 a.m. tee-off at Winged Foot Golf Club, the private club where he had been a member throughout his adult life. To avoid disturbing Alice in the morning, before hitting the sack, he laid out his clothes for the next day.

He considered wearing his Wentworth sweater but rejected the idea, for fear that his golf buddies would think he was a snobbish jerk, rubbing his career success in their faces. He could not help thinking that nothing had changed at Winged Foot in the last three years. His friends and their lives were the same, but that was OK. There was a certain amount of comfort in familiarity, and he valued their unwavering friendship over the years. Jake wished his golf buddies had been able to visit him while he was in London. They would have enjoyed playing the Wentworth course as much he had.

He pulled the duvet over Alice and then climbed into bed next to her and snuggled close. She always smelled good, and he took in her arousing aroma. He started to caress her and hoped she would wake. Then he was struck by the thought that he had not considered her feelings or the fact that she was carrying his baby. Though she was tired, she had never grumbled. He resolved to be a better partner and father to their baby. Jake's fears about how fatherhood would change his life were dissipating, and he did not recoil as much at the thought of the baby. His love for Alice had intensified. He did not want to lose her. He kissed her shoulder and then let her sleep.

Why do I feel so confused? What am I missing? Jake lay there watching her sleep. *I have no doubt that I love her.* Every breath she took was peaceful. *My perfect li'l' honey.* He contemplated marrying Alice, and he contemplated the baby he had fathered. He allowed himself to admit he had played a part. Any feelings of joy bypassed him. He just felt the enormity of responsibility—the fundamental deceit of trying to instill a sense of routine and security in a world that was self-evidently random and the certain knowledge that sooner or later, his child would see through the facade and feel that Jake had let him or her down.

Jake was not sure of the time or how long he had been sleeping, when he felt Alice's warm hand shaking him gently. When his full faculties returned, he realized something was wrong. She was limp and burning with a fever.

"Alice, what's wrong?" He tried to talk to her, but she did not make much sense. He got out of bed, wet a towel, and placed it on her forehead.

"My throat." She slowly raised a hand to her throat.

"Your throat hurts?" Jake heard the hoarseness in her voice, and she responded with a weak nod. When he rested a hand on her leg, she winced. "Is your body aching?"

She struggled but managed to communicate that her joints were painful and felt inflamed. The thermometer registered Alice's body temperature above the normal range.

"I don't know what to give you—the baby." Frightened that he might do more harm than good, Jake dialed the emergency number for his doctor. "Answer the phone." Several seconds passed. "I think I should dial 911."

Jake was relieved when the emergency doctor answered. As luck had it, it was one of the doctors he had seen in the past. The doctor confirmed that Alice's symptoms were not life-threatening to her or the baby and said that Jake should encourage her to use saline gargles and take a painkiller, such as Tylenol. She should also drink plenty of fluids and take a honey-and-lemon mixture.

Armed with the information, Jake nursed Alice through the night. He slept but with one eye open. Around three o'clock in the morning, her temperature went down a little, and she fell asleep.

Alice was still sleeping when Jake's alarm went off. She was still warm, but her temperature had stabilized. She opened her eyes. Able to talk more, she said she felt better and insisted Jake play golf. Jake put several bottles of water on the side table, along with some fresh orange juice. He gave her medication but removed the bottle, leaving only two tablets, as she would not need further medication before he returned. He also drove to the store and bought her honey-and-lemon throat lozenges. He told Alice he was a fifteen-minute drive away and made sure his number was in the automatic redial on her phone.

"Call if you need me," he said before he kissed her goodbye.

When he was gone, Alice slept. With the combination of feeling unwell, jet lag, and baby fatigue, a bomb could have hit the house, and she would not have known.

24

After playing golf that morning, Jake turned off Old Post Road and headed down the road that led to his house. When Jake saw Amanda's car parked outside his house, he pulled off to the side and waited. He could not see whether anyone was in the vehicle, but he guessed Amanda had driven Jessica to his house. What he could not work out was whether they were in the car or in the house. Jake's heart pounded. He tried to take deep breaths to slow his heart rate, but his heart continued to pound as sweat dripped from his brow.

Jessica had a violent temper, and Alice was in no state to receive her. Jake thought about calling Alice. He needed a heads-up before he entered the house. He knew the sight of him could spark an outburst on Jessica's part, and he did not want to subject Alice to an ugly scene.

He picked up his phone, but just as his finger touched the redial button, Amanda's car pulled away. He waited until he was sure Amanda would not see him in her rearview mirror. Then he drove into his driveway and hurried inside to check on Alice.

He found her sound asleep in bed. Jake had planned to go back to New York later in the afternoon, but he could not take the risk that Jessica would return, so he decided he and Alice should leave sooner rather than later. He had picked up a chicken sandwich for Alice from the golf club. It had not occurred to him that it might not work with her sore throat. He picked up his keys and drove to Balducci's grocery store to buy some fresh soup.

When he returned, Alice was sitting up and drinking orange juice and water. She did not have the appetite for soup. Knowing Alice was weak on her legs, Jake prepared a shallow bath and stayed with her while she bathed.

"I was planning to go back to New York on Monday, but I think we should go today." He neglected to mention his run-in with Jessica. "As part of my relocation package, the bank arranged an apartment for me to use for the next three months."

"Is that where you've been living since you moved back to New York?"

"Yes. No. I'm moving in today. I've been staying here on the weekends and in a hotel during the working week."

When Alice was back in the bedroom, he arranged for a car to take them into the city and helped Alice pack her bag. In the half hour they waited for the car, Alice sipped the soup Jake had reheated in the microwave.

"The car is outside. Let's go." Jake helped Alice outside, wrapped a blanket around her, and supported her head with a pillow in the backseat.

"Thank you." It was strenuous on her part, but she smiled.

On the drive, he read the Sunday paper while Alice drifted in and out of sleep.

A few minutes after they passed through Times Square in Midtown Manhattan, the car stopped at a block of apartments. Jake helped Alice to the sofa in the reception area and then walked across to the concierge to collect the keys to his apartment. They took the elevator to the sixth floor.

Jake walked around the apartment that would become his home for the next three months. Then he settled Alice into bed and un-packed their bags. It was a one-bedroom apartment with a sepa-rate kitchen and bathroom and an ample-sized lounge. Alice slept while Jake finished reading the Sunday paper, and he eventually fell asleep too.

He woke up from his nap when Alice walked into the lounge. She still looked unwell, but some color had returned to her cheeks. She sat next to him on the sofa.

"I would like to go for a walk."

He was caught off guard, and his mouth fell open as he looked at her, amazed. He held her hand. "I'm not sure a walk is a good idea."

"Please," she said. Since arriving in New York, she had observed that few windows were opened, and the building temperatures were controlled by air-conditioning. "I need some fresh air."

They walked toward Times Square, New York's theater district. Alice was a little unsteady on her feet, but she held on to Jake's arm. Jake pointed toward Central Park, which he explained was a few blocks away. "We can walk there later in the week when you're feeling better."

She smiled. "I would like that."

Jake, conscious that Alice should rest, turned into an Italian restaurant, even though Alice's appetite was still off.

"Please don't take this the wrong way," Jake said, touching her hand, "but Baby Jake is hungry." He smiled at her. "It's time I took care of you both."

"She could be Baby Alice."

"How do you know? Did my selfishness cause me to miss the first scan? I'm so sorry. Please forgive me."

"No, you didn't miss the first scan." She beamed. "And no, I don't know the sex of the baby." She filled him in on her first two visits to the doctors. The following week would be her sixth week of pregnancy, and her first scan would be at twelve weeks.

"I promise I'll be in London for the scan." He squeezed her hand.

When the waiter arrived at their table, Jake said, "I recommend the lobster bisque, honey; it will be easier on your sore throat. I've eaten it before and found that it tasted rich, but here the chef uses only a small amount of cream, and it's delicious." Jake also ordered fresh bread for Alice before she could say anything. "You can soak bread in the soup to make it easier for you to swallow it."

By the time Jake finished eating his meal, Alice had barely touched hers but had broken off a small piece of bread and eaten it.

The baby, he thought, but he could see she was fatigued. After settling the bill, he helped Alice to her feet and offered his arm as they left the restaurant. He flagged a cab to take them the short distance back to the apartment, questioning his judgment for letting her go out in the first place.

After Jake settled Alice in bed, he called the doctor. The doctor repeated his advice and informed Jake that it would be a couple of days before Alice felt better. Afterward, Jake spent a couple of hours working on a presentation he was giving at work the following day. He also deleted several emails and text messages from Jessica without reading them. When he went to bed later, Alice was sleeping peacefully. He snuggled up beside her, put a hand on her tummy, and gently massaged their baby.

Two days later, Alice walked with Jake the short distance to the subway, and in the afternoon, she walked to Rockefeller Center. A national historic landmark, Rockefeller Center was in the center of Midtown Manhattan.

Alice stopped to rest at Lee Lawrie's statue of Atlas, the centerpiece of Rockefeller Center. She then explored some of the underground pedestrian passages, which were filled with shops and restaurants and surrounded the concourse-level skating rink.

Later in the day, Jake called to check on her and to announce that he had booked a table at Harry Cipriani for a special dinner on Thursday night.

She clapped her hands. "Yippee!" she shouted. *Special* could mean only one thing.

Alice's walk on Thursday morning to Tiffany & Co. seemed to take forever. She hoped to purchase a small gift for Jake to mark the occasion of their engagement. She would have liked more time to shop, but her recent illness had not helped. By the time she arrived at Tiffany, she had already decided to buy him cufflinks. It did not take her long to find the perfect pair. They were round and platinum, with a diamond in the center. Twenty minutes later, she was on her way back to the apartment. Any temptation to go on a shopping spree on Fifth Avenue was put aside by the reality that she would not be able to wear the items for the next nine months.

Thursday evening, Alice flagged a cab. "Fifty-Ninth Street and Fifth Avenue," she said as she climbed into the car. As she approached Harry Cipriani, she was impressed that it was almost an exact duplicate of Harry's Bar in Venice.

Jake walked up to the restaurant as Alice stepped out of the cab. "Hey, honey," he said, smiling. "I thought Harry Cipriani would be a nice touch, given our first date. You look as beautiful now as you did that twenty-seventh day of March."

Alice could not contain her happiness. Jake had arranged for them to sit in a similar position as they had on that first night.

"I love you," he whispered in her ear as they sat down.

"Ditto," she replied.

After Alice and Jake had ordered their meals, they chatted and flirted, and their legs touched under the table, as they had on that first date. The small Tiffany bag Alice handed to Jake and the expression of joy on his face added to her exhilaration. It was apparent he loved the cufflinks.

"I love you, and—"

She reached out and squeezed his hand.

"And I'm blessed to have you in my life."

The special dinner came and went, and Jake did not give Alice a ring. Alice could not comprehend that she had misread him. She did not understand why he had implied he would give her a ring and had not done so. *No! He promised me a ring.* She brought her fist down firmly on the table. *I can't stay quiet any longer. I'll not tolerate his behavior.*

"Jake, have you changed your mind about getting engaged and married?"

"I have money to buy airline tickets. I'll visit you in London. You can visit me here. We need to spend some time getting to know each other better," Jake replied.

His words made perfect sense to Alice, but the shock reverberated throughout her body.

"Yes, getting to know your life partner is the norm," she muttered. She did not realize she was talking quietly to herself. She raised her voice. "Jake, when did you come to this decision? What was the conversation I had with your brother, Patrick—instigated by you—about? You never had any intention of marrying me."

Jake snarled at her like a vicious dog. "Alice, you're so intense!"

Alice was taken aback by Jake's sudden anger. Too afraid and too stunned to respond, she could not stop the tears rolling down her cheeks. She turned to hide her face. She would not let him see her fall apart. A deadly silence hung between them. Confused, Alice could not comprehend Jake's sudden turnabout.

When she turned back, her eyes pieced his. "I want to know what sparked your aggression."

"You backed me into a corner—I don't know you." He paused. "And you don't know me."

You're right about that.

He added, "The options were on the table. On reflection, we should spend some time getting to know each other."

"I backed you into a corner? We talked. How hard is it to say, 'I'm scared. Our relationship is moving too fast'?" A tear rolled down her cheek. "I'm intense? You lack integrity." She stood and put her napkin on the table. "Shame on you that you fooled me once, but shame on me that you did it twice." She turned and walked out of the restaurant.

✦ ✦ ✦

In the days that followed, Jake was oblivious to the fact that he had opened Alice's eyes, oblivious to the hurt she felt, and oblivious that they were not making love.

He was consumed by *Smallville* on Friday night. At midnight, when she came downstairs for a glass of water, the show was blaring on the television, and Jake was asleep on the sofa, surrounded by empty beer bottles. In the kitchen were an empty wineglass and a half-empty bottle of wine.

On Saturday and Sunday morning, Jake played golf at Winged Foot. The weekend paper, TV, and golf filled the remaining hours of the day between naps.

On Saturday evening, Jake took Alice to the golf club for dinner. Winged Foot was one of the oldest golf courses in New England. Jake could not hide his snobbish elitism when he informed Alice that the private club was only open to members and their invited guests. But Alice fell in love with the club for reasons Jake would never understand. It reminded her of Sheffield, South Yorkshire, where she was born. The house in which Alice had grown up had adjoined Graves Park, Sheffield's largest park, located in the southwest part of the city. The park had been gifted to the city by Mr. J. G. Graves, a well-known English watchmaker. Among other features, the park had formal gardens, ancient woodlands, tennis courts, small lakes, and a golf course that reminded her of Winged Foot. The management and staff at Winged Foot were friendly, and for a couple of hours, Alice escaped from Jake to normality.

Jake introduced her to several of his close friends. She could not help noticing that while the other members had brought their partners, Jake's friends dined either with one another or with their sons. Alice and Jake joined Mark and Ritchie for drinks. Mark's son was on suspension from school, having been caught with alcohol at a recent school party.

They discussed the difference between the legal age for drinking alcohol in the United States (twenty-one) and in England (eighteen). Alice said experts in England believed it had created a culture of teenage binge drinking on Friday and Saturday nights, and the problem was growing. Ritchie, like Jake, had worked in London and thought the English consumed enormous amounts of alcohol at social events and that the consequences were often dire. Jake agreed and told the guys he could have stocked a liquor store with the volume of drinks he had purchased for the leaving party he'd had the Monday before he relocated to the United States.

Alice stared at Jake in disbelief. He had lied. Why? He had known when they first met that he was going home within the next two weeks. *He lied*, she thought repeatedly.

Later that night, she encountered the same scene she had encountered on Friday when she came downstairs for water. Jake was asleep on the sofa, surrounded by empty beer bottles. Something had changed in Alice. She felt numb. The will to question Jake did not exist. She contemplated the hours and days until her flight home on Monday.

25

On board the 6:05 p.m. VS60 flight, Alice reached into her flight bag for her mobile phone. On the screen was a text from Jake: "Call me when you land, honey."

She powered off her phone.

As the airplane ascended into the sky en route to London, Alice breathed a sigh of relief. She did not want to be in same country as Jake a minute longer.

With the touch of a button, the flight attendant turned Alice's seat into a bed. Alice snuggled under the duvet and tried to shut Jake out of her mind but could not. He had deceived her. Why? Jake was not eighteen years old; he did not need to practice deceit to get women to have sex with him. *Then again, maybe he does.* Alice pictured the night Jake had been out cold, surrounded by beer bottles. Her mind switched, and she reminisced about the angelic guy who had nursed her through laryngitis—the Jake she loved. She could not control the tears that filled her eyes and wet her pillow. She scolded herself for not ending the relationship in person when she was in New York. Now that chance was but a distant memory.

She tried to draw comfort from the fact that her hormones were making her feel overly emotional, but tears still fell from her eyes, because she knew in her heart that she loved Jake and did not want to end the relationship.

It's not a relationship, she told herself. *Jake is dishonest.*

She resolved not to contact him again.

The smell of bacon and clattering cutlery woke Alice in the morning. She had slept for six hours of the six-hour-and-fifty-minute flight.

After the plane landed, Alice showered and ate breakfast in the Virgin lounge. She had planned to have a car take her to Langley Park, but a growing issue back at the office needed her attention.

It was ten minutes after three in the afternoon when the car set its route for Langley Park. Alice had not texted, emailed, or called Jake. It was 10:10 a.m. in New York, and Jake had not called, emailed, or texted Alice. It was the tenth day following Alice's laryngitis attack, but she still felt uncomfortable, and her temperature had increased throughout the morning. She expected she would have a lingering cough and still feel tired for a further two to three weeks. What she was feeling did not feel like lingering symptoms, though. The muscles in her back ached, and so did her head. She put down the headache to the stress Jake and work were causing. Maybe she needed antibiotics.

Alice dialed the doctor's office for an appointment. It was her lucky day. The receptionist said if she could get there in the next half hour, her doctor could see her. Alice gave the driver the postal code and street address.

Tired but happy that she had managed to get an appointment, Alice waited patiently for her turn. When her name flashed on the screen, she attempted to stand, but her legs could not support her. Alice slumped back into the chair, and her limp body fell onto the empty seats to her right. The woman on her left gasped. One receptionist rushed out from behind her desk to help Alice while the other receptionist called through to the doctor's office.

The doctor rushed over to where the receptionist was helping Alice, who was semiconscious, into a wheelchair. The receptionist pushed Alice into the nurse's room, where she could lie on a bed. After examining Alice, the doctor said to the nurse, "Please call an ambulance."

"Ambulance?" said Alice. "Why?"

"I'm concerned about your high temperature and blood pressure," he replied. "I think you should be admitted to the hospital overnight for observation."

Prior to the ambulance's arrival, the nurse said, "Is there someone we can call to meet you at the hospital?"

Alice gave her Jake's number. Although she had vowed not to call Jake again and he could not meet her at the hospital, he was one of only two people who knew about the baby. *And the one person I can't rely on.*

A few minutes later, the nurse returned and said, "Is there another number I can call? The number you gave me has been disconnected."

"Are you sure?" Alice replied, confused.

Alice tried Jake's number a couple of times but received the same message the nurse had. Finally, she gave up and asked O2 to check the telephone line. The operator confirmed that the line had been disconnected the previous Monday evening. Before Alice could investigate any further, the ambulance arrived.

Alice was admitted to the hospital and settled into a private room.

"Miss Francis, please, can I have next-of-kin contact details?" her nurse asked.

"Jake Logan is the father of my baby," she replied. She paused when she realized she had not answered the nurse's question.

She spoke quickly as she gave the nurse Jake's email address. She paused again, privately acknowledging that he was not her next of kin. Even if he'd had that role, she did not have his number. Feeling embarrassed, she gave the nurse her friend Edward Bernstein's number.

"Please, can you call Mr. Bernstein and let him know where I am?"

Then she relented and provided the nurse with her mother's mobile number, with the understanding that the hospital was prohibited from calling her unless it was to inform her of Alice's pending demise.

"Please, can you call Mr. Bernstein?" Alice asked again.

"Don't worry, Alice. I'll call him." The nurse squeezed Alice's hand gently before leaving the room.

Alice did not feel settled. Wires ran from her chest to a monitor. The doctor who had examined her upon arrival had injected an antibiotic into the drip attached to her arm. Alice did not believe the private room was for her comfort. It was to isolate her. Too exhausted and emotionally disturbed, she did not have the energy to question the nurse or doctor. She would do that later. For the moment, she needed to deal with something she had put off for too long. After the nurse left the room, Alice opened her computer and searched for Jake's contact details at work.

She dialed the switchboard at Jake's bank and asked the operator to put her through to him. She was surprised when the operator gave her Jake's extension in case the call was cut off and then transferred her straight to Jake, bypassing his PA.

"Hello. Jake Logan."

"Hello."

Silence fell over the line. Then it went dead. In that instant, Alice felt a pain across her lower abdomen. She winced.

"Jake!"

Her laptop crashed to the floor, shattering the screen. She felt the pain again as she put a hand to her tummy.

"Nurse!"

Alice reached for the emergency cord and dropped her phone, causing one of the monitor wires to fall out.

The nurse monitoring Alice had seen her patient's blood pressure increase. Shortly before she lost the reading, she beeped the doctor and ran into Alice's room.

"Alice!" the nurse cried.

Alice was unconscious and lying in a pool of blood.

26

lice woke up in the recovery room. The monitors were gone, but the drip in the back of her hand was still in place. A clear liquid passed through it. She guessed it was saline fluid. A nurse smiled at her.

"Alice, you gave us a bit of a scare. How are you feeling? I'm guessing a little groggy from the side effect of the anesthetic. You'll feel better as it wears off. We'll take you back to your room shortly. Your consultant will update you and answer your questions."

Alice was sleepy, but apart from that, she did not feel anything else. She remembered calling Jake and feeling sick. She did not want to think about him. She drifted back to sleep.

The next time Alice opened her eyes, she was back in her private room. No Jake and no messages from him. Her consultant, James Patterson, was standing at her bedside.

"Alice, I'm sorry. We had to terminate your pregnancy. I'm so sorry." He did not say anything else as he allowed her time to register what he had just conveyed.

Slowly, the words rolled out. "My baby is dead? Why? What happened? You can't tell me my baby is dead and not explain. I want to know why."

"You had a miscarriage. There was nothing we could do to save either of the babies."

That was the final sting. "Babies? Are you saying I was carrying twins? And I lost both? I need to know what caused the miscarriage."

Alice's thoughts turned to Jake. *The miscarriage is his fault—the stress he caused me by cutting me out of his life without warning. How could he change his number and hang up on me as if I don't exist?*

"Mr. Patterson, I need to know—could stress have caused my miscarriage?" Her eyes moved down to his hand, which was resting on hers.

"Please try to relax, Alice. You became pregnant once, so the odds are good that you will go on to have a healthy baby in the future and as many healthy babies after that as you want."

Alice lay back in disbelief. Had he considered his audience? "No! Mr. Patterson, you didn't answer my question."

"Alice, you should accept that you may never know why you miscarried. The majority of miscarriages are random, isolated events, and we in the medical profession can't pinpoint a cause. Even with recurrent miscarriages, half the time, there is no known cause."

Great, Alice thought. She would never know why she had miscarried. *Without knowing anything about me, you are advising that two months from now, I can try to get pregnant again.*

"Mr. Patterson, that may be fine in neverland, but I need some indication as to why my babies are gone."

"A possible cause could be chromosomal abnormalities. Mismatched chromosomes account for at least sixty percent of miscarriages. Sometimes when the egg and sperm meet, one or the other is faulty, and then the chromosomes can't line up properly. In this case, the resulting embryo has a chromosomal abnormality, and the pregnancy usually results in a miscarriage."

"Really?"

"Yes, you should be patient. The odds are strongly in your favour that you will get pregnant again and deliver a healthy baby."

Alice clenched her fist and suppressed her urge to punch his lights out.

✦ ✦ ✦

Edward was relieved when he saw Alice sitting up in bed. *I should've told you I loved you before you graduated. I should've taken the risk of finding out you didn't love me. And what if you did?* They had been friends since their university days at Cambridge. His career as a journalist had taken him all over the world. The distance had not broken their strong bond. For the last two years, he had worked for the *New York Times*, but he was back in London, enjoying a vacation before starting his new role with the *Wall Street Journal*.

After Mr. Patterson left the room, Edward walked over to Alice's bed and kissed her.

"Alice—" He stopped when he saw tears roll down her face. "Alice, talk to me. Tell me what's wrong."

Edward sat on the bed and held her hand. He had some knowledge of Jake and Alice's relationship, and she had confided in him before her trip to New York that she was pregnant. But he had known nothing of the recent events in New York. He cared for Alice, and his eyes watered when she told him she had miscarried.

"Alice." He squeezed her shoulder. "I'm so sorry."

He wanted to say what was really on his mind—that Jake didn't appreciate or deserve her—but he appreciated those words were better saved for another day. He stayed with her until late, watching her sleep and then watching her cry. It was ten o'clock at night when he kissed her goodbye and said he would visit the following day.

27

A lice walked out of the hospital with Edward holding her hand. Over the years, it had become clear that sometimes people fell in love only to realize they didn't even like the other person. She squeezed his arm. *I liked you before I loved you. Respected you. And unlike Jake, you respect me. You've integrity. You're honest. We talk about anything and everything. You're a good listener, and I should've told you that I love you.* Tears formed in her eyes. She looked at him and said, "Thank you."

"You're welcome." He smiled at her.

Edward escorted her back to her house in Langley Park, and they talked for a while. When he got up to leave, she thought, *I can't move on, not yet. I don't feel like I ever will, even with time.* When he kissed her lips, she pulled away. *Not now.* She whispered, "I'm not saying never—not now."

Babies? A boy and a girl or two boys or two girls. That had been the final sting from Mr. Patterson: she had been carrying twins. Despite what Mr. Patterson had told her, she wondered if the miscarriage was because of something she had or had not done. *I've been traveling and attending stressful meetings, and then there's Jake.* She had lost something that had been a part of her, albeit for only a short time. She sighed.

Things happen for a reason. I just can't see the reason. Why? Tears rolled down her face.

She could not help feeling guilty for feeling so lost. *Women go through such things all the time. Some even endure worse miscarrying much further into their pregnancies or experience stillbirth. Is it normal to be so confused?* Her emotions ranged from shock and anger to sadness and numbness.

Alice wanted to be by herself. She did not want to see anyone or take any calls. She placed Jake at the top of that list. He was persona non grata. Yet Alice was aware that she could not ignore the office and that without a mobile phone and computer, she was out of touch with the world.

It was after three in the afternoon when she emerged from bed and stepped into the bathroom. She felt marginally better after she showered and dressed, but the reprieve did not last long before the painful grief and sorrow returned to haunt her. If Mr. Patterson was right, she had not done anything to cause her miscarriage, and if it was true that the causes for most miscarriages were out of the mothers' hands, who was at fault? Alice needed someone to blame.

She picked up the bag with the pieces of her computer and phone and then headed to the Apple Store at the Bluewater shopping center in Kent. She turned the car radio to a news station in the hope that catching up on what was happening in the world would take her mind off the miscarriage. It did but not for long. She was hit hard by the realization that she had lost two babies. She wondered if she would ever have a baby. Maybe she was not meant to be a mother. What was it her mother called her? A career woman! She would tell Alice she could not have her cake and eat it too. Alice felt she was being punished for some reason.

As she walked to the Apple Store, she beat herself up for not giving the trip more thought. It was too soon to be out in the world, which did not care that her babies were dead. In the shopping mall, mothers, babies, and pregnant women were everywhere. She turned away whenever she saw families with young children or women who were visibly pregnant. It was a relief when she reached the Apple Store and found a corner in which to hide.

She was in no mood to discuss what had happened to her phone and computer, so repair was out of the equation. She informed the sales assistant that she would like to purchase a new iPhone and a MacBook Pro and have the data transferred from the damaged iPhone and MacBook to her new purchases. She went to the nearby Starbucks to wait until the Apple technicians had completed the task. She sat in a corner, still unable to drink coffee but more tolerant of its aroma. She purchased a bottle of water and fresh orange juice instead.

Alice pondered whether miscarriage was like death in that the pain of her miscarriage would always be with her but would become easier to deal with at some point, just like her father's death. She wondered whether she would be able to look back and feel sad that the miscarriage had happened but not feel nearly as overwhelmed with grief as she felt now. She could not believe that day would ever come. What was happening to her did not seem normal. Tears rolled down her cheeks.

Mother, even for the so-called career girl, this pain is overwhelming. Please, God, give me the strength to deal with this. Please! Over time, please show me how to cope with the miscarriage. Screw terminology—my dead babies.

Alice sat in her bed, catching up on emails from the office. She had not missed much. Nicola had arranged the flight and hotel for her trip to Gibraltar on Sunday evening, and her legal assistant, Paula, had prepared the documents for the bundle. She checked the index. It was all in order. She sent an email with her sign-off and asked Paula to prepare the bundle in accordance with the index. She also sent an email to Nicola, informing her that while she would attend the Gibraltar hearing, she was still feeling unwell, so it was unlikely she would be back in the office before Tuesday or Wednesday, depending on how long the hearing lasted.

Alice scanned her personal email. Jake had sent his contact details, but she ignored the email and powered off her computer. She put her head down on her pillow but remembered she had not checked her iPhone for messages. A few text messages had come through from Edward, along with three from Annabel, reminding her about their upcoming appointment with a hairstylist in Warwickshire, and one from Jake with his new contact details. Alice deleted the message from Jake and buried her head in her pillow.

✦　✦　✦

Gibraltar, Monday

The court hearing was scheduled for 10:00 a.m. It was being held in Gibraltar because the company that had entered the on-demand guarantee was a Gibraltar subsidiary of IG. It was an ex parte hearing, not expected to last more than an hour. IG was hoping the court order restraining the bank from making the first payment to Valencia would be granted after the hearing because of the urgency of preventing payment from being made on Wednesday. A full hearing with notice to all concerned parties would be held at a later date. That was where Alice believed IG's case would fail.

Alice arrived late at the Rock Hotel on Sunday evening. She did not appreciate its beautiful surroundings until the next morning. Of all the Gibraltar hotels, the Rock enjoyed a unique aspect in Gibraltar, with all rooms having magnificent views across the Bay of Gibraltar, the Spanish mainland, and Morocco's Rif Mountains.

After a light breakfast, Alice checked out. She planned to head straight to the airport after the court hearing.

The chairman of the IG group had sworn an affidavit stating that Valencia was in breach of contract and that, consequentially, Valencia was not entitled to payment of the first installment. In the affidavit, the chairman identified the breaches on Valencia's part. He concluded by contending that if the bank made the payment to Valencia, it would cause irreparable damage to IG. He identified that damage as the liquidation of the group of companies, which would result in redundancies for more than three hundred employees. That kind of damage, he asserted, could not be compensated by monetary means.

The court had only heard one side of the story, but if the allegations were proved at a full hearing, it was not inconceivable that damages in terms of money would be inadequate compensation. Injunctions were issued when the mere award of damages at the end of a trial would not be satisfactory or effective or may lead to a greater harm or injustice. The hearing lasted forty-five minutes. The court granted the injunction with a return for the following Tuesday.

No surprises, Alice thought as she walked out of court. Those were yet to come. A likely consequence was that her head would roll, notwithstanding the fact that her legal opinion that this was not a course of action IG should pursue was on record.

After a working lunch with the Gibraltar counsel, Alice went downstairs to her waiting cab. The drive to the airport took no more than ten minutes. Gibraltar Airport was unusual in that it was owned by the Ministry of Defense for use by the Royal Air Force in Gibraltar. Civilian operators used the airport as well, but the only scheduled flights operated to the United Kingdom. Alice found it scary that Winston Churchill Avenue, the main road heading toward the land border with Spain, intersected the airport runway. Consequently, it had to be closed every time a plane landed or departed. She had watched a program on the History Channel called *Most Extreme Airports*, and Gibraltar Airport had ranked as the fifth-most-dangerous airport in the world and the most dangerous in Europe.

Alice received a text from Jake as she sat in the waiting area for her flight: "My PA has booked me on the 6:15 p.m. flight to London Heathrow. Please, will you have dinner with me? Table booked at C London on Tuesday at 7:30 p.m."

She deleted the text immediately after reading it.

Alice's flight was on time. She used the two hours and fifty minutes to prepare a report to the directors on the day's hearing and the forthcoming hearing a week from Tuesday.

Upon her arrival at Gatwick, a car took her to Langley Park. It was a relatively short drive. The roads were clear, and the driver completed the journey in forty minutes.

In the confines of her home, relieved she had made it to Gibraltar and back without a mental breakdown, she allowed her thoughts to return to her lost babies. Alice had friends who had suffered miscarriages. She had not realized how much those women had suffered and how traumatic the losses they had experienced had been. It was taxing her not only emotionally but also physically. Thankfully, her body was healing quickly. Emotionally, the healing process would take much longer. She sat on her bed and cried. When she could not cry anymore, she buried her face in her pillow and screamed.

28

New York

Jake lay in bed but could not sleep. Why had he cut Alice off? Why had he not called her back and apologized? He had not given her his new number, because he was on the run again, running from commitment and from his ultimate fear: rejection. He hated himself, and that was putting it mildly. Alice did not deserve his mean behavior. Now he was being a coward.

Make the call.

What could he say to her? *"Sorry" would be a good place to start. No, saying I'm sorry will not work.* She would still give him a hard time.

You need more time to get yourself out of this mess. Retreat to the cave, Jake. Prepare for a long haul. She'll soften with time.

His mental pep talk did not help him. He still felt rotten, and he had a nagging feeling that something was wrong.

The Thursday following Alice's return to London, Jake sent her a text and an email message with his new contact details. She did not respond. He contemplated calling but did not feel confident about doing that and quickly rejected the idea. He had never been strong when it came to dealing with rejection, even if he deserved it. Jake had a business trip to London the following week. He could contact Alice in person, apologize, and beg for another chance. He believed that if Alice could be patient with him, he would get it right in the end.

He picked up the phone and gave his PA, Elle, instructions to book his flight and hotel. Elle asked if she should aim to schedule his return flight on Friday afternoon. Jake paused. He had planned to spend the weekend with Alice. He told her to book the 9:00 a.m. flight the following Monday morning.

✦   ✦   ✦

JFK Airport, New York

On board the 6:15 flight to London Heathrow, Jake checked his messages before switching his phone to airplane mode. As the airplane taxied down the runway, he wondered why Alice had not responded. His behavior had been selfish and self-centered, but she at least should have taken the time to tell him to get lost. Jake thought that was why he loved her. Alice was not like other women he had known. For the first time, it struck him that he might have lost her permanently.

Jake always had things his way; it was the only way. The Alice situation perplexed him. He snuggled into his bed. He could not contemplate her rejecting him.

Alice is different. She is different, he thought as he drifted off to sleep.

Jake awoke to the flight attendant asking him to put away his bed in preparation for landing. As he settled into his seat, his first thought was of Alice. He wondered if she had called. As the airplane hit the runway, he felt in his pocket for his phone. He disabled the flight mode and found the usual work-related calls and texts but nothing from Alice.

He almost dropped his phone in shock. Then his shock turned to anger. Alice's behavior was unacceptable. Why would he want to be with someone who showed no consideration for his feelings?

Jake was in the car on his way to the Hilton Hotel in Park Lane, when he reconsidered his part in Alice's current standoff. *I changed my contact details without informing her, and I hung up on her when she tried to make contact.* His anger subsided. It hit him with full force that he had overplayed his hand and lost. His chest tightened. He had never lost before.

Across town, Jake showered and dressed for work. He checked his phone every five minutes for a response from Alice. Half an hour later, when she still had not responded, he was mortified. He had to end this here and now. He composed another text message and hit Send.

Jake sat at his desk, confident and feeling pleased with himself. He called the Hilton and gave them Alice's car registration number. He didn't discount that he still had work to do, but he was 90 percent sure of getting her to meet him, and that was half the battle. He ordered flowers to be delivered to the hotel and gave strict instructions that they be held in the lobby until his arrival.

I don't have a plausible excuse for hanging up on her. He reflected on everything that had happened prior to her call. There was the deal for $10 billion that the team had failed to clinch. That setback was exacerbated by the onslaught of calls and texts from Jessica.

Jake appreciated that his fears ran much deeper. *If Navy SEAL psychologists could not penetrate me and I don't understand my fears myself, how the fuck can I explain them to Alice?* He did not know how to explain that where commitment was concerned, he could see the right route, but when it came to taking that path, he freaked out, exhibiting insane behavior. How could he explain that he had never stopped loving her, even when he was hiding in his cave?

29

Tuesday morning, en route to the office, Alice received a text from Jake. "The bird landed" was all she could read of the text without opening it. Alice's anger with him had not subsided. *What will it take for him to get the message? Why can't he leave me alone?* She pulled into the car park and read the full text message.

"The bird landed on time. I am en route to the Hilton Hotel in Park Lane. Shall we meet at the Hilton at 7:00 p.m. for predinner drinks in the rooftop bar?"

Alice deleted the message as she walked into her office. She had not yet set down her jacket and bag, when her phone pinged again.

"Alice, I know where you work. If you don't reply by noon today, I'm coming to your office, where we can talk in public, if you prefer."

Horrified, Alice turned away from her phone. *No!* She could not deal with Jake emotionally. She would take the argument to the gutter. It would be a bad scene. Alice tapped out a quick reply: "Jake, I can't do dinner. Busy at work. It's not a good idea."

"We can skip dinner," Jake replied. "Please! Let's talk."

Alice contemplated Jake's text. Where was this going? She thought he had said everything when he hung up on her. Her fingers moved across the phone's keypad.

"Please! Leave me alone. There's nothing to talk about."

Tears formed in Alice's eyes as she thought about their dead babies. Her phone pinged again. Seeing that it was an email and that it might be work-related, she opened and read its contents. Jake had written an email to Carmen, his PA in the London office, copied to Alice on her work and personal email addresses. The email read, "Please arrange a car for 1:00 p.m. to take me to International Gaming Limited. You'll find the address in my contacts."

Alice dropped the glass of water she had been drinking when she read the email on her screen. She grabbed some tissues to mop up the water. The carpeted floor had cushioned the fall of the glass, preventing it from breaking. She composed herself and typed a reply: "Jake, please don't come to my place of work. We don't have anything to talk about. After all that's happened lately, dinner is not a good idea."

Jake's reply was swift: "Unless you agree to meet, you leave me no alternative but to come to your office."

Reluctantly, Alice agreed to meet him after work. He told her that if she did not show up, he would take a cab to Langley Park. He also told Alice he was sorry for how he had behaved when she called. He asked her to hear him out, and then if she still felt the same, he would not stop her from leaving. They arranged to meet at the Hilton in Park Lane at 6:30 p.m.

No sooner had Alice agreed to meet Jake than she regretted her decision. *Why did I let him bully me?* She already had her answer. *He'll make good on his threats.* Jake was a man who did not take no for an answer. It had brought him success in his career, but it had resulted in an unacceptable arrogance in his relationships. *I can't take any more, but I can't wash my dirty linen in public.* That sentiment applied equally to her neighbors in Langley Park.

Alice had another problem with agreeing to meet him. Tears formed in her eyes. *I still love him.* She could not explain or justify her denial. She stared at the Tiffany cufflinks in her purse, the engagement present Jake had carelessly lost but she had found. *Another pivotal moment in our relationship in which I refused to acknowledge the signals he sent out. I love him, but is love an excuse to turn a blind eye? No! I don't trust my heart to be alone with him.* She tensed and clenched her fists. "I've every reason not to speak to him again." Momentarily, she relaxed, recognizing her anger with him was not strong enough for her to cut him out of her life.

Alice arrived at the Hilton at six fifteen. She was a little taken aback when the doorman informed her there was no valet parking. He directed her to turn right off the driveway, take the first right, and then turn right again into the car park.

The moment she turned into the car park, it was apparent why the hotel did not offer valet parking. A steep spiral decline led into the parking garage. Given her current state of mind, Alice thought it would be a miracle if she made it in and out of the garage without damaging her Porsche.

Minutes later, she stepped into the car park elevator. She could not stop her thoughts from jumping back to her dead babies. Alice knew Jake would regard outward signs of grief as an indication of weakness, so she bottled up her emotions. It was over between Jake and her. She had to appear strong.

When the elevator door opened in the hotel lobby, Alice felt as if she had stepped into a room consumed by Jake. He was waiting for her, holding an enormous bouquet of red roses. Alice had expected the smile and had already steeled her heart, but she had not anticipated the flowers. She felt her cheeks and lips tremble as she forced a smile but sought to repress her true feelings.

Jake kissed her on both cheeks and then handed her the flowers. As soon as she cradled them in one arm, he took her other hand. He suggested they leave the flowers in his room and go up to the rooftop bar for drinks. Alice let Jake lead her toward the elevator. He put a hand out to press the button to call the elevator, but she pulled him back gently.

"Jake, this isn't a good idea."

"What are you talking about? We're going to the rooftop bar for a drink. Where's the harm?"

"You're bullying me into doing something I've told you is not a good idea—we can talk here." She pointed to the chairs and sofa in the lobby. The elevator door opened, and he ushered her in.

The elevator stopped on the nineteenth floor of the twenty-eight-story hotel. She followed Jake down the corridor to his room.

The first thing that hit her when she entered was its stunning view. Set in the heart of Mayfair, the hotel overlooked Hyde Park. In a previous job, Alice had worked for the Hilton Group, and she had learned the London Hilton had an unusual history. Back on September 5, 1975, it had been the target of an IRA bomb that killed two people and injured sixty-three others. It was a concrete-framed building and was regarded by some as an insensitive intrusion on the park. Although members of the royal family visited the hotel regularly, Queen Elizabeth II had made a point of never attending a function staged in the hotel, because it also overlooked the garden in Buckingham Palace, and the palace had opposed its construction.

Jake did not push his luck after Alice set the flowers down to admire the view.

"Let's make our way to the rooftop bar—the view is amazing."

She was impressed when they stepped into the Galvin restaurant and bar. Located on the twenty-eighth floor, it boasted 360-degree views of the London skyline. When the waiter arrived, Alice ordered a pomegranate-apple cocktail. He asked if she would like it with or without alcohol. Before Alice could open her mouth, Jake answered for her.

"Without alcohol."

The smallest things rekindled her grief over the miscarriage. Alice felt a lump in her throat. *Please*, she pleaded silently. *Please, Jake, don't ask about the baby.*

She was relieved when the moment passed. She sat quietly sipping her virgin cocktail while they awaited the small platter of nibbles Jake had ordered with his drink. It was a battle of who would break the silence first, but Alice was not playing that game. She needed answers.

"Jake, can you explain why you hung up on me when I called your office?"

Jake looked as if he had anticipated the question, but still, he could not answer it. "I'm sorry, honey" was all he could muster.

"Why, Jake?"

"I'll make it up to you, honey. I promise."

Alice stared at him; her face was devoid of emotion. Beneath her cold exterior, his words made her blood boil. She leaned forward to throw her drink in his face. *If I act quickly, I can also pour his bottle of beer over his head.*

His eyes caught hers. She tried but could not avoid them. She did not want to see into his soul, feel his sorrow, and accept that he was sorry for what he had done. She stopped dead in her tracks, put down her glass, and looked away. *Why am I inexplicably linked to him? Why? He doesn't have good intentions toward me.*

She had given him time to explain. *Get up now, and walk away. The best he can offer is that he'll make it up to me. What will he do? What has changed?* Part of her felt she should forget the loss of her babies. After all, it had been an unplanned pregnancy, but there was no specific amount of time that a woman was expected to grieve after a pregnancy loss. She was learning that whether it was an early miscarriage or a stillbirth, the pain could be equally acute. How long she would mourn for her babies was not dictated by the length of her pregnancy.

What did he propose to do to make things better? Did he believe he could turn back the hands of time? If he turned back the clock, what did he have in mind that he could do—catch the first available flight to London to be with her? That was it. He would make it up to her by being there in the hospital or when she returned home to comfort her in her time of loss. Except this man, her so-called partner, the man who was sitting at the table with her at the London Hilton, did not know her babies were dead. *It's too late to make it up to me, too late to ease my pain.*

Alice struggled to hold back her emotions. She had almost thrown her cocktail glass and its contents in his face. That was uncharacteristic of her. The appointed time for her exit had arrived. She told Jake she had an early start the following day.

"Please, will you join me for dinner tomorrow?" he asked.

Alice responded that she had a business dinner. Jake suggested Thursday.

"I don't think we should see each other again."

30

Damn it. *She's stone-cold.* He had to get Alice back. If the relationship ended, it would be on his terms. He loved Alice. She was not leaving him.

"Why?" he asked.

For the first time that night, Alice looked into his eyes. "Jake, you were dishonest regarding your proposal of marriage. I would be the first to agree that we did not know each other well enough to get married. But the broken promises and the show you put on with no intention of marrying me, whether now or in the future, were unacceptable. I also have a problem with the fact that you changed your contact details without updating me and the fact that when I called, you hung up. You didn't even give me a chance to talk. You ended the call as soon as you learned it was me! Is that not reason enough to doubt that our relationship has a future? As you requested, we've had drinks, but it's time to bring this evening and this relationship to a close."

Jake acknowledged Alice had reason to be annoyed, yet he could not consider her attitude anything other than rude and cold. He had said he was sorry. His anger subsided when he heard breaking glass. A lady at the next table had dropped her glass. He sensed Alice would have liked to throw a glass or two and maybe even attempt to punch his lights out.

He put a hand out to hold her arm as she got up to leave. Alice pulled away and headed to the elevator. Jake signaled the waiter and gave him his room number with a request to charge the drinks and food to his room. Then he got up and followed her.

Alice took the elevator straight down to the parking garage. She used her remote to open the car, knowing the sound of the opening car would alert her to its location.

As Alice opened the car door and slipped behind the steering wheel, Jake opened the passenger side and got in.

"Jake, you haven't given me a reason as to why you hung up on me."

"I don't have one. Please, Alice."

Jake contemplated his relationship with Grace, the woman he'd thought he would marry, and the Navy SEALs and marines who had died because of her serious error in judgment. When the CIA had terminated Grace, she had terminated their relationship while he lay in a hospital bed, recovering from a serious injury. The Navy SEAL psychologist had tried to help him work through the lingering issues, but he had chosen to the leave the navy and bury the pain. *If I open up to Alice, will she leave me too? What can I say? Emotionally, I'm screwed up.*

Jake opened his mouth, but the words struggled to come out. "Commitment. I have a problem with commitment."

"Jake, you can't make your problem my problem. Please, can you get out of the car?"

"What about the baby? Baby Jake? Alice, can I still be part of his life? When's the scan?"

Alice froze, caught off guard. She gripped the steering wheel as if someone were trying to take it from her.

"Alice, look at me. Alice, talk to me. Alice?"

Tears fell from her eyes. She took a deep breath. "Jake, I'm sorry."

Jake got out of the car and walked around to the driver's side. He opened the door, intending to pry her hands from the steering wheel. Tears continued to roll down Alice's cheeks. He turned her legs, body, and head to face him and then held her hands.

"Talk to me, honey." He studied her and her inability to control her emotions.

"The consultant said it was not my fault—he could not explain why it had happened."

"Honey, you're not making sense. Please tell me why you're upset."

"The babies, Jake. The babies. The babies are gone."

Jake was gripped by fear. He thought about the two occasions when Jessica had aborted a baby. *Jessica has been in contact with Alice? How? When? How much does Alice know?* Jake's fear turned to panic.

"Fuck!" he said under his breath. He could not think straight. *I can work on the assumption that Alice knows about Jessica's abortions and come clean. What if she does not know? I'll be digging my own grave by disclosing them to her.* He thought about calling or texting Jessica, but he had no time. He had to do something.

Jake reached onto the backseat for a box of tissues. He dabbed Alice's tears and kissed her forehead. "Alice, breathe deeply. Take deep breaths."

He made a snap decision to take her to the lobby. It was public, but they could find a quiet place to talk. Jake would have preferred to take her to his room, but he could not help scheming to protect himself. He assumed if Alice had spoken to Jessica and Jessica had told Alice her version of events regarding the babies she had aborted, he would need the protection of being in a public place.

"Alice, you're not in a good state to drive. You should sit for a while in the lobby. I'll order tea or hot chocolate."

Alice allowed Jake to help her out of the car. He locked the car and held her hand as they walked toward the elevator.

Jake found a quiet location in the Hilton lobby to seat Alice. She was still crying into the tissues he had put in her hand. He walked over to reception to order tea for her and a couple of bottles of beer for him. It was not the time for food, but apart from the nibbles in the rooftop bar, he had not eaten since lunch. He looked at the menu and added a couple of club sandwiches to the order.

Jake's heart pounded when he checked his phone and saw the missed calls and text messages from Jessica. One text message stood out: "I know. You're in danger."

He loosened his tie while supporting himself on the reception desk.

"Are you OK, Mr. Logan?" the receptionist asked.

Jake acknowledged her with a nod. He assumed Jessica had spoken to Alice. It was the only explanation for Alice's meltdown. He considered going up to his room and leaving her in the lobby.

She's a big girl, he thought. *She'll work it out, calm down, and go home.*

But he could not do that. Alice was his honey. She was perfect, genuine, and a good person. He had to take what was coming. He had behaved like a coward, and the duplicity of his behavior had caught up with him. His eyes watered when he contemplated the idea that Alice and Baby Jake would be lost to him.

As he approached Alice, she appeared to have calmed down. The waiter arrived simultaneously with part of Jake's order. He placed the tea and beer on the table. Jake wasted no time in picking up the first bottle. He needed it to calm his nerves so he could face what was coming. He sat next to Alice, observing her as she sipped her tea. His knee touched hers, and she did not pull away. He put the beer bottle down and held her hand.

Alice looked directly into his eyes. "Jake, I'm sorry."

He could not understand why Alice was sorry, but he stayed silent. She was talking, and that was good.

"That day I called you—"

"Alice, I'm sorry. How many times do you want me to say I'm sorry?"

"Sh!" She put a finger to his lips. "I called you from the hospital."

Jake picked up the second bottle of beer, forcing more than the normal amount down his throat. When the waiter arrived with the sandwiches, Jake had lost his appetite. He was holding both of Alice's hands.

Alice told Jake she had felt unwell the Tuesday she arrived back in London after her trip to New York. Thinking she was having a relapse and needed antibiotics for the laryngitis, she had made an appointment with her doctor on her way home. She told him she had fainted in the waiting room, which had resulted in her admission to the hospital. She had called him as her next of kin to let him know she was in the hospital.

"Jake, you hung up on me."

Tears poured down Alice's cheeks. Jake put his arms around her. He waited until she was calm.

"I tried to talk, and you hung up on me."

"Honey, I'm sorry."

"The computer dropped; the phone dropped; and when I woke up, the babies were gone."

Jake frowned in confusion. "Babies?"

"Yes, Jake. I was carrying twins."

Jake let Alice's hands go and turned to hide the tears forming in his eyes. Once he had composed himself, he stood up and held out a hand. She took it and followed him to the elevator.

In Jake's room, Alice sat down on the bed. She had been naive about many things, but she understood that miscarriages could make men nervous to talk to their partner. Not only was Jake visibly upset about the loss, but she saw he was also grieving for her. Alice picked up the box of tissues on the table. She wanted to stop crying but could not control the emotions Jake had unleashed. *I'm not coping—how can I help you?* For the most part of the evening, she had managed to keep a light tone—one that fit a simple ending to a short-lived relationship. *What can I tell you about our babies, when I'm struggling with why?* In that moment, she blamed herself for the miscarriage. She felt it was her fault. If only she had behaved differently. If only she had not allowed herself to become so stressed. She had not prepared her body for pregnancy. If she had taken vitamins before becoming pregnant, she might not have miscarried. Such thoughts had been ringing in her mind ever since the miscarriage, making it even harder to get over her loss.

"Jake, I don't have answers, but if you want to talk, I'll talk."

Now that her miscarriage was out in the open, he sat in silence, apparently scared to broach the topic. She guessed he was fearful that he might upset her, and when she looked at him, she saw that he was trying to hold back the tears that had formed in his eyes.

Alice had made the offer to discuss her miscarriage, but Jake didn't take it up. She assumed he sought warmth and comfort, because he lay close to her and held her when she cried. She tenderly squeezed his hand when his tears fell.

31

New York

Jessica sat in the reception room in Beth's office as she read Jake's reply to her most recent email for the sixth time. She thought he had read her email carefully, because he had acknowledged that she had been expansive and that he was pleased she had expressed her feelings. *I think he is wrong that much of it has nothing to do with the points he's often raised, but that's OK.* He had said that he was genuinely sorry she was unhappy and that he had been pained when he read her email. Tears formed in her eyes when she read the next paragraph. He said he cared about her and had tested himself, saying—she repeated the words, "If we were on the same page—wanted the same things—would I want to be with Jessica because I feel sorry for her or because I really want to be with her? I go back and forth and think it wouldn't be because I feel sorry for you. But despite that, we want different things. I can't tell you how often I think about you—a lot."

She sat up straight and wiped the tears from her eyes. She thought, *But Jake left the door open when he wrote that if it will help me move on, he's willing to go to counseling with me.* The email did not make sense to her. *If we go to counseling and work out our issues, why would I need to move on?*

She opened her text messages and reread the text Jake had sent shortly after the email: "Hey, Jessica. Hope you're OK. Just checking in. Lunch tomorrow?"

After she'd received the email from Jake stating that he would go to the therapist with her, she'd decided to give Beth another chance. If Beth saw that Jake cared, she might understand why Jessica could not let him go. She was hopeful. If Jake still cared about her, things could turn around. He would do right by her.

Jessica entered Beth's office and sat on the sofa. Jessica had tears in her eyes when she looked up. "Beth, I've had no contact with Jake since his text suggesting we meet for lunch." She could not remember whether it had been a week or two weeks ago. "I can't function. These fucking pills are not working." She threw the bottle at Beth.

Beth caught the bottle and was about to speak, but then Jessica let the outburst fly.

Jessica told Beth that she had replied to Jake's text, letting him know she was available to have lunch. "All I wanted was to have fucking lunch. He's so weak—a pussy, a spineless coward. He couldn't be a fucking man and fucking show up or call? Who the fuck acts like that? He's a fucking loser, an idiot, an asshole, a piece of trash."

"Why do you continue to force a relationship with Jake?"

Ignoring the question, Jessica raved on, saying Jake was garbage, a manipulative liar who played head games. She had been calling and texting Jake since her eyes had opened that morning.

"Have you considered letting Jake go and moving on with your life?" Beth asked.

Jessica said she had something important to tell Jake. "I need to alert him. He's walking into a dangerous situation,"

"What's the danger?"

Jessica ignored that question as well. "He won't take my calls or answer my texts. How can I get him to talk to me?"

32

lice opened her eyes at around six o'clock in the morning. Jake was sitting at the desk, working. She went to the bathroom and emerged wrapped in a white terry cloth robe. Jake turned to her. "Good morning, honey. Did you sleep?"

She smiled. "Yes." *No! What the hell is he thinking or feeling?*

A knock sounded at the door. Jake had ordered room service. The waiter brought in coffee, orange juice, and toast. Alice silently ate and sipped coffee. She noticed that Jake had brought up her sports bag from the car. He worked throughout breakfast. Alice was relieved when he asked if she felt like running. She did not, but she needed to get out of the confines of the room, so she gave him a thumbs-up.

Alice and Jake crossed Park Lane and jogged into Hyde Park, heading northeast toward Speakers' Corner. They had run for just over a mile, when Jake turned to Alice.

"You must hate me."

Alice was taken aback. She had grown used to the man who shied away from emotional discussions. "No, Jake. I don't hate you." She told him she felt a strong bond with him and not just because of the babies. She had felt it the moment they met. A lot had happened since then. Now, if she was being honest with herself, she realized she did not know him, and that unsettled her.

Jake ran in silence for a while before speaking. "Do you want to talk? Tell me what I can do to help."

It took a while before she found the courage to confess that she had formed an early bond with the babies. She felt incredibly sad that she and Jake would never know their twins.

"I'm still prone to frequent episodes of uncontrollable crying, as you witnessed last night."

"Do you have to go into the office today?" he asked. Before she could reply, Jake told her that he had a short meeting he could not avoid but that he would like her to spend the day with him. "Please, honey," he pleaded. "Help me make sense of what's happened."

"Jake—" She paused. *I'm not in the mood for his pleading.* Her voice lacked enthusiasm when she said, "I need to check my work email before I can commit." She thought it would give her time to think.

Back in the hotel room, Alice showered and then sat in her dressing robe, reading the onslaught of emails from the directors. She was frustrated. It did not matter how many times she advised them, backed by an opinion from external counsel; the directors refused to face the possibility that they would not win the inter partes hearing the following week. Alice had a meeting request for 3:00 p.m. with the board of directors. *There, in black and white, is my excuse to get away.* She explained to Jake that she had to go back to Langley Park so she would be suitably dressed for a scheduled meeting.

33

J ake had not slept last night; he was still in shock from what Alice had told him. Nine days earlier, she had been carrying his baby. Seven hours earlier, she had announced that there had been two babies, and she had miscarried both. *Did she have that correct? What happened in the twenty-four hours after she left the United States that Monday evening?* Reality hit him. There was no reason Alice would have gotten it wrong.

With both babies gone, he felt numb. He had tried to comfort himself and put his arm around the waist of her warm sleeping body. He shared her pain but was powerless to help her. *The pregnancy was entirely unplanned—I was unhappy. Now …* He was overcome with grief. He felt the miscarriage was his fault somehow, because for a while, he had neither acknowledged nor wanted the baby. *Babies,* he thought, correcting himself. Now he did not want to accept that she had miscarried. He was guilt-ridden; his thoughts about not wanting the baby haunted him. Jake could not control his tears or his grief.

He slipped out of bed, dressed in jogging pants, and picked up the car keys before leaving the room. *If she stirs, I can't let her see me break down.*

When he returned to the room, he sat at the desk and forced himself to work. He heard when she climbed out of the bed but did not initiate conversation. Eventually, he broke the silence and encouraged her to go running with him. Jake wanted to believe her that she had a meeting later that day, but he was skeptical and thought it was an excuse to escape from him, never to be seen again. Following the events of the previous twenty-four hours, Jake understood that Alice was upset and that he could not fix the problem. As a man, he wanted to fix problems, but he knew Alice, and the best he could do was provide a shoulder on which she could cry and a listening ear. He accepted that he could not make her forget. He resolved to be supportive, understanding, and loving and appreciate that there would be a grieving process, which would take time.

He suggested that after their late night, it was crazy to drive home and that they should have brunch. He set a timetable for their afternoon. After brunch, they could go to Harrods to purchase clothing for her to wear to her meeting. *Alice can prepare for her meeting at my office during my meeting. Then we can go to her meeting.* Jake schemed that he could not trust Alice to be by herself. She might run.

Alice reached into her bag and pulled out her last pair of fresh jogging pants. Fortunately, because she often worked out during lunch or immediately after work, she always carried an abundance of sportswear in her bag.

At brunch, Jake could feel Alice's stare piercing him. He had no idea what she was thinking, until she said, "Where are you going with this? You haven't addressed any of my concerns regarding our past relationship."

Past relationship? Jake put a hand on hers. "Alice, I still want to marry you."

"Do you expect bells of jubilation? Maybe I don't want to marry you." There was no emotion in her voice. She took a deep breath.

"Jake, you encouraged me to order a seven-thousand-pound wedding dress and then disappeared, leaving me to pick up the bill."

"When you were in the United States, you canceled the dress."

"No. I found a more suitable dress."

"How much do you need?"

"Oh, now I'm supposed to be relieved that I'll not have to pay for the fiasco of your broken promises? The money isn't the point." Her voice rose. "You've failed to grasp what I'm trying to convey."

"I get it, and I'm sorry."

"I don't have the energy to argue with you." She raised a hand and waved him off.

"No—no arguments. I'll settle the bill when we go to Harrods today."

After brunch, they walked across Hyde Park to Harrods. Alice needed underwear and a shirt. After the lingerie department, she headed to Thomas Pink to purchase a shirt for her afternoon meeting. As they were leaving Thomas Pink with three shirts and enough underwear to last a week, he observed her swift movement. Jake hoped the shopping had been therapeutic and taken her focus off the babies she had lost. *There's no denying I took Alice and her pregnancy for granted, and now I could lose her as well.* When Alice glanced over her shoulder to see if Jake was keeping up with her, it was too late for him to hide the pained look on his face. She stopped dead in her tracks and grabbed his hand.

"Are you OK? I'm so sorry. I've discounted the mix of emotions—which I've had time to deal with—that might be puzzling you. Do you want to grab a coffee and talk?"

No! I want to get out of here. "I'm OK," he said with a smile. He was uncomfortable expressing painful emotions in the same way she did. He was alarmed that his usually closed exterior was on full display, and she had observed he was grieving.

Before they left Harrods, Jake insisted they go to Pronovias to pay for the wedding dress. Even though he did not hand his credit card over as a happy groom-to-be, he gave an outward appearance of joy. Jake had to convince Alice he wanted to marry her and that this was not a simple case of his not wanting to lose her. It had not gone unnoticed by him that she was examining him closely for signs that this was just another parking ticket to him. To receive her forgiveness, he had to let Alice see and feel his renewed commitment to her.

✦ ✦ ✦

They showered and then got dressed in their work attire. Alice had several hours before her meeting.

"Alice, I think you should prepare for your meeting in my office."

Silence fell over the room. Outrage screamed at him when he dared to let his eyes meet hers.

"Did you just order me to work out of your office?"

"No. Please, will you? I think—I mean, don't leave me. I need you by my side. Nine days have passed since your miscarriage. Do you understand that you shouldn't, and can't, face a miscarriage alone?" He believed she needed to allow herself plenty of time to grieve and feel whatever she was feeling. "Have you told your family?"

When she did not reply, he said, "I thought that was the case. I'm not telling you what to do, but this is our issue." Right now, Jake was the only person to whom she was able to confide her deepest feelings. For all his faults, he neither judged her nor told her how she should feel. "Trust me. You must find a way to begin the healing process. I can help you."

After Jake's meeting, they took a taxi across London to Alice's office. Jake waited patiently in Starbucks for her.

In the car on the way back to the Hilton, he suggested they should get away and spend a few days in Florida. Alice could meet his parents and spend some time relaxing and healing. Alice, exhausted by the events of the last nine days, did not resist and agreed to spend a long weekend on Sanibel Island with him.

34

Sanibel Island, June, two weeks later

Alice and Jake spent the weekend running, cycling, and taking long walks on the beach. Each day, they ran six miles, cycled six miles, and then walked six miles along the pure-white sand that edged the turquoise waters of the Gulf of Mexico. In the evening, they experienced the Sanibel Island bars and restaurants. Jake was supportive, and Alice was handling things much better than she had expected.

On Sunday, Alice had lunch with Jake at the beach before he disappeared to play golf, leaving Alice to relax. Alice smiled when she thought about meeting Jake's mother and father. She had been nervous at first, but they made her feel welcome. Jake's father was an attorney, so he and Alice shared a love of the law. His mother appeared to be a good woman, and conversation between them flowed naturally. Alice was at ease. They were generations apart but were brought together by their love for Jake.

Her thoughts were interrupted when her phone vibrated. It was Edward.

"Alice, it's Edward. How are you?"

"Good. I'm enjoying a long weekend in Florida."

There was a long silence before he said, "With Jake? Alice, how could you forgive him?"

"Sorry, but you're breaking up. I can't hear you. I'm on the beach. I didn't hear the entire question." Alice walked quickly to the beach house as she asked, "Did you ask how I could take Jake back?" *How can I look at him lovingly when I still have memories of his behavior?* The line went quiet for a moment.

"Alice, can you hear me?"

"Yes." *I want to be loved.* "You're wrong to blame all my pain on Jake. I want to be loved, and Jake makes me feel loved."

"He has a strange way of loving you."

"And Mother's love? You don't find that strange? You have no idea of the damage done by the feeling that my mother doesn't love me. The more successful I've become in my career, the greater the distance between us has grown. Throughout my achievements, my mother has never said she's proud of me. That hurts."

"You're changing the subject. You know your mother loves you."

"If you want to talk about Jake, I will. Jake has a fear of commitment. Something painful happened in his past to cause it. When he's ready, he'll tell me about it."

"You're making excuses for him."

"That's unfair. Just because I don't agree that Jake isn't a nice person, you're saying I'm making excuses. Do I believe he's arrogant, yes. Still—" She paused, thinking about her next words. "Everyone carries his or her own pain, which influences the decisions he or she makes. That doesn't condone thoughtless, insensitive, or selfish decisions, but it makes them easier to understand."

"Alice, you're being naive. Even if I give Jake the benefit of the doubt regarding his commitment issues, when you were in the hospital alone, crying, you told me that in the beginning, he was angelic, and then, over time, you witnessed Jake turn into a person you didn't recognize. You said the occasions when this happened had intensified and become more frequent over time."

"I've forgiven Jake. That's all. But he's far from off the hook."

"Why? You're setting yourself up for more hurt."

"My present happiness is more important than my past suffering. Forgiving Jake is not condoning the hurtful things he has done."

"I refuse to have this debate with you. Do you remember when I had my issues with Mel? You made me listen to 'Breathe' by Blu Cantrell. You wanted me to take on board the message in the lyrics: 'When love hurts, it won't work.' I listened to that track until the point hit home. You're not hearing your own advice."

"Edward, I can't give you a cogent reason or tell you what you want to hear. I can't explain why I've forgiven Jake so many times. You and I have been friends forever. Don't let Jake come between us. Please don't ask why again. I can't process that pain."

"All I'm saying is—"

She did not let him finish his sentence. "I have to run. I'll call when I'm back in London. Speak soon." Alice ended the call.

London

Alice sat behind her office desk. Time had been the best healer—time and the long weekend she had shared with Jake on Sanibel Island. They had relaxed and laughed in their paradise. Alice was taking the first steps back to normality and a world that waited for no person.

Annabel's wedding was approaching quickly. The invitations had long since been sent to the invitees, including Jake. He had neither declined nor accepted. Alice had emailed reminders to him a couple of times, asking him to let Annabel know one way or the other. Annabel needed to confirm her wedding breakfast number. Alice could not deal with the drama she would face if Annabel did not receive a response.

The day was quiet. Alice realized she might have been paranoid, but her workload had diminished recently. She thought it might have had something to do with losing the injunction case in the Gibraltar courts. Bored, she wished she had the study material for the New

York bar exam. Advanced reading would have been beneficial. Jake, though not overly enthusiastic, had participated in plans for Alice to move to the United States. During the visit to Sanibel Island, they had discussed how she would fill her days if she made the move. They had decided she should continue her legal career, which would involve taking the New York bar exam. He'd asked her to identify a suitable course and email the details.

Alice found a course provider in London that offered the BARBRI program. BARBRI had a good reputation in London and the United States, based on its extensive history in bar exam preparation. Excited at the prospect of her new life with Jake, she wasted little time in providing Jake with the course enrollment details.

35

New York

Jake sat in his office on the forty-second floor of the bank's global headquarters. He stared out the window at the crane standing at Ground Zero. Rebuilding at the World Trade Center site was taking longer than expected.

He had just finished going through his emails for the day, including several related to the final stages of a merger-and-acquisition deal. He needed to follow up on the calls that had to be set up between the buyer and the seller and other parties, including the lawyers and accountants.

He continued to peruse his emails. He counted six emails from Jessica and two from Alice. He opened one of the two emails from Alice. It was a reminder to return the acceptance card to Annabel. Jake deleted the email. He opened the second email from Alice. The subject line read, "BARBRI." Alice had not received the check to enroll in the BARBRI bar exam preparation course. Jake was aware she had not received the check, because despite what he had confirmed to her in emails, he had not put it in the mail.

He thought about Jessica. Things had become complicated since he had reconnected with her to help her move on with her life. At first, their contact had been limited to exchanging texts and emails, and then he'd found himself agreeing to lunch. Lunches had turned into a dinner. He could not deny that he still had strong feelings for her.

Jake's thoughts turned back to his conversation with her at their recent dinner. He had tried to be constructive, explaining that she should address her attitude toward him, because it was having a negative effect on their friendship. She needed to be aware of her behavior, because it could impact relationships with her other friends and other potential partners.

He had been honest when he told her that he had shied away from talking to her, because it was too painful. She was always crying, highlighting how bad her life was or asking him for money. He'd stressed that he would like to be there for her as a friend and not a lover but that their relationship, at present, was not even close to a fair trade. Jake did not expect a fifty-fifty relationship between them, but he felt that in terms of psychic energy and support, the total was 90 percent from him, with only 10 percent from her.

He did not want to hurt Alice, but he knew it would be wrong to encourage her to move to the United States if Jessica was still in his life. Jake had observed Jessica's increasingly sudden mood changes and suicide threats. He suspected she might be mentally ill. He could not make that diagnosis; he needed to speak to her therapist.

Jake's thoughts turned to their last dinner and Jessica's chilling words: *You abandoned me. Jake, abandonment caused and increased my anxiety and depression.* He could not deny that her mental state was deteriorating. She needed help. How could he push her away now? Jessica had invited him to attend a session with her therapist. He would follow through. Until she moved on, he could not contemplate a relationship with Alice.

Jake contemplated an excuse he could give Alice for not sending the check. If he could not find an excuse, she would realize something was wrong. He was not about to explain Jessica to her. The course cost £5,000.

It's a speeding ticket. Five thousand pounds to keep Alice happy and blissfully unaware was nothing. He searched for his checkbook and signed the check before asking Elle to mail it to Alice.

Jake had just picked up his phone to call Jessica, when one of the bank's equity research analysts, Matthew, knocked on his office door. After speaking with him, Jake decided the team needed to add more analysis to the IPO pitch they were giving the next afternoon and focus on completely different metrics.

Fuck, he thought as Matthew left the room. The team would need to redo most of their work. Jessica went completely out of his mind as he revised the pitch.

It was approaching six o'clock in the evening when Jake received the last-minute changes from everyone on the team. The pitch would not take too long to process. The production team would not start printing until after eight o'clock that night, which meant he would be working for the rest of the evening, even if he left the office now.

Fuck! Jessica will not let this one go.

Rather than deal with the inevitable onslaught of abuse, Jake made a snap decision not to call Jessica to let her know he could not keep their dinner engagement.

When the first of several texts, emails, and telephone calls arrived, he justified ignoring her by using the importance of his work as an excuse. He had noticed an inconsistency on the second slide: stock prices had been updated earlier in the presentation but not there. It was time for him to check over everything again.

After Jake finished, acutely aware that Jessica would give him grief for the next two weeks, he called Alice. It did not matter that it was three o'clock in the morning Greenwich mean time. He needed her softness, not Jessica's abuse. "Honey, how are you?"

"It's three in the morning. Did something happen?"

"No. No, just wanted to hear your voice. I sent the check. Call tomorrow if it does not arrive, and I'll track the delay. Night night." *I love you.* He played the role of a perfect partner but was careful not to say, "I love you," when he ended the conversation. Lately, he'd kept those words back for emergency situations. Jake continued to work late into the night.

The next day, he overslept. He looked at his phone. He had received several voice mails from Julian, one of his team members, asking why he had not sent the final details of the merger and acquisition to the buyer and the seller. Now Elle was on his case on behalf of Julian. He thought about telling her in a sarcastic tone that he would email the buyer and the seller to inform them that he had been up all night working on another pitch and that he was going to send the final details of their deal by 9:00 a.m. but that he needed an hour of sleep first. Before he replied to Elle, however, he remembered that she did not have a sense of humor. Instead, he informed her that he would deal with it immediately.

While traveling into the office, he traded aggressive emails with Julian. Julian had forgotten the pecking order and was jostling for Jake's job. He reprimanded Jake, arguing that Jake should have emailed the entire group to say the presentation would be late. Jake chuckled to himself. Julian might have won the battle, but the war was far from over. It was review time. He could hurt Julian in the pocket. Perhaps Julian needed reminding of Jake's position in the bank and of the fact that he was at Jake's mercy. Julian reminded Jake of a younger version of himself. Julian's failing was that he had forgotten that everyone had to pay his or her dues. If he wanted to climb the greasy pole, he needed to learn respect for his seniors.

36

London

Alice stopped at the traffic light and tried to process what the chairman, Richard, had said to her. She hit the redial button to call the mobile phone of the CEO, Margaret, on her car phone. When Margaret answered, Alice exchanged pleasantries and then asked if she had read the transfer-pricing report.

"Yes, why?"

"Did you read the letter from HM Revenue and Customs?"

"Where are you going with this?"

"I read the letter from HM Revenue and Customs in Richard's office. It mentioned that HM Revenue and Customs will be conducting an audit. Richard also had in hand the transfer-pricing report. He asked me to explain the connection."

"What did you say?"

"I explained that the audit is routine, but with knowledge of the issues revealed by the transfer-pricing report, the audit will be anything but routine."

"I still don't understand why you're calling me; you seem to have the matter in hand."

"Richard ordered me to protect the company and brief the

employees on what they should not reveal to HM Revenue and Customs." She paused.

"And?"

"To carry out his request will compromise my professional standing as a lawyer."

Margaret was sympathetic but told Alice she could not help, because she had just handed in her resignation to Richard.

Alice hit the redial for the CFO. When he answered, she dispensed with the pleasantries and asked if he had read the transfer-pricing report.

"Yes," Bob replied.

"We need to talk," Alice said. He agreed to meet her for a drink—she was two minutes from where he lived.

"Smile. It can't be that bad, can it?" Bob said as he approached her table minutes later.

"Park that question until we've had our drink," Alice replied.

Alice did not believe things could get any worse, until Bob told her that for the second time that month, one of his team members had informed him they had banked several thousand euros in cash. Alice sipped her white wine spritzer and asked Bob to start at the beginning. He explained that several of the company's clients refused to use traditional banking methods. With or without the company's permission, a company agent had met with the client to collect the payment in cash. Alice found it hard to believe the company did not know. She asked how the employee had brought the money into England.

Embarrassed, Bob looked at Alice. "The employee in question stuffed the cash into her panties."

"Money-laundering—I think I can top that. Correct me if I'm wrong, but IG owes the Exchequer one million pounds on account of transfer pricing."

"Correct."

"In our meeting earlier today, I asked Richard if he had considered the implications flowing from the transfer-pricing report. He looked at me as if I'd advised him to murder his mother."

"What did he say?"

"He said, 'You are either with the company or against it. If you have a problem with my request, there's little or no point in you being the company's in-house counsel.' And with that, he pushed his chair back and walked out of the boardroom."

"I'm sorry. I had a similar conversation with him."

"And?"

"I informed him that I was retiring, and I'll consult on an ad hoc basis to ensure a smooth transition to the newly appointed chief financial officer."

"Will you be attending any of the meetings with HM Revenue and Customs?"

"No! That's the reason I resigned."

"So I comply or resign?" *It's illegal what he's asking.*

When he did not reply, the answer was clear. The mind was a funny thing. For months, she had been considering changing her career. *At minimum, I was planning to dust off my curriculum vitae and embark on a job search. But now that it has become clear my job is being taken away from me, I want to fight for it.*

Alice was not sure what to do next, but that issue had become redundant. By the time she reached home and checked her email, the matter was out of her hands. Richard's PA had emailed to inform her that since the company's interests and her interests no longer coincided, he would prefer if she did not return to the office. Alice sat at her kitchen table in disbelief. *IG fired me without reason. Jake—how do I tell him, and what will he think?*

One week later

Alice could not work out whether Jake was in his cave. A week earlier, she had broken down and told him what had happened at work.

He'd agreed and supported her when she told him she was issuing legal proceedings against the chairman and IG for unfair dismissal.

Alice heeded the words "A man who is his own lawyer has a fool for a client," and she had instructed lawyers to act on her behalf. She had held several meetings with her lawyers, who had advised that her case had reasonable prospects of success. Proceedings were underway against Richard and the company.

In the days that followed, Alice had also enrolled in the BARBRI New York bar exam course. It did not start until mid-September, but she had started reading in advance.

The day before Jake's most recent standoff, they had discussed taking a holiday in Europe after Annabel's wedding. She thought they had agreed on Italy, but they had not made any firm plans, and her last conversation with him had been Friday night. He had neither texted nor called since. Alice still did not know whether he would be at Annabel's wedding. She tried, without success, to call and text him on Monday and Tuesday. She had long since stopped thinking she had done something wrong when he retreated to his cave.

37

Greenwich, Connecticut, two weeks later

With his feet resting on the coffee table as he drank beer, ate pizza, and watched golf, Jake was in his happy place. He jumped when a knock sounded at the door. It was late for salespeople to be calling. He looked out the window, but a shrub blocked his view to the door. Jake thought about ignoring the caller, but the lights and television were on, so whoever it was would know he was home. The knock came again.

He opened the door to find Jessica standing on his doorstep. He was not sure whether to shut the door or welcome her in. It was too late. She opened the screen door and kissed him on the cheek.

"Hi, big babe," she said as she pushed her way into the house. She threw her bag onto the armchair and went straight to the wine fridge.

Jake followed her into the kitchen. "I don't recall making plans to see you tonight."

"That's just it. You say you want to get back together, but if I don't call, you don't call." She told him she had spent thousands of dollars remodeling the closet so he would have room for his clothes, yet he had made no attempt to move back in.

"I paid to remodel the closet," Jake said, "and I don't recall any reconciliation conversations."

Jessica did not reply. She continued opening the expensive bottle of wine she had in her hand.

Jake turned and walked out of the kitchen. "I wish I hadn't opened the door," he muttered.

Jessica followed with the bottle and a glass. Jake continued to watch golf as if she were not there.

"So, big babe, have you figured out when you'll be moving in? I'm thinking we could have a little party."

"What are you talking about?" His phone was in his hand, and he scrolled through his emails. She continued to press him for a date when he would be moving into her New York apartment. "Not now," he snapped at her. "I'm working."

It was just after midnight when they both fell asleep, too drunk to make it to the bedroom. Jake was the first to wake and go to bed. She stirred from her drunken stupor around two o'clock in the morning and climbed, uninvited, into Jake's bed.

Jake often played golf on the weekends, usually teeing off at seven in the morning. When the alarm sounded, he opened his eyes to find Jessica naked in his bed. The events of the previous evening flooded back. He crept out of bed, hoping not to wake her. His plan did not work. She was awake and determined that they were going to have sex. Jake did not find Jessica repulsive, so getting an erection was no problem. He cared deeply about her, but lovemaking had become merely sex to him because of her betrayal, and it would always be just sex, no matter how he or Jessica tried to dress it up.

The sex did satisfy a need, though. He kissed Jessica afterward to show his appreciation.

"Jake, that was great. Was it good for you?"

"Yes, it was awesome," Jake lied. He did not have time to discuss sex. She must have known it was just sex. To stay and cuddle would have complicated the act. He had to go. He did not like to keep his golf buddies waiting. He showered and told Jessica he would probably see her the following day and that maybe they could have lunch.

Jake got back to the house just after noon. He sensed immediately that something was wrong. The garage door and the door to the den were open. Inside the den, two of Jessica's pictures on loan from her art gallery were gone. He hated them and did not care that she had removed them. Leaving his golf clubs in the den, he went up to the bedroom.

"Jessica!" he called as he approached the bedroom.

His response came in the form of a running shoe in the chest. The second running shoe, which he recognized as one of Alice's, hit his arm. Jessica was stuffing the clothes that remained from the last time she had moved out into a bag. The door of the closet where her clothes had been was broken.

"Fuck you, Jake." Jessica picked up the lamp to throw it.

"Jessica, stop!"

She pushed past him as he stood in the doorway, causing his head to hit the wall hard.

"Fuck off, Jake!"

Downstairs in the kitchen, Jessica pushed crockery into the bag she was carrying. She picked up the Jeep keys and carried her bag and the pictures out to the vehicle. Before Jake could stop her, she got into the Jeep, reversed onto the road, and drove off, leaving him standing in the driveway, rubbing his sore head.

Jake was still trying to register the events of the past weekend. He was angry with Alice for leaving her running shoes at his house. He loved Alice, but he could not offer her commitment. He feared betrayal. He feared she would leave him eventually, as Grace and Jessica had. Added to that were the fact that he did not know how to explain his on-and-off relationship with Jessica and the guilt he carried in relation to her. Each time Jessica begged, against his better judgment, he allowed her back into his life. He knew that no matter what Jessica or he desired, their relationship could not go beyond platonic. Yet acting on what he knew to be true had been difficult for him. He pondered how long it would take for Jessica to come crawling back to him. The timescale would depend on the level of cash she had in her bank account.

His niece, Victoria, had called four days ago and berated him for not leaving the Jeep at the train station last Monday morning. *My Jeep!* She had not accepted his apology or explanation that Jessica had taken it when she left last Sunday. *My Jeep!* He was annoyed with Victoria for making him feel bad about the fact that Jessica had taken the Jeep. He understood and did not mind that she used the Jeep while he was in New York, but if it was unavailable, he felt his sister-in-law should improvise. After all, Victoria was her responsibility, not his.

His thoughts flicked back to Jessica. He cared about her, but their time together was over. The relationship did not work. It hurt Jake that she was gone, and he felt rejected again. He thought about calling Alice but could not take the grief. He opened a bottle of beer while contemplating what he should have for dinner.

Many of Jake's colleagues were on their August vacation. He had not been in contact with Jessica since Sunday, when she'd stormed out. He had no intention of calling or texting her. He had done nothing wrong. He'd told her that he had dated a couple of women after he moved back to the United States from London and that those relationships had ended. Jessica believed he could not survive without her, but she was wrong. His thoughts turned to Alice. He had to text her to inquire about the dress code for Annabel's wedding.

38

New York

Beth asked Jessica if she would stay away from Jake this time and if she had any plans to rebuild her career.

"Jake had that fucking bitch in my bed! I'm done with that fucking asshole!" She told Beth she had suspected something was wrong that morning. He had not made love to her; Jake had used her for sex. "Does he think I don't know the difference?" she shouted as tears formed in her eyes. "I took the Jeep and moved all my shit out of that fucker's life."

Beth, as Jessica's therapist, strove to help, but Jessica's refusal to move forward was causing stagnation. That and her foul language were becoming problems for Beth to continue treating her. "Did you return the Jeep, Jessica?" She raised her voice. "Keeping the Jeep might result in Jake reporting it as stolen, and police action could result."

"That nerd? Call the police? I don't think so." Jessica told Beth the Jeep was a piece of crap and that it had long since broken down. "The Jeep is at the garage. He can pay the bill to retrieve it."

Greenwich, Connecticut

Amanda parked her car in Jake's driveway. She told Jessica she did not think it was a good idea. She tried to point out that the house was dark. It was unlikely he was home.

"Shut up, Amanda. If he's home, I'm here to collect the rest of my things. If he's not, I want to find out if he's still seeing that London bitch."

Jessica entered the house through the garage door. She stopped and went back to the car. "Keep a lookout, and honk the horn if Jake approaches. Amanda!"

Amanda had her head in her phone.

"I'm counting on you to keep a lookout." Back inside the garage, she took the key from the place where Jake hid it and let herself into the house.

Inside the kitchen, Jessica saw the invitation to Annabel's wedding. "Fuck! He's in London." Was there a connection with the running-shoes bitch?

She turned on the lights and climbed the stairs to the master bedroom. She found no evidence that the running-shoes bitch had been there since she had moved out last Sunday, but she did notice renovations underway.

"Fuck you, Jake. You make me live in a dump and remodel for your London bitch." She ruffled the bed to give the appearance that two people had slept in it, pulled a thong out of her bag, and threw it into the laundry. That would be a surprise for that bitch if he brought her home.

Jessica locked the door and replaced the key.

"He's in London with that bitch," she said when she got back into the car. "We might as well go back to your place."

The Hamptons, two weeks later

Jessica joined her sister, Susan, for a long weekend in the Hamptons. Jessica seized the opportunity to talk to Susan. Jessica told her that

Jake was moving into her New York apartment when he returned from a business trip to London.

Susan looked puzzled. "I thought Jake was dating an English woman."

"It's over with that bitch."

"Jessica, we've been here before. Jake has let you down too many times. I don't want you to get hurt again." Susan appeared genuinely concerned for Jessica. "I wish you would forget Jake and move on."

"Why can't you support me?"

"Have you confronted the irreconcilable differences between Jake and you?"

Jessica did not reply, which was reply enough.

"Why do you have to be so fucking downbeat?" Jessica asked. She told Susan that Jake's text two weeks earlier had been positive. He'd said they needed to have a serious talk to sort things out, because they both deserved to be happy.

"I agree—by taking your own separate paths."

"It is easy for you to say that—you have a husband and two beautiful children."

Susan looked at her sister with a sad expression. "I love you, Jessica, but fear you're losing your mind. This obsession with Jake must stop."

39

Langley Park

Alice and Annabel were in the reception room, going back and forth on the seating plan for the wedding breakfast. If they got the seating plan right, the guests would have a fantastic afternoon, which would spill into the evening. If they got it wrong, the guests would dread the next wedding they were invited to attend. Annabel was insistent that Jake sit at a table with family, but the only family member Jake had met was Mother, and she would be at the bridal table.

That Jake had yet to signal that he was attending the wedding posed a problem. Alice had lived for weeks with Annabel's constant reminder that the wedding breakfast was £150 per head and that she needed to finalize the number. Alice had accepted on Jake's behalf and resolved to pay the £150 if he did not show up.

After their fourth glass of bubbly, they decided they were having an unnecessary meltdown over a guest who might not show. IG had done Alice a favor. With the pressure of work gone, she relaxed, enjoying the time she was spending with her baby sister, something she had not done for a while.

✦ ✦ ✦

Alice had just finished a job interview for a six-month commercial contract position starting in mid-September. Walking back to the tube station, she reached into her handbag for her phone to give the recruitment agent her feedback in relation to the interview. She switched the phone on and noticed a missed text and a call from Jake.

"Honey, tried to call. What's the dress code for your sister's wedding?"

Alice read the text a second time to make sure she had not made a mistake. Excited that he was coming, she moved to call him. In that split second, reality hit home. He had not been in contact for the past few days. She should not chase after him. Alice ignored the text and made her way home.

By the time she reached Eden Park station, her feet ached. She thought about taking her heels off and walking home barefoot. It was a relief when her phone rang. She sat down on a bench to take the call.

It was the recruitment agent, Alistair, to let her know the company had offered her the position, subject to financial checks.

The instant she ended the call with Alistair, her phone rang again. It was Jake, and he was right on form. His conversation was a continuation of a dialogue he believed had taken place the day before. In his mind, there had been no four-day gap.

"Did you speak to Annabel regarding the dress code for the wedding?" he asked.

"Did you return your acceptance?"

Jake did not hesitate when he replied, "Yes. Did Annabel not receive it?"

"Can I suggest you wear a dark navy suit?"

"Perfect. Elle has made a reservation on the six o'clock flight to London on Thursday evening. I'll email my flight details."

Alice thought it might be pushing her luck, but she had nothing to lose and asked him if he had made the arrangements for their vacation.

"Yes, honey. It's a surprise."

That was all it took for the little girl in Alice to emerge. Jake's rude behavior over the past week was forgiven. She begged him to give her clues about their holiday destination. Alice hated but also loved surprises. Yes, it was a contradiction. For the moment, the surprise vacation distracted her. Alice was happy.

On Thursday afternoon, the manicurists cleaned, cut, filed, polished, and painted Alice's and Annabel's fingernails. Alice's fingers were drying, and her pedicure was almost finished, when her phone rang. She recognized the number as Jake's bank but not his direct number. Her mood sank.

Here comes his excuse.

Her nails were wet. She asked the manicurist to answer the phone and hold it to her ear. To Alice's relief, it was Elle, asking for details from her passport to book flights. Alice gave the details she could remember and told Elle she would email the remaining details within the next ten minutes.

Later that night, Annabel and Alice finished the final seating arrangement for the wedding breakfast and discussed dinner arrangements for Friday night at Coombe Abbey.

The next morning, Jake arrived in London. Three hours later, they were en route to Coombe Abbey, and the next day, they attended Annabel and Marcus's wedding.

Heathrow Airport, London

The Virgin limousine approached the airport. Jake and Alice entered the Virgin lounge via the VIP entrance. Once they were inside, it was not difficult for Alice to rule out Italy as their holiday destination. Virgin Atlantic operated long-haul services to several destinations but not to Europe. She thought about the choice of destinations, hoping it was the Caribbean, Montego Bay in specific. By the time they boarded the aircraft, there was no hiding that their destination was New York. Jake said, "I've an important meeting that dictates I return to the office before our vacation." Her disappointment was visible. "Annabel's wedding was beautiful," he said to remind her that he had made the effort to come to attend the wedding.

Jake was relieved that there were individual seating arrangements. He would not have to deal with Alice making noise in his head for the next six hours. He needed time to come up with a vacation on short notice.

"Jake—"

He cut her off. "Honey, can we talk about the vacation once the bird is up in the air?" It was not just the lack of a planned vacation he would have to explain. For the next two days, she would have to live with the workmen in the house. Jessica had hated the house. It was too late for that relationship, but he could make a home for Alice. It was time to move on.

The air hostess had just finished serving drinks, when Alice put her head over the seat divide. Jake was fond of her; it was not her fault she was a female. The only way he would get any peace was to come clean.

"Honey, we're spending two nights in Connecticut, and then we're flying to—honey, you'll have to wait. The holiday destination is a surprise."

Then he reminded her that the Connecticut house was under construction and that two of the bathrooms and two rooms were being renovated.

"Remember? I told you, honey," he added. "Last week."

Jake had not told her anything, but he thought he had, so that was OK. If he had mentioned the renovations, Alice could have stayed in the comfort of her home and joined him Tuesday evening. She let the conversation fly and continued to read her BARBRI textbook on American constitutional law.

It was late when they finally arrived at his house in Connecticut. Jake had not been jesting. The bathroom in the master bedroom was a building site, and the furniture and floor in the dining and reception rooms were covered with drop cloths.

In the master bedroom, it was impossible not to notice the unmade bed. An unmade bed was not unusual, especially given Jake's busy lifestyle. It was the fact that it appeared as if two people had been sleeping in it that caught Alice's attention. It was late, so she did not broach the subject. They were both tired, and Jake had an early start. She found clean sheets and remade the bed.

Jake woke fifteen minutes before his alarm clock sounded. He parted Alice's legs gently and slid between them. When she opened her sleepy eyes, he kissed her lips softly and with all the love he felt in his heart. He moved slowly and romantically until her body woke up and joined him in climax. He held her in his arms until she drifted back to sleep before he slid out of bed to shower and dress for work. He bent over and kissed her before leaving at six fifteen.

Alice was forced out of bed at seven; she had to be showered and dressed before the workmen arrived to commence work at eight. The builders were working on the master bedroom, so she thought it wise to move everything she needed downstairs to one of the other bedrooms. Alice was puzzled when she could not find her running shoes in the closet. In addition, the closet doors were broken. Upon closer inspection, it appeared as if someone had tried to kick them down. The broken closet doors were probably none of her business, but the running shoes were. She made a mental note to ask about them when Jake called later. For the moment, she would have to settle for a long walk along the beach without her shoes. Running was not an option.

Alice walked past the kitchen sink and stopped cold. She stared at the wineglasses in the sink. *How many wineglasses are there in the sink?* She counted. *Six.* Jake didn't drink that much wine, and she doubted he'd have used a glass each time if he had. *Has he had a female guest in here? The bed. The door. My shoes.* She shook her head. *Would he? Nah. Crazy. And paranoid.* She returned to the bedroom and began to study for the bar.

Midmorning, she explored Greenwich on foot, taking a walk

along the beach. The missing running shoes, broken closet doors, and wineglasses continued to prey on her mind.

When Jake called at lunch, he downplayed the missing running shoes, claiming he had moved them because the builders were working in the master bedroom. Alice's suspicions were raised, but she let it go for the moment, knowing there was no basis on which to make allegations.

She was in the bedroom, packing her suitcase for their vacation, when Jake returned from work that evening. The car was picking them up at 5:00 a.m. the following morning. That left her limited time, so she thought it best to get ready the night before.

She could tell Jake was in a good mood as he looked forward to their vacation. Maybe she should have let her suspicions regarding the unmade bed, damaged closet doors, missing running shoes, and wineglasses for two go, but she could not, especially since she had done the laundry.

"Why was this in your laundry?" she asked, holding up the thong Jessica had planted.

She regretted opening her mouth immediately. Jake flew into a rage. His face turned red. For a few seconds, she thought he might punch her.

"Jessica was here," he snarled. "She came to move her things out last Sunday."

Jake told Alice that Jessica had taken the drinking glasses and wineglasses she had chosen, although he had bought them. Alice asked why he had not stopped her.

"She put them in the Jeep and drove off before I could do or say anything."

"Did you have sex with her?"

"No!"

"On Sunday night, the bed looked as if two people had slept in it."

"I don't know what you're talking about." He told her the maid came on Wednesdays. If she was coming, there was no point in making the bed. Further, his leaving at six fifteen in the morning meant sometimes the bed did not get made.

She did not push the issue. She had no way of knowing if he was telling the truth. The bed would have looked that way if he had not made it over several days. It could have been the truth.

"What happened to my running shoes and the closet doors?"

Jake had nowhere to run. He came clean. He explained that Jessica had found the running shoes when she was packing her things. She had gone crazy. She had thrown the running shoes at him and kicked the closet doors, causing the damage.

Alice stared at Jake, a little stunned by his tale. She did not respond. *Incredible!* Her eyes pieced his. *I can't read him, and I've no proof he's not telling the truth.*

✦ ✦ ✦

That night, they had dinner at a local restaurant. Jake stared at her intently. She had not let him off the hook and refused to behave as if the day's events had not happened. Unprompted, Jake said, "I'm certain I made the bed."

"What?"

"I can't rule out that Jessica went back to the house after I left."

"Please tell me she isn't walking around with keys to your house."

"No, I asked her for my keys, and yes, she gave them to me. I have a spare key hidden in the garage, and Jessica is aware of it."

"Jake! Are you out of your mind?"

"It's over with Jessica. She has moved the last of her things out of the house. Please don't let Jessica spoil the vacation."

Alice had not expected so much information from Jake. It was good that he was talking.

"Believe me. Jessica and I have no future."

Clearly, his past relationship with Jessica was still a sensitive subject. Despite their differences, Alice sensed he still cared deeply for her. *That's a problem, but I've come too far to turn back now.*

In physical injury, shock was the body's way of protecting one against the reality of hurt, in case the pain became too great to bear. Just as the body grew numb, so could the human heart when it needed protection against emotional pain. Alice's denial was her numbing her heart.

Two minutes before their car arrived the following morning, they were ready to go. Alice was still trying to guess their holiday destination. When the driver confirmed they were headed to the Virgin Atlantic terminal, her bet was on the Caribbean. Jake was tight-lipped, determined to keep the surprise a secret for as long as possible.

Alice could not contain her excitement when he printed their boarding passes to Montego Bay, Jamaica. Joy radiated on Jake's face too; he had made Alice happy.

"Thank you." She appreciated the finer things in life but did not take them for granted.

Three hours and forty minutes after their flight departed from the United States, they landed at Sir Donald Sangster International Airport. A car was waiting to take them to the Ritz-Carlton, Montego Bay. During the fifteen-minute drive, they admired the city's picturesque low mountains. As they approached Rose Hall Plantation, where the Ritz-Carlton Golf and Spa Resort was located, she saw on Jake's face the joy of a child opening a Christmas present.

"Honey, I've booked the spa for you on the day I play the eighteen-hole championship White Witch Golf Course. You'll enjoy it."

That was the start to one of the best vacations Alice had ever experienced. Being with Jake was the icing on the cake. During the days, they walked on a secluded, warm, sandy beach and waded in the shimmering waters with the lush green mountains rising in the background. In the evenings, they unwound to the rhythmic sounds of reggae.

They completed their idyllic seven-day vacation at Dunn's River Falls, the famous waterfall near Ocho Rios, Jamaica. They climbed up the waterfalls. About 180 feet high and 600 feet long, the falls were terraced like giant steps, some of which were man-made improvements. Several small lagoons were interspersed among the vertical sections of the falls. The falls were bordered by lush green vegetation that shaded the area from the sun. It also helped to keep them cool as they climbed.

At the top, Jake held Alice in an embrace. "You and me forever," he whispered into her ear.

Seven days later, Jake and Alice sat in Sir Donald Sangster International Airport, wishing they could spend seven more days in the Caribbean. Jake had been fielding work emails all morning. He had not discussed his work with Alice. It appeared to her that a deal was closing, and Jake's sign-off was required. A facsimile had been sent to him in the airport lounge, and he had gone to collect it. Jake's text alert buzzed. Alice raised her head. Realizing it was Jake's phone on the table, she returned her attention to the holiday photos she was emailing to Annabel.

Unseen by Alice, the text from Jessica on the screen of Jake's phone read, "Love you, big babe."

Jake picked up his iPhone. The panic was over with the deal the bank was closing, but another one was looming. A message from Jessica was on the screen. *Did Alice see it?* He was hesitant to turn and face her. He had known Jessica would be back, but her timing was poor. He would have preferred Alice to be back in London. He had called Jessica before he and Alice boarded the flight to Montego Bay. He'd informed her that if she called at his house uninvited again, he would have her arrested. He was unsure whether Jessica had heeded his words. After their flight had landed in Montego Bay and Jake had been permitted to turn flight mode off, he had read her text: "Did your London bitch find my thong before or after you fucked her?"

Jake guessed Jessica had spent the last seven days recharging her batteries. He ignored the text, determined she would not spoil his holiday. He would confront her once back in the United States.

Finally, he mustered the courage to turn and face Alice. "Hi, honey. Boarding to JFK is delayed. Can I get you a drink?"

He was relieved when Alice looked up from her phone and smiled.

"Jake, we have some great photographs both from Montego Bay and Coombe Abbey." She handed him her phone.

40

JFK Airport, New York, Sunday evening

J ake watched the bartender mix cocktails in the airport lounge while he waited for his departure gate to be announced. His flight was still delayed. His phone rang. It was Jessica. He had dodged her for the last two weeks, because she believed he was in London on business. He hesitated, knowing that if he did not speak to her, the facade would fall apart.

"Jessica, it's late. Can we talk tomorrow?"

"You promise to call, but you don't."

"It's late, Jessica. I'll call from the Mayfair tomorrow afternoon, two o'clock eastern time."

"Bye, Jake. Love you. We can talk tomorrow."

HK Bank, London, Monday

Jake had a business meeting in London. He had arranged to meet Alice at the Mayfair Hotel later that evening. He stared at his computer monitor. He bypassed Jessica's emails and opened the emails relating to his forthcoming meeting in London. He could not believe that his ex-girlfriend, Michelle, would be attending the afternoon meeting. He and Michelle had dated after she was involved in several transactions in which her law firm had acted on behalf of the bank. Jake found her contact details and sent her a text message.

"Hey, girlfriend. Dinner Monday night?"

She responded twenty minutes later. "Yes. It's short notice. Awaiting confirmation from the babysitter."

Jake smiled as he typed his reply: "Can you stay for dessert?"

"Dessert? It has been a while since our last date."

"Do you remember when I put my head between your legs for dessert?"

"We should treat dinner as a first date. Save dessert for the next date."

Jake checked the time. It was too late to stop Alice from meeting him at the Mayfair. He felt unapologetic that he would have to stand her up. He needed a good excuse—or did he? On all his recent business trips to London, she'd had an exclusive on his time. The more time he spent with her, the closer they became. Sooner or later, she would raise the issue of commitment. He needed to maintain his independence. Dinner with Michelle, as far as he was concerned, was an unplanned but important meeting with a business colleague. Alice could order room service and read about American constitutional law. That would keep her occupied. Studying seemed to excite her more than he did these days.

Early that evening, Jake walked into the Mayfair Hotel and crossed the contemporary, chic lobby to reception. He did not notice Alice on his left until he turned to walk to the elevator. He studied her. Alice was his English rose. He was overcome with remorse. Why did he fight the inevitable? It was too late to cancel dinner with Michelle. Across the room, their eyes met. He had to take Alice upstairs to his room, express his feelings, and let her know how much he missed her every minute they were apart.

In the privacy of their room, Jake peeled off Alice's clothes layer by layer. They did not make it to the bedroom. He made love to her in the reception area of his suite. Afterward, she lay in his arms. Jake hated himself when he lied to her about dinner.

Jake had long since forgotten about dessert with Michelle. They were on the third bottle of wine, and he needed an excuse to leave. Why he had ended the relationship with Michelle came rushing back to him. If he stayed, three bottles would become five, and he would be the only one with the memory of their one-sided night of passion. Though she drank too much to hide her inhibitions, the net effect was that the only way they could have sex was if she was drunk.

He called the waiter. Michelle was not ready to leave. He suggested she finish the bottle at home. As he put her into a taxi, she suggested dinner with dessert on Friday night. Jake kicked himself for opening that can of worms. Michelle was too drunk to appreciate he had not replied, but he was cognizant that he was not off the hook. Michelle's texts might exceed Jessica's the following day.

"Fuck!" he said as Michelle's taxi accelerated away. He had not called Jessica.

Shortly thereafter, Jake returned to the Mayfair, tired and having had one glass of wine too many. It did not stop him from hitting the minibar. As soon as he sat down, his phone rang again.

"Don't answer it, honey," Alice said. "It's late. I'm tired."

Jake lay on the bed. Before his head hit the pillow, he was out cold.

New York

Jessica could not sleep. She could not get the image of Jake with another woman out of her head. There had been another person in the hotel room. That was why the operator had suggested she call back. Playing in the background was the Whitney Houston and Deborah Cox duet "Same Script, Different Cast," in which Whitney played the former lover of Cox's current boyfriend and warned Cox of his hurtful ways.

> This is a retake of my life.
> I was his star for many nights.
> Now the roles have changed,
> and you're the leading lady in his life.

At least the antidepressants were working. What was happening was making sense now. She could not sleep, because it was her duty to warn that fucking bitch about Jake.

What do you care? Jess said. *What do you gain by warning Jake's bitch?*

"I can't hear you!" Jessica put her hands over her ears.

I know you can hear me, Jessica. I need to know why you want to warn that bitch. Be a clever girl, Jessica. You're trying to get her out of the way.

"Jess, can you please go away? I can't hear you."

Oh? I know you can hear me. The bitch must go to make room for Jake and you to be happy.

"Shut up, Jess. You don't know what you're talking about. Get out of my head!"

Jessica, it will not work.

"What do you know? It's your fucking fault he dumped us."

If you two were meant to be, we would all be together, singing from the same hymn sheet.

"How can Jake be happy with that bitch? They're not on the same page."

Jake and I were on the same page. Have you forgotten those beautiful wedding invitations—platinum rings joined together? Mr. and Mrs. Logan?

"Jess, Jake has moved on. Same book, huh? Which page do we share?"

Let me answer that one for you. It's the page where Jake lives his life as ordained by Jessica.

"Fuck! Jess, why do we argue like this? You, Jake, and I all want the same things. I just need to make him see that his life is with us."

OK, now you're back on plan. Good luck, Jessica. I'll sit this one out. Let me know how it goes.

"If you don't mind, Jess, I have a phone call to make."

Jessica dialed the Mayfair Hotel and asked to be put through to Mr. and Mrs. Logan's room.

Jessica lay on her bed, crying. "Jess, it's fucking unacceptable for Jake's bitch to speak to me in that manner. I'm calling his mother."

When Jess did not answer, Jessica called Jake's mother. When Jake's mother did not answer the phone, she called Jake. His phone went to voice mail.

"Jake, you need to control that bitch! There's no point in you moving into my apartment if you're dating bitches in every fucking country your cock touches. I want a fucking date when you're moving in. No more bullshit."

41

After Jake left, Alice called room service before relaxing in her bath filled with Mayfair aromatic oils. Earlier that day, she had received the reading list for the weekend BARBRI lectures. Between contracting and studying, she did not have much time to play, so it did not upset her that Jake had a business dinner. She had just settled down to work, when the room's phone rang. When Alice answered, the operator informed her there was a call for Jake. Alice asked the operator to inform the caller that Jake was unavailable and that the person should call back later. She went back to her manuals and studied until he returned.

It was still dark when Jake and Alice opened their eyes at six o'clock the next morning. Jake had a meeting at 9:00. Alice's meeting was not until noon. Outside, the dark morning crept into the bedrooms while the gardens prepared to sleep, and the vivid autumn colors loomed strong, reminding them that summer was departing. Alice and Jake treasured the limited days they would have to run.

Their morning run started with a run through Green Park down to Westminster Bridge and back to the Mayfair gym. After a quick workout, Jake showered and dressed. He said he would have liked to have breakfast with Alice, but he had twenty minutes to reach the city for his meeting.

She poured another cup of coffee, opened her bag, and added the final touches to her materials for her noon meeting in the city. Alice was in office mode, when the landline in the hotel room rang. She lifted the receiver from its cradle without giving it a second thought.

"Hello?"

There was a pause before a female with an American accent said, "Please don't put the receiver down."

"Can I help you?" Alice asked. "To whom am I speaking?"

"I'm Jake's partner—Jessica. Who are you?"

Alice took deep breaths, trying to maintain her composure. She realized that was the only way she would get answers. "I'm Jake's friend."

"This bitch is stupid," Jessica said with her hand over the microphone. *You're going to regret the day you set eyes on Jake.* Her confidence was growing. "I hope you don't mind me asking, but if you're a friend, why are you in my boyfriend's hotel room?"

"If you're in a relationship with Jake, it strikes me as odd that you don't know he's sharing his room with a woman," Alice said, her impatience showing in her voice. "Are you and Jake really in a relationship, or is it just your imagination? Are you and Jake intimate?"

She started to say, "Yes, we are intimate," but she paused. *I forced myself on Jake. Even I know it doesn't count as being intimate.* "No," she replied. "No."

Alice thought she detected a sob in the background. She was correct. Above her sobs, Jessica said, "Jake was supposed to be moving into my apartment after his business trip to London." She told Alice he had spent thousands of dollars remodeling her closet so he would have room for his clothes. To Alice's amazement, Jessica did not stop there, not even to breathe. She said, "Are you aware that Jake sleeps with prostitutes? That's why he's staying at the Mayfair; the Mayfair is known for its abundance of high-class prostitutes."

"Those are serious allegations to be making against Jake and the Mayfair."

"He said you were a lawyer."

Her response threw Alice off guard. "You don't know anything about me," she replied.

Jessica had the upper hand, but she wasted her advantage by seeking confirmation of her knowledge. "Do you own a Porsche?"

"No."

"Did you leave a pair of running shoes in a Prada shoe bag in our master bedroom? Do you have long dark brown hair? There was a long brown hair in the bed Jake and I share."

"No."

In God's name, what's she talking about? She called me, and now ... Jessica had to be strictly on a need-to-know basis. There was no way Jessica was putting her in the witness box. Alice was determined to throw the pressure back on Jessica. "How do you know Jake sleeps with prostitutes?"

Jessica's response was quick. She said she had hired a detective to follow him. "Have you met that bitch, Victoria, his niece?"

Alice wished she had put the phone down.

"Did he give you a ring? You should get the ring. He'll never marry you. Do you have children?" Jessica did not wait for replies. "He'll never be a father to your children."

Jessica's cry was so loud that Alice pulled the phone away from her ear. It was not far enough.

"Jake made me have an abortion. He made me kill my baby."

The phone went dead but not before Jessica's words numbed Alice's very being.

42

New York

Jessica stared into her coffee. Her thoughts were focused on the previous twelve hours. She was not sure how she had sunk so low. Jess, the voice in her head, was getting stronger. She did not understand why she and Jess argued. She had been best friends with Jess since the age of five. Now Jess shouted at her.

Jess, why can't we be friends again? I need you.

Jessica feared admitting she might be mentally ill. Such an admission would destroy what remained of her fading career. Her dream of owning an art gallery had become a figment of her imagination. Jessica thought about how she sat in a room full of art all day long. Being surrounded by original art enhanced her creative expression, and she had produced a few pieces of her own. Selling and creating art as a livelihood was her sweetest dream come true.

Her life and career had been going well until she persuaded Pete to let her hold an exhibition that carried art exclusively by Luke, an up-and-coming artist and her lover at the time. Pete owned the premises from which she operated. He had also invested in her work. The deal was that when he had recouped his investment in the premises with a return, he would sell the premises to Jessica.

She had met Luke at one of her exhibitions. At first, they had just been friends, but they quickly had become lovers. Luke and Jessica had spent many hours together at his house in the Hamptons while Jake was traveling on business. Jessica believed in having another olive branch to hold on to before ending any relationship.

It had all gone wrong when a critic and several reviewers made comments on Luke's art that he did not like. Jessica, unable to be objective, had refused to accept the way things had gone. She'd wanted to show her support for Luke, so she'd removed anyone who spoke unfavorably about Luke's work from the mailing list. One of the reviewers, Luke's ex-girlfriend, had argued with Jessica, criticizing her lack of objectivity. The argument had become heated. Jessica had informed the other woman that she was no longer welcome in the gallery. Jessica had not realized how stupid she had been until the morning reviews. Not only had Luke's reviews been poor, but one of the reviewers had accused Jessica of attempting to control her own press. Jessica had forgotten the most basic rule: the press always had the last word.

The reviewer she had upset had spread the word to other critics. Jessica had underestimated their influence; they had the power to destroy her. They had done just that, leaving her pregnant and alone. Luke had not stayed around to help her pick up the pieces.

Jessica asked herself if Jess had played a part in her outburst with the reviewer. She tried to remember when she first had encountered Jess's hostility. She made a mental note to find a way to discuss Jess with Beth. If she could control Jess, maybe she could kick-start her career. People did not remember the content of reviews nearly as well as they remembered the names of galleries that were the subjects of those reviews. She had put on some good exhibitions, and she would do so again.

"I'll give you a penny for your thoughts."

When she heard the voice in the background of her thoughts, she panicked. *Jess!* She looked up to find a man standing at her table.

"Penny for your thoughts?" he asked. "I'm Tom. Mind if I join you?"

Jessica felt lousy. She was inclined to refuse—until her eyes caught his.

"It's OK if you prefer to sit alone. I was watching you from afar." His gaze slipped down the length of Jessica's body and back up to meet her eyes. "You're too beautiful to drink coffee alone."

The posh, residential Upper East Side was known for its wealthy denizens, and it was unusual for an attractive woman to be out drinking coffee in the early morning hours alone. Tom's job training as a CIA officer gave him the skill to profile people in an instant. He observed that she was upset about something but not upset enough for it to be a recent breakup. The lack of makeup and her nails, which were overdue for a manicure, on a woman of her class, suggested she was single. There was no one in her life for whom she needed to make the effort at this hour of the morning. For him, the interesting question was whether her last partner was insane or whether it was her insanity that had driven him away. Friends had told him that his reasoning was cynical, but he made no apology. Cynicism was a hazard of his work. He had sat in enough coffeehouses, not just in New York but around the world, to call on his expertise and state that women of her caliber usually drank coffee in the morning with husbands, boyfriends, or girlfriends.

"I'm Jessica," she said finally. "Sit down. Your company would be appreciated."

43

Coffee ended with breakfast, which ended with an invitation to dinner. Jessica discovered that Tom was from a family who had been successful in business. Although he had not joined the family's business, their wealth was at his disposal, and he was not afraid to spend it. Jessica liked that. He was perfect. He promised to take her shopping. Jessica also discovered that Tom held a high position in the federal government. He traveled frequently and hoped Jessica would travel with him. She felt a rush of adrenaline when he suggested a future together.

By the time she was dressed for dinner, Jessica had convinced herself that Tom was husband material. He was falling for her. They would marry and have a house in the Hamptons, two children, and a dog.

Jessica was no stranger to nice restaurants, but she could not restrain a "Wow!" when she and Tom walked into 230 Fifth. The view of the skyline through the floor-to-ceiling windows in the penthouse lounge was amazing.

Tom expressed his admiration for Jessica's little black dress, but it was obvious that it would not work in the outdoor space, even with heat lamps.

Jessica could not believe her luck was changing. She had told him a little about her likes and dislikes, and he had shown attention to detail. Had Tom remembered that she loved Malaysian food? The restaurant had an impressive Malaysian menu. The two of them shared small plates of crispy shrimp, pork meatballs, and noodles. Tom talked about the countries around the world where he had lived.

When he excused himself and went to the restroom, Jess asked Jessica why she was ignoring her. Not sure if the voice was back, Jessica looked around to check if she was alone.

Those fruity house cocktails are making me sick, Jessica. Stop pretending to be virtuous. It doesn't suit you.

"Go away, Jess. You're not invited to this dinner," Jessica hissed under her breath.

Oh, I am, Jessica. If you want me to have sex with Tom, you'll dump the fruity cocktails. The red wine list is excellent.

Jessica was relieved when Tom returned. Worried that Jess would spoil dinner, she shared a bottle of red wine with him.

Later, when the cab pulled up in front of Jessica's apartment, she invited Tom up for a nightcap. The door to the apartment had barely closed, when Tom put his arms around her and pulled her close. He kissed her neck and lips as he unzipped her dress. Jessica took Tom's hand and guided him to the bedroom.

"I'll give you a reason you can love me forever," he whispered as he kissed her ear.

"I want to make love," Jessica whispered back. She thought about making babies.

As Tom slept, Jessica thought about his performance as a lover. While he was not Jake, Tom knew what to do. She thought back to her first time with Jake, when she had asked if he did not know what he should do to satisfy a woman. She had shown him what to do.

Yes! Jess replied. *Now he's fucking that bitch in London.*

"Jess!" Jessica needed to control her.

Jessica, the sex with Tom was good.

"Go away," Jessica whispered. "He's falling in love."

Tom lifted his head and asked Jessica whom she was talking to.

"I wasn't talking, Tom."

To distract him, she slid her hand down to his semierect penis and fondled it to an erection. Tom enjoyed every inch of Jessica's body again.

✦   ✦   ✦

Tom woke up just after two in the morning. That was the point when he should have gotten dressed to leave, with or without a goodbye note. His work did not allow him to commit to any woman. He did not know how to tell Jessica he was leaving for Egypt in two days. He watched her sleep. They had fallen asleep with music playing in the background. The lyrics of Az Yet's "Last Night" played in his memory.

Making love to Jessica had been amazing. He wondered if he should stay and enjoy her body in the morning before saying good-bye. She made him feel—Tom blanked his mind. He did not want to continue that line of thought. He felt something for her that he had not felt for a long time. He closed his eyes.

Jessica and Tom made love again that morning.

"Coffee or maybe breakfast?" Jessica asked.

"Jessica, I have to go."

"Lunch or dinner?"

"Sorry, but I'm leaving the country in two days. I have a lot to do."

"Is that it then?"

Tom paused to consider the question before replying. He enjoyed Jessica's company, and the sex was good. "Yes. Unless you want to come to Egypt."

Tears of joy filled her eyes. Jessica put her arms around Tom.

44

London

Jake saw missed calls from Alice and Jessica. He read Alice's text first: "Tried to call. It's important. Please return my call."

Jake's heart raced. He punched Alice's number into his phone. It went to voice mail. After the miscarriage and his regret for not being there for her, he'd vowed never to ignore a call again if she flagged it as important. She appeared to be coping with the miscarriage, but he still worried about her and prayed all was well. Although he feared commitment and tried to run away from time to time, Jake could no longer fight his love for Alice. He shot her a quick text.

"Are you OK? Call!"

He listened to his voice mail. Jessica's message was confusing. He thought she had calmed down about the running shoes and his dating other women. To calm her, he had reassured her by lying. He had informed her that he was not in a relationship or dating now. He had said nothing about moving into her New York apartment and did not understand why she believed he was.

Jake had just finished lunch with his work colleagues, when he saw the text from Alice: "I'm OK. Jessica called the Mayfair."

Shit! How could he have been so careless? He had told Jessica which hotel he was staying at while he was in London. His phone vibrated when another text arrived from Alice.

"I've booked a table—7:00 at Scott's restaurant. We should talk over dinner. I have back-to-back meetings this afternoon."

Jake was relieved. At least she was still talking to him. He would deal with Jessica later.

Later that evening, Jake found Alice sitting at the table she had re-served. He thought she looked relaxed for a woman who had just spoken to Jessica. He smiled and thought maybe he should ask her what drug she was on.

When Alice saw him approach, she stood up so he could kiss her on the cheek. They exchanged pleasantries. The weather was good for the time of year. Alice probably had another week on the project she was supervising with the company for which she was consulting, and then she could join him in the United States for a couple of weeks. The food arrived. Alice loved English fish and chips. It was the only dish she had yet to find to her satisfaction at an American restaurant. As they began to eat, Alice got down to business.

"Jake, Jessica claims you made her abort her baby."

Jake had nowhere to run. "Honey, there's something you need to know."

Why had he struggled to acknowledge what had happened? Why could he not tell her the truth? He had done no wrong. It was because of what Jessica had done to offend his masculinity.

"The baby wasn't mine."

Alice saw the awkwardness in Jake's eyes. He sipped his wine before backing up to tell Alice the parts of the story Jessica had ne-glected to mention.

He explained that during the first two years of his relationship with Jessica, his work had required frequent business trips to London. Jessica had not seemed to mind, because she had been busy at the art gallery. She had gone with him on his business trips occasionally, particularly if one coincided with one of her art exhibitions, which she held periodically in Europe.

"The weekend it happened …" Jake fell silent.

Alice's facial features appeared questioning. She opened her mouth to ask what had happened, but she allowed him time to compose himself.

He explained that Jessica had not had to work that weekend, and he had not been required to travel on business. The plan had been to go house hunting in Connecticut, but Jessica had canceled at the last minute. She'd said one of her friends was having a birthday party in the Hamptons. "I found it strange that I'd not been invited, but then again, it was not so strange, because she did not like my friends, and I didn't like hers."

He'd spent that Saturday afternoon playing golf. Later in evening, while catching up on work matters on his home office computer, he had seen an email from Luke confirming his and Jessica's plans for the weekend in the Hamptons.

"Alice, for all her faults, I loved Jessica."

Jake blamed himself for what had happened. He had put business before Jessica. The constant traveling had resulted in her feeling neglected. The guilt he carried and his love for Jessica had enabled him to forgive her and continue the relationship.

Six weeks later, she'd announced she was pregnant. Ultimately, he'd discovered she sought his forgiveness because Luke had moved on, so she'd needed financial support for her and the baby. Jake said he would not have ruled out supporting another man's child, but under those circumstances, he could not do it.

"She believes you're moving into her apartment in New York."

"Jessica's delusional," he replied. He explained that Jessica had sought to come back into his life recently after another failed relationship. She had called, pleading for reconciliation. When that had failed, she'd told him she had financial difficulties. Believing she was about to be made homeless, he had helped her out as a friend. Jessica had used the money to remodel her closet.

"Where is she now? Have you spoken to her?"

"No, and I have no intention of calling her."

This time, she went too far.

45

A year passed. The seasons—winter, spring, summer, and autumn—came and went. Jake had no contact with Jessica. He guessed she had finally accepted their breakup, and he did not wish to stir things up or give her any false hope by contacting her.

Then, at the end of November, he received an email from her, informing him that she was in Egypt.

Hi, Jake,

I've been living in Egypt this last year with my boyfriend, Tom. For now, we're living in the capital city, Cairo. Tom's work has meant we travel frequently. He's a high-level government official and from a wealthy family.

Babe, this is an exciting time in my life. Modern and contemporary Egyptian art can be as diverse as any works in the world. I'm collecting pieces for an exhibition when I get back to New York. I'm learning heaps about art. The Egyptians were one of the first major civilizations to codify design elements in art and architecture. Egyptian blue, also known as calcium copper silicate, is a pigment that has been used by Egyptians for thousands of years. It's considered to be the first synthetic pigment. The wall paintings done in the service of the pharaohs followed a rigid code of visual rules and meanings.

We're going to the Cairo Opera House tonight. It's amazing. Cairo is the Hollywood of the Middle East. Tom has promised to take me to the Cairo International Film Festival.

Jessica

Jake stared at the words he had just read. If the email had come from anybody other than Jessica, he would have conveyed best wishes for the future. Was she taunting him? Was this her way of making him aware that he now had competition? He cleared the screen. For both their sakes, he hoped she had finally moved on with her life. But he was not going to hold his breath.

In mid-December, Jessica called Jake. He hesitated before answering. *Stop! It's simple—a call from your ex to brag about the wonderful life she's living that you couldn't give her. Take the call, be happy for her, and then go back to the peaceful life you're living.*

"Hey, how are you?"

"Babe, I've moved back to New York. Lunch?"

He hesitated again and then thought, *What harm can it do? She's cheerful, and what I've hoped for these last years has finally played out: a platonic friendship.*

He agreed to lunch, and they agreed on a restaurant. "I'll text you a time after I check my calendar."

After the lunch, he thought traveling had changed her. She seemed like the exciting woman he had once loved, and he could not help feeling a twinge of jealousy that she was with Tom. He missed her in a way he had not before. She had been so mean in the days and months that followed their breakup that he had not had time to miss her or grieve the end of their relationship. *I'm with Alice now.* Still, he felt immense sadness for what could have been with Jessica. He had to pull himself together. He had no regrets about moving on with life; his difficulty was in balancing his renewed pining for Jessica with his relationship with Alice.

That said, it was the fourth night Alice had gone to bed alone. Jake cracked his sixth bottle of beer. It was not her fault; he had been avoiding her. He drank three-quarters of the bottle before going into the kitchen to pour a glass of wine. Jake put his feet up on the coffee table, put earphones in his ears, and hit Play when he found Lady Antebellum's "Need You Now."

Eventually, he clambered upstairs and into bed. He kissed the back of her neck. "Sorry, honey. I haven't been fair to you."

Alice pulled the sheet around her shoulders. She was glad Jake's holiday leave had started. He seemed not only stressed but also distant. She knew only too well the damage high-pressure jobs could do to employees' well-being. She hoped Christmas among family and their upcoming vacation would restore his balance.

As she drifted off to sleep, Jake snuggled up to her. He was warm, but the stench of alcohol hit her nostrils. Her first instinct was to chastise him for his increased drinking, but she decided to save the tongue-lashing. She had felt his absence in bed the past four nights.

Alice continued consultancy work for various companies. Between contracts that lasted two to three weeks, she spent time in the United States with Jake. Jake's work also brought him to London at least once a month. Their relationship was blissful, but they both recognized that the long-distance dating could not continue forever. They discussed plans for her to move to the States on a more permanent basis.

Alice's mother did not receive the news well. The past issues in their relationship did not matter. The problem was not that Alice's mother did not wish to see her daughter happy. It was simple: she did not want Alice to move across the pond. She had traveled the six hours and fifty minutes to the United States, but seeing how easy it would be to visit her daughter in her new home had no effect, nor did new technology—the internet, texts, and cheap or free overseas calls. When she could not talk Alice out of moving to the States, their relationship found a renewed tension. She accused Alice of breaking up the family. Alice felt isolated from her mother and her sisters. Nevertheless, just before Christmas, she moved to the United States.

It would be her second Christmas in the States. With Jake, it was romantic, like the fairy tales in the movies. Jake, like many Americans, cut down his tree in a nearby forest. They drove back to the house with it and decorated it together with a variety of traditional ornaments, beads, candy canes, and Christmas lights. Jake lifted Alice so she could place the star on top of the tree to represent the star of Bethlehem. The spirit of Christmas graced their home. Wherever they went, they brought a feeling of joy and holiday cheer.

Hamilton Wright Mabie's quote "Blessed is the season which engages the whole world in a conspiracy of love" summarized Alice's feelings about Christmas. Each evening, Jake waited for Alice inside the front door to give her one of many Christmas kisses under the mistletoe. Then everything changed—at least for a moment.

Christmas Eve and Christmas Day were fun, relaxing days with family. On Christmas morning, they went to church, and in the evening, after Jake's family left, Jake and Alice sat in front of the fire. The bright firelight lit up the room, and the aroma of burning wood filtered throughout the house. The crackling of the wood was audible above the background music—Shola's "Celebrate."

"Celebrate our love tonight," the singer crooned. It warmed the essence of their beings and reached deep into their hearts and souls, driving away the winter cold. The flames danced, hypnotizing them and fueling their passion. The fire flickered in Alice's eyes, reflecting off her dark brown hair. His lips found hers. Their bodies entwined. At climax, the fire burned within.

The day after Christmas, Alice and Jake started their four-day vacation in Miami, Florida. They arrived at the Ritz-Carlton, Key Biscayne, in the south part of Miami. Jake had chosen the location because of the magnificent beaches and stunning landscape. But there was another reason Jake was at the Ritz-Carlton: the hotel sat close to the award-winning Crandon Golf Course. He had also booked Alice into the hotel's spa, which described itself as "ahead of the game."

It was Alice's first stay in Miami. Previously, she had pit-stopped at the airport to collect a rental car before driving on to Orlando. Miami was a unique city with its own sense of style. She understood why it appealed to Jake. Its laid-back vibe allowed visitors to forget about the busyness back home. Alice would have scheduled their next holiday in Miami again just to indulge in its melting pot of South American cuisine.

Toward the end of their vacation, Jake rented a car and showed Alice Everglades National Park, located between Naples and Miami. It was one of the largest wetland ecosystems in the United States. Many of the animals, birds, fish, and reptiles in the park were on the endangered species list.

"American crocodiles are rarely seen, and fewer than six hundred crocodiles remain in the Everglades," Jake said. "Within a few years, if the US government doesn't take steps to protect them, they'll go extinct."

"It would be sad if that were to happen," she replied.

He smiled. "I have my own campaign to save the crocodiles. I will, for the sake of their survival, feed you to the crocs."

"Jake!"

"I'm teasing." He squeezed her hand. "I love you."

"Ditto." She put her hand on his.

After visiting his parents, they returned to Connecticut to kick-start the new year.

Soon it was the last day of the Christmas holidays. They brought the New Year in with a bang—and paid the price the following morning. Although neither Alice nor Jake was in the mood for any more parties, they did not want the holidays to end, but the last day of any holiday always ended long before it had started. Jake put papers together, preparing for his early start the following morning. Alice did not have an office to which she needed to go, but she had to find the discipline to study while continuing to develop her e-commerce practice with clients in the United Kingdom.

As she sat on the bed, observing Jake, her heart filled with love for her boy. It was late, and they had enjoyed the holidays together. Her expectation was that he would join her in bed, and they would make love.

When he did not, Alice was disappointed. He selected the sports channel on the bedroom television and cracked a Sierra Nevada. With the holidays over, the stressed-out late-night drinker was back.

"Jake, it's a new year. A resolution to cut down the drink would not be a bad thing."

That was all Jake needed. The vicious dog showed his teeth. He was swift when he turned, put his feet on the floor, and poured the remains of his beer down his throat.

"Fuck you," he snarled. "Are you calling me an alcoholic?"

She looked on as anger raged through him. He turned to face her.

"You have no idea—I read multiple emails today. Of late, ninety-nine percent of my emails bring doom and gloom. Twenty percent of the shit show comes from that self-centered bitch Jessica."

Did he just mention Jessica?

"Neither you nor Jessica can comprehend the stress or the pressure I'm carrying right now."

Alice opened her mouth to respond.

"Fuck you!" Jake shouted again before leaving the bedroom.

46

New York, Tuesday morning

Jessica arrived at Beth's office at the appointed time. She had not seen her for more than a year. Beth observed her urgency immediately. It was as if she had spent the holidays waiting for the office to open. Beth initiated the conversation, wishing Jessica a happy New Year.

"Are you fucking joking?" Jessica asked.

Nothing has changed. Not that she'd expected Jessica was there to report progress in her life.

"I don't believe that lowlife Tom has any intention of marrying me anytime soon. He claims he needs more time. I gave him more time. He's fucked up."

"How long have you been dating?"

"What difference does it make?" Jessica went on to say that she and Tom had been dating for just over a year and that he had not given her an engagement ring during the holidays. "I challenged his lack of commitment. His response was that he loved me and wanted children but that he needs more time. Beth, I was accommodating and agreed to give him more time if, in return, he would lay out the expenditure to freeze my eggs."

"Freeze your eggs?"

"Yes! That's what I said: freeze my eggs. I haven't heard from that lowlife since our discussion."

Beth observed Jessica's genuine surprise that she had not heard from or seen Tom since then.

"I don't understand why, of late, Jake will not agree to lunch. There are things about Tom I want to discuss with him. Jake still has feelings for me. He's always been my insurance policy. Anyway, yesterday I sent an email to that fucking loser Jake to let him know that I don't have any money and that it would force the sale of my apartment. Fucking homeless. The fucker didn't even acknowledge me."

"When did Jake last communicate with you?"

"How the fuck do I know? Occasionally, he sends a text to see if I'm OK. I can't keep track of dates or even time now that Jess has resurfaced."

"Jess?" Beth asked. "Who's that?"

"A friend. I'm hoping we can be reconciled."

"I don't understand what Jess has to do with your ability to remember dates and keep track of time."

Jessica, if you mention my fucking name again, I'll hurt your fucking head.

"Beth, these questions aren't helping to solve my problem with that lowlife Tom. I'm exhausted. Can we arrange another session later this week?"

New York, two days later

"Leave the fucking key when you go!" Jessica yelled at Tom.

The door slammed behind him.

Jessica sobbed into her pillow. "What the fuck did I do wrong? Do I have *stupid* printed on my head?"

Jess was quick to respond. *I told you to keep your fucking legs shut. You have absolutely no self-respect. Fucking Tom before you had a promise of babies.*

"Jess, he called me a crazy bitch."

You scared him with all that frozen-eggs talk.

Jessica opened her second bottle of wine. She used it to wash down the antidepressants. She stared at the money order for $2,000 from Jake. He had not bothered to put a message in the envelope.

"Asshole."

Jessica searched for a reason to get out of bed. She had lost count of how many text messages she had sent and how many phone calls she had made to Jake. His response had been a money order, followed by a text message that told her to leave him alone. Tom had run. Jake had been mean to her. He had dumped her at the altar and made her have abortions. He owed her. Jessica resolved that she would not be right until Jake did right by her.

Jessica, you're pathetic, Jess said. *Why do you keep getting fucked? You need a plan. Call the fucking HK Bank, and tell them Jake is an asshole.*

"Jess, it's not my fault. We should talk to Beth."

Beth? Did you mention fucking Beth, your pacifier? It's your fault. If you don't stop that fucking weak act, I'll terminate your fucking ass. Do you think I want a baby? A ball and chain around my neck? I'm done with this poverty. I'll take out the obstacles. This is my survival. I'll kill, starting with you, Jessica. Call the fucking bank.

47

lice's eyes opened around six thirty on Tuesday. Her head pounded. She had not heard Jake leave the house fifteen minutes earlier. After his outburst, he had not come to bed. She noticed on her way down to the kitchen that the bed in the guest room was unmade. Beer and wineglasses littered the granite work surfaces. The keys to both the new and the old Jeeps were gone, so she assumed Victoria had come to collect the old Jeep, and he had taken the new one.

When she climbed onto a kitchen chair to reach into the cabinet, she was greeted with a banging headache. She picked up a bottle of painkillers, grabbed water from the fridge, and proceeded back up the stairs. She went into the guest room and confirmed when she looked through the guest bedroom window that he had taken the Jeep. The light hurt her eyes, sending a sharp pain through her head. She dropped the blind back in place and swallowed a couple of Tylenol PMs, hoping to sleep off the headache. It hurt so badly that she had to lie on the bed in the guest room to settle it before going up to the master bedroom.

The room was dark when Alice emerged from sleep. It was late. Her head still hurt. She slipped out of bed. The darkness was kinder on her eyes. She picked up her phone. It was 9:30 p.m. Jake had neither texted nor called. Alice's head hurt too much for her to give his childish behavior much thought. She was more concerned that her headache had progressed to a migraine. Her nausea was more than a sensation. She dropped her phone, rushed to the bathroom, and vomited.

Afterward, she lay on the bed. She needed targeted medication to control her migraine. The pain, the thumping in her head, and the light beaming into the room prevented her from making a survival call to Jake to ask him to bring her the medicine she needed. She lay still, scared to move her head, fearing the pain and rush of nausea that would result. Finally, she slept, too weak to go downstairs. The water she had brought upstairs was gone, and she no longer had the strength to open the Tylenol bottle.

When she woke up Thursday morning, the headache was subsiding, but two days of sleeping had made no difference to her energy level; she was exhausted. When she tried to stand, she fell back onto the bed and lay there in a semiconscious state.

Tuesday morning, Jake caught the 6:40 a.m. Metro North train to Grand Central. He sat on the train with his earphones in, sipping coffee. He listened to Boomer and Carton discuss and debate sports topics and then switched his phone on and perused his emails. Until then, he had been relaxed, with no heart palpitations.

He had already read Jessica's email the day before. He had no intention of revisiting it. Jessica's email and Alice's selfish behavior had him wondering if women had any concept of a world beyond themselves. He bypassed Jessica's email and went to the email that had raised the subject of a head count in the London and New York offices. From what he was reading, he would be directly responsible for reducing his London and New York teams by half. It was his decision as to how he did it, but do it he must.

Settled at his desk on Thursday morning, Jake reviewed his London team's performance. He was still under pressure to indicate where his knife would fall. He switched his attention to check the onslaught of emails. His head went down to the desktop when his phone vibrated. A test message from Victoria was on the screen. She did not normally text him. She assumed he knew what was happening in her world from her Facebook updates. She failed to register that he did not use Facebook. There must have been a good reason why she had sent him a text. Jake opened it and read it.

Victoria said she had been trying to contact Alice since Tuesday to meet for lunch, but Alice had not replied to any of her text messages or calls. Jake sent a text to Victoria, informing her that he would check with Alice. Maybe she was having technical problems with her phone and had not received the messages.

Panic struck. He knew Alice would not ignore Victoria deliberately. He called Alice, but she did not answer. He sent her a text, but she did not reply. He waited half an hour before calling her again. No answer. Jake's concern for her escalated. He had no meetings after two o'clock. When his final meeting ended, he would take the first available train to Greenwich. He sent Alice another text, telling her to contact Victoria, and then called her, but once again, all he got was her voice mail.

When Jake boarded the Metro North train, he called Alice again. He hesitated over whether he should call 911. He also considered sending Victoria over to the house but then remembered she was in New York. Part of him believed Alice was angry and punishing him for his outburst. He thought of the countless times he had run home to Jessica to find her in a dressing robe, drinking red wine and cursing. He fought with his demons. The damaged side of him that had been so abused by Jessica refused to accept that women were individuals. His refusal not to tar Alice with the same brush had led him to their current standoff. The other part of him, the meek and loving part, knew Alice was in trouble. He would have to live with the consequences that flowed from his ugly behavior.

The house was dark as he approached. Inside, he found Alice in the master bedroom. She appeared to be asleep. It was only when he called out to her and shook her shoulder gently that he realized she was not well. His suspicion had been correct.

"Alice, what's wrong? What pills have you swallowed?" Jake could not help but liken every situation to his experiences with Jessica. "What's wrong, Alice?"

She slurred her words. Eventually, he understood that she had experienced a migraine attack. He noticed the empty water bottle. He shook the bottle of painkillers by her bedside. It was still three-quarters full. It all started to fall into place. She had not eaten since their last meal on Monday night. The only fluids in her body were from the empty water bottle.

Jake went to the kitchen and returned shortly with a bottle of water. He helped Alice sip the water. She was very weak. He called a doctor and then followed through on the doctor's instructions. He needed to hydrate her and then slowly introduce food. The doctor had recommended he start with soup. *God, forgive me. I'm so sorry.* Tuesday morning, he had walked out of the house, leaving her without food, money, or transportation.

He started the Jeep and headed to the grocery store. Suppose Victoria had not tried to contact Alice? When exactly had he planned to apologize? *If I'd not come back when I did …*

Jake could not contemplate the consequences. His foot hit the brake—he stopped suddenly. He had almost crashed his Jeep into the vehicle in front of him.

When he returned home with the soup, Alice was sitting up in bed. She had not brushed her hair in two days, but to him, she still looked beautiful. She was a strong woman but fragile in many ways. At times, he was a danger to her. She deserved better. Alice thanked him for the soup. She did not say anything else.

Jake went out and then returned a half hour later with rotisserie chicken and salad. He searched inside himself for words to make amends with her but found none. He feared that he had gone too far this time and that forgiveness was not on the horizon. As he walked out of the bedroom, he turned to Alice. "If you're feeling stronger, I would like you to come downstairs to eat with me."

Downstairs, Jake cleared the beer bottles, wine bottles, and glasses. If she joined him for dinner, he could not let her meet the slob of three nights ago.

Alice did not join him, but she did come down later to put her plate in the kitchen. She had not eaten all the food he had brought her, but he was grateful she had eaten something.

The next morning, Jake arranged for a taxi to pick him up ten minutes after nine. Alice was lying in the bed but awake when he walked in with fresh coffee from Starbucks. He informed her that the Jeep keys were downstairs in the kitchen, and he was taking a taxi to the train station. He had put soup and other supplies in the fridge but also had left some money in the kitchen in case she needed to buy anything.

"Thank you." She did not initiate a conversation.

"I'm sorry, Alice," Jake said, and then he walked out of the bedroom.

48

Fearing the stress of the last three days would prolong her migraine, Alice had tried to block out Jake's outburst. Now her emotions were going back and forth from anger at him to feeling sorry for herself.

She stepped out of the shower and wrapped a towel around her body. His weak apology that morning had bounced off her. She was regretting her decision to move to the United States. She picked up her phone to text him.

She wrote, "Your behavior toward me was unacceptable. I can't continue living with you. Can you recommend a shipper to send my things back to England?"

She hesitated and then hit Send.

After she had dressed and made the bed, she made her way down to the kitchen. Resting under the key for the Jeep was $500. Everything was after the fact. He did wrong and then threw money at the problem. Alice opened her computer. She was already a day behind with the advisory opinion she was preparing for an internet start-up. She sat down to work.

Midafternoon, she received a text from Jake: "Sorry! I'm sorry for my behavior. Unless you want to, I don't want you to leave."

She mumbled, "Unless you want to, I don't want you to. Your

behavior is forcing me to leave." She called Jake. He answered on the second ring.

"I'm sorry. A lot of things had built up that, unfortunately, I took out on you. During the vacation, I was thinking about work and under pressure from different people. Then I felt as if you didn't support me, coupled with your offhand, out-of-the-blue statement. I took offense and, frankly, overreacted."

"I didn't support you?" She laughed hysterically.

"Alice. Alice?"

She stopped laughing.

"I can't talk now; I have a meeting in two minutes. I've emailed you the information for the shipping company. If you want to do this, it might be much easier to go to the UPS store across from Stop & Shop and see if they can ship stuff. I'm sure they do that. I know people who have shipped ski equipment and luggage to holiday destinations." He said he had also forwarded an email from a colleague, Mark Duggan, with information about his recent international move. The line went dead.

Alice was dumfounded. She put her phone on the table. *My love for you is unconditional and always will be, but you make it difficult for me to support you. This, whatever it is, is not done because you have a meeting.*

She powered up her computer and tried to work, but her mind drifted. He had spent the last two years making it clear that he did not need or want anything from her. She had tried many times to get him to be open with her, whether about Jessica or about his work. He had persistently rejected her attempts to reach out to him. She closed her computer and contemplated calling him back. She looked at her watch: ten minutes had passed since their conversation. *If—and that is a big if—he is in a meeting, it would not be over yet.*

She paced around the kitchen, willing herself to calm down and let it go. She mumbled to herself, "I was aware that he was under work-related stress, but for fear of rejection or his snapping at me, the only thing I felt able to do was to touch his arm and say there would be plenty of time to be stressed when he returned to work." She questioned her behavior toward him. *Maybe it was not good enough. I don't know. What else could I have done or said?*

Alice's annoyance increased when her phone pinged, and she read Jake's text.

"Not sure what your plans are. How do drinks at the Gray Goose and takeout sound?"

Alice replied, "I'm going back to England; I think we should be friends."

Jake's response was quick: "If I need another friend, I'll call."

Why was he behaving as if she had wronged him? She was still shocked over his outburst on Monday night. He'd apologized and said he did not want her to leave, but he had not said why she should stay. As usual, he expected her to accept his apology. *His behavior is alarming. Tuesday and the days that followed felt like he was physically punching me.*

It was clear from his text that if she went home, friendship was not in the cards. "My heart is bleeding," she said sarcastically. How could they be friends now or in the future? There were a few truths she had to face. If he had loved her and wanted them to have a future, he would not have hurt her. She had thought that in the fullness of time, they would get engaged and marry, but he had grown further away from that goal by the day and used his commitment issues as an excuse for not wanting to get married. *And as an excuse to abuse me.*

Her phone pinged again.

"I've said sorry several times. I overreacted! I want you to stay."

Why did he want her to stay? He was an intelligent man. It was not as simple as saying he did not want her to go. Without an adequate explanation, she had no choice but to leave. Prior to several of his outbursts, she had mentioned commitment. He had not sought to say he loved her. *No, you would not say those words, because it's not the norm to hurt the people you love.* He had pushed her away as he asserted that he wanted her to stay, provided she accept his behavior, no matter how ugly it was and no matter how aghast or insecure she felt. "No!" She shook her head. "No self-respecting person would stay without commitment or a cogent reason why you can't commit."

✦　✦　✦

Alice jumped when she heard the door from the garage to the house open and close. *Jake!* She looked at her watch; it was just after seven in the evening. She closed her computer and moved into the reception room.

Jake appeared amped up when he walked into the reception room. "Sorry. I've admitted that I overreacted. I love you and want you to stay. I'm not going to get into a big debate and psychodrama."

Alice forced herself to look directly into his eyes. "The last thing I want is a big debate and psychodrama, but for the last three days, I've felt scared and alone, and I believe I made a big mistake in moving to the United States."

He said that he was sorry again and that he had overreacted. "I certainly don't expect you to stay and accept such behavior as the norm. It's safe to say that my behavior was out of bounds and extremely unusual. Don't believe that such behavior is consistent with how I want to live or have lived my life. I love you." He paused. "You're reading way too much into issues of commitment. I'll say it again: I'm sorry about Monday night. Please forgive, and let's move on. I made a mistake and was big enough to admit it."

She was exhausted by their interactions of the day; she was still hurt. The reality was that she was so terrified of losing the relationship that she was not able to think rationally. Still engaging him directly in his eyes, she said, "I believe you're sorry, and I believe that, like me, you feel this deep connection—a bond that has kept us together. But the bottom line—"

"I'm working on my issues. I'm sorry."

She raised a hand. "Listen. I'm not—" She thought about what she was trying to convey. "I've acknowledged that without trust, there cannot be commitment. And that is probably why you are not able to commit to me and, consequently, feel I don't support you." She sighed. "Sometimes we do our best, but it's still not enough. I don't know where we can go from here unless and until you trust me."

The following week, Alice met Edward in New York. She stepped into the restaurant and was led to a table for two overlooking the street. Edward was already seated. When Alice approached, Edward stood up to embrace her.

"Edward, how are you? How are you enjoying life at the *Wall Street Journal*?"

"I'm good, and you? How's Jake? I hope he's treating you well."

"I'm OK. Life with Jake is like riding a roller coaster—up and down." Alice paused and silently relived the recent drama in her life. "Edward, you don't know how pleased I am that you're living in New York."

"Is there something you're not telling me?"

She shrugged. "I'm living in a new country. Occasionally, I feel isolated and alone. To be honest, after my last spat with Jake, moving home crossed my mind, but as you know, my family did not approve when I moved to the United States without solid plans for a wedding. Mother's 'I told you so' is the one 'I told you so' I can't face."

Edward sighed. "Alice, whatever I say will fall on deaf ears."

"Can't you show some compassion?" Alice asked. "Don't you understand the concept of forgiveness—giving a person another chance? Jake can't be a better person if everybody says, 'Kill.'"

"Forgiveness is good but not when your loyalty is being taken for granted. How many chances do you plan to give him?"

"Relationships are not always clear sailing," Alice said. "Let's change the subject. Tell me about your new apartment."

After he had relayed the details about his apartment, she thought, *I'm jealous. I'm still committed to taking the New York bar. Maybe I'll stay here, build a law practice, and get an apartment.*

After their meal, she kissed Edward and said, "Let's catch up again soon."

He hugged her tightly and whispered in her ear, "You have no idea how much I care about you. I would treat you with the respect you deserve."

49

Beth had five minutes before her therapy session with Jessica. She scanned her notes in preparation. Jessica's reference to Jess in the last session had troubled her. Jessica had not answered the question as to when she had first encountered Jess. Beth wondered why Jessica was unwilling to talk about Jess if she was one of her acquaintances. Also, the similarity of the names raised alarm bells. She debated whether Jess was a figment of Jessica's imagination. She decided to address the issue at the start of their session.

"Jessica, at the end of our last session, you mentioned you were having trouble remembering dates and times because of Jess. How long have you and Jess been friends? Where did Jess go, and how long was she gone?"

When Jessica remained silent, Beth said, "Take your time, Jessica. Can you remember how and when you and Jess became friends? Is Jess bullying you? I would like to help you take control of your life."

No! Jessica jerked her body up. "Beth, I'm meeting a client at the gallery. Can we pick up this conversation later?"

After Jessica left Beth's clinic, she flagged a cab and asked the driver to take her to Harry's, Wall Street. Seated in the back of the cab, she thought about the answers to Beth's questions and the consequences she would have faced if she had responded. She concluded that upsetting Jess was not in her best interest. Jess was unpredictable and had threatened her. Jess was also stronger. Jessica had no doubt that Jess could dominate her. It was a risk she could not take. The deal was that she could have her time with Beth in return for not discussing Jess. She had already gone too far by revealing Jess's existence.

Jessica could not work out why Jess hated Beth. It had become a little clearer when Beth informed her that she could not help Jessica control Jess if she refused to acknowledge her presence. Jessica felt pleased with herself with the idea that with Beth's help, she could bring about Jess's demise.

Bitch! Jess shrilled in Jessica's head. *Has that fucking bitch done anything to help you get Jake back?*

Jessica congratulated herself. She had found Jess's weakness. Jess was scared. She could and would dominate her. She could get rid of her right then and there—or at least try.

Then she paused. Jess was right. Beth had not helped her get Jake back. Jake had started taking the occasional call and replying to her text messages, but that progress was due to Jess.

Jessica was waiting for Jake when he arrived at Harry's for lunch. Even from a distance, he could see that she had made an effort with her appearance. But a sleeveless black dress and heels were inappropriate for the time of day and the winter season.

Jessica stood and pouted her lips, expecting Jake to kiss her. He did not. His annoyance registered on his face. Jessica's distress meter crept up.

Stop it! No fucking tears! Jess screamed. *Threaten to call the bank if you do not get what you want.*

Jake stepped back. "What the fuck do you think you're doing? Have you lost your mind?" He pulled out his chair. "I thought you understood the boundaries."

That was it. Tears streamed down her face.

"I can't take this." Jake threw a money order for $2,000 onto the table and then turned and walked out of the restaurant.

It worked, Jessica.

"Jess, he's gone."

You have a money order.

"But I don't have Jake—or the babies."

Shut the fuck up! You need money for babies. Call Jake. Confirm lunch tomorrow, or we'll call the bank.

Jessica smiled as she pressed the End button on her phone.

How the mighty has fallen, Jess said. *I told you we could break Jake.*

"Yes, we're a team." Jessica smiled to herself. "We need to dig out the information on the freezing of human eggs so we can discuss the procedure with Jake."

You don't waste time, do you? Jessica, you're crazy. All that baby talk makes me want to vomit. Initially, to make you happy, I approved of having babies, but you're far from happy. Get money, yes. Babies? I don't think so. If we can't agree, one of us will have to go. And, Jessica, I'm fucking sure it won't be me.

"It's not crazy to freeze eggs; it's normal," Jessica replied. "I need to be prepared—Jake will ask if I've done my homework."

Jessica! Jake does not need to know you want his sperm. Think! Use your brain. I don't want fucking babies! I won't help you if you screw up. No second chances.

She did not want to upset Jess, especially since everything was going so well. Any thoughts of trying to control Jess frightened her. Jess could read her mind. How could she talk to Beth without Jess finding out?

50

J ake cast his thoughts back to Monday morning. Elle had not been at her desk for the last hour. She had not called in sick and was in the office that day. This was not like her. Generally, Elle let him know if she was going to be away from her desk for a prolonged period. Jake was growing impatient. He needed confirmation on the two meetings he had asked her to set up for the afternoon. He was relieved when she walked into his office but a little surprised when she asked if she could speak to him privately and then closed the door.

Elle sat down opposite Jake. "Please say if you think I'm overstepping the mark. It's not my business." Elle looked down and fumbled with the file in her hands.

Jake leaned forward. "Elle, what is the problem?"

Elle cleared her throat. "Jessica has called a member of the bank's board of directors."

Jake's heart sank. "Who? Who did she call?"

"Roberto. Fortunately, Roberto's PA, Jenny, picked up the call."

"Do you know why she called?"

"Jessica told Jenny that she was a friend of Roberto."

Jake did not confirm whether that part of the conversation was true. Jessica's assertion had been a twist on the truth. Roberto and

Jessica were not friends. It was true that he had met Jessica, because she was a friend of Roberto's wife, Meghan. Roberto only tolerated her because of his wife's friendship with her.

Elle said, "When Jenny informed Jessica that Roberto was un-available, Jessica said it was important that she speak to him. She left a message: 'Please ask Roberto to call me. I need to make him aware that Jake Logan is an asshole.' Jake, the point is, next time, Jenny might not be around to filter the call. Also, there's no guarantee she won't use the call as a source of gossip."

Jake thanked Elle for her discretion and assured her that he would speak to Jessica and let her know her behavior was inappropriate.

Jake's deliberately long walk back to the bank after his aborted lunch with Jessica did not clear his mind. He struggled to concentrate during his afternoon meeting. He had underestimated her. There had been a time when he could walk away and not hear anything from her for several months. Now she would not go away without money or lunch. *Where will it stop?* He had lost count of how many times she had begged him to have dinner. Yesterday she had suggested cooking dinner and said he should stay over at her apartment. She would want sex for dessert.

Jake tried to work out how he had arrived at that point. Between leaving the restaurant and getting back to his office, Jessica had made it clear that if he did not call, she would call the bank. Jessica was fully cognizant of the embarrassment she could cause Jake and that he would shy away from his personal life being played out in public. Sure, he could warn the bank's human resources that his mentally unstable ex-girlfriend was stalking him, and they would appear sympathetic to his face, but behind his back, they would talk about his lack of judg-ment in becoming involved with her in the first place. Before long, the board members, while discussing his long-term future with the bank, would conclude that a man who could not exercise judgment in his personal life was unlikely to exercise professional judgment. Their appraisal would be neither rational nor fair, but it would not matter. The career ladder would be pushed back from the wall, leaving him to fall. Jake had hit an all-time low.

Back in his office, he called Jessica and asked if there was a problem. Jessica said there was not, but lunch had not turned out the way she had expected. She hoped they could meet for dinner.

"I have a business dinner with colleagues tonight. Lunch tomorrow could work."

"Perfect," Jessica replied.

Jake's stress level escalated. What would he tell Alice? Jessica's behavior was blackmail. Her ability to embarrass him and, consequently, damage his reputation at the bank was not what he needed in the current financial climate.

The following day, Jake ate lunch with Jessica. His thoughts were on her. Where did she think their relationship was going? Why could she not recognize that beyond a platonic relationship, they had no future? Jessica continued to talk, oblivious to the fact that Jake was not listening. His head was overrun with his upcoming meeting with human resources in the London office. English employees had entrenched rights; he could not simply walk into the office and fire the team. He did not hear Jessica until she said the word *embryo*.

"What? Sorry, but I missed part of the conversation. Repeat what you just said."

"Jake, hundreds of babies have been born from treatment using previously frozen, thawed, and mature eggs from various centers around the world." Jessica took a deep breath and explained that she, like many women in their thirties who were freezing eggs because they were still hunting for Mr. Right, did not want to lose out on her ability to have children. "It will take the pressure off finding a partner."

Jessica had his attention. He heard what she was saying. He asked her to correct him if he was wrong. His understanding was that egg freezing was still a relatively new technology.

"The chance of success is good," Jessica replied. "Think about it. I'm opting for egg freezing as a last resort."

Jake was dumbfounded and did not respond.

"Attend the consultation with me. I'm just asking—not begging—you to support me in exploring this option."

He reluctantly agreed.

51

Greenwich, Connecticut, two days later

Alice decided not to join Jake on his business trip to London. The legal opinion she had produced for an American company, advising it in relation to setting up an online service aimed at the UK market, had resulted in follow-up work. She could not spare the time to travel. She had promised herself she would keep the peace and achieve her goal of passing the New York bar. After Jake returned from London, she had agreed they would take a ski vacation to Colorado. It would also enable her to achieve another goal: she had planned a stopover in Vegas to attend a business conference.

Jake had informed her that he had a reservation on the 6:15 p.m. Sunday flight to London and that he'd arranged for the car to pick him up at 3:00 p.m. Alice did not waste what little time they had to relax before his trip. After their workout at the gym, they had brunch. The sun shone brightly on the cold winter day. Wrapped up, they walked along the beachfront. The forecast promised snow.

It was winter, and it appeared the world was already in hibernation; it was unusually quiet for a Sunday. No dogs ran among the seemingly dead but sleeping trees and plants. It was not their usual long walk. The cold turned them back to the house to light a fire and thaw out.

Amanda's Honda turned onto the road leading to Jake's house. Jessica watched as Jake dropped the pile of fire logs he had picked up when he looked up and saw the Honda. She laughed hysterically when he darted behind the garage door and hit the switch to close it while pulling out his phone.

Jessica answered on the first ring. "Jake." She looked at Amanda with a beaming smile across her face.

"I asked you not to turn up at the house unannounced."

"Did you? I don't remember that conversation. It would be nice to spend Sunday afternoon together. I thought you would prefer Sunday lunch to an unannounced visit at the bank tomorrow."

"A car is picking me up at three. I'm flying to London this evening."

"Liar—I saw you picking up fire logs."

"I don't care if you believe me. I've a bag to pack."

"Don't forget our consultation with the fertility clinic."

Jessica ended the call. She was in control. She instructed Amanda to park the car farther away from the house.

"Jess is curious as to whether he's telling the truth. She thinks the bitch is in the house."

"Jess?" said Amanda.

Jessica's face flushed. Feeling embarrassed, she said, "Jess? What are you talking about? Let's have lunch. We can come back at two forty-five to confirm that a car has collected Jake."

52

eth sat in her office, reading her notes on Jessica. She had been treating her on and off for almost three years for depression, mood swings, suicidal tendencies, and alcohol abuse. *Jessica's condition has evolved.* Beth observed that Jessica's sense of identity and reality as well as her thoughts, sensations, perceptions, and memories had become disconnected from one another.

Her preliminary diagnosis was dissociative identity disorder, or DID. The research had informed Beth that some individuals with DID spent years in the mental health system prior to diagnosis. She was also aware that diagnosing DID accurately took time because the symptoms that caused a person with DID to seek treatment were like those of many other psychiatric disorders. Given that Jessica's history of mental illness was patchy, Beth thought, *Before I refer her to a specialist, I'll discuss my observations with Steve.*

Steve Lopez Dunhill, MD, was a longtime colleague. She invited Steve to her office. Steve had watched Jessica enter and then storm out of Beth's office on previous occasions. That was the extent of his knowledge.

"Back in January, I observed in Jessica an uncertainty—an apparent identity confusion," Beth said. "The episodes were infrequent, but there appeared to be a struggle within her to define herself."

Steve asked about Beth's use of the term *infrequent* and how many times Beth had noticed the behavior.

"I witnessed two distinct identities on two occasions in January," Beth replied. "Through January and February, the incidents when the two identities struggled to control her behavior increased. At times, Jessica is unable to recall important personal information—memory lapses that are too extensive to be explained by ordinary forgetfulness. Jessica is, in my opinion, exhibiting signs of DID."

"Are you sure?" Steve appeared surprised and sought to confirm what Beth had just revealed. "Are you saying Jessica is showing signs of multiple personality disorder?"

"Yes," she replied, a little impatient. "Subject to Jessica's agreement, I'd like you to observe a session."

"Me?" he said, displaying his elation. "Many therapists study but rarely see a verifiable case of DID."

She nodded. "I've observed severe changes of identity in Jessica. The disturbance was not caused by the direct physiological effects of a substance. In one session, she broke down, admitting she had shifts of identity as separate personalities. She referred to the other personality as Jess. During that session, Jess asserted control of her behavior and thoughts at different times."

"Did Jessica remember the episode?"

"Yes. She had complete awareness of what happened when the other identity had control. Jessica's awareness is a problem in itself. She appeared to be apprehensive of the other identity."

Beth confirmed that at times, Jessica had experienced depression, mood swings, anxiety, and panic attacks. To Beth's knowledge, Jessica also had suicidal tendencies, heard voices, experienced sleep disorders, and indulged in alcohol abuse.

Five days later, Steve again joined Beth in her office. Jessica had refused to allow him to join a session. He said he was still interested in discussing the case and had not ruled out the possibility of Jessica reversing her decision.

"The causes of dissociative identity disorder are complex," he said. "Studies show that a history of trauma, usually abuse in childhood, is almost always the case for people who have severe dissociative symptoms. Jessica hasn't made you aware of or hinted at any childhood abuse, has she?"

"Not all abused children have dissociative identity disorder," Beth replied. "The relationship is not one of simple cause and effect."

"You're missing my point. Not all abused children have dissociative identity disorder, but most children with DID were abused."

Beth told Steve that she believed Jessica, like others who suffered from dissociative difficulties, was trying to keep it hidden. She had observed her making excuses to cut sessions short. She suspected Jessica was trying to avoid revealing the other identity.

"Add to that the fact that even when asked, many DID sufferers deny a history of abuse," Beth said. "It could also be that Jessica has dissociative amnesia and doesn't remember the abuse."

"What are the chances of getting her admitted to a clinic where we can observe her and prescribe medication?"

"I have that under consideration. We must be careful, though. Any mention of medication triggers an identity change, and Jessica immediately leaves the session."

53

Grand Central Station, New York

Jessica's train pulled into Grand Central. Staying in Connecticut had produced pleasing results. A car had collected Jake from the house at three o'clock, which confirmed his trip to London. If he had a girlfriend, she was nowhere to be seen. She had instructed Amanda to do the occasional drive-by. Jessica contemplated that she would take out any bitch who crossed her path. The babies were her priority.

Jessica, this talk is insane, but I like your fighting spirit.

"Jess, we work together. If you have a problem, I talk to Beth."

Fucking bitch. Who do you think you're threatening? I can and will take you out. Think again. You're too fucking weak to fight me. Don't mention Beth again. If you cross me again, no baby and no consultation Friday. Fuck you, bitch.

Apologize to her—the baby. "Jess, I'm sorry."

Four days later

On Friday, Jessica, accompanied by Jake, sat in the clinic, waiting to be called in for their consultation. The clinic had recommended counseling. The issues underlying the need to consider egg freezing were complex. Most doctors insisted on counseling sessions. Jake had argued with Jessica about his need to be present if it was simply a case of her freezing eggs until Mr. Right came along. Jessica was ecstatic he had shown up for the consultation. It did not escape her that she still had the task of getting him to pay for not only this session but also the others that would follow. On another level, she had observed his discomfort and feared he would abruptly depart.

She had been waiting for twenty minutes, when Jake said, "I must get back to the office. How much does this consultation cost—can I give you a money order?"

"No! The doctor needs to assess my suitability to undergo the procedure. There will be questions about my personal circumstances. I want you to understand all the details—this is not our only option."

"Jessica, what are you talking about? You and I are not in a relationship. You are implying this is not just money and support. If you push this beyond what a platonic friend might offer, I'm out."

You're here now. That's all that matters.

Jessica stared out her bedroom window. "Jess, Jake isn't answering my texts. He isn't backing out now! Jess, can you hear me?"

Fuck off, Jessica. You spoke to that bitch Beth.

"Sorry, Jess."

Fuck off. You're a liar. I don't trust you. Lying bitch! Stupid bitch! You're not sorry, but you will be. Jess chuckled. *Go ahead. Let bitch Beth medicate me. I don't want fucking babies.*

"Sorry, Jess. What should I do about Jake?"

Stupid asshole. You should go to Greenwich. If that doesn't work, call the fucking bank. Teach Jake some fucking manners. Did you call his mother?

"No."

Did you threaten to call his mother?

"No."

You're a fucking idiot! Let me guess. That fucking bitch Beth. Did she tell you it wasn't a good idea?

Jessica picked up her purse. Jess was right. There was no point in talking to Beth. It was setting her back. She had to freeze her eggs. Jake owed her. She needed money. She did not want to spend her savings. She was sure he would come around to the idea of donating sperm if she did not find a life partner. If she traveled by taxi, she could get the next train to Greenwich.

✦ ✦ ✦

Greenwich, Connecticut

Amanda was in the bedroom, getting her daughter ready for soccer practice. Jessica sat in the kitchen, sobbing. She had been calling, emailing, and texting Jake since leaving New York but had not gotten a reply. The antidepressants Beth had prescribed were not working.

Fucking Beth. She has no idea.

If Jessica complained, Beth would tell her to give the antidepressants time to work. It was Beth's fucking standard answer.

She doesn't understand; time is not on my side.

Jessica felt as if her world were crashing in on her. "Jess, Jake has turned his phone off!"

Jessica, stop that fucking screeching. It is pathetic. Amanda will hear us. Bitch Beth is enough of a problem. The bank is closed. Call his mother. Jake knows if you shout loudly enough and long enough, somebody might hear you and believe you. Lie! He won't want his mom to know he sleeps with prostitutes.

Jessica searched through her contacts for the telephone number for Jake's mother. She paused at the text from Jake that said he was on vacation and would reach out when he returned. She was annoyed that Jake had taken a vacation without discussing it with her. He was fucking around on her time, and she had wasted a journey to Greenwich. "I need a vacation. If he put more effort into our relationship, it would work," she whined.

Stop! You need to stop swallowing pills. He threatened you. I can't take your crap.

"He agreed to support me and go with me to the egg-freezing procedure."

He threatened you. Which part do you not understand?

"He loves me."

OK, there's no point in me attending the clinic next week. As a matter of fact, make an appointment with Beth to terminate my ass.

"Jess, I didn't mean … I was just—"

What were you just saying? Tell that fucker Jake you'll call the bank.

"Sorry, Jess. I will."

54

Greenwich, Connecticut, Saturday morning

Jake stepped out of the shower and walked over to the night-stand, looking for the remote control so he could change the television channel. His chest tightened when he saw six text messages from Jessica on his phone. *A big mistake. Huge!* He had been careless in leaving his phone on the nightstand. Alice was in the bedroom, packing her bag for their vacation. She could easily have seen the messages. There was no escaping Jessica. Anger rose in him. He swore that if she wrecked his vacation, it would be the last thing she did.

He went to the bedroom window to check for Amanda's Honda and then let out a sigh of relief. It was nowhere to be seen; however, the car to take them to the airport was waiting in the driveway. The driver was twenty minutes early, but he appeared content, reading his newspaper. When the driver looked up, Jake recognized him as Douglas, one of the three men from the limousine company that had driven him for more than ten years.

Jake turned away from the window. He did not want to spend a minute longer than necessary in the house. He feared Jessica would show up. Making sure his phone was on silent, he shoved it into his computer bag.

✦   ✦   ✦

JFK Airport, New York

Despite the stress Jake had been under from the end of the year through January and into February, he had spared no expense or time in finding the perfect winter vacation for Alice. He had chosen Colorado. They were spending five nights at the Broadmoor, a resort known as the Grand Dame of the Rockies. Jake had been to Colorado many times. He thought it would be fun to explore the picturesque mountains, streams, and canyons with Alice before going to Las Vegas for her business trip.

Jake sent a flurry of text messages and emails in the car and at the airport, to the point that Alice asked whether he would be able to take a break and relax while on vacation.

Jake contemplated the twenty text messages and two emails he had received from Jessica that morning. He did billion-dollar deals daily, and he never lost his nerve or buckled under pressure. Jessica was an acquisition he had acquired but could not dispose of, even at a price. If he did not respond immediately to her texts, she reacted with a tirade of abuse. He found himself sending a minimum of three texts each day. He would text her "Hi" in the mornings, "How are you doing?" at lunch, and "Night night" at the end of the day.

He had promised to pay for the egg-freezing procedure. She had made it clear in her email at 11:30 a.m. that day that the money was not enough and threatened to call his mother and the bank. What did she want from him? What did she hope to achieve by calling his mother? His mother would never side with her against him. Surely she had heard of family loyalty.

The bank was another issue. He did not want the embarrassment.

An old and respected institution like the one at which he worked would not tolerate scandal at any level. Jake felt a heavy burden. He thought about the process of getting rid of Jessica. Damage control was his priority. He did not owe her anything, did he?

Broadmoor Resort, Colorado

It was late evening when the four-hour flight touched down at Denver International Airport. The airport was located ninety minutes from the Broadmoor. Jake had arranged a shuttle service to the resort. The Broadmoor was home to the Tavern, which was reputed to serve the best steaks and seafood in Colorado Springs, coupled with live music from the Tavern Orchestra. The Tavern was the perfect end to the day for Jake and Alice, who were tired after their journey.

Jake's peace was broken when he checked his texts before retiring to bed. Stressed, he told Alice he had to make a quick call. He kissed her, and Alice's concerned expression was unmissable. He went into the living room, closing the bedroom door on his way out.

During Jake's conversation, Alice heard him say, "I'm in Colorado. If you call my … you'll regret it. No, I'm not threatening you. I'm giving advance warning. If you go down that road, things will change."

Alice strained to hear Jake's conversation. She heard him say, "I'm in Colorado. If you call my … you'll regret it. No, I'm not threatening you. I'm giving advance warning. If you go down that road, things will change."

She did not catch the word after *my*, but it sounded like *mother*. She could not work out with whom he was speaking but guessed it was Jessica.

When Jake walked back into the bedroom, she asked if everything was OK.

"Yes," he replied.

She did not push the issue. *I can't confess to eavesdropping.*

The conversation she overheard on Saturday brought some calm to the five nights they spent at the Broadmoor. The stress, fluctuating moods, and discomfort she had seen him experience when he checked his text messages or email dissipated; he appeared relaxed and enjoyed the vacation.

The highlight of the vacation was on Sunday, when they attended Pauline Memorial Chapel. The chapel had been dedicated as a Catholic church when Saint Paul's Catholic Parish of Springs was established. It had been designed in a Spanish mission style and exhibited many examples of religious art and artifacts.

Colorado Springs's only in-town ski resort, Ski Broadmoor, had closed. The closest ski resort was Monarch Mountain, located west of the city, in the Sangre de Cristo Mountains. On two days of the vacation, Alice rose early, joined by Jake, to do the two-hour drive. She spent the rest of the days exploring the mountains, streams, and canyons with him. After another memorable vacation, on Thursday, they boarded a flight to Las Vegas.

✦ ✦ ✦

Las Vegas

Alice had been torn between the Cosmopolitan and the Bellagio. At a previous conference, she had stayed at the Bellagio. In the end, they had opted for the Cosmopolitan. She thought they would enjoy the great view of the Strip from one of the Cosmopolitan's two high-rise towers.

The night after their arrival, Jake stepped into the shower and offered to wash Alice's back. She did not resist when his hands turned her around gently and massaged her body. Lifting her, he united his body with hers, thrusting until they reached a climax in unison.

Afterward, Alice, wrapped in a terry cloth robe, applied makeup. Jake called to her from the shower to pass his shaving kit, which was in the pocket of his travel bag. When Alice pulled it out, a box of condoms came out as well. Alice stared at the box on the carpet, stunned.

Jake called again from the shower, bringing her back to reality. She picked up the shaving kit, took it to the bathroom, and handed it to him. He did not see the look on her face.

When she returned to the bedroom, her shock was overcome by anger. Alice took a deep breath. She needed to calm herself and decide what to do next. Although she could not think of one, perhaps there was a perfectly logical reason for Jake to have condoms in his travel bag. An outburst from her could result in his lying. She picked up the box and put it back in his bag.

Alice and Jake explored the Cosmopolitan with minimal conversation. Eventually, they settled at the Chandelier Bar. They had chosen it due to the playground atmosphere, which was coupled with an art exhibit. After their cocktails were set in front of them, Jake asked Alice if she was OK, because she had been quiet. This was Alice's opportunity. She did not waste it.

"Jake, are you seeing another woman?"

"No. Why?"

"You have condoms in your bag. They fell out when you asked me to get your shaving kit." Alice's eyes filled with tears.

"Alice, it's not what you think."

"What? You're reading my mind now? Tell me what I'm thinking—I'm waiting."

"The condoms have been in my bag since we stayed at the Hilton."

"You're lying—the condoms you bought in London were sensitive."

He sighed. "You're not going to believe the truth."

"Try me."

He explained that after Jessica had called the Mayfair Hotel back in September a year ago, she had started dating a man named Tom, a high-level government employee who traveled frequently and lived in other jurisdictions for his work. Jessica had traveled with him wherever he went. Then, out of the blue, during December and January, she had started contacting him, stating she had broken up with Tom, she was broke, and her apartment was about to be repossessed.

"What does any of this have to do with the condoms in your bag?"

"I met Jessica for lunch a couple of times as a friend." He looked down. "The first time I met her, it was to give her a money order. The second time, she was very distressed, alone, and threatening suicide. I took her to lunch as a friend. I care about her as a platonic friend. Jessica put the condoms in my bag."

"I don't believe you. How convenient. You're lying." She watched as his calm dissipated.

His face flushed, and he clenched his fists. "I don't give a fuck what you believe."

With that, he got up and stalked off, leaving Alice alone in the bar.

55

The walls were closing in around Jake. He had to get out of there. He was already dealing with one crazy woman. His head could not take another. Jake was struggling to understand Alice. He had told the truth, and she had called him a liar. He walked to the Bellagio and stood outside the hotel, viewing the show of water, music, and lights. It was mesmerizing. Jake wished Alice was with him.

No, scratch that. Alice is going to be here. This romantic setting is too good to be missed. He pulled his phone out of his jacket pocket and started to dial her number but then stopped. Anger stirred within him. How could he be with a woman who could not accept the simple truth? *Fuck her. This is Las Vegas, America's playground. People come here to have fun, and fun is what I'm going to have.*

Jake put Alice out of his mind. He had not done anything remotely wrong. *Forget Alice. Forget the crazy woman who caused the problem.* He had told Alice she had nothing to be concerned about.

His selfishness prevented him from seeing beyond his assertion that Alice's discovery of the condoms should not have been an issue, because he had done nothing wrong. He could not comprehend why, after receiving an explanation, she would turn it into a serious issue.

Jake hit the casino tables in the Bellagio. From the Bellagio, he went to the Venetian and then across to Caesar's Palace.

A boy does not have to be unhappy in Las Vegas, he thought as he sat at one of the tables. He leaned forward and asked the croupier for directions to the best gentleman's club in town. The croupier asked Jake if he had ever been to a gentleman's club before.

"A gentleman never tells," Jake replied, and he burst into laughter.

The croupier laughed with him. On the assumption that Jake had been to other gentleman's clubs, he promised Jake he had not seen anything like Sapphire. Jake did not need any more information. He cashed in his chips and headed there.

Sapphire was enormous. In the main room were three stages. Jake opted for a champagne room, a specialized VIP service. It was located on the second level and overlooked the main room. It appealed to Jake because of the privacy and the intimacy. It was fitted with flat-screen televisions, plush seating, and a private bar. Jake spared no expense. His plan to forget his troubles was working. His problems with Alice and Jessica were distant memories. He settled himself in the champagne room and purchased time in half-hour increments with an exotic dancer.

At six in the morning, Jake sat at the bar in the Cosmopolitan. He had some explaining to do—first about why he had stayed out all night and second about the condoms in his bag, given that Alice had not been convinced by the Jessica story. He asked the bartender which of two explanations he would give to a partner who was already seeing red: that he had spent the rest of the night watching an exotic dancer after hitting the casinos or the truth that after hitting the casinos and watching an exotic dancer for ten minutes, he had fallen asleep in Sapphire's champagne room for four hours and twenty minutes.

The bartender said, "How much did it cost you?"

"Seven thousand dollars," Jake replied. He explained that the dancer had claimed she had entertained him for four and a half hours.

The joke was on him. She had not danced; she had not done anything other than drink champagne and watch television. He had been too tired and embarrassed when he woke up to complain to Sapphire's management.

The bartender advised him, "Go with scenario two." He laughed, saying it was too pathetic not to be the truth, and then caught himself. "Sorry, sir. I didn't mean—"

"It's OK," Jake said. "It was lame."

"Suffice it to say the boys at work will hear version one."

Thank God that what happens in Vegas stays in Vegas.

Jake went up to the hotel room at seven o'clock. His wallet was $9,000 lighter—the total cost since he had left the Chandelier Bar. He heard Alice taking a shower. Jake wished he could get into the shower with her, but he dared not even go into the bathroom. He knew for sure that the minute he opened the shower door, she would punch his lights out. He sat on the sofa and waited for her to come out of the bathroom. He had decided he would show Alice the evidence she needed to believe Jessica had put the condoms into his bag. He would also explain where he had been all night. Once she saw he was not lying about the condoms, she would know he was telling the truth about his night out.

Alice was not expecting to see Jake when she walked out of the bathroom. "Dammit, Jake! You frightened me. Where have you been?"

He cut her off. "I don't want to fight. Please hear me out. I can explain."

"Really? You think I've time to scream at you? Did you forget I came to Vegas for business?" Her tone was sarcastic. "Make it quick. I need to get dressed for the conference."

Jake walked toward her, holding out his phone. "You need to read these texts."

Alice took the phone and sat at the desk, scrolling through the string of messages.

Jessica had written, "Hi, hon," followed by "Lunch tomorrow?"

When he had not replied, Jessica had said, "Jake, pick up the fucking phone. I don't feel good."

Jake finally had responded, saying, "I'm in a meeting."

Jessica had replied, "Fucking liar." With no response, she had added, "Are you still seeing that London bitch?" and then "Pick up the fucking phone."

Later, she had written, "Lunch was fun. Thought we could do it again."

Finally, with no response, she had said, "Fuck you, Jake!" and "Hope the bitch finds the condoms. Fuck you."

"Jessica called twenty times while sending these texts," he said. "She was calling the landline and mobile simultaneously. Elle has been instructed not to put her calls through to me or anyone else in the office. Alice, you have no idea."

"Jake, you need to sort this problem out. Is she mentally ill? I couldn't help noticing that you didn't tell Jessica you're in relationship."

"You have no idea—"

"Jake, sort the problem out before she destroys our relationship, not to mention your career. I must get dressed."

"Yes, honey."

"You're not off the hook. It's seven thirty. You didn't sleep in our bed. You owe me an explanation."

"Honey—"

"Later, Jake. I'm running late."

56

New York, four days later

The taxi pulled up in front of the New York Life Clinic. When Jake walked into the building, Jessica was waiting for him in the reception area. Jessica appeared nervous. Her legs were crossed, and her arms were wrapped around her chest. Relief spread across her face when she saw him walk through the revolving glass doors.

"You're late," she said with a raised voice, but then she lowered it after a visible effort to regain control of herself. "It's OK. You're here now."

Jake looked at his watch. He was late by seconds. He did not respond to her. The sooner this appointment was over the better.

Soon they sat in the consultation room, waiting for the doctor. With renewed confidence because of Jake's attendance at the clinic, Jessica seated herself comfortably. She talked to Jake as if they were a couple. She was in total denial. It failed to compute that Jake was no longer her life partner. Onlookers would have believed they were Mr. and Mrs. Logan. But if their eyes had fallen to the third finger of her left hand, their assumption would not have been verified.

When the doctor entered the room, he was accompanied by the

clinic's accounts manager. After introductions, the accounts manager opened his file and handed Jake a brochure that detailed the costs involved in the procedure Jessica was about to undergo. He broke the costs down, explaining that it was $9,000 per attempt to freeze the eggs. He emphasized that Jake's "wife" might have to undergo up to three cycles to preserve a good number of eggs.

At that point, the focus was on Jake. The accounts manager paid little or no attention to Jessica. He assumed Jake would be picking up the bill, and to that end, Jessica was irrelevant.

Jake started by correcting the accounts manager's false assumption regarding their marital status. "We're not married. Miss Brooks is a platonic friend."

Jessica's face contorted with anger.

Desperate to leave, Jake pretended not to notice Jessica's discomfort. "Where do you want me to sign?"

"Right here, Mr. Logan."

After the payment authorization had been collected, the accounts manager wished them good luck and exited the room.

The doctor reviewed his notes before directing his attention to Jessica. "Based on the information you gave during your previous consultation, I understand that the reason for freezing your eggs is nonmedical."

Jessica looked at Jake.

"Miss Brooks, please, can you confirm that my understanding is correct?"

"Yes, the reason for freezing my eggs is nonmedical."

The doctor also drew their attention to the fact that the notes recorded that she was undergoing the procedure to delay having children until a more appropriate time in her life.

Jessica twisted her hands nervously, wishing she had gone to Beth to get a prescription to keep her calm.

Jessica! That bitch asks too many questions.

Jess was not supposed to be there, but with Jake and the doctor in the room, Jessica considered it too risky to attempt to chase her away.

Don't worry. I'll get you through this ordeal, Jess said. *I can deal with both you and that bitch Beth down the road.*

Jessica wanted to ask Jess what she was planning to do with Beth, but now was not the time. Jessica was worried. She needed Beth to help her get rid of Jess.

Jessica, you can't get rid of me. If I go, so do the babies.

"Sh," Jessica said.

"I'm sorry, Miss Brooks," the doctor said. "Did you say something?"

"No," Jessica blurted out.

He asked Jessica if she viewed freezing her eggs as a safety net.

"Yes," Jessica replied.

He continued reading through the notes. He paused to ask Jessica if she had given serious consideration to the age factor. He said it was his understanding that during the first consultation, she had been told that the probability of getting pregnant declined with age. In addition, the risks of miscarriage and of certain abnormalities, such as Down syndrome, increased.

Jake looked at his watch, obviously eager to get the meeting done as quickly as possible. "Doctor, Jessica is thirty-three. That's why she would like to freeze her eggs now, before it's too late."

"Sorry, Mr. Logan," the doctor replied. "There appears to be some confusion here. The information recorded in the file indicates that Miss Brooks has passed the age we would recommend for a woman to freeze eggs. The purpose of this consultation is to confirm that this is the correct procedure for her."

"I don't understand," Jake said, looking at Jessica for an explanation.

Her mouth opened, but no words came out.

The doctor explained that age had a major bearing on in vitro fertilization success and on the success of the egg-freezing process. It was especially relevant for women in their late thirties or early forties, which was the time when Miss Brooks or any woman would see a decline in the number of eggs collected, egg quality, and viability.

"There are various tests available—scans and blood tests—that will enable us to assess whether good numbers of eggs are available to be collected," he said. "However, the clinic would rarely recommend egg freezing for women over forty-one." He said he could carry out the tests, but he would not advise egg freezing if the results suggested low numbers of eggs were likely to be produced.

"I still don't understand," Jake said. "Jessica is thirty-three. Where's the problem?"

"The notes state Miss Brooks is forty-three."

Thunk! Jake's phone dropped to the floor. His stare pierced her. "Jessica?"

She did not reply.

"Jessica?" When she still refused to reply, Jake stood up. "Thank you, Doctor." He walked out of the room.

Jessica lay in bed with a pillow pulled securely around her ears. After Jake had walked out of the consulting room, she had followed close on his heels. He had stopped; turned; and said to Jessica that when he'd walked into the clinic, his brain had told him to turn and run, but his heart had called out to her, the monster he believed he had played a part in creating.

"Jess, he called me a monster!" she sobbed. "Yes, a monster—not said to be cruel, he claimed. Jess, I can't read that statement any other way." Since then, she had been in bed, crying. She had no reason to live.

"Go away, Jess!" she screamed, pulling the pillow tighter around her ears. "Please go away. I can't take any more."

Fuck you, Jessica. Fuck you! Kill yourself, but you're not killing me. Fuck you, Jessica. I got the money to freeze the eggs. I made Jake go to the clinic with you. Now you want to kill me? Fuck you, Jessica. Get the fuck out of bed, or I'll kill you. I'll hurt your fucking head so hard you'll be a fucking cabbage. Get up, you pathetic fuck.

"Jess, I can't. I don't have a job. I don't have a man. I don't have children."

You stupid bitch! Make Jake come back. He owes you. What is it you tell yourself? Jake loves you? Jess taunted.

"How?"

Get out of the way. I'll email him. If he doesn't respond, I'll call the fucking bank.

Jessica pulled out her computer and typed an email.

Jake,

Please read this email. Sorry I deceived you about my age. I can't turn back the clock. I lied. Sorry.

I get upset when I'm with you. It's not the case when I'm with other people. People tell me I'm a nice person. Being with you brings up all the pain you've put me through and continue to put me through. I have extreme anxiety problems. You've hurt me in ways I didn't know people could hurt each other. I have serious self-esteem issues. I cry every day and see Beth for counseling most days.

When I meet you for lunch, it's very stressful—because of the pain you've put me through and continue to put me through. You're giving me mixed signals. You're unreliable in your love for me. You have no idea what it's like to be on the receiving end.

You ignore me, run away from me, hang up on me, keep me hanging on plans, stand me up, ignore my calls, don't take my calls at work, don't return texts, and shut off your phone. You've taken me to the brink of hell and back more times than I can count.

I let my emotions out with you because I can truly be myself with you. Jake, you know what I've been through, and you're the source of my pain. Do you think Beth or Jess want to hear about my problems? I keep my pain inside and walk around with a fake smile on my face.

I hope that one day you'll finally understand, support me, and right the wrongs you've done to me. I need you to support me with the egg freezing. None of my friends or family will support me. Tom fucked off when I mentioned freezing eggs. I only have you.

Part of me really believes you'll make all the bad things you did right. Another part of me thinks I'm going insane. I thought we would work through our relationship problems. I see us together, and I see you as the father of my baby. How could I not? You already were my "husband" for the years we were together, and in my mind, you were father to my dead babies.

Jessica stopped typing for a moment. "Does that make sense, Jess?"

Jessica, Jake understands what you're writing. I believe he went to school. Jake knows what's required of him. Finish the email.

With a sigh, Jessica continued.

I need professional help. I lost my babies, and I lost the person I love. I don't care what you think. You're still in a relationship with me. I have no family. When I see babies, young moms, or kids being pushed in strollers, I start crying in broad daylight. I have no man who loves me besides you, whenever you feel like it. I have no friends except Jess, and she comes and goes.

I'm fucked up because I don't work much these days, and my career isn't what it used to be. I'm a loser personally, so I don't feel confident. Every time you hurt me, like when you walked out of the clinic today, it chips away at my ability to get up and be successful. It really affects me deeply.

Anyhow, back to my point. Please go with me to the clinic to finish the egg-freezing procedure. The doctor said my chance of success would be better if I was younger, but he did not say it was impossible for me to have a healthy baby. I'll find a job and use a sperm donor if we don't work things out in our relationship or if I don't find the right man. Even if it's just on the days I go to the hospital, please go with me. Please say yes.

Jessica

Finished typing, Jessica paused to reread the message before sending. She was startled when Jess's voice sounded in her head.

Send the fucking email. I'll back you up if he doesn't respond.

57

Greenwich, Connecticut

lice stepped out of the shower and grabbed her robe before she ran into the bedroom to answer the phone. "Edward, hi!"

"How are you? Tell me about Vegas. Did you have a good time?"

"A long story. Do you have the time?"

It did not take long to narrate the details of the business trip tacked on to the end of her most recent vacation with Jake.

"Did Jake offer an explanation as to where he spent Thursday night?"

Alice's face lit up, and she burst into laughter. Several seconds later, she calmed down and told him that Jake had arranged to meet her after the conference at the Henry, a restaurant located in the Cosmopolitan. She burst into laughter again when she relayed how she had watched Jake squirm when he explained where he had been that night.

"How can you laugh?" Edward asked when she was finished. "Did you get upset when you found out he'd gone to a strip club?"

"No! Should I be?"

"Some women get upset if their partner or husband goes to a strip club."

"I never understood why." She teased him. "If you and I were dating, would you be upset if I went to Sapphire?"

"You and me dating? I wish. Two of the many reasons I love you are your free spirit and your open mind—you don't judge."

"Edward, society's morals have changed." She informed him that Sapphire offered packages for women as well as men. Many women held their bachelorette parties at Sapphire. Alice laughed again. "Jake slept for four hours. That was a tough one for him to live down. He made me promise not to share his antics with our friends at dinner parties."

Alice's tone changed when the subject of Jessica was raised. "Dinner at the Henry revealed more than where Jake had spent Thursday night." She paused. "Over time, I've come to understand more about Jake's personality. He's emotionally immature. On one level, I fell in love with that emotional immaturity, the boyishness. On another level, it makes having a grown-up relationship difficult."

There was a long silence.

"Edward, are you still there?"

"Yes. I beg you—please don't take this the wrong way, but are you signaling that you're leaving him? I detected a change in your mood when I mentioned Jessica."

She didn't answer the question. "Jake's immaturity goes beyond not understanding women. He has a simplistic view of relationships."

"I don't understand," he said.

Alice gave him an example. "As far as Jake is concerned, he comes home every night to me. He claims he doesn't have sex with his ex and cares about her only as a platonic friend. So he can't comprehend any issues with his seeing her for the occasional lunch or dinner. He doesn't see any issues with helping her financially either."

If she took a step back and looked at the situation objectively, she did not argue with the quotation "There but for the grace of God go I." Even though she was not happy about Jake's involvement, if Jessica was in need, she would not object to his helping her. But Jake's idea of benevolence differed from hers.

"Edward, he paid to freeze her eggs!"

Alice struggled with Jake's compassion toward Jessica on two levels. First, Jessica had not accepted that her intimate relationship with Jake was over. She still appeared to have strong feelings for him. She sought to reconcile with him, and Jake had unintentionally given her false hope. Second, Alice was uncomfortable with the way Jake was approaching the problem.

"Jessica appears to need psychiatric help. Other than giving her subsistence money, he is not equipped to help her, but he can't accept that he is making the situation worse."

Nothing Jake said about ongoing contact with Jessica made sense. Jake claimed he cared about Jessica and did not want to see her suffer. Alice struggled to understand why Jake believed that if he helped Jessica with the egg-freezing procedure, Jake's philanthropy would give her hope for her future and empower Jessica to move on and relax in the knowledge that when she found Mr. Right, she could have a family.

What about the risk of birth defects? Jake had been in the consultant's room when the doctor informed Jessica that she had waited too long to have the procedure.

Jake continued to renew and compound the mistakes of the past.

After Jake had revealed to Alice that he was helping Jessica with the cost to freeze her eggs, they had discussed the obvious implications, and Alice had tried to get Jake to appreciate the danger of what he had done. Jake refused to acknowledge that it was likely Jessica would not stop pursuing him until he had fertilized those eggs. He insisted he had made it clear that he was helping her as a friend and that he could not be a father to her children.

Two months later

Edward's text message notified Alice that he was running ten minutes late and that she should order a Caesar salad with grilled chicken for him. He arrived at the restaurant on cue with the salad. When the waiter left, Alice and Edward engaged in conversation about their respective jobs. Alice quickly lost her focus. Jake was dominating her thoughts, and she needed to unburden. The writing was on the wall. She could no longer offer an explanation or justification for her continued presence in Jake's life.

"Jake didn't heed my warning. His reactions to Jessica's pleas are shrouded in a high degree of naivete."

"Are you telling me Jake is continuing to see Jessica?"

"No, the lunches have stopped. He hasn't seen Jessica since the eggs were frozen. He went to the hospital with her. He was adamant that it was purely for moral support. Jessica continues to text and call Jake, but overall, he stays away from her."

"But doesn't the fact that he paid to freeze his ex-girlfriend's eggs raise any alarm bells?" he asked.

Alice replied that the answer to the question varied according to the year in which Edward required an answer. "When I first found out about the egg freezing, I was shocked. Given Jessica and Jake's history, I was stunned that she would ask and even more surprised that he would agree to pay." Jessica had been jilted at the altar but still was chasing the man who had abandoned her, and Jake's girlfriend had jilted him and become pregnant by another man. Jessica had asked him to be the father to that baby because the biological father did not want to be with her. When he'd refused, she'd aborted the baby. As if that were not enough, as soon as the grass had appeared greener on the other side, she'd jilted him a second time.

A relationship between Jessica and Jake was a recipe for disaster, yet neither one could let the other go. Jake continued to be charitable to her, and she continued to chase him, desiring him to father her babies. Alice said she did not feel threatened, because while the trust in her relationship with Jake had hit an all-time low, she could state with certainty that he did not want to have children with Jessica. That, no matter what she felt, ensured he would never contemplate reconciliation with her. It was truly out of charity that Jake had paid to freeze Jessica's eggs, even if the gesture had been misguided.

In hindsight, Alice wished she would have insisted that Jake have no further contact with Jessica. Any failure on his part to accept her ultimatum would have resulted in her return to England. Jessica was mentally unstable. She refused to allow her relationship with Jake to end. Now she was blackmailing him emotionally and stalking him. Although Jake refused to see it, Alice realized Jessica had developed an obsession.

The expression on Edward's face indicated something did not add up. He recounted Alice's narrative and asked her why—if she was sure Jake was not interested in reconciling with Jessica—the level of trust in their relationship had hit an all-time low.

Alice fell silent.

"Alice," Edward said, "if Jake isn't interested in reconciliation with Jessica, why don't you trust him?"

Alice paused before answering. "It was the turning point in our relationship."

Edward waited for her to continue.

She looked down at her hands, which were clasped together. "At times, Jake can be very childish."

"Yes, you've said that before. And?"

She went on to say he reminded her of boisterous boys playing. "One of the boys breaks another boy's toy. The boy with the broken toy grabs a toy belonging to the boy who broke his toy and breaks it." Jake was the boy who grabbed the toy and broke it. But Jake was no longer a little boy; he was an adult. Yet he was incapable of understanding or communicating his true feelings. He only expressed his feelings in black or white—angry or happy. He was unable to differentiate the emotional shades of gray in between. He would convince himself that he was feeling a certain way to mask his true feelings. Where relationships were concerned, if called upon to exercise emotional maturity, he could not. Jake reacted without thinking of the consequences and then regretted his actions.

"OK, Alice." Edward touched her hand and stared into her eyes as she raised her head. "You didn't answer my question. If Jake isn't interested in reconciling with Jessica, why don't you trust him?"

"Foolishly, I didn't believe Jake would set out to deliberately and maliciously hurt me."

She explained that two days earlier, on Saturday, when she had been due to take the New York bar exam, Jake had spent the day and evening with Jessica. He had walked out in one of his temper tantrums and taken the Jeep, the only means of transport. By late Saturday night, when he had not returned, Alice had called him.

"He let me believe he had stayed with Jessica the entire night. Can you believe that? He did it for no other reason than to cause maximum hurt. Jake interpreted my distance over the previous three days, when my studying intensified and I was focused on the forthcoming exam, as my rejecting him."

Alice could not acknowledge that based on Jake's past record, she was splitting hairs. Until that moment, in her mind, Jake's vindictive behavior had been spontaneous. However, his recent behavior had all the hallmarks of premeditation. He could not deny his intent to hurt her. He understood the consequences of his actions and had made no apology in the immediate aftermath.

✦   ✦   ✦

Two days later

Alice closed the bedroom door. Seated on the bed, she removed the letter from the open envelope. She had grown accustomed to Jake's disrespect for her feelings. Earlier that day, he had opened his weekly mail. When Jake had opened the letter Alice now had in her hands, he had scanned its contents and then placed it back in the envelope. Then he'd put the letter on top of the rest of the mail, with the sender's address face up, before walking out of the kitchen. Alice unfolded the letter and read it.

> Dear Jake,
>
> Thanks for remembering my birthday. You're a good friend. I just love the diamond Tiffany necklace. It's

gorgeous, and the heart is perfect! Every time I wear the necklace, I'll think of you.

Someone knocked on the door immediately after I opened your gift. When I saw the flowers and Belgian chocolates, I was surprised and delighted. How did you remember they were my very favorite chocolates? What an awesome treat! I truly enjoyed every one of them. Thank you for thinking of me in such a meaningful way. You're the best!

Thanks so much for the lovely gift. I look forward to seeing you soon.

Love,
Jessica

Alice dropped the letter and ran downstairs to confront Jake.

"Why did you buy Jessica a romantic present for her birthday?" Before Jake could answer, she shouted at him. "Jake, you gave me gift vouchers for my birthday! You bought your ex-girlfriend a romantic present. I want an explanation."

"I bought you a Tiffany necklace for Christmas, and you returned it two days later!"

Alice let out all her pent-up anger. She reminded Jake that he had bought her the necklace out of guilt. It had been an appeasement for the commitment he had failed to make to her once again.

"How could you buy Jessica a romantic gift and give me gift vouchers?"

"I didn't buy you a present for your birthday because we had argued. Don't you remember? We weren't talking for two days before your birthday."

Alice knew Jake was right on that point, but it did not matter. "That doesn't make it right for you to buy Jessica a romantic gift. What does it say about your feelings for me?"

Jake tried to explain that the two events were unrelated. He told Alice that on one of the occasions when he had eaten lunch with Jessica, she had been emotional and talked about taking her life. They had talked at length, and eventually, she'd acknowledged that she needed professional help to cope with losing her babies. Jessica had said that she had no family, and when she saw babies, young moms, or kids being pushed in strollers in the street, she would start crying. Losing her babies, coupled with not having a career, was also causing self-esteem issues.

"I thought it would make her feel better about herself if I gave her a nice present for her birthday. I was trying to help her."

"So you put her feelings before mine?"

Jake's patience ran out. "Fuck you. I did nothing wrong." He picked up his telephone and wallet, grabbed his coat, and walked out of the house. "I did nothing wrong!" he repeated on his way out the door.

"You never do anything wrong, Jake! It was an inappropriate gift. Can't you see that?"

"Fuck you."

With that, he slammed the door.

✦   ✦   ✦

New York, two days later

Alice had tried to convince Edward she was OK, but her attempt to disguise her unsettledness when speaking to him early that morning had been poor. When she'd declined to have lunch with him later in the week or in the early part of the following week, she had raised his suspicion that something was wrong. Edward called her again, and she agreed reluctantly to meet him at Molto restaurant and wine bar for dinner.

Alice sat at the bar, staring into her glass. Edward greeted her. He did not sit down, because upon his entry into the restaurant, he had planned for them to sit in a booth.

"I'm guessing your melancholy was brought on by Jake," Edward said. "Talk to me. I promise not to say, 'I told you so.'"

As Alice brought Edward up to speed on Jake's most recent deplorable behavior, Edward stared at her in disbelief.

"When I read the letter, Jake's act of cruelty and deceit reverberated to the core of my being," she said.

"Are you saying that after the way Jake has treated you, the letter was a shock? Is that what you're expecting me to believe?"

"No! For a while now, I have had a sense of foreboding. My denial was stupid. I refused to admit the truth. The clock did not stop ticking. It was only a matter of time before Jake committed the ultimate act of betrayal."

Alice already had one foot out the door. She was looking for confidence to take out the other foot and run. The beginning of the end had already begun. She was not shocked, just disappointed.

Alice lifted her head and looked into Edward's eyes. She would not make excuses for staying. For her, it came down to a line she had drawn. In every relationship, couples drew lines, but the lines were rarely the same for both parties. Sometimes a line was discernible only if one partner crossed it. Jake was touching Alice's line, but he had yet to cross it.

"Where did you draw the line, Alice?" Edward asked.

"It's simple. It was intimacy in the beginning. If I discovered Jake had had sex with another woman, the relationship was finished."

"Why did you move the goalposts?"

"Jake's childish, clandestine, and cruel behavior."

Alice reminded Edward of the week of the New York bar examination in July. Where had Jake's respect for her feelings been? Why had he not cut her some slack and given some consideration to the stress she was under because of the upcoming exam? He'd led her to believe he had stayed with Jessica the entire night. That night and the days that followed had been stressful. Alice had been unable to sleep.

"I arrived at the examination center and was refused admission because I didn't have identification. My passport was in Connecticut."

Jake had not had sex with Jessica. He had stayed at his New York apartment. She had seen enough texts and emails prior to that night, the following day, and subsequently to know that what Jessica had wanted to happen had not happened. Jake understood that if the other person was not on the same page, it was cruel to have a one-night stand, and he and Jessica certainly were not on the same page. Where Jessica was concerned, he had come to realize the responsibility that came with sex. He cared enough about her not to hurt her in that way.

It could have been a play on words, but it had upset Alice when Jake explained that he had not slept with Jessica because he did not want to give her false hope. Alice would have felt better if his reasoning had been that he was in a loving relationship with her.

Alice tried to explain why she had stayed. It was easy for someone like Edward, on the outside looking in, to say what she should or should not do. Alice recounted how many times she or another person had repeated the words "There are plenty more fish in the sea." But she did not want to go fishing; she had caught her fish. He had not had sex with Jessica, so he would live to fight another day.

She looked at Edward. She had seen that expression before. He would not let this rest until he had a narrative in relation to the events surrounding the birthday gift to Jessica. She could see the letter was bugging him.

In hindsight, Alice was able to refer to her birthday to try to explain, not justify, Jake's behavior. Prior to her birthday, Jake had called to say he would be late because he was having dinner with colleagues. Alice could not explain why, but something he had or had not said had made her suspicious. Maybe she had seen a text message. She asked Edward to accept that she realized Jake was lying to her. Her suspicions about Jake had been raised during the telephone conversation. Jake had not been able to reassure her that he was having dinner with colleagues. Alice had questioned him, and consequences had followed.

Jessica had become passive; she would take the financial handouts and whatever time Jake could spare for her. She did not question

Jake, so she had received jewelry, flowers, and chocolates. Alice had challenged Jake's veracity—a wrong move. Jake had punished Alice by deliberately ignoring her birthday. She subsequently had received a belated birthday present: gift vouchers from a store in which she shopped on rare occasions.

"There were many things that should have pushed me over the edge," she said. "That was the one that made me see red. When I finished reading the letter, something inside me died. From that point on, our relationship has not been the same. Jake has extinguished what remained of our innocent love. He has no idea how much he hurt me."

Edward squeezed her hand tightly. "Jake has a twisted view of right and wrong. In fact, he has no regard at all for right and wrong. He will always disregard your wishes and feelings. My dear friend, run, and don't stop."

Going forward, it would not be easy, but Jake was living in New York and coming home occasionally on the weekends to play golf. Alice had done the work and vowed to take the New York bar at the next sitting and then either go home or find an apartment in New York.

58

New York, two days later

Jessica was seated on the sofa in Beth's office. Once again, she had refused to allow Steve to attend the session. She was agitated. Her demeanor had become one of the key and visible indicators that she had not come alone.

Beth wrote on her notepad, "Ninety percent confident of Jessica's diagnosis—second opinion before acting."

Jessica, you must tell Beth to fuck off. She'll put you in a hospital for insane people if Steve confirms you're crazy. Remember, you told Jake you were insane in that email. An admission is all they need. Tell Beth to go fuck herself.

"Jess, I need help." Jessica's eyes darted to her clasped hands.

Beth smiled and scribbled on her notepad: "Confirmed that the other identity is present." She said, "Yes, Jessica, you need help. Is it Jess who doesn't want Steve to observe?"

"Fuck you, Beth! Jessica doesn't need your help!" Jess shouted.

"Jess, this is Beth. I can help you both."

"I know who you are," Jess replied. "I don't need your fucking help."

Beth had recorded the parts of the conversation in which Jess had been vocal. Jessica was silent for the moment, a signal that Jess was gone.

Jessica, I'm out of here. You talk to that bitch if it helps you. If you fuck with me, those fucking eggs stay on ice.

Jessica told Beth that the past weekend was probably the meanest Jake had ever been to her.

Jessica! That's a lie. You should tell Beth about the horrible actions he inflicted on me and you. Yes, tell the bitch. Perhaps it'll remind you why you need me.

Jessica became agitated again and was too scared to answer Jess. Jess caused her head to hurt if she upset her. Jessica continued by correcting what she had just said to Beth.

"There were other occasions when Jake caused me severe pain, but this weekend came close to the meanest Jake has ever been to me."

"Tell me about the other occasions," Beth said.

Jessica said that by far, the worst act Jake had ever done had been leaving her at the altar on their wedding day. The second horrible act had been leaving her with a baby and forcing her to give it up.

Beth started her reply by saying it did not make what Jake had done right, but to enable her to get a full picture, she needed to know whether Jessica had had any indication that Jake would not show up for the wedding.

The bitch is trying to blame you and make out that it's your fault.

Jessica did not hesitate. "No! What sane person does that to someone he claims to love?"

"So you don't believe he loved you?" Beth asked.

She's trying to fucking trap you! Don't answer.

Beth had refreshed her knowledge of dissociative identity disorder. From that update, she was aware that the alters, or different identities, could have their own age, sex, or race. Each also had his or her own posture, gestures, and distinct way of talking. Now she understood how Jessica might have concealed Jess during her childhood as her imaginary friend or animal. Beth also had discovered that as each personality revealed itself, it controlled the individual's behavior and thoughts by switching. The switching could take anywhere from seconds to days.

After a silence, Beth asked Jessica if Jake had been the father of her baby.

"Jessica is not answering that question!" Jess shouted. "It's none of your fucking business who Jessica was fucking!"

Beth studied Jessica's facial features carefully. Although Jess had replied, Jessica looked terrified. She presumed that the intervals of switching were seconds apart and at Jess's behest to prevent Jessica from revealing information that would help with her diagnosis and treatment. The pained expression could also have been on account of Jess's voice in her head.

Jessica shook her head from side to side in reply. "Beth, can we change the subject? Your questions are upsetting and cause offense." She mumbled, "Can't anger Jess. Jess is the only person who can get me a baby."

"Sorry, but I didn't hear the last part of what you said."

"I said that it doesn't matter whether Jake has been drinking or not; he's abusive toward me. One day he loves me. The next day, he acts like he hates me. It is damaging me mentally."

Beth chose to ignore Jess's earlier intervention. She knew the process of getting both identities to trust her could be slow. "Jessica, why do you refuse to let Jake go?"

Jessica said she could not forget what she had been through. "I'm not giving Jake permission to leave after all that has happened, and I'll never forget it until he makes it right. I believe that is the only way I'll be whole."

"Pursuing Jake, holding him responsible for your happiness, is not the only way to get your life back," she said. "You have to take control of your life."

That's the first sensible piece of advice that bitch has offered, Jess said. *You need to get your head out of your ass and call the bank. I can call for you. We don't have much money, and you don't have your baby.*

"I was hurt by the first abortion that Jake wanted me to have. I've buried that pain so deeply that I only have a numb feeling. It's disturbing that I'm experiencing the pain now so long after the event. It was only recently that I started grieving. It's difficult to explain. The second abortion was so traumatic that the pain of it superseded the first," said Jessica.

You're making me sick, Jess said. *Get the fuck out of this office. You aborted the babies. Live with it. Stop feeling sorry for yourself. Call the fucking bank, and make Jake give you his fucking sperm.*

Beth struggled to hide her shock at the revelation. She wrote on her notepad, "Explanation for Jessica's constant reference to babies—two abortions." She asked, "Jessica, did you have two abortions?"

59

J ake could not help asking himself how he had arrived at his current situation. His relationship with Alice was falling apart. On each occasion when he had gone back to Connecticut to make amends, Alice had appeared indifferent to his presence. Why could she not understand that he felt responsible for Jessica's well-being and that his concern for Jessica was charitable and purely platonic?

Jake was in his New York apartment, sprawled out on the sofa with a beer bottle in his hand. His anger had subsided. Still, why had Jessica lied about her age? She had dated him on and off for five years, and it had never occurred to her to come clean. He contemplated what else she had lied about.

Jake held that thought. Did he really care about Jessica, or was he merely carrying around unjustified guilt perpetuated by her continual emotional blackmail? Jessica misinterpreted every act of benevolence. He thought about the multiple text messages and calls he received daily. He was alone in his apartment and could not turn on his phone, or he would receive a flood of abuse from her. He had to accept that he was mishandling the situation. He was haunted by the events of that Friday when Alice had confronted him about the gifts to her and Jessica for their respective birthdays. He was struggling to get a grip on the problem. The person he wished he could call or text remained aloof. Finally, he walked over to his computer to check his email.

There was the usual onslaught of emails from work, which he processed quickly. He was about to shut down his computer, when an email from Jessica hit his inbox. Jake hesitated. He did not open it. He could not take much more of the emotional crap and was on the verge of imploding. *The fucking nightmare must stop.* His thoughts were broken by his flashing phone. He grabbed at it to power if off but inadvertently answered the incoming call. His finger hovered over the End Call icon for a few seconds. He heard Jessica's voice.

"I'm trying to understand why you humiliated me in the bank's reception area on Friday," she said.

When Jake did not respond immediately, she added, "Your behavior was a living nightmare all over again."

Jake took a deep breath and exhaled. "Sorry I embarrassed you, but you can't show up at my place of work or house unannounced." He leaned back on the sofa and put the phone on the armrest but grabbed it when he heard a female voice scream.

"Jessica, he ignored you!"

"Jessica? Who was that?"

"Don't change the subject. You knew the security guards were within earshot. Fuck! You asked if we had met before. How could you say, 'Sorry, lady, but I don't know you'?" Jessica did not pause to catch her breath. "I didn't deserve to be treated that way, and you have no idea how painful it was to hear you talk like that. Your words were unnecessarily mean. They sounded like acid in my ears."

Frustrated, Jake tapped his fingers on the sofa arm. What he had said had not registered with her. He repeated, "You can't show up at my place of work or house unannounced."

"Words hurt, and you've never been crueler and more heartless. It was shocking and below the belt, even for you. I don't deserve that kind of treatment from you. In fact, nobody on the planet does. Your behavior was seriously wrong! I don't think I can explain how sickening it was."

Stop! He put a hand over his chest. He massaged it and forced himself to breathe deeply.

"You can't answer any calls? You can't speak to me in person? How do you let somebody call you over and over without addressing it? It's fucked-up behavior. It's abuse."

"Not true," he replied.

"You have no idea how your selfish indifference hurts. I should be used to your behavior. The tightness in my chest it gives me, the nausea, the anxiety, and the total drowning feeling are things I've experienced multiple times. For some fucked-up reason, dealing with your behavior never gets easier. Being murdered emotionally is the same over and over again. It hurts! Like hell on earth."

"Excuse me? I give you tightness in your chest? Do you think I'm sitting here laughing?" Jake realized the conversation was devolving into a pointless argument. He took another deep breath, exhaled, and said, "You and I have discussed countless times, in a way that is very painful, that we want different things. The conflict in terms of wanting different things is not something that is reconcilable." He paused as he regulated his breathing to ease the pain he was experiencing in his chest. "I'm sorry for past mistakes, but given our irreconcilable differences, it doesn't make any sense for you and me to be in a relationship."

Jessica's voice whined when she said, "What about me? What about what I want? I know you're capable of understanding. You're the man I want to take care of me. We can work this out, but you don't call or return my calls. How do you think that makes me feel? No wonder I walk around crying all the time."

He clenched his fists to suppress his anger. "Stop, Jessica. It's too late. I don't trust your motives, and it's clear your behavior toward me isn't as much because of how you feel about me as it is about the fact that your other options didn't work out. In essence, I'm a backup plan for you. You and I have dated on and off for several years. We've had our time, but the relationship didn't work. I've moved on, and you need to do the same. How can I get you to accept that? There's no future for us. You must look forward, not back." He heard her sob. "Once again, I'm sorry I upset you and hope we can be friends going forward."

"Every time you hurt me, I swear it's the last time, but you always get me again. Why do you do it? I don't understand. You ignore me like I don't exist. How would you feel if someone did that to you? You make me feel horrible. I feel unworthy of happiness, like a loser, and as if nobody loves me. Your attitude and behavior toward me suck. What did I do? Nothing. Nothing!"

The line was quiet. He did not reply. It was apparent that Jessica was oblivious to the fact that she was engaged in a one-sided conversation.

"Jake, you're going to right the wrongs you've inflicted on me. Jess promises that if you don't, it'll get ugly. Jake, do you hear me? Fuck you!"

As he moved his right index finger over the phone icon to end the call, he heard glass breaking, followed by the voice he had heard earlier in their conversation.

"Jessica, you're fucking unhinged! Another fucking mess for me to clean up."

60

eth played the recording of her recent sessions with Jessica. Steve asked if she had been able to confirm that Jessica had had two abortions. Beth replied that she had not.

"I need confirmation on my diagnosis," Beth said. "Jess, the other identity, is getting stronger. She's helping Jessica cope with life's dilemmas. Any reference made to her abortion, or abortions, or any other stressful event triggers a sudden shift from one alter, Jessica, to the other, Jess. There will come a point when I won't be able to medicate Jessica." Beth was of the opinion that if that happened, they would lose Jessica. "We can't force Jess to medicate. At this point, there's no evidence that Jessica is a danger to herself or others. Can you see my dilemma?"

"Is Jess violent?"

"Not to my knowledge, but she's abusive and destructive in terms of getting Jessica to deal with her trauma. I'm worried about Jessica."

"There's no known history of trauma or abuse in her childhood?"

"No, but I suspect from my last session with Jessica and from the information she inadvertently let slip out that she had two abortions, which she perceives as forced terminations."

Beth reiterated that Jessica had been traumatized by the knowledge that through her own hand, she could not have children. She could not process that she was responsible on any level. To help her cope, Jess had emerged. Jessica blamed her ex-partner and refused to move forward.

"It doesn't matter which label we put on her diagnosis. She is severely disturbed," Beth said. "What do we know about the long-term effects of abortions on women?"

"The research is inconclusive," Steve responded.

"Abortion, like miscarriage, can cause severe trauma," Beth said.

"We don't know that. What do we know?" Steve asked. "We know that the causes of dissociative disorders are complex. Studies show that a history of trauma, usually abuse in childhood, is almost always the case for people who have moderate to severe dissociative symptoms. Beth, if we're to go out on a limb with this, we need more information. Can you get her permission for the ex-partner and me to attend one of the sessions?"

Beth told Steve that the ex-partner attending a session was a possibility but that Jessica had made it clear Jess would not tolerate Steve attending any of their sessions. Beth assured him that she would update him but said he had to leave because she was expecting Jessica.

Beth did not have to question Jessica about Jess. They had barely exchanged pleasantries, when Jess made her presence known.

"I don't want to be friends with that fucker Jake. Jessica needs sperm. What the fuck is he talking about? Friends? I hate that nerd. We need money and sperm."

Beth did not reply.

Jessica's contorted face softened. "I'm struggling emotionally and suffer from frequent headaches—I think it's because Jess is stronger, and I can't control her." Jessica had one hand partially over her head and eyes to block out the light emanating from the window. "Jess promised to get me a baby."

"Can you bring me up to date on what has happened since our last session?"

Jessica told Beth that she had written and spoken to Jake after he ignored her in the bank's reception area. Tears fell down her cheeks.

Jessica cried uncontrollably and then stopped suddenly, mumbling to herself, "Jessica, I should kick your ass."

"Jess, stop blaming me. You were careless with that outburst about friendship with Jake."

Beth did a quick check to make sure the conversation was being recorded. She looked startled. Jessica's voice was louder and angry.

"Why the fuck does Jake think Jessica or I want to be his friend? He's Jessica's backup plan? What the fuck is he talking about? Jessica's plan? Is Jake serious? Jessica is a bimbo."

Jessica's face was flushed and tensed. "Jessica, Beth wants to medicate me." The voice fell to an inaudible level. "I need Jessica to get more money from Jake, and then I'll nuke her and that therapist."

Beth observed as Jessica pushed paper facial tissues in her purse and looked at her.

Her voice had softened when she said, "Jake walked past me in the bank's reception area as if he did not know me, and when he replied to my email, he said I viewed him as my insurance policy. It was a total shock, and I'm sad to know he thinks I consider him my last option."

Beth said, "You've often talked about Jake being financially responsible for you."

Jessica, she's tricking you. Get a grip. You don't need to answer that bitch. Tell her to fuck off!

"Beth, since I met Jake, nobody has been the center of my life. Period!"

"What about Tom? I thought he made you happy."

"Yes, I've gone out with other men; that's obvious. There isn't an issue with dating. There're tons of men in this city—they're freaking everywhere—and I get asked out constantly!"

Way to go, Jessica. Tell that bitch we have options.

As Jessica told Beth that she had been asked out multiple times, she described herself as friendly and said that guys always wanted to call her.

Some of the tension went out of Jessica, but it did not last long. She tensed again when she said she hated the idea of going out with guys other than Jake.

You've been forced to date! You forced yourself to date because Jake let you down. Tell the bitch you've been proposed to multiple times by men you just met.

"Why can't you let Jake go?" Beth asked.

It is a trick! The fucking bitch is trying to trick you. Don't answer. Fuck Beth. You don't need her.

"Jess, I'm OK. I can handle this."

Jessica told Beth that she thought of the other men as distractions. She flirted and went out because her friends and family forced her to do so. "What else am I supposed to do? I get lonely. I'm alone and stuck in the city. I'm pathetic and ridiculous. I hate my life and myself."

Speak for yourself, Jess said. *It was my decision to terminate those relationships.*

"I didn't want them to work out," said Jess. "Jessica doesn't know what's good for her, so I terminated the losers she was dating."

"Jess, you have to let me speak," Jessica said. "Yes, there are assholes out there, and I have pretty much figured out now what a lot of these pricks are about. I really never knew until after I met Jake."

You're fucked up, Jessica. Just could not keep your legs closed.

"Jess, I have zero interest in dealing with any bullshit."

Jessica, the doctor said you're too old to freeze eggs. You need a man now. That's why you want Jake back. You don't love him. You want sperm. Beth isn't stupid. She won't say it, so I will.

"I want a monogamous relationship. Jake has never faltered in his love for me. I want a baby."

"Would Jake be willing to attend one of our sessions?"

Don't trust that bitch! She'll tell Jake we want sperm for babies and money.

"No!" Jessica shouted. "Jess, Beth is trying to help us."

61

Greenwich, Connecticut

Alice wrapped Jake's birthday present and signed the card with *XX*. She thought about writing, "For the one I love—you're not perfect, but I love you." *Love?*

She put the pen down and said, "No longer am I turning a blind eye and allowing him to chip away at my self-esteem. I'll take the New York bar exam." She was looking forward—if she established a law practice, getting a green card and an apartment in New York was an attainable goal.

She put her thoughts aside. She was expecting him back in Connecticut that night. They were back on speaking terms but sleeping in separate beds. She had not overlooked that Jake would attempt to rekindle their love. She had no idea how she would react, because she was looking for a fundamental change, not his excuses.

Later, when Alice met Jake at the train station, she did not pull away when he kissed her on the cheek. On the drive to the grocery store, he asked if she would like to have dinner for his birthday the following night. Alice's anger toward him had started to subside, so she agreed and asked if he had a restaurant in mind. He said he would think about it and let her know.

The evening passed without incident, and life seemed to be returning to some semblance of normality. In the morning, Alice gave Jake his birthday present. He appeared genuinely pleased. For the man who had everything, simple things in life—such as a T-shirt in his favorite color and a pair of running shorts that replicated his favorite shorts, which had seen better days—made him happy. Alice had scored on both counts. When Jake kissed her goodbye that morning, his outward appearance was happy, and he seemed to be looking forward to their dinner later that evening.

Seven o'clock came and went. Jake had not called to say which train he would be catching so Alice could pick him up at the station. He had not sent a text saying he was delayed at work either. Alice's frustration mounted.

Seven thirty came. She reached over to the table for her phone to call Jake but was distracted by a knock at the door. She opened it, and on the doorstep was a lady with blonde hair. It took several seconds before her brain registered who it was.

Jessica!

Jessica did not wait to be invited inside. She opened the screen door, pushed past Alice, and threw her bag onto the armchair in the front reception room.

"Where's Jake? And who are you?"

Alice was surprised by Jessica's hostile disposition but quickly regained her composure. "I'm Alice, Jake's partner. Are you Jessica?"

"Yes!"

"Fuck! Did you know he had installed the London bitch?" Jess asked Jessica.

"Sorry—did you say something?" Alice asked.

"No," Jessica replied quietly. She mumbled, "I must deflect Jess. She doesn't do diplomacy. If she thinks I'm handling the situation, she'll have no reason to intervene."

Alice stared at Jessica, who appeared panicked and was muttering. "Are you OK? I'm sorry, but I didn't catch what you said."

Jessica picked up her bag. She mumbled, "Jess, I've got this." She spoke to Alice as she turned toward the kitchen. "You're English, right? I guess American English is your second language, and you struggle with it. Where's Jake?" she asked a second time as she continued into the kitchen. "We're having dinner tonight. It's his birthday. I have his present right here." She spoke to Alice as if there were no chance she knew it was Jake's birthday. "Don't make me ask again. Where's Jake? What have you done with him?"

Jessica's face softened when Alice did not reply. "You don't know where he is, do you?"

Alice thought she behaved as if they had something in common. Jake was playing them both.

Jessica removed her phone from her bag and called Jake. She gawked at Alice as she waited for the call to connect. Alice realized the phone had not connected when Jessica pulled the phone away from her ear.

"Jake told me he wasn't in a relationship. We're supposed to be having dinner tonight." Her voice dropped to a barely audible mumble. "I'm not whining. Jess, no! Don't take over—I've got this." Jessica's face contorted. She appeared to be in some sort of pain.

"Are you OK?" Alice asked again. When Jessica did not answer, she picked up the landline and called Jake. The phone rang twice before he answered. She asked if he was OK. "Are you coming back to Connecticut tonight? Jessica is at the house."

"What?" he replied. "I will call you back."

Alice replaced the receiver and looked up as Jessica stepped forward. Shock registered on Jessica's face, presumably because Jake had picked up.

"Jess, Jake is calling."

Alice looked over her shoulder. For a second, she thought somebody had entered the room. She turned her head back when she realized Jessica was talking to herself; her face was beaming.

"Yes!" Jessica said with a raised voice.

Alice observed her strange behavior and backed slowly away from Jessica. *Do I need a weapon?* she thought. What would work? Her eyes cut to the desk. There was a heavy paperweight. *Maybe I can get over there.*

"Happy birthday, babe," Jessica said. "What happened? We were supposed to meet for dinner tonight. I brought you a birthday present."

Jessica continued talking to Jake as if they were lovers. Alice could see that Jessica's eyes had a deadness, a glint that scared her to the core.

Careful to keep her face impassive, Alice moved toward the desk.

"Jessica, get out of my house now!" Jake said. "If you don't leave now, I'm calling the police."

Although Alice was not holding the cell phone, she heard Jake shout at Jessica.

The shrill of the landline made her jump. Jessica had hung up, and her face was bewildered.

Taking one step over, Alice picked up the ringing phone.

Jake said, "I'm so sorry. Call me if she doesn't leave." The line went dead.

Alice's eyes darted back to Jessica when she heard her talking to Jess. Alice maintained her focus on Jessica as she replaced the receiver. She stepped back and, with her hand lowered and pointing in the direction of the door, indicated that Jessica should leave. "Please leave."

Alice tensed when Jessica raised a hand, pulled her purse off her shoulder, placed it on the table, and burst into tears. Within seconds, her crying turned to hysteria.

"Sh. Sh." Alice stepped toward her to console her but quickly backed away. *Throwing her out is not going to be easy.*

"Jake made me murder my babies."

Alice's outward display of sympathy dissipated and was replaced by anger. That was not what she needed to hear. Painful memories flooded back about her miscarriage. She did not want to hear about Jessica's abortion. *Did she say* babies? "You had two abortions?"

"Yes. Jake made me have two abortions. My babies are dead."

"Jake told me it wasn't his baby. The baby you aborted—was it his?"

The pitch of Jessica's sobs increased. "No."

Alice was appalled. "You are looking for sympathy," she muttered under her breath.

Jake's most recent email had renewed Jessica's confidence. He had said he wanted to be friends. As far as she was concerned, that was a start. Jess had a different opinion, which she refused to dismiss, but friendship was a start. After Jake's birthday, she would talk to him about having therapy sessions. Why had she not thought of it before? Relationship counseling—that was all they needed. She spent the day shopping for Jake's birthday present. She also sent several text messages to him about having dinner that night. This was the story of her life; everything had gone south.

Jessica!

Jessica heard Jess but ignored her.

Jessica, you stupid bitch!

"I can't hear you!"

Yes, you can, you stupid fuck. I'll say this once and once only. Jake is not coming to your fucking birthday dinner, and we don't want Alice's pity. Get your head in the game. Do you comprehend?

"I can't hear you."

You will hear me. It will be my decision whether to save your fucking ass. Get your head in the game!

Jessica's face contorted. "Jake doesn't want you in his life. Why are you still here? He said you were going back to England."

"Why did you continue chasing Jake after he jilted you at the altar? It seems to me you're the one he doesn't want in his life," Alice said with discernable anger in her voice. "You've no right to come into this house uninvited and speak to me in this manner—please leave."

Jessica did not respond. Instead, tears began to fall from her eyes. Alice's face was aghast.

"Let me set the record straight," Jessica said, raising her voice. "Jake did not jilt me at the altar. The relationship was not working. I wanted out and divorced him shortly after we married."

Jessica stared at Alice, waiting for her to react to what she had just revealed. Initially, she thought Alice looked confused, as if something she had said did not add up, and then Alice's face registered disgust.

Alice said, "Why didn't you keep the baby, given your age and the fact that you wanted so desperately to have children? And you had a second abortion?" she asked softly. "For all of Jake's faults, he would have accepted financial responsibility for his child."

Get some wine, Jessica, and get out. The bitch is on to you.

Alice asked Jessica if the second baby had also belonged to someone other than Jake.

Jess had had enough. "It's none of your fucking business."

When Alice stepped back, Jess smiled with satisfaction. She stepped forward. Alice's fear that she might harm her registered on her face.

Alice took another step back and said, "I did not intend to offend you." Her voice was a little shaky. "I asked because I don't want to be with a man who would leave a woman at the altar while she was carrying his baby."

Jess saw an opportunity to get rid of the London bitch. *Jessica, if we play the jilting at the altar and the abortion right, Alice will hate Jake and go back to London.*

Before Jess could seize the opportunity to deal with the situation, Jessica informed Alice that the second baby had not been Jake's either. Jessica felt pleased with herself. She was sure by the stunned expression on Alice's face that she believed Jake had married her. She had saved her dignity in relation to being jilted at the altar.

The paternity of the babies was a fundamental detail to leave out, and Alice could not resist asking, "What woman in her right mind would expect a man to be father to a child who was not his, given the deceitful circumstances?"

"I told Jake that he wasn't the father. That's why we argued and eventually divorced."

You stupid bitch! Jess screamed. She could not believe what she had just heard. *I'll deal with you later. Get the wine, and get the fuck out.*

As a means of misdirection, Jessica told Alice she had decorated the house. "Did Jake tell you? This is all my furniture." Jessica bragged that it all had been her idea. "I bet Jake didn't tell you we used to cook together either." Jessica went to the kitchen to grab one of the cookbooks, walking around the house as if it were hers and as if Alice were merely a guest. She returned with the Jamie Oliver cookbook Alice had bought Jake for Christmas.

"Give me your telephone number," Jessica said. "We can stay in touch. You may need a shoulder to cry on one day soon."

She went to a drawer, opened it, and searched for a pen. Jessica came across Jake's gun. She stroked it but left it in situ; she had to remain focused on continuing the conversation with Alice while she believed she had the upper hand. Alice let out a sigh of relief when Jessica removed only a pen from the drawer. The gun did not escape Jess's attention, though. She was interested in the plan going forward.

Jessica handed the pen and a piece of paper to Alice.

Take the gun, Jessica.

"What is Jake doing with this gun?" Jessica asked, holding it up. "I told him not to keep it in the house. Let me dispose of it for you." She put the gun in her bag. "Write your cell number." It was an order, not a request.

Alice's hesitation was visible, but she wrote down her number. Jessica entered it into her phone and then called Alice to see if the number was correct.

Jessica smiled. "Now you have my number too." She walked over to the wine fridge and removed two bottles of Jake's nine-hundred-dollar wine. "Jake owes me. Bye, Alice. Nice meeting you."

Jessica and Jess discussed the situation as they walked to Amanda's car.

Jessica, you need to email Jake and set him straight. Tonight was unacceptable. I'll help with the situation. We'll deal with Jake first. As a matter of fact, it's better if I write the email. Just stay off those fucking pills.

Jessica was in no mood to argue. Her eggs would not stay frozen forever. Had the doctor said ten months or ten years? Either way, Jessica did not feel she could take the risk. Given her age, the quality of the eggs she had frozen could not be guaranteed. Chances were she would have to defrost several eggs. She would work on ten months.

Jessica thought Jess was distracted by Amanda's babbling about having to wait so long while Jessica was in the house. Jessica had asked her to wait so she could drop Jake and her off at the restaurant. As Amanda talked, Jessica sent a text message to Jake.

"Why do you think disappearing is OK?"

"I don't," Jake replied, "but being backed into something you're not comfortable with is wrong and unfair. So is having your concerns met with attacks or crying."

Jessica! Jess shouted. *I told you I'd deal with this situation. Back off. Cross me one more time, and I'm done. You're out of here. Do you fucking understand?*

Seconds after they stepped into Amanda's house, Jess's eyes darted around the room for a computer. After getting Amanda's permission to use it, she sat down in front of it.

Get out of the way. I'm writing this email. You fucked up big-time tonight.

Jessica's head hurt. She gave way to Jess.

Jake,

You're so rude. Jessica backed you into seeing her? Is that a joke? You wanted to see Jessica! How about this, Jake? Learn how not to lie to Jessica or yourself. Learn! Grow up!

Back up here, why don't you, Jake? Is it my fault Jessica got pregnant twice? Do you think that didn't affect me? You think I'm supposed to be fine? To be normal now? Do you understand that has severely hurt Jessica? I'm doing pretty fucking well, considering you deeply and permanently hurt Jessica. Do you get that, you stupid asshole? Do you think I should be skipping down the street all day long? I'm struggling hard to get through the abuse you inflicted on Jessica! Sorry, but it's normal to have a hard time because of the trauma you put us through!

Jessica has fucking dissociative identity disorder (DID). That's what bitch Beth thinks. Jessica's DID is because of what you put her through! She's in serious therapy with that bitch. Jessica is totally alone. Fuck you. I'm not her friend. Don't even think it. She will never get over your abuse—never! She's so weak. I have no choice but to nuke her. I suffer every single minute of every single goddamned day. Jessica cries constantly. What you see is nothing!

Jessica can't work. She dreams about some amazing career. Then there are the babies. Why the fuck did you waste money on freezing eggs? Jessica is so screwed up; she can't look after babies. But you'll give her babies if it's the last thing you do. I'll shoot the fucking sperm out of you if I have to. We're not dealing with this alone. No fucking way. It's your fault! Jessica didn't get pregnant and leave you! You left her alone! You! And you kept coming back for more, telling her you cared about her and giving her hope and signs that we were going to get back together. Stop being an asshole, the liar that you can never stop being! Stop lying! You're such scum! You asshole! I know you told Jessica you didn't want kids, but Jessica wants them. Fuck you! Somebody needs to kill you!

Tonight Jessica just wanted to have fucking dinner. And you're such a weak pussy, a spineless coward, that you can't even be a fucking man and fucking show up or call—not even call! Who the fuck acts like that? You are a fucking douche bag—a loser, idiot, asshole, and piece of trash! You're a complete piece of garbage to treat us to more of your sick manipulation, lies, and bullshit games. We don't deserve to be abused and lied to!

You should be fucking arrested, you psycho, lying piece of trash. You have no goddamned balls and no goddamned manners! Go fuck yourself, Jake Logan. You really can't ever be a fucking gentleman, can you? It's literally impossible.

You are ugly inside. Evil! A hateful, ungodly, evil, sick man. Get mental help, and learn some goddamned manners. You're sick. I just noticed how you basically hate all the women in your life. Clearly, you hate us. You don't love Jessica at all.

Have a great night! Kisses! Love you! You're the best! How did Jessica get so lucky to find somebody like you?

Asshole! XOXOX

In Jessica's head, it felt as if Jess had brought her friends around to party. She could hear only people screaming and shouting. She could not think straight. This was not the time to party. She had to find a way to defrost her eggs.

✦   ✦   ✦

Jessica called Alice and asked her if she had spoken to Jake. "Now that you know we're still in a relationship, what are your plans? Jake and I are having IVF."

Alice had heard enough. "That's nice, Jessica. You don't have to concern yourself about me. I'm going back to England. I wish you a good night." She ended the call.

Score!

Jess was happy. Jessica appeared to be getting her act together. It was a shame she would have to go.

62

A lice walked around the house, locking all the doors and windows. She was not sure whether to feel hostility or pity toward Jessica. The woman she had observed had appeared unbalanced and, at times, dangerous. *The gun!* Alice picked up her phone and sent Jake a text: "Jessica has taken your gun and two bottles of expensive wine."

Seconds later, Jake replied, "I'm sorry for what happened. Are you OK?"

Alice put her head down on the pillow and tried to sleep, but no matter how hard she tried, she could not make the terrible ordeal she had experienced go away. Her eyes filled with tears. It was time to go home.

She drifted off to sleep, but the ring of her telephone brought her back.

"Alice, it's Jessica."

"It's late. What do you want? I thought you said all there was to say, and I've made my position clear." Alice sat up suddenly. "Where are you? It sounds like you're outside. Where's your friend? When you left the house earlier, you mentioned your friend Amanda was waiting in the car." *Is she outside the house?* Alice rushed over to a window.

"Jake canceled my authority to use the cab service on his account.

It's expensive to get a car back to New York. I shouldn't have to spend my money on a car."

But it's OK to make Jake pay without prior permission? For a split second, Alice considered calling the police. *What would I say? If she's outside, she's not causing a disturbance. I found her strange, and at times, I was frightened, but she didn't physically threaten me. What's my complaint?* She thought about the gun. *It's Jake's responsibility to report the gun stolen.* She ducked down. *I don't want her to see me.* She crouched down with her back against the wall. *Did I lock the doors? Yes—did I?* She made her way downstairs to check.

"Can you stay with your friend?"

"Yes. I don't have any choice. But right now, I can't stay in the house with Amanda's kids screaming in my head. I will go back after she has put them to bed."

The night seemed long. Jake did not come home for his birthday dinner. Alice slept on and off. She climbed out of bed at five o'clock in the morning, having decided it was a waste of time to try to sleep and wash away the events of the previous night. She had tried but could not recognize Jake as Jessica described him or understand why his relationship with her had ever left first base. Jake was not totally without blame. He had done nothing to defend Alice from Jessica, and he had made no effort to come home when he realized the horrible situation. Now he was letting this crazy woman run her out of town.

This is not me being a jealous bitch. Something is seriously wrong with Jessica. Alice was curious whether Jake had ever heard her talking to Jess. Alice pondered whether it was her fault—if she could have done something differently. She had not sought an explanation from Jake as to why he had continued to see Jessica or tried to help him understand that by not moving on, he was harming Jessica. Bottom line, she had not demanded that Jake stop seeing Jessica. But she told herself that on countless occasions, she had told Jake that where Jessica was concerned, he was playing with fire. It was one thing for Jake to be saddled with his crazy ex-girlfriend, but to leave Alice to deal with the fallout was quite another. No, dealing with Jessica was too much. *There's no reason for me to hang around. I'll call Victoria later and ask if I can leave my things at her house for the shippers to collect.* She was ready to go home.

She called the airline to book her flight to England. Her hands trembled as she removed the credit card from her wallet and read the numbers to the agent. With the flight booked, she sat and stared at the name on the card: Jake Logan. He had given it to her to use at will until her card arrived. Alice had not slept well last night, and she attributed her nervousness to that. She thought the alternative was untenable. *I love him and don't want to go home, but I don't have a choice.* A tear rolled down her cheek. She wiped it away with the back of her hand and called the shipping company.

Feeling depressed, alone, and tired, Alice crawled back into bed, but she did not get the peace she sought. The phone rang.

"Alice, it's Jessica. Has Jake called? He isn't taking my calls. When are you leaving for London?"

Alice told Jessica she had shipping arrangements to finalize. She was hoping to leave Friday. Jessica asked why she could not check extra baggage.

"Is Jake paying for the flight and shipping? He'll hurt you if you stay. Jake and I are trying to work things out—rekindle our love."

"Is your relationship intimate?" Alice asked.

"Yes," Jessica replied hesitantly. "No."

"Yes or no?" Alice said. She realized she could be winding Jessica up but did not care.

"It's not about sex, you fucking bitch," Jess replied.

Before the line went dead, Alice heard, "Jess!" and then "Shut the fuck up. I warned you."

Alice's phone pinged. Jessica had sent a text message: "Sorry. I didn't mean to be rude. I'm so stressed. I'm worried that Jake won't attend our IVF appointment."

Alice switched off her phone and unplugged the landline. She had not slept the previous night, and she had no desire to deal with texts or emails from Jessica or Jake.

The next day, when she opened her eyes, Jake was sitting on the end of the bed, staring at her. He smiled. He was holding two cups of Starbucks coffee and reached over to hand one to her.

"We need to talk," he said. "I read your text message. Jessica was not honest with you. The things she said aren't true. Jessica's babies were not mine. I did not marry her or get her pregnant. I did not arrange to have dinner with her on the night of my birthday. I have not had sex with her and did not agree to go to her IVF appointments. I could go on and on."

Alice swung her legs off the bed and accepted the coffee. "Even if I could move beyond your denials, when the dust settles, you will still be chasing Jessica and lying to me. We've been here too many times before."

"Please don't leave." He moved closer to her and placed a hand on her thigh. "I'm very sorry and can't begin to explain myself. I obviously have made grievous errors, and words can't begin to express how sorry I am. You've been nothing but kind, loving, and considerate. I'm not trying to make excuses about my failings, but at a minimum, I owe you an explanation."

Alice sipped her coffee and did not look at him.

"How did we get into this position?" he said.

She looked up suddenly. "We!"

"It was poor character on my part and a lack of courage, which I guess go hand in hand. When Jessica reemerged nine months ago—after she went away with a guy who I think is a CIA officer—she was in a tough spot and wanted to get back together."

Alice gently pulled her leg away, separating it from Jake's hand. *I've been here before.* She blurted out, "Nothing has changed."

He said that was not accurate. He had not minced his words when he spoke to Jessica and verbalized that their relationship was toxic. His head lowered. "I lacked the courage to tell her I had found someone else, because I didn't want to hurt her any more than I already had." He articulated that Jessica had nothing. "I was worried that finding out about our relationship would push her over the edge. My deception, which is what it was, had nothing to do with fooling around. I was trying to protect her feelings."

"At the expense of my feelings and well-being." Her anger spilled out.

"Clearly, I overlooked your feelings in the process, but I rationalized that it didn't matter, because I was with you. Sorry. That was an error on my part." As time went on, he said, he had seen Jessica periodically for lunch or the occasional dinner, and he had attended counseling with her because she'd assured him she was trying to work through her emotional issues. "I was weak and didn't do the right thing. I'm not trying to justify what was an error of judgment. I'm just trying to explain how I got here. I was doing what I thought was the kind thing to do, but I lacked the courage to do what was really required, and unfortunately, you were hurt in the process. For that, I'm very sorry." He said he cared about Jessica but recognized that he could never be with her. "The relationship between her and me is irreparable, coupled with the fact that she is not always stable, as you, unfortunately, have witnessed."

Alice was still avoiding eye contact with him. She said, "I appreciate your explanation, but what has changed? How is today different from yesterday or the day before that?"

"I wrote an email earlier today that I didn't send, because I didn't think you would answer it. It fell under the category of a Saint Jude email," he said, referring to the patron saint of lost causes. "In essence, while I have no reason for you to reconsider, despite my terrible behavior, I love you, and the thought of not being with you makes me very sad. Please. I only have myself to blame. I'm willing to get married and buy you a ring today. I'd be happy to fly your mother and sisters over to be part of the wedding celebrations. I've thought about getting married a lot. I'm willing to do this now, not next month or next year."

Alice moved her lips from the coffee. "Is this declaration the same as the one made after you moved back to New York without discussing it with me? No." She shook her head. "It sounds more like the special dinner declaration when I gave you cuff links, and minutes later, you snarled at me because you had broken a promise of marriage. Do you even have those cuff links?"

"Despite my behavior, which is inexcusable, I do love you and worry about you."

"Why? I take care of myself."

"I understand why you want to leave. I don't blame you. However, I would regret it for the rest of my life if I didn't come here and ask you to reconsider."

"You didn't answer my question—fundamentally, nothing has changed." She put her coffee down and headed to the bathroom.

63

Wall Street, New York

J ake turned off his phone. He felt he would collapse under
the weight of Jessica's texts and calls. Seconds later, his PA
buzzed and said, "Jessica's on line one."

"Please inform her I'm in a meeting, and hold all calls from her."
He refused to respond to any of her communications; still, she was
relentless. What did he have to do for her to get the message?

As the day went on, she did not stop. She threatened to call
Roberto. Jake could see his new PA, Tracy, whispering with the other
PAs. He no longer had Elle to cover his back.

Her resignation to advance her career is inconvenient!

He turned his mind to the head count and the consequential job
losses. He had watched several members of his team escorted off the
premises. On a good note, he had used the downsizing to purge the
backstabbers. The downside was a smaller team, which meant an
increased workload. He could cope with the demands, but he would
insist that his compensation reflect his efforts. Was the bank's board
deliberately trying to crush his ego?

No! I'm in charge professionally. It's my personal life that's fucked up.

Exhausted, he went back to his apartment at four o'clock. The plan was to regroup and then go out to Connecticut. If he was out of the office, instead of gossiping, Tracy would simply pass the message to Jessica that he was unavailable.

The day following Jake's birthday and Jessica's impromptu visit to Greenwich, Connecticut, Anthony, the bank's in-house counsel, walked into Jake's office and closed the door behind him. The minute the door closed, Tracy walked away from her workstation to gossip.

"Jake, if you want to escalate this and take legal action, we have to be sure we have a case," Anthony said. "Are you sure you want to go down this road?"

Jake was distracted, thinking about how he could get Alice to meet him in New York.

"Stalking is unwanted or obsessive attention by an individual toward another person," Anthony said. "Is Jenny—sorry, Jessica— following or monitoring you? Is that what we have here? How many times has she shown up at the bank? If this is what we have, it's a criminal offense."

"I'm forwarding a recent email from Jessica," Jake said. "FYI, this is one of a hundred emails, texts, and calls I receive from her on a daily basis."

> Subject: Please don't make me suffer anymore!
>
> Jake, I swear to God I think I'm having a heart attack or stroke! Should I go to the hospital? Will you come?

Jake forwarded Anthony his reply as well, marking both as "for internal use only."

> I have nothing to talk to you about and refuse to be manipulated by you. You don't care about me, and I don't want to be blackmailed.

Anthony quoted from the document he held in his hand. He informed Jake that if Jessica was harassing or intimidating Alice or him and that harassment or intimidation was causing substantial emotional distress, he could get Jessica arrested under US stalking laws.

"You said Jessica had been to the Connecticut house and that she had taken your gun," Anthony said, referring to his conversation with Jake earlier that day. "Is that correct? Have you reported the theft?"

"No."

"You need to report the gun missing."

Anthony said Jake would have no problem in pursuing a legal remedy against Jessica. He told Jake to call if he needed any assistance to bring the matter to a close.

Before he left, Anthony tossed a copy of the legislation onto Jake's desk. He agreed with Jake that pursuing legal action against Jessica might push her over the edge. They both thought the sensible course of action would be to use the threat of legal action first, because that might be enough to solve the problem.

New York, two days later

Edward arrived at Colony Grill just after eight thirty in the evening. Alice had had a work-related deadline to meet and was tired after a long day. They had decided to get pizza together for a quick dinner. The waiter led Edward to the booth where he had seated Alice five minutes earlier.

After they ordered drinks and pizza, Edward looked at Alice's left hand. He pointed to the classic three-and-a-half-carat Tiffany diamond ring on Alice's ring finger. "Is that your engagement ring?"

Alice smiled. She removed the ring from her finger and handed it to him so he could inspect it.

She explained that the day Jake had spoken to Anthony about Jessica's stalking, he had called Alice and insisted that as a matter of urgency, she meet him at his New York apartment. That evening, he had come home with his arms filled with red roses, a bottle of champagne, and the engagement ring. He had also made a reservation at the Waverly Inn.

"Maybe on another occasion, I'll tell you the details," Alice said. "For now, I can say the evening was beautiful, and I will always remember it that way." *And too late*, she thought. She was thinking about Jessica when Edward handed the ring back. She put it on the table. *I told Jake to lock his shit down—I did not sign up for Jessica.*

"The day was also memorable for another reason. Jake had received a strange text message from Jessica." Alice showed the message that Jake had forwarded to her to Edward: "Jake, Gemma made Jessica take too many painkillers. Get your fucking ass over here if you don't want her to die. Jess."

"Who's Gemma?" Edward asked.

"Jessica's baby sister. She died when Jessica was a little girl."

"Who's Jess?"

"I don't know. She wrote a vile email to me recently. It came from Jessica's email account."

Alice told Edward she had observed Jessica argue with an imaginary person, Jess, while at the house in Greenwich. "Something wasn't right, and I told Jake to call her. He called Jessica a few times before she answered. She sounded drowsy. My spidey sense told me something was wrong."

"And?" said Edward.

"I said to Jake, 'What are we waiting for? Go. I'll call the ambulance.' I dialed 911 and explained the strange text message and the subsequent calls Jake had made to Jessica and gave Jessica's contact details. I did not feel there was anything more I could do."

In the taxi to Jessica's apartment, Alice said, Jake had called Nathan, Jessica's brother-in-law. In the past, Jessica had shared many of the arguments she'd had with Jake with Susan. Susan had consoled Jessica when Jake jilted her at the altar.

"As a result, Jake has a poor relationship with Susan. It was unlikely she would take his call," said Alice. "Once Jake conveyed to

Nathan what he thought might be happening, Susan agreed to meet Jake at the apartment. Jake arrived before the ambulance. Jessica had taken painkillers and sleeping pills. She was barely conscious. Jake said he forced her to vomit and talk until Susan and the ambulance arrived. Jake told me that Susan gave him a cold stare and said, 'Thank you. We can take it from here.'

"Jake and I learned later that on many occasions, Jessica had ended a conversation with Susan so she could attend a therapy session with Beth. Susan searched Jessica's phone contacts for Beth's number and then called her. I assume that naturally, she would want to get the best treatment for her sister. Jake said the conversation with Beth was brief, but at Beth's request, Jessica was taken to New York Presbyterian Hospital. Beth reassured Susan that New York Presbyterian delivered the best psychiatric care in New York. In fact, Jake said it was ranked among the top four hospitals in the United States for psychiatry."

"What happened to Jessica?" said Edward.

"Oh yes, Jessica. Jake was out of the loop, but he discovered that the doctors had pumped Jessica's stomach to clean out its contents and eliminate the drugs from her system. She was also given activated charcoal to absorb any drugs that remained. Afterward, they observed Jessica for any signs of toxic effects from the two bottles of pills she had consumed.

"After consultation, Beth and the psychiatric department monitored Jessica for twenty-four hours. There was also a debate about her emotional state. Susan wanted Jessica to have an evaluation by a mental health professional before her discharge. Jessica did not want to stay beyond the twenty-four hours.

"Jessica won the debate, and twenty-four hours later, she was discharged. She refused to talk to Beth. I imagine Susan was disappointed. Jake was disgusted that Susan didn't stay around. She hugged her sister goodbye. I guess she realized she could not help her if Jessica did not want to be helped."

Edward signed the bill; they stood up and readied themselves to leave. He bent toward Alice and kissed her lips. She moved closer to him and embraced him to hold the kiss. Several seconds later, she broke away and stared intently into his eyes. *Is it too late for you and me?* He held her stare as he reached to his side, picked up the ring, and dropped it into her purse.

64

Jess finally spoke to Jessica. *I don't want any more sessions with the bitch Beth. She can't help us.*

"Jess, Jake won't talk to me since you sent that email. I call and text him a hundred times a day."

Stupid bitch! He didn't call you before I sent the email either, Jess said.

Then a different voice said, *Jessica, you need to be around people who love you.*

Jessica recognized the new voice immediately. It was her baby sister.

"Gemma?" she called. "Is that you, Gemma? I've accepted the fact that Jake doesn't want me now, especially if I have a child."

Why do I have to deal with you? Jess shouted. She wanted to make Jessica's head hurt. *You haven't accepted that he doesn't want you. Fact! He hasn't wanted you for a while. He never wanted you.*

Tears rolled down Jessica's face.

Jessica, I can't take this crap. Why the fuck is Gemma involved in this? If you wanted her in your life, you shouldn't have pushed her into the stream.

"It was an accident."

Accident? Then why did Mom and Dad shout at you? You didn't look out for your sister. If you couldn't look out for your baby sister, how are you planning to look after a baby?

"I would raise a baby by myself. I really would. I have savings, all the clothes, and all the equipment and books. Obviously, I would get a job and sell my apartment for money. I could easily move down south with the money and live very well. It's all I think about."

Fuck off, Jessica. I'm not living in poverty.

Jessica, Gemma said, *take the pills.*

Jessica opened the bottle of painkillers.

Yes, Jessica, take the pain away. Swallow the pills. We'll be together again. It's not fair that I died and you survived. I'm your baby sister. We should be together. This is the only way you can make everything right. You need to take more pills.

✦ ✦ ✦

Forty-eight hours later

Jessica rode home alone in a taxi. To the outside world, she was Jessica, the shell. Inside, she was Jess. Jess was not ready to die. The only way she could survive was to suppress Jessica.

Jess was angry that Jessica had made her body weak. All that fucking stomach pumping had made her throat sore. Jess felt she should have taken charge sooner. She had given Jessica too many chances, and Jessica had screwed up every time. Jess thought about her shopping list. First, Jake had to get his priorities right. He could start by visiting Jessica in her apartment. Second, she had to run Alice out of town. Third, she had to let that bitch Beth know she was running the show now. She believed things would have worked out differently if Jake had attended more sessions with Beth. Jess was not happy that she had to clean up Jessica's mess, but it could have been worse.

"Fuck you, Jessica. You tried to kill me."

Jess opened her laptop and wrote an email to Jake.

> Jake, will you come? Susan's gone. I have nobody.
>
> Jessica tried to kill herself two days ago. She fired a gun at my head. Nothing happened. She thought

there were no bullets in the gun. Jessica went crazy when the gun didn't work. She fired the gun at a wall and put a bullet in the wall. A minute later, she and I found some painkillers and sleeping pills in the medicine cabinet. I listened to music as she took the pills one by one. I shouted at Jessica to fucking stop, but she wouldn't listen.

You found me and woke me up. I couldn't open my eyes or move, but I heard everything. I remember you shaking me and saying, "Oh my God." I remember the ambulance people taking off my clothes and making me throw up. Was that you, Jake? There wasn't any pain. I don't remember having my stomach pumped.

When I woke up, it was twenty-four hours later. Susan kept tickling me. "'Bout time you woke up," she said. "I've been tickling you all night." Susan used to tickle Jessica, and she liked being tickled. When I didn't see you, I thought I was in heaven. The room looked like some place in heaven for fucking misfits, but I was in a hospital, a long room with rows of beds with all kinds of fucking crazy people—teenagers, pregnant girls, suicide attempters, drug addicts. They made me walk around in a white gown and watch TV. Jessica tried to kill us because she was angry with you. When Susan came back from the workstation, she just said, "Why'd you do this? To try to get attention?"

Am I glad you rescued me? Yes. That fucking bitch tried to kill me. I am glad I didn't die. It made me realize how much I appreciate myself, because I had a glimpse of what I might have fucking lost. I have no friends, so nothing to miss there. But I would have missed you. I checked myself out of the hospital. Susan tried to make me go to a psychiatrist. When that failed, she suggested that bitch Beth. I never liked Beth. I think she has more problems than Jessica. She has done nothing but drug Jessica for a year now. She should have set Jessica straight with those frozen eggs. Both you and I know you never intended to defrost them. I'm in charge now. No more baby talk. Will you come to the apartment, Jake?

Jessica is still suicidal. I've asked her why. Why does Jessica feel she has no alternatives? I hate to say this, but we need to get her to that bitch Beth, and you need to attend. I'm not doing this on my own. Next time, I'll nuke Jessica's ass.

Jess smiled to herself before she hit Send.

65

A lice walked out of Headliners, her place of solace, feeling like a million bucks. Now she was ready to face Jake and Jessica.

Alice drove down Post Road en route to Jake's house, thinking about Jake and the events of the past week. She tried to put aside Jessica's suicide attempt. She had her routine set until the New York bar exam. Alice didn't enjoy the test prep waiting for her: 150 multiple-choice questions and two practice essays each day tended to bore her. But she couldn't do what she had done in England, and she was determined to at least finish what she'd started.

Jake had called earlier in the day to say he had received another strange message from Jessica. *What's new?* Susan had not given an update on her progress, so he'd decided to pass by her apartment to look in on her. Alice and Jake had exchanged heated words over who should be responsible for Jessica. Alice had done her utmost to make Jake understand that he could not shoulder the responsibility for Jessica by himself. She found it hard to believe Jessica had no friends or family to keep an eye on her. Jake did not disagree. He'd said that Anthony had also stressed to him that he was too involved and that he should pull out of the situation. Jake had said that Jessica's email indicated Susan was not around. She thought, *Did Jessica purposely write an email that gave the impression Susan was not around?*

Later that day, halfway through the New York bar test prep, her phone rang. "Jake, this had better be important."

"Jessica appears stable—there was no more suicide talk. I've retrieved the two bottles of wine she took from the house."

"What about the gun?"

"Jessica said she could not remember where Jess had hidden it. I didn't want to hang about at the apartment, so I did a quick search for the gun, and when I didn't find it, I said goodbye and told her to take care." He paused. "I want to be up front with you: I have decided to give Jessica the money."

"What money?" Alice asked. Not that it mattered. It was his money to do with as he wished. She just wanted to finish the bar and see what was next.

"I left a check for two thousand dollars because there was no food in the apartment, and there were several opened but unpaid bills on the coffee table. When I left, Jessica was rocking back and forth in her rocking chair, reading her book on art. She published the book ten years ago. I have serious doubts she will ever be all right again." Jake took a deep breath. "Alice, I agreed to do another therapy session with her."

"Why?" Alice asked. "Don't you think that will make things worse, based on the advice Anthony gave you?"

"I just feel I should be there for her during this difficult time." Jake pleaded with Alice to understand. There was nothing between Jessica and him. It was a simple case of his not wanting her death on his hands.

"I disagree with the way you're handling the situation, but I feel for you, and I've sympathy for Jessica's suffering." She was determined not to make Jessica's problem her problem. The few occasions when she had spoken to Jessica on the phone had been mentally draining. She did not need that kind of stress in her life. Alice had resolved that this time, neither Jake nor Jessica would get in the way of her attempt at the New York bar exam.

Alice woke at 5:50 a.m. on Saturday morning. Jake was still sleeping. She was easing out of the bed, when Jake snuggled up to her. She was aroused when he pressed and massaged his erection against her body. He kissed her bare shoulders and neck. His hands gently massaged her thighs while parting her legs. When Alice groaned with pleasure, Jake entered and slowly brought her to a climax. She did not want the feeling to end. She lay in his arms until the alarm clock forced him out of bed. Jake was teeing off with his friends Mark, Ritchie, and Pete seven o'clock.

Alice dropped Jake at Winged Foot, got a Starbucks coffee, and then settled in to begin her first set of timed questions. Just as she began, the landline rang. Alice tried to ignore the phone but then hit the Postpone button on the test. The course providers had suggested taking the test with a slight distraction, but she was sure they did not have a ringing phone in mind. Before she could lift the receiver, the phone's speaker announced, "Jessica Brooks calling." Alice's finger immediately hit the end-call icon.

The phone rang again, this time announcing, "Private caller."

Alice answered, but when she realized it was Jessica, she hung up. Thereafter, every time she tried to resume her mock test, the phone rang. Finally, Alice unplugged it.

She resumed the test, thinking she had taken care of the problem, but she had answered only two questions, when her mobile rang. Alice switched it to silent mode. When Alice failed to answer the phone, Jessica sent several text messages.

"Did you hang up when I called? Why aren't you picking up, Alice? I need to speak with you."

Alice did not reply. A minute later, a second text arrived.

"I hope you'll call me. Please let me know what your plans are re: Jake and living in Connecticut. I deserve to know. I'm still involved with him and would like you to have the decency to step aside and out of our lives. You've caused enough damage."

Alice ignored the second text. Jessica had already managed to ruin a day of study, but she did not stop.

"Have Jake call me. Jess."

Alice asked herself how she had become caught up in this madness. A minute later, a fourth text arrived: "Are you still with him or not?"

Two minutes later, she received a fifth: "I suggest you call me, Alice, or this is not going to be fun for anybody. I've had enough bullshit from you and Jake, and I want to be done with you."

Alice picked up her bag. She needed to get out of the house.

Later, as she sat in a Barnes & Noble bookstore, studying, she switched on her phone to check for messages, knowing she had to pick up Jake after he was done at Winged Foot. A sixth text message from Jessica was waiting for her: "Hey, I assume it was you who answered Jake's phone earlier today. Please give me a call. Thanks."

And a seventh: "I don't bite."

Then came an eighth: "Alice, I'm looking for clarity in this very confusing and ridiculous situation. I don't want to be in your life—trust me. I don't want Jess to take you out. Under different circumstances, we could have been friends. It's impossible to get the truth from Jake. I won't stop until I know what's going on."

And a ninth: "Seriously, Alice, how does this help anybody? Ignoring me doesn't work. I'm not going away."

Finally, a tenth and final text arrived: "You're a fool to hang up. Denial gets you nowhere. Tell Jake to call me. And stop telling him lies about me. I can and will take you out."

The words sent a chill down Alice's spine. Her eyes filled with tears. This was not a normal life. She could not spend her days looking over her shoulder. *But*, she thought, *I'm so close to taking the bar exam. After I pass, my career prospects will be enhanced both here and back in England.*

Later that evening, though she wished it had been different, Jake rehashed the events of his day. He explained that he had just finished putting in a drink order, when Mark waved at him.

"As he neared, he said I had a call but then waved me off as if he had made a mistake."

"And?" Alice asked when he remained silent for several minutes.

"Mark had a brief conversation with the person who had called," Jake said. "When I arrived back at the table, Mark was already re-counting his conversation with Jessica to Richie and Pete. Both had been seated at the table when she called. Mark said Jessica had asked if he was aware I was dating a woman called Alice. She did not give Mark a chance to reply. She shouted, 'Alice is not good for Jake! Jake is in danger. Alice is dangerous.'"

Alice reached over and placed a hand on his. She thought, *How many times have I told you? What will it take?*

Mark had turned to him and asked in jest if he needed his Navy SEAL buddies to give him secure passage home. "Alice, you have no idea. 'Remind me,' Mark said. 'Jessica is the ex-girlfriend who produced that kindergarten picture book and then claimed to be an expert on art, right?' They all laughed. I smiled to hide my embarrassment."

66

New York

Fuck that mean Wall Street banker. He earns all that fucking money and leaves two thousand dollars. Fuck Jake.

Two thousand dollars would not buy a dress. Jess remembered the sunglasses she had seen for $800. She had told that stupid bitch Jessica to buy them so Jake would not recognize her in public. Had she listened? No. Then the fucker had tried to kill her. *Screw Jessica.* On Monday, she would make that bitch Beth tell her how to take Jessica out.

Jess told Jessica to get her lazy ass down to the bank to deposit Jake's check. *I've dealt with task one. Now we run that bitch Alice out of town.*

"Jess, she's not taking your calls."

Jessica felt better. Jake cared. She wanted to get back into the show. She was seeing Beth on Monday. She would come clean about Jess and tell Beth everything.

Did I ask for your opinion? Shut the fuck up, and get yourself down to the bank. I told you what would happen if you didn't shape up. You tried to kill me. You're fucking done. Bitch Beth is going to tell me how to nuke you.

Since Alice had not answered the phone, Jess would move to plan

B and get back to the bitch Beth later. Jess searched through Jessica's phone contacts. She remembered when Jessica had met Barbara, Mark's wife. She hated Jake's friends, but for some strange reason, she had taken to Barbara.

This bitch will do.

She called Barbara. When she did not answer, Jess sent a text, asking her to call because Jake was in trouble. When Barbara did not call, Jess called Mark.

Jake had joined Jessica in Beth's consulting room. Jessica tried to maintain her composure, with her hands in her lap and her legs crossed. She relented and put a hand on her head and squinted. *Why can't I remember?* She had been having problems with her memory recently and suffering chronic headaches Even now, a week after the overdose, she could not remember some things. She tried to remember where Jess had hidden the gun, but she could not. Starting a week before the overdose, she did not remember anything at all. Jessica's knowledge was limited to what Jake claimed she had written in emails and texts.

"I can forward text messages and emails to Beth, including the texts you sent Alice last weekend," he said.

Jessica fell silent. She was too scared to reply, not to mention that Jess would punish her if she did. The pain in her head was sharp and piercing—so unbearable that she often blacked out and remained in a semiconscious state for several hours. She could not remember anything when she came back.

Observing that Jessica was in excruciating pain, Beth recommended that Jessica be admitted to a psychiatric hospital for a full evaluation. "Jessica, it can't wait any longer. Please don't deny that Jess is getting stronger."

"Jess?" Jake asked.

Jessica shot Beth a look that told her he did not need to know. "I can't go into a psychiatric hospital. If I'm in the hospital, my clients will drop me, and once I'm out of the hospital, businesses won't hire me. I'll be forced to lie on business proposals and applications. I won't be able to get health insurance. People will look at me like I'm dangerous." Jessica's eyes filled with tears.

"How can we make you see that you're a danger to yourself?"

Jessica composed herself. "I don't care what happens to me." She turned to Jake. "I wanted to have a baby. Life without a baby is more than I can bear. I've tried so hard to make you provide sperm for my baby, but you don't seem to care. You have plans that don't include me. I let you know my intentions, when I shouldn't have. Jess begged me not to tell you about our plan. Without a baby, life is unbearable."

Jessica ignored the tears forming in Jake's eyes as she continued talking. "Jess's mind is warped and twisted. She's reached the point where I can't control her any longer. I can't challenge her. Since the overdose, Jess's hatred for me has grown. We used to be friends. She thinks I tried to kill her. You must control her. I dare not wait any longer—until the final twist comes and she snaps. I don't want to spend the rest of my life in some psychiatric hospital."

"Jessica," Beth said, "Jake is here for you, but he can't help if you're unwilling to explore and discuss your dissociative identity disorder diagnosis." When Jessica remained silent, she glanced at Jake. "DID is a mental illness that involves Jessica experiencing at least two clear identities or personality states. I believe you would think of them as alter egos." Beth said that Jake would see each alter in Jessica, one being Jess and the other being Jessica. Each had her own way of viewing and relating to the world.

Jake nodded. "Yes, it makes sense now. It explains the calls, texts, and emails."

Steve joined them in Beth's office. After bringing him up to speed on recent events, Beth turned the discussion to treatment for Jessica going forward.

Jess had had enough. *I had one ask: shut your fucking mouth, Jessica.* Enraged, she stood up and walked out of Beth's office.

The phone rang, but before Beth could take the call, Jess barged into the room.

"Are you bitching about me, Beth? I thought so. I told Jessica you were a bitch." Jess walked up to Beth and got in her face.

Beth pushed her chair back.

Jake stood up slowly and moved forward to restrain Jess.

"Well! How's this, Bitch Beth? Your authorization to discuss my case with Jake is revoked. Until Jake finds some fucking manners, he's out of Jessica's life." Jess marched out of the room.

There was silence in the room. Beth opened a desk drawer and handed Jake her business card. "I'm sorry. If Jessica is not present, it puts me in a position of conflict. I could be compromised professionally if I continue this discussion with you."

"What? It's obvious Jessica's not right."

"Yes, but I can't discuss her case. I would understand if you want to distance yourself from her," she said, "but now you're probably the only person who can reach Jessica."

In the taxi, Jess muttered to herself. "Death is too good for you, Jessica. I warned you to keep your mouth shut. You can forget about a baby. No more fucking tears or moaning. You don't exist."

She gave the taxi driver her apartment address. She needed to stop there to collect something.

"I'm going to Connecticut to make sure that bitch Alice has gone."

What will you do if she's at the house?

"Shut up, Jessica."

Jessica's phone rang. She was about to answer, when Jess stopped her.

"Put the fucking phone down, Jessica. I told you: Jake is going to learn some fucking manners."

Jessica obeyed.

Later, she sat in a chair, rocking. A text alert sounded. She looked at the message: "I'll pass by your apartment on my way home. Jake."

"Fuck you, Jake!" Jess shouted. "Jessica is coming with me to Connecticut."

Jess picked up the phone to send him a text. Then it occurred to her that if Alice had ignored her request that she go back to London, she would most likely be in New York with Jake. On second thought, she postponed her trip to Connecticut until the weekend. It would be nice to see Jake. The $2,000 had not gone far.

"Jessica, clean yourself up. Jake is on his way."

When Jake rang the door buzzer, Jessica's spirits lifted. Jess had not lied to her. Jake said he was staying in New York that night. He suggested they go for a walk.

"Get your coat, Jessica. We can find somewhere nice to have a drink and grab something to nibble," said Jake.

Over drinks, Jessica turned the conversation to Jake's relationship with Alice. "Are you still seeing her?"

Jake could not take the grief. "I'm not seeing anybody at the moment."

Jessica shook her head. "Jake, I don't understand you. Why do you tell lies? She's living in your house."

Part of Jake was a coward. He could not take Jessica's verbal abuse. He did not want her to have another emotional breakdown, so he lied. The other part of him wanted to protect Alice from Jessica. If Jessica thought Alice had gone back to England, she would not stalk her.

"She's staying at the house until she finishes making arrangements to ship her things to England." He showed Jessica a copy of Alice's plane ticket. It indicated that Alice had a flight to London.

Thank God for organized Alice. She had anticipated and planned for her next visit to England and had locked down the ticket price and date of travel. The ticket was not open, but if necessary, the flight date could be changed for a small fee.

The time he spent with Jessica was no different from any time he met with her. It always came down to money and the wrongs she perceived he had done.

"It saddens me that you think I want something from you every time we meet," Jessica said. "I can see how you might think that, but it's part and parcel of my relationship with you. I didn't create this situation; you did. If you're referring to money, I don't ask for it, but if I allude to it, it's an expression of my love for you. I count on you for support. It makes me feel like you love me when you give it. I look to you for support because I feel like I'm married to you."

What is she talking about? It's rubbish. The only person Jessica cares about is Jessica.

Jake counted to ten before responding. He wanted Jessica back from the clutches of Jess, so he chose not to defend himself. When he walked her back to the apartment, he gave her the $500 he had in his pocket.

67

As Steve walked out of Beth's office, he noticed Jessica in the waiting room. At least he thought it was her.

When he passed by, Jess glared at him and then turned to the receptionist. "Some people don't have any fucking manners. He's pissing on my time."

Steve averted his eyes from the flushed face of the receptionist and assumed she was embarrassed by Jessica's rude behavior, because she lowered her head. Steve observed how Jessica's demeanor was different from the first time he had seen her walk into Beth's office. He felt a twinge of excitement and paused to reflect on his discussion with Beth. The trauma of not being able to have children after having an abortion, or abortions, might have been the cause of Jess's emergence. He agreed with Beth up to that point.

In his opinion, the abortions had not caused the dissociation. Steve needed to review Jessica's personal history. Somewhere in that history, it was likely he would discover recurring, overpowering, or life-threatening disturbances at a sensitive developmental stage of her childhood, which would explain the dissociation. He was frustrated that Jessica was not his patient.

He reentered Beth's office and closed the door after Jake left. Steve was not impressed when Beth told him she was looking for an expert in DID. "Why can't we deal with this case? I've done a mountain of research and even started writing a paper on it. Psychotherapy is generally considered to be the main component of treatment for DID. Why are you dropping the case? You're more than qualified."

"Steven, my goal was reintegration of the personalities. It backfired. Jessica's identity has almost been consumed, and Jess asserts that my goal is to get rid of, or kill, parts of her."

"Then let's make our goal achieving a more peaceful coexistence between Jessica and Jess," Steve said. "If we can find a way to have them coexist and work together, we might get Jessica back. Give it twenty-four hours, please. I have other ideas."

"We can't experiment with Jessica's mental health."

"Give me twenty-four hours. That's all I am asking."

Steve was annoyed with Beth. Statistics regarding the disorder indicated that the incidence of DID was only about 3 percent of patients in psychiatric hospitals. A case had fallen into her hands, and she did not have the balls to deal with it. What he was about to do was not professional, but he could not let such an opportunity slip by just because Beth did not want to do her homework.

Steve flagged a taxi and gave the drive his destination: Jessica's apartment. He saw Jake and Jessica approach the apartment. When he was sure Jake was gone, he rang the buzzer. "Jessica, this is Steve. I'm a colleague of Beth's."

"I know who you are. What do you want?"

"To talk."

"I have nothing to say."

"Jessica, where are your fucking brains?" Jess asked. "I'm not going back to that bitch Beth. You need somebody to talk to you. I won't stand by while you try to kill me again. Let him in. We can throw his fucking ass out if he turns out to be as stupid as Beth." Jess spoke quietly. She did not want Steve to hear her.

Minutes later, Steve sat down beside Jessica. He flirted with her and observed as her confidence returned. *Jessica, I don't like him—you'll have sex with any man who's willing. Tomorrow you'll be talking about Mr. and Mrs. Steve Dunhill. It's making me sick—I don't want to sleep with Steve. Surely he would not. It would be unethical.* Still, Jessica was not his patient. *Cut it out, Jessica, or I'll intervene.*

Steve explained hypnosis to Jessica as a successful form of treatment. He said it was used sometimes to help increase the information a person with DID had about his or her symptoms or identity states. "With this information, you can increase the control you have over those states when they change from one personality state to another."

Anger raged in Jess. *He wants to teach Jessica how to control me! There's no fucking way he's treating Jessica.*

Steve looked on as Jessica's demeanor changed. "Jess is present." His utterance was inaudible to Jessica. He looked startled; his inexperience was displayed. It was apparent he had given no consideration to the consequences of the conversation he had had with Jessica. He tried to walk it back and said, "It would enhance your communications with Jess."

Jess sat placidly, paying attention to Steve and nodding. Meanwhile, anger consumed her. *How dare he try to control me? Why me and not Jessica? She's the one who's crazy because she can't have babies.*

Steve observed Jessica's calm manner—he was getting through to her. She offered him a drink, and he accepted a Coke Zero.

When Jess walked back into the room, Steve had his back to her. She walked over to the sofa. Steve turned in time to see the iron in Jess's hand. His reaction was not quick enough to stop it from coming down and hitting him in the head. Steve slumped down onto the sofa.

Jess made her way into the kitchen and put the iron away. Then she went to the freezer and emptied its contents. Afterward, she returned to the living room.

The blow to Steve's head had not broken the skin, but the unbroken skin that surrounded the fragmented blood vessels had swollen and turned dark shades of blue, red, and purple. Jess dragged Steve into the kitchen and pushed him into the freezer.

"Sorry!" she screeched. "Not! You were making my head hurt. You didn't care about Jessica; you just wanted to use her for your own ends. I didn't like you, but I gave you a chance because of Jessica."

She moved back into the living room and adjusted the cushions on the rocking chair. She caught sight of Steve's wallet and phone, which had fallen out of his pocket. Jess switched his phone off, emptied his wallet of $200, and then threw the phone and wallet into the freezer with Steve.

Jess was tired. It had been an exhausting day. It was just after eleven o'clock when she snuggled into bed.

68

Jessica sipped her coffee in Starbucks. Later, she was meeting Jake for lunch. Jess had been quiet since her outburst in Beth's office. Without Jess screaming in her head, Jessica felt good. Meeting Jake was the icing on the cake. She wished Jess would let her see Beth. The memory lapses were increasing, and she pondered if she could get medication. Jessica did not understand. How could it be good for Jess to have memory lapses? Jessica thought Jess would benefit from treatment as well. She thought it was strange that Jess complained about the headaches but not the memory lapses. Jessica failed to realize that Jess did not suffer from the memory lapses. Jess was happy about Jessica's memory lapses; they worked in her favor.

Jessica contemplated asking Jess about her loss of memory. She remembered that Jess had suggested Jessica have a therapy session with Steve. Jessica had doubts that she or Jess would benefit from sessions with him. Steve made Jessica feel like an experiment he wanted to write up for *Psychology Review*. However, Jessica was desperate to talk with someone, so in the end, it did not matter whether it was Steve or Beth who treated her. It was not worth having an argument with Jess. For the moment, she would have to postpone going to Beth. It could not hurt to make an appointment, though, she thought. Jess could cancel if she decided she did not want to see Beth.

Jessica contemplated raising the question of Jake providing his sperm for the frozen eggs. Amanda had been driving by Jake's house daily. There was no sign of Alice. Maybe Jake had been telling the truth when he informed Jessica that Alice had gone back to London. She was not sure whether he had said that she was going or that she had gone. Jess planned on going to Connecticut on Friday. Jessica speculated whether Jess would stay quiet. Jess had something in mind to deal with Jake, but she refused to share the details of her plan with Jessica. Jessica prayed Jess would stay quiet until after lunch with Jake.

Jess was keeping a low profile. No one had inquired about Steve, which was good. The freezer was a good place for him; he needed to cool down. Jess's plan was to lie low. She would stay out of Jessica's head for a few days. Staying away was the perfect alibi.

Jess considered letting Jessica see Beth. Jessica would not be able to resist the temptation to boast that she had taken control of her life. Jess could hear her sickening talk: "Jake and I are working on the relationship." How could she have based her conjecture on one drink and a few nibbles of food? Jess could not believe she shared a body with the stupid bitch. Jess laughed to herself. Jessica's boasting could benefit Jess. Jessica would interpret Jess's silence as her increasing strength over Jess. She would boast that she had Jess under control.

Jess imagined how the session with Beth would play out. Jessica would squeak with that kindergarten voice, "Jess hasn't been around for four days." At that point, Jess would think, *Score!* Jess would have her alibi. Then Jessica would start talking about memory lapses. Jessica was fucked up. She could not remember even simple events, such as ridding the world of that wannabe celebrity psychologist Steve. She should have been proud they had saved Steve's patients from more insanity inflicted by his hands.

Jess's reprieve from babysitting Jessica came to an abrupt halt when Jessica received a text message from Jake: "Jessica, how are you? I can't do lunch today. Are you free on Monday?"

She typed a quick response: "I'm free Saturday."

Jessica cried when Jake did not respond.

Jessica, I'm warning you. Quit that screaming. I know you have some brain cells. He can't do Saturday because he's with that bitch Alice. I suggest you get your stupid ass to Connecticut. We have business that can't wait. Stop that fucking crying. I can't think. We need to make plans to send that bitch back to London. She can fly business or cargo; I don't care.

Jess wanted to take the gun to threaten the bitch and show Alice that she was serious about her leaving town, but then she thought better of the idea. If she took the gun out now, Jessica might tell Jake where she had been hiding it. Jake was not getting the gun back. Jess resolved that she would get the gun the next time Jessica had a blackout.

Greenwich, Connecticut

Jess watched as Alice drove the Jeep into the driveway. She searched in her bag for her phone. "Stay out of this, Jessica."

Amanda, who thought she had heard Jessica talking to her, asked Jessica to repeat what she had just said.

"Nothing," Jessica replied. "I was talking to myself."

Jess sent a text message to Jake: "Jessica doesn't deserve to be abused and lied to! You told her the bitch Alice was gone. You should be fucking arrested, you psycho, lying piece of trash. Jess."

Jess wanted to go into Jake's house now to deal with Alice. Alice needed to know that Jess was not joking about her going back to England.

"The bitch needs to leave now," Jess muttered as she opened the car door.

"Jessica, where are you going?" Amanda asked.

It was enough to stop Jess and make her think about her timing. If Alice refused to leave, things could get nasty, and Amanda would be a witness. Jess got back in and closed the door. She would give Alice one more warning.

"Let's go," she said to Amanda. "She's not worth my time."

Amanda suggested they go to Polpo restaurant later. There was a good chance Jake would be there, and she could confront him.

Jess was tiring of struggling to keep up with Amanda. All the fucking dining out was wearing her out. Amanda did not take Jess's business in Connecticut seriously. She was a bad role model for Jessica. Amanda had two small children, and all she did was socialize. Jess thought she should have been an expert on the restaurant bars in Connecticut, not a mother. Amanda had ditched her husband so she could party. Unlike that dumb bitch Jessica, Amanda had made sure she had an insurance policy before shooting her mouth off and marching to the divorce courts.

Jess blamed Jessica's nasty demeanor for Jake having jilted them at the altar. Why couldn't she have just taken the money and been nice to him? Instead, she had tried to crush his Wall Street balls. Jess laughed to herself. Jessica was a stupid bitch. The only thing Mr. Wall Street understood was money. He had lots of it. Jessica did not, but she wanted some. Jessica had no leverage, though. She could not do the math.

Jess thought about silencing Amanda. She would get the use of her house and her car. But she did not know what to do with the screaming children. They had done nothing wrong. Her problem was Amanda. Amanda, like Jessica, was a stupid bitch. It did not matter how often they opened their legs and lost the man. They failed to comprehend that no man would want to be with a woman who would leave her children night after night to drink or do drugs and have sex on the tennis court with the instructor. Then Jess had a thought: *Maybe the father could take the children.*

Jess made a mental note to discuss the matter with Jessica without mentioning Amanda's potential demise. She needed transportation in Connecticut to keep an eye on Jake. Amanda was not serious. She wanted to piss around on Jess's time. Jess had explained to Amanda why she was in Connecticut, yet Amanda had refused to follow Jake that evening. How could Amanda not have seen Jake drive out of the parking lot?

Fuck Amanda. Jess would take care of her later. For the moment, she needed to warn Alice. She wrote a text to her: "You could say thanks for the lovely text I sent you. You're a psycho bitch. You have no manners, like that fucking Jake. Have a great night in my bed!"

On Saturday morning, Jess discreetly trailed Alice from her house. When Alice turned off I-95 on exit 18, Jess realized where she was headed. Jess carried on driving until she reached the next exit.

"Fucking coward!" she yelled. "I'll get the bitch later."

Jess thought about the children. She had to get back to the house before the sleeping pills she had put in their chocolate milk wore off. She had found the number for Amanda's ex-husband in Jessica's contacts. He was collecting the children at one o'clock. Jess felt guilty about what she had done, but it was the best course of action. Amanda was an awful mother. Her ex-husband, Henry, had been genuinely concerned when she told him Amanda had gone off with some man and had not come home. He'd said he could take care of the children. Jess had suggested he consider seeking sole custody. She believed the children deserved better care than Amanda could provide.

The children were still sleepy from the sleeping pills. When Henry arrived to collect them, Jess told him they were tired because they had stayed up late waiting for Amanda to come home. Henry could not thank Jess enough for taking care of the children.

"Thank you," he said again as he loaded the children into his car.

"That's OK. I'd love to stay and chat, but I'm meeting a friend. I must lock up. I'll leave a note for Amanda, so she'll know you have the children. Bye, Henry. Give the children the love and care they deserve." Jess closed the door. She then said, "Jessica, I thought Henry would never leave. The coast is clear. We should get Amanda."

"What about Alice?" Jessica asked.

"I'll say this once: stop whining. You don't need to worry about her. I have a plan. I have things to do. We can't leave Amanda in the Honda."

69

Greenwich, Connecticut

Jake called Alice to make sure she was OK. He had not revealed any of his recent findings about Jessica. He found it hard to believe there was anything wrong with Jessica beyond her usual selfishness. He was relieved to hear that Alice was well and totally unaware of the possibility of Jessica's presence in the locality.

"I'll be on the two o'clock Metro North train," he said. "I'll collect you, and we can have drinks at Winged Foot."

Later, when Jake arrived home, he found Alice in the bedroom, crying. He was cognizant that Alice did not deserve Jessica's cruel medicine, or was it Jess's? Jake was still struggling to accept the reality of what Beth had told him about Jessica. Alice had received multiple texts from Jessica's cell phone informing her that Jessica was in a relationship with him and that Alice should go back to England. She handed her phone to him. It displayed a text from Jessica: "You are ugly inside. Evil! A hateful, ungodlike, evil, sick woman to take another woman's man. Jake wants you to leave. I want you to leave. It's time you left us alone, Alice. You're not wanted here. Go home. Leave."

After they left Winged Foot later that day, Jake and Alice went to Polpo to collect their carryout meal. Without discussing the matter with Alice, Jake opted not to stay for a drink, because he was apprehensive that Jessica was in the area, likely to stalk Alice and him.

As they pulled away from Polpo, Amanda and Jessica drove into the parking lot. Jake saw the Honda in his rearview mirror.

"Duck!" he shouted to Alice.

"What?" Alice obeyed and ducked.

"I don't think they saw you."

"Who? Who are you hiding from?" Alice asked.

"Let's drive by Victoria's house. I told Jessica I was having dinner with Victoria tonight."

"Why? Why do you lie to Jessica? How does it help her?" Alice asked, annoyed.

"She's stalking me."

"Jake, you should talk to the police. For all your intelligence, you still can't see the seriousness of this situation. If you did, you would lock it down."

"I'm sorry."

"Jake! Are you listening? Her behavior is downright scary, and that's putting it mildly."

Jake again apologized to her.

"Stop apologizing; it's not a solution. I need you, Jake, to snap out of this denial and act. In the beginning, I ignored the calls and text messages. I didn't want to. I tried hard not to overdramatize the matter, but now I'm terrified Jessica will hurt either you or me." She paused. "Or even herself."

"I'll speak to Anthony on Monday."

The anger in Alice's tone lightened. "I'll say it again: I don't believe Jessica set out to be menacing. It's more that she seeks attention. If she doesn't get that attention, she escalates the situation by any means necessary."

"I know," said Jake. "Jessica would commit suicide not because she had a desire to die but simply to prove a point. Jessica is selfish."

"Yes, but open your eyes to the fact that her selfishness is becoming dangerous to anyone intimately connected to you."

✦ ✦ ✦

The next day, Jake followed his Saturday morning routine. Alice drove him to Winged Foot and then went back to the house to study. She locked all the doors for peace of mind. Around eleven o'clock, needing a break from studying, she drove to Starbucks.

On the way back, she noticed a black Honda driving too close behind her. Initially, she did not recognize Jessica behind the wheel. Then she saw the blonde hair. As the Honda pulled closer to her vehicle, she recognized the face as Jessica's. Frightened, she gripped the steering wheel hard. *Think, Alice. Think. You must get off this road. No, you're safer in public. When the light changes, change lanes, and let her go ahead.* When Alice stopped at the traffic light, the Honda narrowly missed hitting the Jeep's bumper.

In her rearview mirror, she looked to see if Amanda was in the passenger seat, but Amanda did not appear to be in the vehicle. "Please. Please," she pleaded. "Let the adjacent lane stay free." When the traffic light changed, Alice signaled and changed lanes. As Jessica eased forward slowly, Alice watched as Jessica reached into the back of the Honda. She grabbed a blanket and threw it over a woman. "Oh my God! I think—no, I'm sure—that was Amanda, passed out on the backseat." Alice bypassed the turn for Jake's house and headed to Winged Foot.

When Jessica did not turn off at exit 18, Alice was relieved. She continued driving until she saw a point where she could turn the Jeep around and head home. Alice considered whether she should tell Jake about the morning's events, but Alice understood he would play down her narrative. *He said he would call Anthony, but I bet he won't.* It was not that he did not care, but he lacked the strength to act. After Jessica had called Mark and his wife with her crazy story that Jake was in danger from Alice, Jake had done nothing to protect Alice or himself. Not even the embarrassment of Mark, Ritchie, and Pete laughing at Jessica's lack of intelligence and her "picture book," which Jessica claimed demonstrated her expertise in art, had stirred Jake to act.

What does Jessica have on Jake? Why would he allow her to destroy our lives? What chance do I have, when Jake's friends and family have been telling him for years that he should let Jessica go because he does not owe her anything? Jake appeared ready to stand by and watch Jessica destroy his career and his relationships with his family and partner. Alice did not want the uncomfortable feeling she was experiencing. She sensed this was the calm before the storm. She did not want to be held responsible if anything bad happened. It was better to look like a fool than answer awkward questions if Jessica spiraled out of control and hurt somebody. *Amanda! What happened to Amanda? Was she sleeping? Does she need help?*

Alice was, and would always be, a lawyer. She imagined herself as a witness on the stand. The prosecution would destroy what she had left of her sanity. "You recognized that Jessica was a danger and did not act," the prosecutor would say. "You could have prevented Jessica from getting into the car. That fatal accident occurred because you did not act."

Upon reflection, she decided that this time, she would tell Jake. The next time, she would call the police.

New York, two weeks later

Jake's refusal to deal with Jessica intensified the tension growing between him and Alice. For her peace of mind, she was spending her time in New York.

"What?" she said when she raised her head from the book she was reading. Jake was staring her at her.

"We can't put our lives on hold. I gave the concierge for the building a description of Jessica and told the doormen not to give her access to the apartment if she stops by."

She put the book down. "Thank you. I appreciate that you did that, but you have given zero consideration to the fact that I feel like a prisoner. If I mention Jessica has sent an abusive text message or called, your reaction is to pull out the phone cord and show me the hundreds of texts and calls you receive daily. My family call the landline."

"I'm doing my best. Can you not see that? Don't let Jessica come between us."

"Oh, so now it's my fault? I'm not being considerate of your feelings?"

"I'm not saying that."

"Yes, you are. You make me feel that if I don't sympathize, you'll show me the door."

"Not true."

"You think nothing of having lunches and, increasingly, dinners with Jessica. Your justification is that Jessica is alone and doesn't have any family or friends close by. What about me? My social calendar is not overflowing—my friends and family are in England. Maybe you should ask why she does not have friends."

Jake slammed his beer can on the table and walked out of the apartment. He showed little regard for Alice's feelings or the impact his continued presence in Jessica's life was having on her mental state.

Alice was desperate to get out of the prison the New York apartment was becoming. Later that week, she took the Metro North train to Connecticut. Jessica's stalking was disturbing. Alice was having difficulty concentrating. She had three contracts to review before the end of the day. Her client would not accept her fear of Jessica as an excuse for late delivery of work she had promised. Alice downloaded the first contract and perused it on the train.

70

New York

Whan the last member of Jake's team walked out of the room, his mind turned to Alice and Jessica. Alice had no idea about the number of calls, text messages, and emails he had to field from Jessica daily. Many of them were offensive. He also had to deal with her persistent threats of suicide. Jake did not want Jessica's blood on his hands. Her family members had long since washed their hands of her. He found Alice's refusal to be understanding and accept that he had to spend time with Jessica selfish. What he perceived as jealous outbursts by Alice had become unbearable. Both Alice and Jessica were suffocating him. Jake wanted to run from them.

Jake had been dodging Jessica for more than a week. He had emailed her earlier in the week and told her that until she stopped the threats of suicide, he did not want to see her again. He could not face another lunch or dinner spent listening to her tell him she had nothing for which to live. He sent Alice a text asking her to pick him up at the station at 7:30 p.m.

Later that evening, Jake boarded the Metro North train to Connecticut. He found a seat and settled down to read his newspaper.

"Is this seat taken?"

He looked up from his newspaper in shock. "Jessica!"

He was unable to absorb his thoughts or focus on anything other than Jessica standing in the aisle. He felt nauseated. Moments later, his brain registered the event and put it into perspective. He could not arrive in Connecticut and get off the train with Jessica, knowing Alice would be waiting to pick him up.

"Jessica, what are you doing here? You must get off this train."

"Why?"

He decided to change his tack. "Jessica, will you please get off the train?"

When Jessica refused to leave, Jake put his newspaper down and pushed past her as he disembarked.

Jessica followed Jake into a nearby bar. He could not get back on the train without her also boarding. She stuck close to him, preventing him from using his phone to let Alice know he was not on the train.

After a couple of drinks, he told Jessica it was too late to go back to Connecticut. He said goodbye and boarded a subway train to his apartment. Jessica followed. She watched him go inside. He observed her for thirty minutes from his apartment window before she moved away. He did not leave the window until he saw her flag a taxi.

Jake picked up his phone to call Alice and saw a text messages from Jessica.

"You were going to see that bitch Alice. I don't want to continue seeing you if you're with Alice."

Just as he finished reading it, his phone vibrated again.

"If you go to see that bitch, I'll know. Jake, I'm pleading with you. Don't force Jess to act."

Jake put his hands over his head. "Leave me alone!" he screamed. "Leave me alone!"

When a text message from Alice hit his phone, Jake responded with three simple words, not caring whose feelings he hurt: "Leave me alone."

71

Alice recognized the end had come. She did not pick up the phone to call or text Jake. He did not call or text Alice either. She lay in bed, listening to Keri Hilson's "Beautiful Mistake."

Her phone sounded a text alert. *Jake!* She snatched up the phone, but her mood changed when she saw the sender's name.

"Alice, how many times do I have to tell you? Jake wants you to leave. I want you to leave. It's time you left us alone. Alice, you are not wanted here. Go home. Leave. Now."

Alice did not respond. She sent a text to Jake instead: "Make Jessica stop. I've had enough."

Seconds later, he replied, "I can't. I am dealing with an onslaught of abusive texts from her. Leave me alone—I want you both to leave me alone."

Alice struggled to comprehend why Jake was treating her as if she were Jessica. Her text had not been abusive in any way. She had merely asked him to stop Jessica from sending more abusive texts. The phone sounded another text alert.

"Where's Jake, Alice? This is so crazy. Jake is not OK. Alice, if you don't call me, I'm calling the police."

A minute later, another text arrived: "Alice, if you don't tell me where I can find Jake, the police are coming to find out what's going on. You have two minutes."

Alice switched her phone to silent and tried to sleep. She thought about Jessica's words. *Jake is not OK.* Anger swelled in her. She did not know where Jake was, and more to the point, she did not really care.

The doorbell rang. Alice jumped. She could not see the front door from the bedroom, but a flashing blue light made her go to the window and look out. A police car was parked on the side street. The doorbell rang again. As Alice approached the front door, she saw another police car parked out front. She jumped as someone banged on the door.

"Police! Open up!"

Alice opened the door. The flashing lights of the two police cars hit her eyes. Farther down the road, she saw another police car.

The officer at her door said, "Ma'am, we received a report that violent screaming and shouting were coming from the house and that the owner had not been seen for a few days. Are you the house owner? Can we come in and look around?"

Alice noticed four policemen walk to the back of the house. She opened the screen door to allow the officer inside. Holding a flashlight in his hand, he pointed it just below Alice's eyes.

"Please, Mrs. Logan, can you turn some lights on?"

"Yes," she replied. "And my name is Francis—Alice Francis." It was not until Alice switched on the lights that she felt vulnerable and uncomfortable. She was wearing nothing but Jake's large white T-shirt.

The other police officer asked if he could speak to Mr. Logan.

"He isn't here," Alice replied. Then she asked the policeman if she could go upstairs to put on some jogging pants, to which he agreed.

When Alice returned, the police officer asked when she had last seen Jake. The other officer asked if he could look around the house.

Alice gave him permission to search the house and confirmed that the last time she had seen Jake had been seven days earlier. "Did Jessica Brooks reported the disturbance?" When the officer did not say yes or no, Alice had her confirmation that Jessica was likely behind the saga.

Alice handed her phone to the officer. It displayed all the text messages she had received from Jessica.

Annoyance registered on the officer's face. He turned to his colleague. "False alarm. Ms. Brooks is wasting police time and resources."

The hoax call was serious enough for the Greenwich Police Department to contact the New York Police Department to set in motion a chain of events that resulted in an order preventing Jessica from contacting Alice again, whether by text, email, or phone or in person.

After the police left, tears rolled down Alice's cheeks. She was angry with Jake. Angry because he had shown no regard for her feelings and had neither called nor texted. Angry because he had allowed things to get out of hand with Jessica to the point that Jessica had caused the police to invade her privacy. The officer had said he would contact Jake to make sure he was OK.

Even after the police contacted Jake, Jake neither called nor texted Alice.

"That's it. I'm getting an apartment, passing the bar, and then ..." She paused. "Screw it. I'm going home."

New York, two days later

Early Sunday afternoon, Alice arrived at Jake's apartment. Some things never changed. Jake was watching sports on TV and was surrounded by the morning paper. The only noticeable difference was his anger—or lack thereof. He appeared indifferent to Alice's presence. She could see something was wrong, and she lost the confidence to confront him and bring their relationship to a close. She suggested they get out of the apartment for a drink.

Despite her trepidation, it turned out to be a lovely afternoon. They had drinks in the Meatpacking District and then walked along the Hudson River. Jake was shocked when Alice told him about the events that had taken place at his house. He could not and did not defend Jessica. He admitted she was out of control and that he had underestimated the extent of the problem. Alice saw the burden he was carrying when he recounted how many times a day Jessica called the office and sent him abusive text messages. He said that even if he had done the things she accused him of, it did not warrant the sick, cruel messages she sent.

He showed Alice a text message Jessica had sent recently when he was boarding a flight: "I hope the flight crashes. That's what I wish. But the plane crashing and you burning to death would be too fucking good for you, Jake."

"Jessica does not know that the flight I was on was forced to make an emergency landing shortly after it took off. She almost got her wish."

The look in his eyes told Alice he was genuinely scared. She did not have the heart to tell him that she had reached her limit.

Later that evening, they had dinner at Pastis. Alice could not help feeling that her life in the United States of America had come full circle. It was ending where it had begun.

When they arrived back at the apartment, Jake said he was feeling unwell and went to bed. It was eleven o'clock, too late for Alice to go back to Connecticut.

Alice did not sleep. She spent the night thinking about the happier moments in her relationship with Jake.

In the morning, Alice awoke feeling aroused. She closed her eyes and moaned softly. Her fingers brought her orgasm closer; her body ached for him. But for recent events, she would have reached out to him and kissed him. Now she feared relighting her feelings for him. She lay still, waiting for the moment to pass.

A few minutes later, when Jake's hands moved down her body and lifted her T-shirt above her head, she did not resist. He kissed and caressed every part of her. His head moved down her torso. He kissed and teased with his tongue until their bodies begged to be entwined. Just as they had the first time, they made love; she felt the lower part of her body throb when she climaxed. Her muscles tightened, teasing him and causing his explosion.

Afterward, they lay motionless.

"Forgive me," he whispered. "I love you."

She was silent, but she snuggled close to him. *I love you. Forgive me, but I'm going home.*

Jake moved first but only because he had to go to work for a meeting.

Forty-five minutes later, Alice kissed him goodbye and then turned and walked away so he would not see the tears rolling down her cheeks.

72

Jessica woke up, drowsy from taking sleeping pills and drinking red wine. She could not remember the last time she had taken her antidepressants. Jess still had a total ban on sessions with Beth, but she had been forced back to reality. Jess needed money.

Jessica, when did you last speak to Jake?

"You know he's not taking my calls."

You stupid bitch! Did you ask yourself why?

"No!"

I guessed as much. He's with that English bitch. I have some texts to send. Where did you put the fucking phone?

Jessica swallowed a cocktail of sleeping pills and antidepressants. She was desperate to shut Jess out. Jess had been screaming and shouting since she had found out Jessica had called the police and sent them to Jake's house in Connecticut.

Jessica, you're a stupid bitch. Jess kept repeating it like a damaged CD. *Do you know what will happen if the police come to the apartment? If the police don't find Jake at the house, they'll come to your apartment to search for him. That bitch Alice will send them here. If the police find out what we did, they'll send us to prison, and it'll be your fault.*

When Jessica told Jess she was stupid, because people did not go to prison for making hoax calls, Jess went crazy, screaming and smashing plates and glasses. Jessica's head hurt. She wanted to get medication, but Jess would not let her see Beth. Jess said Jessica was a loose cannon who would get them both in trouble.

Fucking prison! I'm not going to prison. I'll kill you before I go to prison. Fucking prison. I did what was necessary. I'd do it again too. I am not going to prison. Do you hear me? I'm not going to prison!

Jessica, answer the fucking intercom. I'm not going to fucking prison.

"Jess, we are not going to prison. I made a hoax call. We did not commit an offense punishable by imprisonment."

That's what you think. You're fucking stupid. I know differently. I'm not going to prison. It was your stupidity that got us into this mess.

Jessica had no idea what had upset Jess, but she could not take the screaming in her head any longer. She did not have the energy to argue. Jessica picked up the telephone intercom. The voice on the other end of the line announced that her visitors were from the NYPD, Officer Brian Nicolas and Officer Chris Gigs. Officer Nicolas asked if he could speak to Miss Jessica Brooks. Jessica pressed the door release to let the officers into the apartment. They flashed their identification before entering.

Once they were inside her apartment, Officer Gigs asked Jessica about the hoax calls and informed her that she would be notified in due course whether charges would be brought against her regarding the calls she had made.

Jessica sat on the sofa, nervously twisting her tightly clasped hands. Officer Gigs stared at the rumpled carpet and its pile, which appeared to have had something dragged across. There were an unopened can of Coke Zero and several empty red wine bottles and glasses on the table. He nudged his colleague, drawing his attention to the hole in the wall.

Officer Nicolas switched the conversation to the text messages she had sent to Alice. He said her text messages were unjustified, threatening, and abusive. He left Jessica with no doubt that if she contacted Alice again, whether by phone, email, or text or in person, she would be arrested.

Officer Gigs did not see any remorse on Jessica's face. "Ma'am, do you understand that your behavior was unacceptable, and if it's repeated, you'll be arrested and charged?" He paused, waiting for her to apologize for wasting police time and maybe offer an explanation that what she had done was uncharacteristic of her. Nothing. He glanced at his colleague and silently mouthed, "She's weird."

Jess had been thrown into a state of panic that Jessica might draw attention to their guest in the freezer. Jess had not wasted any time in exercising her domination over Jessica when she started behaving nervously. Jess was the one dealing with the police officers. She felt no remorse for Alice. Alice had stolen Jake from Jessica and was standing in the way of Jessica and Jake's reconciliation. Jess willed herself to stay calm until the officers were gone.

She had unfinished business with Alice. When Jessica had spoken to Jake, he had made excuses about Alice making plans to ship her things to London, saying that was the reason she had not moved out of the house. Jess was prepared to store Alice's belongings at the apartment until the shippers were able to collect them. She would not listen to any more excuses for her not leaving.

Jess did not try to defend or apologize for her actions. She waited patiently until Officer Nicolas finished giving her a verbal warning. He asked Jess to confirm that she understood that she would find herself in serious trouble if the police received any further reports that she had phoned, emailed, texted, or made personal contact with Alice Francis.

Jess looked at Officer Nicolas. "If you're finished, I'd like you to leave."

Get out of my apartment!

As Nicolas and Gigs entered the elevator, they agreed that something was not right. Their uneasy feelings made them want to go back to

Jessica's apartment and poke around. Gigs asked Nicolas whether the NYPD had any background information on her. Nicolas said he had run a check on Jessica, and the database had flagged her as a domestic violence perpetrator. Various boyfriends over the years had been on the receiving end of her fists or had the entire contents of the kitchen hurled at them.

"Brian, we can't justify going back into the apartment, but I'm telling you now: something isn't right."

"Let's talk to Mr. Logan," Nicolas said. "If we get nothing from him, we have to drop it."

Speaking to Jake Logan did not quell Gigs's suspicions. Jake was evasive. He pointed them in the direction of Dr. Jones, Jessica's therapist. As they exited the lobby of Jake's building, Gigs said, "Logan was holding something back."

"So we keep digging," replied Nicolas.

From Jake's apartment, they drove to Jones's office on the Upper East Side. Jones was forthcoming.

After introductions, she said, "Officers, please call me Beth."

"We would like to talk to you about Jessica Brooks. I understand she's your patient," said Gigs.

"Yes. I hope you understand that doctor-patient privilege protects the communication between Jessica and me."

Nicolas had seen the threatening texts Jessica had sent Alice. He cut to the chase. "Do you believe Jessica Brooks is capable of unprovoked aggression?"

"No, but—" Beth paused. She did not finish her sentence, because doing so would have forced her to reveal Jess and Jessica's DID diagnosis.

"But?" said Nicolas.

"Jessica is not violent—she's better categorized as a danger to herself." Beth said she had recently consulted with Dr. Steve Dunhill in relation to Jessica's diagnosis, and she had reached out to him several times over the last two days without success. He lived alone in the West Village.

"I don't understand the relevance and where you are going with this," said Gigs.

Beth explained that Dunhill had asked for twenty-four hours before she acted on Jessica's case. "He was writing a paper, which he planned to publish. That said, Jessica refused to allow him to attend any of our sessions. He was hoping to convince her otherwise."

Nicolas asked, "Would you say there was hostility between them?"

"Jessica did not like Steve." Beth paused. "Steve was adamant he could help her." She paused again. Jessica's right to confidentiality was paramount. "When the twenty-four hours came and went, I called Steve, but he did not answer; the phone went to voice mail. I called Steve's office, and his PA said he had not come into the office recently or called in."

"Why the concern?" said Gigs.

"I don't know—call it gut instinct. Steve displayed enthusiasm—obsession—to keep Jessica as a patient, but he did not contact me. If he had a change of mind and elected to abandon the project, why didn't he inform me? Not communicating—well, that's not the Steve I know. Something went seriously wrong."

73

J ess stared out the apartment window until she saw the police car pull away. Feeling safe, she went back into her bedroom. She had spent several days chasing down Milton, a friend of Jessica's ex-boyfriend Luke. Milton was known in the art world for creating and selling works of art he credited falsely to other famous artists. Jess had money she had saved over the years while she made that stupid fuck Jessica spend Jake's money. For $50,000, Milton had provided her with a Social Security number, an identification card, a driver's license, and a passport in the name of Gemma Brooks. Jessica had resurrected Gemma, and that had given Jess the idea to obtain the documents in Gemma's name. After the incident with Steve, she needed a backup plan. She warned that stupid bitch Jessica that she was not spending time in the fucking state penitentiary. She removed the passport; the gun; $30,000; and the other items. From now on, she needed to be always prepared.

Jess did not have a detailed plan. She would brandish the gun to show Alice she was serious about her leaving and to shut her mouth. Alice had to understand that talking to the police was unacceptable. Jess was not prepared to be held liable for Jessica's stalking. Jess did not believe she needed to do anything rash, provided Alice boarded a plane back to London.

She placed the gun at the bottom of Jessica's purse. Jess could not guarantee she could go to Connecticut and return without Jessica interfering. Jessica was unlikely to find the gun in that stupid oversized purse she dragged everywhere. Jess packed an overnight bag with the other items. Ten minutes later, she was in a taxi en route to Connecticut.

The taxi stopped outside Amanda's house. Jess paid the driver and watched him drive away before engaging Jessica.

I need you to go inside the house. Once inside, give Amanda a dose of sleeping pills. Do you understand your instructions?

"Jess, it's dangerous. We almost had to call the ambulance the last time we gave her sleeping pills."

Stop the fucking bullshit. Either you do as I ask, or I'll take care of Amanda in a permanent way. I need the car. I don't want to hear your bullshit.

"Jess, she hasn't spoken to me since you called Henry. He has custody of the children. Amanda's visitation rights have been limited by the family court. She only sees the children on alternative weekends."

Hooray. She was a fucking terrible mom. You go in there and tell that fucking bitch she was out of her mind on drugs. You didn't have a choice. Would she have preferred we called the child protection agency? I don't have time for this bullshit. If you cross me, it'll be the last time you see your fucking precious Amanda alive.

At first, Amanda argued with Jessica, but it was not long before they were sitting at the kitchen table, drinking red wine and planning their weekend exploits. Minutes later, Amanda told Jessica she was tired. She appeared unaware that it was midafternoon. As far as she was concerned, she was having an early night. She suggested they agree to resume their conversation at breakfast.

Jess did not waste time in putting Amanda to bed.

It was two thirty in the afternoon when Jessica drove the Honda past Jake's house. She smiled when she saw the Jeep parked in the driveway. In front of it, a limousine was parked.

"Ha ha." She had finally reached Alice's pea brain. The bitch was leaving. Jess did not discount that the limousine could have been for Jake, but that was unlikely; it was a workday.

Jess parked on a side road that bordered the house. She reached into Jessica's purse. Her hand cradled the gun in the bottom.

Jess held the gun in her hand as she crossed the lawn, sneaking past the limousine. She entered through the garage door and closed it behind her.

Jess removed the key from the place where Jake always hid it. She opened the door and walked inside. She felt it was her right to be there.

As she entered the kitchen, she watched Alice enter the reception room. Alice had her back to Jess. She crossed the reception room and turned left into the dining room. Jess smiled; her next turn would bring them face-to-face.

74

A lice took her final walk around the house to make sure she had packed all her belongings. She fought back tears. The house had been her home for the last twenty months. She would have changed some things if she'd had a free hand, but her relationship with Jake had never been about material things, whether to do with the house or generally. Alice's tears were not about losing a standard of living; they were about losing the man she loved. She didn't feel any person, man or woman, could have lived with Jake's refusal to address Jessica and her unacceptable behavior. Time and time again, he had made excuses for her and put her before Alice.

Alice's sweep of the house ended in the kitchen. She turned left into the kitchen and found Jessica standing there, waving Jake's gun. Gripped with fear, she stepped back. Her heart thumped hard and fast against her chest.

"I know Jessica has asked you to leave on several occasions. Why are you still here? Why haven't you gone back to London? You're an intelligent woman. Did you not understand the request?"

Jess did not give Alice the opportunity to reply. She lowered the gun as she stepped toward her. Jess's eyes darted from Alice to the knife on the table.

By the time Alice saw the knife, it was too late. She turned to move away, but her timing was wrong. Jess picked up the knife from the kitchen table and slipped it into Alice's side. She twisted it. Pain sliced into Alice's side. "Augh!" She staggered forward, fell to her knees, and slipped to the floor. Her stomach felt queasy, and her side burned.

Jess knelt by her. "I didn't plan this. Jessica and I wanted you to leave of your own accord. I don't understand why you couldn't just leave. Can you tell me why? Jessica asked you to leave. I didn't come here to harm you. I just came to talk, but I know you won't leave. How many times did Jessica ask you to leave?" Then her voice turned soft and toneless, as if she were speaking from far away. "You're still here. I guess we were asking too much."

Jess moved Alice's hair away from her face. "I thought about shooting you," she said in a jovial tone. "Do you know why I didn't? Shooting someone is too quick. I want you to suffer, just like Jessica had to suffer. Plus, if I'd shot you, you wouldn't have known why or who had done it. Alice, you needed to learn a lesson. This is the lesson: if a situation is explained to you and a person makes a simple request of you, don't disregard that request." Jess smiled at her. "I believe in God. Do you? You look like you do. I taught you a lesson for the next life."

Jess stood up, looking down at Alice, who lay in a growing pool of blood. "Why didn't you leave?"

Jess walked out of the house and crossed the lawn. She glimpsed the limousine driver with a phone in his hand. "Did he see me enter the house?" She picked up her pace. "I'm out of here—I can't take the chance he saw me."

Douglas, the driver, caught sight of a woman's backside as she slipped into the garage with a gun in her hand. He jerked upward. His eyes had not deceived him.

Several minutes later, he observed a woman he had chauffeured before emerge from the house, still holding a gun. He picked up his phone and dialed 911. He gave a detailed account of what he had seen. He confirmed that he had not heard any gunshots but that the person he was picking up to take to the airport was still in the house, and it was several minutes after the appointed time for departure. The dispatcher said, "The police will be with you shortly. Sir, wait. Don't go inside the house."

Douglas did not wait. He opened the limousine door and stepped out with the phone still in his hand.

Alice was semiconscious. A muzzy blackness slowly covered her eyes.

"Jake?" Her voice was barely audible. "Hold my hand. I don't want to die alone."

She tried to fight the darkness. Her hand reached out to touch him. She could not feel him, but in her delirious state, she thought she could see him.

"It's time for me to leave."

Douglas dialed 911 again. "Miss Alice has been stabbed." Sirens sounded in the background as he took her hand. "Miss Alice, hold on. Help is on its way."

Douglas made one more call, to the office. He asked them to get in touch with Jake Logan to let him know what had happened. Then he cradled Miss Alice, the woman he had met once eighteen months earlier when he picked her up from JFK and dropped her at Mr. Logan's house.

Alice thought she felt Jake's hand. She eyed him suspiciously. "Jake, I don't belong here."

75

J ake Logan arrived at Greenwich Hospital Association two minutes before the ambulance pulled up to the entrance. He stood inside the entrance and watched as the paramedics whisked the stretcher into the emergency department's operating theater. Fifty-five minutes later, Dr. Milner opened the door to the waiting room. Jake jumped up, anxious for an update.

"Miss Francis's condition is stable but critical." The doctor paused. "I'm sorry, but there's a chance she won't make it through the night. The nurse will take you to her room."

Armed police officers were posted outside Alice's room. Jake walked inside, sat by Alice's bed, and held her hand. He could not hold back his emotions, and his eyes filled with tears. He wiped them away and then surveyed his surroundings.

His eyes caught the television monitor. The news media had already picked up the story. Jake was aware that although he had walked into the hospital anonymously, he would be part of the media circus when he tried to leave. This was not simply another stabbing in the inner city. Jake imagined the following day's headline: "Wall Street Banker's Fiancée Stabbed in Connecticut Suburb." The enormity of the situation hit him. That was devastating, but when he looked up at the silent screen in Alice's room, he saw Jessica's apartment building surrounded by police. The breaking news was that a dead body had been found in the freezer of a New York socialite's apartment.

When Officer Nicolas and Officer Gigs walked into Alice's hospital room to ask if they could speak to Jake in private, his phone vibrated. It was the bank's human resources department. Seconds later, another call came from Anthony, the bank's in-house counsel. He also had a missed call from Alice's mother. The walls were closing in on him. He felt as if he were suffocating. He did not want to leave Alice's bedside. Losing his career because the bank would not tolerate scandal was one thing. Losing Alice was something else altogether. In the past, she had argued with him, saying that where Jessica was concerned, he justified all that there was to justify. There was no way he could justify losing Alice.

When Jake left her room to talk to the police, his phone sounded a text alert from Anthony.

"Jake, this does not look good for you. Call."

Anthony had sent the message from his private iPhone.

"Thank you, Anthony, for your concern. My time at HK Bank is over."

Jake was aware of HK's unwritten code. The bank would not fire him. They expected him to resign.

76

In the Delta lounge, Jess stared up at the breaking news. A photo of her younger self flashed up on the screen. The reporter said the police were looking for her. They wanted to speak to her in connection with a body found in her apartment and a stabbing in Connecticut.

Jess boarded the international flight to Paris as Gemma Brooks. After she fastened her seat belt, Gemma asked Jess if Alice lived in Connecticut.

Yes, Jess replied.

What did you do to Alice? Gemma asked. *Your hair is shorter now, and it's brunette, but I'm sure that was a picture of you on the news.*

Gemma, do you remember Jessica?

Yes, of course I do. She's my sister.

If you don't want to end up like Jessica, you won't ask too many questions. I need your image and name. You have no other fucking use to me, but I think we can be friends. I know what Jessica did to you. Are you a schemer? Jessica was a schemer. Steve was a schemer. Fucking shenanigans. I clean up. No loose ends remain.

Ingram Content Group UK Ltd.
Milton Keynes UK
UKHW012133280623
424228UK00013B/247/J

9 781665 741361